WHAT SHE NEEDED

Isabel waited while Jaret secured the door behind them. In the moonlight, she could see the stretch and play of muscle beneath his shirt as he blew out the lantern and returned it to its peg. She wanted to touch him, to see if he was as strong as he seemed when she'd fallen against him in Lucifer's stall. The desire was so overpowering, she had to clasp her fingers together to keep from reaching out.

Then he offered his arm to escort her back to the house, giving her the excuse she needed to feel the muscles hidden by black cloth . . .

Also by Tracy Garrett

TOUCH OF TEXAS

Published by Zebra Books

TOUCHED BY LOVE

TRACY GARRETT

ZEBRA BOOKS
Kensington Publishing Corp.
www.kensingtonbooks.com

ZEBRA BOOKS are published by

Kensington Publishing Corp.
850 Third Avenue
New York, NY 10022

All Kensington titles, imprints, and distributed lines are available at special quantity discounts for bulk purchases for sales promotion, premiums, fund-raising, educational, or institutional use.

Special book excerpts or customized printings can also be created to fit specific needs. For details, write or phone the office of the Kensington Special Sales Manager: Attn. Special Sales Department. Kensington Publishing Corp., 850 Third Avenue, New York, NY 10022. Phone: 1-800-221-2647.

ISBN-13: 978-1-4201-0101-0
ISBN-10: 1-4201-0101-3

First Printing: November 2008
10 9 8 7 6 5 4 3 2 1

Printed in the United States of America

To Mom and Dad,
for all your love, support, and cheering
along the way.
You always believed I could do it,
and I did.

Acknowledgments

To my editor, Hilary Sares, for making my dream a reality; to Sha-Shana Crichton, my agent, for believing in me; to Jo Davis, my critique partner and dearest friend; to Terry Gongaware, for your invaluable research assistance on all things with bullets; to the WriterFoxes, the greatest cheering section a girl can ask for; to Dallas Area Romance Authors, for your generosity and unwavering support;

And to my husband, Dan. Everyone should have someone like you in their life.

Prologue

Sierra Madre Mountains, Mexico, February 1847

Jaret Walker crested the last hill and hauled back on the reins. His exhausted horse stood still beneath him, sides heaving as it tried to breathe in the thin mountain air. Eighteen days on the trail dodging bandits and the Mexican Army had worn the mare pretty thin. Jaret wasn't in much better shape. He shoved cold hands into his coat pockets and ducked his chin beneath his collar, out of the icy wind. Below him, on the dry plain, spread Perote Prison, a place of death and ghosts.

The once white stone of the Spanish castle was gray and pitted by the centuries of sand the wind flung at its walls. In the early morning light, the place looked deserted, but Jaret knew better. Within those walls, hopeless men clung to life, if you could call it that. Many of the unfortunate prisoners had been captured in the various raids and skirmishes in the contested lands of Texas. And few would ever know freedom again.

For the thousandth time since he left Texas behind, he questioned his sanity. What he was about to do could land him in that prime piece of hell for good, but he had no choice. He'd been lied to, duped, and an innocent man was down there, paying the price.

Tugging his hat lower on his brow, Jaret lifted the reins and covered the last mile to the gate of the prison. A deep moat, filled with rocks and bones, guarded the high wall. A single bridge spanned the grisly pond. At its end, two stone soldiers kept permanent watch, the macabre statues portraying the remains of the men after they were hacked to death for falling asleep on duty. He reassured his mare when she sidestepped, picking up on his uneasiness. "It's okay, girl. I'm just praying I don't end up displayed next to them."

He guided his horse across the bridge and up to the imposing gate. Two soldiers came through the small door in the entry, weapons pointed at Jaret. He eased back in the saddle to stop the horse and held his hands out to the sides where they could be seen.

"*Me llamo* Jaret Walker," he identified himself in halting Spanish. "*Tengo una carta para el general.*" He pulled a sealed envelope from his jacket, keeping his movements slow and easy. On the front of the letter was the name of the general in command of the prison. "It's important. *Importante,*" he added, hoping to move them along a little faster. He wanted to put this place well behind him before the sun went down.

Jaret handed the letter over to one of the soldiers. Then both disappeared back inside the prison gate. He waited.

Ten minutes passed. Twenty. A trickle of sweat worked its way down Jaret's neck, in spite of the cold wind that never seemed to stop. If the general figured out the letter was a forgery, he was as good as dead. Finally the door reopened.

"Inside," the soldier ordered, leveling his rifle at Jaret's middle. A torrent of Spanish was flung at him as one side of the massive gate opened with a scream of rusty hinges.

Jaret's command of the language might be limited, but he understood enough to know the general was waiting. The question was did the soldier mean he'd been granted an interview, or would he be trapped inside for good? Jaret dismounted, stomped some feeling back into his feet and led his horse through the opening. He couldn't stop the shiver that skated down his spine when the gate boomed shut behind him.

He breathed a little easier when the general met him in the promenade. Their business went quickly, and with the exchange of gold, a prisoner was delivered into Jaret's keeping.

Nick Bennett looked a lot thinner than when Jaret left him here three months ago. This place could do that to a man. Suck him down to dry bones in no time. Jaret had no intention of giving the general time to change his mind. Ignoring Bennett's glare, Jaret led him out the gate to freedom. "Don't say a word," he hissed under his breath. "Just follow me."

They mounted and rode double as soon as they cleared the bridge. The mare seemed to want to get away from the prison, too, and kept to a steady trot over the first hill and out of sight. Jaret guided her back to where he'd concealed another horse before he slowed the pace.

"Why?" The single word held all of Nick Bennett's hatred and fury and confusion.

"You didn't belong in there."

Bennett accepted Jaret's help off the horse, balancing against the saddle until his knees would hold him. "I told you that before you brought me here."

"True, but I expected you to say that. I'd been told different." Jaret drew a knife from his boot and sliced through the ropes binding Nick's wrists.

"What changed your mind?"

"I found out someone wants you dead and I was the way they chose to do it. I don't hire out for murder." He handed

Nick a dark hat to cover his blond hair and dug out the extra coat he'd brought along. It was too large, especially with the weight Bennett had lost, but the dark wool would keep him warm.

The two men mounted up and took to the trail in silence. Jaret wanted as many miles as possible between them and the prison. They pushed on into the evening, until darkness forced them to make camp. They ate jerky and hard tack, and washed it down with icy water from the stream they'd crossed an hour before. Jaret refused to light a fire, even when Nick started to shiver.

"It's damn cold." Nick rubbed his arms and legs with hands chafed raw by the winter wind, trying to get warm.

"I know, but the bandits in this stretch of hell love to work at night." Jaret held out a revolver. "Here. I'm going to scout the area, make sure we're alone. I'll warn you before I come back in."

Nick checked the load and tested the weight of the gun. "How do you know I won't shoot you?"

"I don't."

One corner of Nick's mouth kicked up at Jaret's stark reply. Before he could extend the conversation, Jaret slipped into the night. He made three circuits of the camp, varying his route and speed each time. Nothing moved but him and the moon overhead. By the time he got back, Bennett was sound asleep.

The days ran together, each one longer than the last. While Bennett slept and regained a little of his strength, Jaret was wearing thin. He hadn't slept more than a few minutes at a time, trying to remain alert for the thieves that plagued travelers on this route. It took nearly four weeks, but finally they were so close to the Rio Grande they could smell it.

The morning sun helped raise their spirits. "Will we

make the river today?" Bennett groomed his horse and spread the saddle blanket over its gleaming hide.

"Easily. It's just out of sight, an hour at the most." Jaret lifted Nick's saddle to save him the effort.

"I never thanked you for bringing Micah with you." Nick patted his horse's neck and tickled its ear, distracting it before tightening the cinch around the reluctant animal. "Stand still, you stubborn mule," he scolded when the horse sidestepped to avoid the bit.

"You needed a mount. Couldn't see the sense in leaving him behind and having him disappear before we got back."

Bennett nodded. "I appreciate it. This horse is a particular favorite of mine. I'd have hated to lose him."

They fell silent, working side by side in a pattern they'd developed over the long weeks on the trail. Much to their mutual surprise, the two had also developed a friendship of sorts. It probably wouldn't be a lasting one, but Jaret never expected it to be. No one in his life ever cared enough to stick around.

The closer they got to the river, the faster they rode. "Come on, Walker, pick it up." Nick laughed as he urged his horse to a gallop. "Last one to get wet buys the whiskey."

They thundered over the slight rise in the land and straight into a trap. Gunfire erupted from both sides, separating them. Bennett dove from his horse and rolled under some scrub bushes. Jaret managed to find a pile of rocks that offered a little better protection.

From his vantage point, he picked off two of the bandits. Bennett took out a third when the man presented his back while changing positions to get a better angle to shoot Jaret.

Everything fell silent. "Bennett?"

"Still in one piece. You?"

"Yeah." Jaret shifted, trying to draw any remaining fire.

When nothing moved, he worked his way to where Nick lay sprawled in the dirt, careful to stay out of sight.

"Is it over?

Jaret studied the land, checking out every shadow. "I'm not sure. Stay put."

He balanced on the balls of his feet, ready to make a run for another spot of cover.

"Look out!"

Nick dove at Jaret, hitting him in the back. Jaret felt the bullet slam into Nick as they fell. Jaret rolled away and came up firing. The bandit was dead before he hit the ground. In the silence, Jaret heard the sound of a single horse, galloping away toward Texas. At least one man had escaped to carry the tale.

"Bennett?" Blood was everywhere, running from the gaping wound in Nick's shoulder.

"How bad?" Bennett was conscious, but just barely.

Jaret did what he could to stop the flow of blood. "Pretty bad. You need doctoring that I can't do. Let me make sure we're done here, then I'll get you across the river."

"Don't take too long." Bennett took a shallow breath and closed his eyes.

Cursing at the delay, Jaret searched out every bandit to be certain they were dead. He removed guns, ammunition, anything that might be used to shoot them in the back. As he rolled over the last attacker, a chill ran down his spine. He recognized the man. He'd been in the room when Jaret was hired to kidnap Bennett and deliver him to that hell on earth. Jaret glanced around, studying the setup.

This trap had been laid for him, to eliminate the only witness to Bennett's disappearance. Jaret blistered the air with curses. He'd been set up and Bennett paid the price.

Again.

Chapter One

Wild Horse Desert, South Texas, April 1847

"No, Uncle. I won't be bullied into this."

Isabel Bennett faced her uncle across the spacious sitting room. "I told you I won't marry anyone until Nicolas is safely home. I meant what I said."

The twitch under Don Enrique Antonio Ferdinand de la Rosa's eye grew more pronounced despite his smile. "My dear child, you must face the truth. Your brother is dead."

"No! Nicolas is alive and he will come home." She carefully enunciated every word in an effort to control her temper. The folds of her skirt hid her clenched fists. She almost hated her uncle for forcing this argument again.

When he first came to Two Roses, she'd been so happy to have family around her again. Her brother, Nicolas, had just left on a trip to buy breeding stock. The next morning her uncle arrived. Though she saw no real family resemblance, he claimed to be her mother's brother. She wasn't convinced, but he knew all about her family and he quoted parts of the last letter she'd written to him.

Don Enrique's appearance had been a complete surprise. He'd never mentioned his intention to visit the ranch. As the eldest, he had inherited the family's minor title and position and, she assumed, he preferred life in the Spanish court to living in the Americas.

Still, Isabel welcomed him to the large horse ranch she called home. Unfortunately, he wasn't much help. Though he claimed to want only to preserve and prosper the family's holdings, he'd completely ignored the ranch and dedicated himself to finding Isabel a husband. The man was driving her to distraction.

Watching him now, she admitted her uncle was not what she'd expected. His smooth round face glistened with perspiration, emphasizing the fact that most of his remaining hair grew low on the sides of his head. He wore his typical dark brown woolen trousers and waistcoat, with a starched cotton shirt buttoned all the way to his prominent double chin.

Isabel patted the dampness on her neck with a handkerchief. How could he stand wearing so many layers in this heat? With his fancy clothes, slicked back hair, and a belly that hid his silver-inlaid belt, she saw nothing of her mother in him. Still, he was family. She struggled not to give voice to her frustration.

"Until Nicolas is home safely, I will concentrate on running the ranch. I don't require a husband for that. I've made my decision," she spoke over his interruption. "I won't discuss it again."

Isabel fanned her heated face with her handkerchief. Though all the windows were open to catch the breeze, no air moved in the large house. She narrowed her eyes against the sunlight beating down on the hard-packed dirt outside the window. The headache that had plagued her all morning pounded behind her eyes, but she tried to ignore it. To acknowledge the pain was a very female sign of weakness, to her mind, and she refused to give in.

She swiped a bead of perspiration from her brow. Another trickled between her breasts. The heat was unusual for April, even for the middle of the day, and it made tolerating her uncle's meddling even more difficult.

"My dear, be reasonable," he wheedled. "You are twenty-four, well beyond the age to marry, and Silas Williams is a wealthy man. As the owner of the largest ranch in this part of the world, he will see that you are cared for in style. You'll have the very best of everything available at a whim."

"His ranch is not larger that mine," she muttered under her breath. Isabel gritted her teeth as he sipped from the cut crystal glass of whiskey that was never far from his hand.

"His land borders our own, so you would be able to visit on occasion. You would be very busy, no doubt, setting up your new home and starting a family, but I'm certain you could return, should you wish to. My dear, you must forgive me for being indelicate, but you are not getting any younger. Mr. Williams may well be your last opportunity to marry. Maintaining this ridiculous hope that your brother will return will only see you into a life of spinsterhood."

As if she would marry that miserly old goat, Isabel fumed silently. True, Silas Williams owned an impressive number of acres bordering her ranch to the north and west. But the last time he'd been on her ranch, he'd glanced at the stock, taken a much longer look at her, and then offered his unsolicited advice on managing expenses by feeding the horses less and her employees nothing at all—unless they paid for it.

She would hear his grating voice in her nightmares, lecturing her on her proper place. *"Girlie, you don't need a cook when you could be doing the job yourself."*

Reining in her temper, she'd calmly pointed out that she couldn't take on the responsibilities of the kitchen, since running the ranch was more than a full-time job.

"Exactly," he'd countered. *"That's why it should be left to someone who is knowledgeable in such things. Your*

foreman could handle the ranch. That would free you to devote your attention to matters more fitting for a woman." His leer had left no doubt to what *matters* he referred.

Add his aversion to bathing, which he tried to cover up with copious amounts of cologne, and he was no woman's idea of a good catch.

But she didn't voice her opinion of Silas Williams to her uncle. It would only toss more fuel on the fire.

Isabel stared out the window behind her uncle's chair while he continued his lecture. Lately he seemed determined to marry her off to anyone who would take her away from the ranch. Anyone with enough money to see *him* settled nicely as well, of course.

For as long as she could remember, Two Roses had been all she'd wanted. She loved everything about the remote Texas ranch. Though the land was rough and unforgiving, and her nearest neighbors were a hard day's ride away, she knew in her soul this was where she belonged.

After her father had succumbed to his broken heart while on a trip to Austin, the land had been left to Isabel and her brother equally. Nicolas didn't seem interested in running the ranch. He only cared about the horses, so the land and everyone on it became her responsibility.

Isabel saw nothing wrong with letting Nicolas concentrate on what he loved while she took on the rest. As her hopes of having a family of her own faded, she'd consoled herself with dreams of someday being an indulgent aunt to her brother's children.

"Isabel, what is the matter with you? You haven't heard a word I've said. Are you ill?" Her uncle assumed a tone of concern and solicitude. "Perhaps you should lie down if you aren't feeling well."

She wound her fingers together to keep from rubbing at the headache pounding in her temples. "It's only the heat," she assured her uncle as she lowered herself onto a brocade settee. "Uncle Enrique, it isn't ridiculous to believe Nicolas is alive. I know he is. I can feel it."

Her uncle snorted in disdain, drained the whiskey in his glass and turned to the decanter. She offered up a silent prayer that he wouldn't drink too much today, but knew her words were wasted. His drunkenness was becoming a common occurrence.

He lifted the decanter and stared hard at his glass, as if trying to bring it into focus. Before he could pour more liquor, the sound of an approaching horse came through the open window.

"Who on earth could that be?" Her uncle twisted in his chair to look out the window.

Isabel rushed across the room, hoping against all reason that it was Nicolas. She bit back a cry of disappointment when she saw a stranger on horseback rather than her brother. "I've never seen him before, Uncle."

"Well, then . . ." Her uncle set his glass on the side table, pushed to his feet and tugged his vest down over his ample stomach. Smoothing his sparse hair into place, he glanced at his reflection in the large gilt mirror across the room. Satisfied with what he saw, he went to greet their visitor, weaving slightly as he made his way to the door.

Isabel sank into the chair he'd vacated. It wasn't Nicolas. She took a couple of deep breaths to rein in the fear and worry that threatened to engulf her. Rising again, Isabel pushed the curtain aside to take a closer look at the stranger. He was tall, sitting easily in the saddle of an equally leggy buckskin horse. He'd been on the trail for a while, judging by the dust on his clothes and the sheen of sweat on the animal's coat.

The sun sharpened the angles of the man's face, making his high cheekbones and square jaw look as if they'd been carved of granite. A long mustache framed his upper lip, setting off his sharp, straight nose.

The muscles in his arms shifted beneath his black shirt as he brought the horse to a stop. His sleeves were turned back to combat the rising heat, and tanned skin showed below the roll of fabric. Then he tipped back his hat with one finger and turned toward the window where she stood.

"Oh, my," she whispered. Even from this distance she could see his eyes were the icy blue of a winter lake, and his hair was the color of the sable fur her mother had loved, dark brown and luxurious. It brushed the collar of his shirt and she was embarrassed to find she wanted to run her fingers through it. Unfamiliar warmth that had nothing to do with the sun washed over her.

Straightening with a jerk, she stepped away from the window and smoothed her skirts. Her hands were shaking. Who was this man? How could he affect her with only a look? She shook her head to try and break the spell he'd cast over her. Whoever he was, he was a guest on her ranch. She should be welcoming him, not ogling from behind a window curtain. Hoping her upset didn't somehow show, she followed her uncle outside to greet him.

Jaret Walker set up a stir among the ranch hands when he rode his dun-colored mare into the yard. The horse's dark mane lifted with each step as he guided her toward the house. Without moving more than his eyes, he counted a dozen. There should be ten more working close to the house and another thirty or so out with the herds, if his friend's information was accurate.

He ignored the urge to turn back to the east and ride hard to get far away from this remote spot on the Texas desert. Being among people made him itchy. Give him the wide open prairie and his horse for company, and he'd ask for nothing more. But he was here because of a promise, and he always kept his word.

One of the ranch hands stepped out of the shadows, directly into his path. Jaret stopped his horse with a slight tug on the reins. Though he was taller than most men and broad enough to intimidate people just by being, this man looked to be nearly his equal. When he reached up to grab the bridle to hold the horse in place, Jaret moved the animal out of reach with a touch of one heel.

"Afternoon." He nodded in the general direction of the other hands who'd stopped what they were doing to size him up. "I have business with Nick Bennett. Would he be around?"

"Perhaps I can be of assistance?" A short, rather round man separated from the shade of the porch. "I am his uncle, Don Enrique Antonio Ferdinand de la Rosa." The man puffed up with importance and lost his balance, staggering into the porch railing. "I run the estate in his absence."

Estate? The man had a pretty high opinion of this plot of dirt in the Texas desert. While it looked like decent grazing land with the only water he'd seen for hours, it was still only dirt. True, someone had put a lot of caring into the place. The dusty wagon road leading to the house had been lined with smooth-cut fence rails that were placed with precision for nearly a quarter of a mile. And the fence was nothing compared to the house.

It looked like it had started life as a small, stone and mud shotgun house, with a door at each end of the hallway to let the breeze through. But the structure had been added to over the years. The two-story extension in front of him was part wood, part native rock, and sported large glass windows and lace curtains. There was a stone building off to the right of the main house and the dozen or so structures spread out on both sides were probably the homes of the ranch hands and their families. Each building was painted a different color, bright splotches on the dry brown land offering plenty of places to hide, and lots of eyes to see you, too. He turned away from the layout of the homestead. It wasn't his problem at the moment. The man watching him from the porch steps was.

"Jaret Walker." He touched the brim of his hat but didn't bother to take it off. "No offense, Mr. de la Rosa, but my business is with Nick Bennett."

"My nephew is not here, nor, sadly, is he expected to return. You'll have to take your business up with me."

"Any business on this ranch will be handled by me, Uncle."

Though Jaret couldn't see who was standing in the shadow of the doorway, it was definitely a woman who spoke. Her warm, rich voice carried the authority of one accustomed to being in charge.

"Welcome, Mr. Walker. Won't you come inside? I want to hear how you know my brother."

Jaret pulled the dusty hat from his head automatically as she stepped into view. She was a sight worth a three-day ride. Eyes the color of obsidian sparkled in the sunlight. Her long black hair was tied back with a silk scarf and looked as rich and soft as the fabric that bound it. The light yellow dress she wore made her skin glow like sun-warmed honey. Its puffed sleeves accented her straight shoulders and made her waist seem small enough for his hands to span. She was taller than the man she called uncle and well formed, with enough curves in all the right places to get a man's attention. She met his stare with a look of confidence and more than a little arrogance, to his thinking. She was going to give him trouble.

The uncle made a perfunctory introduction. "This is my

niece, Isabel Bennett, the true rose of this ranch, according to most of the men around here."

Jaret saw the woman's smile tighten at her uncle's sarcastic tone, confirming a piece of information from Nick Bennett. His sister was polite and proper, but she didn't suffer fools lightly.

"Ma'am." He nodded his head in greeting.

"A pleasure, Mr. Walker. Come into the house where it's a little cooler. Manuel, will you take care of our guest's horse, please?"

While he was registering the fact that she'd asked an employee to do something rather than ordering it done, a man came forward. His round brown face spoke of his Mexican heritage. He had a stocky build and a gait that testified to a life spent on horseback. The gray scattered through the black hair at his temples told Jaret that his life had been a fairly long one.

Jaret committed the old vaquero's face to memory. This was the man Nick Bennett had sworn Jaret could trust with his life—and Isabel's.

Jaret swung out of the saddle and stretched. He'd been riding since first light and it felt good to have his feet on the ground again. When he climbed the steps onto the porch, Isabel held out her hand. He grasped it and was struck by the contrast of a firm grip and very soft skin that held the faint scent of roses. Jaret held her hand long enough for her look of politeness to turn to curiosity. She tilted her head slightly and both eyebrows lifted. He released her before she could ask any of the questions he read in her eyes.

He turned when she did and waited for the older man to go ahead of him into the house. The coolness of the foyer swept over him. Jaret was grateful for the respite from the sun. He dropped his hat onto a small marble table near the door and shoved his fingers through his hair. He supposed it was too long to be considered in fashion, but then he'd never really cared what others thought of him.

The spurs on his boots rang on the wood floor and echoed through the high-ceilinged rooms as they crossed the wide hallway. Several doors could be seen down the length of it, most open to allow the light breeze to move unhindered through the house. At the far end he glimpsed the garden through the open back door. The walls were made of the same stone as the exterior. They were the color of the surrounding desert, and still held the coolness of the night even though the sun was nearly overhead. Vases of roses were set on several tables, adding color and perfume to the air.

"Nice place."

Isabel smiled over her shoulder. "Thank you. The land has been in my mother's family for nearly ninety years. The grant was secured as a wedding gift for my great-great-grandmother. They built the original house together." She indicated the stone walls of the hallway and another small room to their left. "We've expanded over the generations." Her smile was gentle with memory, with love of her home and her legacy.

"So you grew up here?"

"I was born here, as was my brother. Now, with my parents gone and Nicolas missing, it falls to me to keep it running until he returns."

"Missing?" Jaret feigned surprise. He knew exactly where her brother was, but he wasn't ready to trust anyone on the ranch with the information.

"He went to the coast in October to buy breeding stock. The horses were delivered, but Nicolas didn't return." Her shoulders shook with her breath. "I had men searching from here to Galveston for weeks, but we found no sign of him." She stared past his shoulder, down the long, empty hallway. "I still haven't heard from him."

She preceded Jaret into the parlor. It was nothing like he expected, not that he had much to compare it to. He hadn't been invited into many. The room was big and airy, dominated on one side by the windows that looked onto the yard. A massive fireplace, made of the same stone that lined the entry hall, took up most of the far wall, which was painted the same soft yellow as Isabel's dress. It was a welcoming room, and the chairs were large enough to make even a man his size comfortable.

Jaret watched Isabel visibly compose herself. Her worry for her brother was obvious. The deep breath she took lifted her shoulders and drew his gaze to the long line of her back, from her elegant neck to the curve of her hips.

"May I offer you something cool to drink, Mr. Walker?"

"Or perhaps something a bit stronger?" De la Rosa lowered his bulk into a chair by the window and gestured toward a decanter and two empty glasses.

Jaret glanced at Isabel. While he didn't care what she thought of him, he didn't want to risk alienating her. It would only make the job he'd come here to do more difficult. She inclined her head slightly at his unspoken question, so he accepted.

"Whiskey would be welcome."

Jaret accepted the glass with a nod. He didn't really want it, but he'd found alcohol was often a good way to open a man up. When you drank with someone, they were more willing to talk. And he was here for information.

"Please tell me how you know my brother." Isabel's voice pulled him out of his thoughts. She motioned him into a chair, then perched on the edge of a small sofa and smoothed her fingers over the neck of the swan carved into the armrest. "When did you last see him? Where was he?"

He declined the chair she indicated, surprised she wasn't worried about the dust on her fine furniture. Instead, he crossed the room to lean against the fireplace mantel.

"I met Nick some months back in Galveston. We got to talking about horses and he mentioned that he raised a fine Spanish-mix breed. He invited me to come and look them over if I was ever interested in purchasing one or two."

He swallowed some of the whiskey and waited for it to sear a path to his stomach. But the burn never came. The liquor felt cool and warm at the same time, and blazed a pleasant trail down his throat. Must be damned expensive stuff.

"I've been working on building my own spread, and I'm in a position to consider adding some stock. I thought I'd accept his invitation and see what he has for sale."

At least part of the story was true. He was interested in the horses being bred on the Bennett ranch. But he didn't own any land, probably never would. And he wasn't here because of an invitation to buy stock. He had a debt to repay.

He wandered to the window and looked out toward the barn. Most of the hands had returned to work, but the one who had first spoken to him was sitting on the porch with a rifle across his knees. Did the ranch hand think the old man or the woman required an armed guard? Or was it a standard precaution at this spread whenever a stranger rode in?

"I would have preferred knowing you were planning to come, sir." De la Rosa waved his glass in Jaret's direction.

Isabel made a soft sound of protest as her uncle drained his glass and reached for the decanter to pour more. Jaret wondered if she disliked the unfriendly comment or the drinking.

"I wrote to Nick more than a month ago, telling him I planned to arrive by the twentieth. I apologize for the delay, but it couldn't be helped."

"Really? We received no letter." The older man settled back into his chair, balancing a full glass on his belly.

Jaret wasn't surprised to hear it, since he'd never sent one. But he was counting on the hospitality that was an unwritten rule in this part of the country. As the invited guest of the ranch's heir, he wouldn't be turned away unless this man was a fool, or too greedy to be smart.

"I sent it in plenty of time to arrive before I did."

Isabel waved away his explanation. "It doesn't matter, Mr. Walker. You're welcome on Two Roses as long as you wish to remain. Now, please, tell me about Nicolas."

Jaret thanked her for the invitation he'd expected to receive. He needed time to decide if his friend was right in thinking that someone here preferred the ranch's other heir never return. Watching Isabel, he wondered if she was the one trying to steal her brother's birthright. Maybe she really was unaware of everything happening around her.

Nick Bennett had been adamant about his sister's innocence, insisting that she would do nothing to harm him. Jaret didn't really care one way or the other. He would do what he'd promised, regardless of how she felt about it.

"Where did you meet Nicolas? Have you seen him since your first meeting, or heard anything of him? Did he tell you when he planned to return home?" Isabel leaned toward Jaret, obviously anxious to hear his answers.

"Isabel, stop badgering the man."

"I am not *badgering,* Uncle." She smiled an apology to Jaret even as she denied it. "I'm just so worried about my brother, and I thought you might know what happened to him."

Her uncle started to protest again, but Jaret interrupted. "It's all right, Mr. de la Rosa. I don't mind telling what I know." *Or part of it,* his conscience added.

Jaret turned back to Isabel. "I ducked into a saloon in

Galveston to get out of a storm. This would have been five—no, six months ago. The only open chair in the place was at your brother's table, so I took it."

He sipped at the whiskey to buy some time and to wash the taste of the lie from his mouth. As a rule, Jaret detested liars, and to his mind, no matter how good the reason, he was walking a razor edge right now. He stuck as close to the truth as he could.

"He struck up a conversation, talked about the rain, horses, this place, even you."

Isabel smiled and he was momentarily distracted. She had a smile that could give a man ideas. He ignored his natural response and concentrated on his story. "We got on pretty well."

"My brother has always made friends easily. Where did he go when the storm let up?"

"I don't know, ma'am." That was a bald-faced lie. He swallowed more whiskey. "I think he had a room in the hotel across the street, so he may have gone there. I didn't see him in town after that, so I assumed he'd headed home." He returned to staring out the window.

In truth, Jaret had followed Nick as he rode out of town the next morning and taken him prisoner with very little trouble. Two days before that, a man approached him about doing a job for him. They needed a thief caught and delivered to justice. He'd been told Nick Bennett was a good-for-nothing gambler who needed to be dumped in prison for killing a Mexican general to avoid paying a debt. He'd sworn, on his mother's deathbed, to take men like that off the street. It was one of the reasons he wore a gun and was willing to use it. Though he never saw him with the money, Bennett fit the description on the wanted poster they'd shown him, so he accepted the assignment. Jaret had nothing special waiting to be done and a little extra money, honestly earned, was always useful.

Catching Nick had been so easy Jaret had begun to doubt the tale he'd been told almost from the start. But he'd given his word and taken a man's money, so he finished the job. Only a few weeks after delivering Bennett to prison, their story began to fall apart. Jaret tried to make it right by getting Nick out of prison again, but they'd ridden into an ambush and by the time he'd finished meddling in Nick Bennett's life, the man had been too shot up and weak to go anywhere.

Jaret tossed back the rest of his whiskey but it churned in his gut, keeping pace with the memories rolling in his mind.

For days they weren't sure Bennett would survive. Jaret stuck close by while the man fought an enemy seen only in feverish nightmares. The minute Bennett regained consciousness, he began struggling to get out of bed, raving on about his ranch and land grabbers. When they'd calmed him down, Nick spilled everything he'd discovered while in Austin and explained the danger his sister was in, finally convincing Jaret to come and protect her.

The voice of his host interrupted the flood of memories. "Isabel, you have asked enough questions."

"But Uncle—"

He raised a hand to silence her protest. "You may continue this conversation at dinner. Run along and rest until you are feeling better."

Jaret turned back in time to see Isabel's eyes narrow, but he couldn't tell if it was in pain or irritation. Her feelings were quickly hidden behind a polite smile.

"Very well, Uncle Enrique. Mr. Walker, I'll have a room prepared for you. I hope you'll stay with us for a while. I expect Nicolas to return soon, and I'm certain he'll want to see you again."

She didn't wait for an answer. With a nod to both men, she rose with the grace of royalty and walked from the room. Jaret stood where he was and watched until the door closed behind her. He inhaled deeply, enjoying the scent of roses that remained after she'd gone, wondering where on her soft skin she dabbed the perfume. His body hardened at the thought of discovering all the places for himself. He cursed in silence and tried to rein in his reaction. Such a beautiful flower wasn't meant for the likes of him.

He turned to find de la Rosa pouring yet another drink. Jaret declined the man's offer to join him. "Is she all right?"

"Isabel?" The man dropped his bulk back into his chair. "She's quite all right. My niece is plagued with headaches, but it is nothing serious. I told her it's brought on by her constant worrying over things she cannot change, but she refuses to listen to my counsel. In her best interests, I have instructed her maid on the proper way to administer laudanum at such times as this, but Isabel refuses to take it. I'm certain she will join us for dinner, have no fear."

Jaret fought to hide the revulsion that filled him. Laudanum. He knew from experience how it could destroy a family—or what remained of one—how it could steal a person's will to live. Maybe his friend was right about what was happening here after all.

"Isabel is a lovely creature, don't you agree?"

Jaret pulled his attention away from the door. If the man thought he was being subtle, the whiskey had gone to his head.

De la Rosa didn't wait for a reply. "She insists that her brother will return, but to speak plainly, gentleman to gentleman, I am certain he's dead." He gulped down half the contents of his glass. "I am, of course, trying to look out for her best interests, but it is difficult when she refuses to consider her own future instead of that of a brother who'll never be seen again."

De la Rosa waved his glass in the air to emphasize his words, nearly sloshing the liquor onto the floor. "The girl even keeps her brother's room in readiness for his return." He took another healthy swallow of whiskey. "Such accommodations would better serve me," he muttered, "but that old shrew of a housekeeper won't hear of it."

Jaret needed to get out of the house, away from the greed that filled this room, before he suffocated. He set his glass on a nearby table.

"I'd like a look at those horses now, if you don't mind."

De la Rosa attempted to rise, but couldn't manage it through the haze of the whiskey. Instead, he waved Jaret toward the door. "See Mr. Hardin, my foreman. He'll show you what you want to see."

Isabel wanted to crumple into a heap and cry. She made it to the top of the stairs, out of sight of the hallway below, before the disappointment won out. With a soft sob, she leaned against the stone wall.

Where was Nicolas? The headache began to pound behind her eyes. Her uncle insisted she was needlessly making herself ill and she supposed he was right. But for a few blessed minutes, when she was talking with Jaret Walker, the worry had faded and she'd been able to relax.

The housekeeper appeared at her side and urged Isabel into her bedroom. The plump old woman hurried to pull the drapes and block out the brilliant spring sunlight.

"Thank you, Lydia." Sinking to the bed, she didn't protest when the woman removed her shoes and lifted her legs onto the feather mattress, but she refused the laudanum her loyal friend pressed on her.

"Please, little one. Don Enrique says it will help you."

"I don't want it. The headache isn't too bad. Besides, the pain will make me stronger. Isn't that what you always told me?"

"Yes, but I meant a scraped knee or a burned finger." Lydia brushed away Isabel's hands and loosened the front of her dress to make her more comfortable. Because of the heat, Isabel didn't wear a corset. She detested the things in the winter; she refused to even consider one in the summer.

She should probably be embarrassed that she'd greeted a guest with only a muslin chemise and a single petticoat beneath her gown, but at the moment, as Lydia fanned cool air over her skin, she was very grateful for her decision.

"I'm just so afraid for Nicolas. Why doesn't he come home, or at least send word?"

"I know. I worry, too, little one."

Isabel tried to set aside her fear and concentrate instead on the here and now. "Lydia, Jaret Walker will be staying with us for several days. He's a friend of Nicolas's and is here to consider the purchase of some horses. Please show him to Nicolas's room."

Lydia looked scandalized. "But that's right across the hall from you. The south bedroom would be better."

Isabel arched an eyebrow and stopped the woman's protest. Lydia had been a part of this household since before Isabel was born and was protective of the occupants and their reputations, but Isabel was in charge.

"It's the best empty bedroom in the house and I want Mr. Walker to be comfortable."

"Your uncle will not be happy about the arrangement."

Isabel felt a burst of perverse pleasure at the thought. "I know."

Lydia's wheezing laugh echoed in the room.

"He's seen Nicolas," Isabel whispered, grasping the gnarled hand of her dearest friend. "Do you think Nicolas is dead? Uncle Enrique tells me every day he is, and that I must accept the fact that he won't return. Do you think he's dead, too?"

Wise old eyes lifted to meet hers. "No, child, he isn't dead. I'm sure of it." She pressed a hand to her heart. "I would know it in here if he were. He'll come home soon."

Isabel smiled. "Thank you, Lydia. I'll sleep for a little while now. Wake me in an hour, please."

Isabel closed her eyes and willed herself to relax. She heard the old woman cross the room, and the door click shut behind her. Then came silence, and blessed relief.

When Isabel awoke, the walls were painted with the soft pink light of sunset. Far more than an hour had passed. She stretched, easing the stiffness in her body from lying in bed so long. At least her headache was gone.

She swung her legs off the bed and crossed to her dressing table. Pouring water into the washbasin, she splashed some on her face and neck, washing away the last of her grogginess.

The sounds of horses and men outside her open window drew her attention. Glancing down, she spotted a tall figure near the corral. He'd rolled up his sleeves a little more in deference to the afternoon heat, and his hat sat low on his forehead, but she recognized Jaret Walker.

What kind of a man wore black on a day as hot as this one? A man who wanted to be noticed, perhaps. Or maybe one who wants to go unnoticed in shadows and darkness. She was very curious to know the kind of man Nicolas chose as his friend.

Even from this distance she could feel the impact of

seeing him again. When he rode up to the house this afternoon, he'd merely been a tall man on an even taller horse. Then he'd looked at her and a shiver had run through her all the way to her toes.

As she watched him now, Jaret said something to Hank Hardin and the men laughed together. Isabel's lips curved in automatic response. It was the first time she could recall the unpleasant foreman even so much as smiling. Nicolas's friend certainly had a way about him.

Thoughts of her brother were replaced by concern as Jaret climbed over the corral fence and moved toward the young stallion she'd named Lucifer. What was he doing? Lucifer was an unpredictable beast, prone to nipping and kicking. Isabel had raised him from the day he was born, when his mother refused to nurse. Though the stallion would do anything for her, the ranch hands were always careful to stay out of his reach when she wasn't around. What was Mr. Hardin thinking to let Jaret go into the corral?

She stared in disbelief as Jaret advanced. Though she couldn't hear the words, she could see his lips moving as he spoke to the horse. When he reached out a hand, Lucifer shied away, but Jaret just closed the distance again. She leaned out the window to call a warning, but it was too late.

The horse swung its massive head, striking Jaret in the chest and knocking him into the dust. Before he could recover, Lucifer reared to strike out with deadly hooves.

Chapter Two

Isabel's cry of warning stuck in her throat. She'd never seen a man move so quickly. Almost before he hit the ground, Jaret rolled to his feet. Lucifer reared again and trumpeted a challenge.

She didn't wait to see what happened next. She ran down the stairs, struggling to fasten the front of her dress as she went. If Lucifer decided to kill Jaret and dismantel the corral one board at a time, she was the only person who could stop him.

By the time Isabel reached the yard, Jaret was safely outside the fence. A couple of the ranch hands were trying to check him over, but he waved them away. Other than the dust on his shirt, and the hat that was even now being crushed under flailing hooves, he seemed to be fine.

Isabel slowed her headlong rush, but headed into the corral without hesitating. The moment one of the hands opened the gate, she concentrated only on Lucifer. She heard a shout and sounds of a scuffle behind her, but she didn't allow herself to be distracted. Even though she knew this animal as well as she knew herself, she didn't take her safety for granted.

The horse pawed the ground, already worked into an

impressive frenzy. Clumps of dirt flew from his slashing hooves each time he reared. The huge animal spun to face her and trumpeted his displeasure as she stepped through the gate, but it didn't deter Isabel.

Murmuring softly of cool water and treats, she approached cautiously. At the first sound of her voice, Lucifer ceased his equine display of temper, but still quivered and snorted. Isabel slowed her steps a bit more and finally stopped a few feet in front of the horse.

Isabel stood perfectly still, talking to him until his rolling eyes focused on her, then called his name in a quiet voice. The horse's ears flicked forward and he came to her like a well-trained hound. She stroked his neck when he laid his head over her shoulder and scolded him for losing his temper. When she was sure he was calm once more, she turned toward the men gathered around.

Jaret shrugged off the two men restraining him. He'd made it back inside the corral, but they'd caught him before he could intervene. When Isabel glanced his way, he started to speak, but she cut him off with a slight shake of her head.

Leading Lucifer by no more than a hand on his neck, she walked directly to Jaret, retrieving his mangled hat as she passed.

"Lucifer, this is my guest, Mr. Walker." The big equine head dropped in something very close to a bow. She held out Jaret's hat with a smile of apology. "Mr. Walker, meet Lucifer, the pride of our herd."

Jaret reached out slowly. His hand was steady, which she thought showed admirable control considering how close he'd come to being as flat as his hat. He laid his large hand over hers where it rested on the horse's neck and moved only the tips of his fingers to stroke Lucifer. Isabel found herself watching him instead of the horse.

His hand covered hers completely. It looked strong and the roughness she could feel against her own told her he wasn't afraid of hard work. His skin was tanned from the Texas sun, and she could see the dark hair on his arm where his sleeve was rolled back.

She was startled out of her reverie when Lucifer shied away. Jaret's other arm wrapped around her to pull her from danger. She twisted at the same instant, reaching for Lucifer's mane to calm him again. Her sharp movements succeeded in pulling apart her hastily fastened dress and Jaret's hand came to rest inside her bodice, against the thin fabric of her chemise. All the sounds of the corral and the men gathered at the fence faded into the background.

Sensation rippled through her at his intimate touch. The heat of his palm seemed to burn her skin through the fine cloth. What was wrong with her? The touch was impersonal, designed to protect, not arouse, but she couldn't stop the shiver that raced up her spine.

Had Jaret felt her response? She searched his face, but his total concentration was on the horse. He held her close until Lucifer calmed again, then began to stroke the animal in the same motion as before, but without her hand beneath his. It took a few more moments before Lucifer accepted his touch, then Jaret released the horse, and her.

"Why don't we take him inside the barn, Miss Bennett? He's had enough for one day."

Nodding her agreement, Isabel led Lucifer away, with Jaret following close behind, one hand on the muscular flank of the horse. The instant the stall door closed behind Lucifer, Jaret turned furious eyes on her.

"What the hell were you thinking, woman, running into the corral like that? That beast could have killed you without knowing who it was he was stomping on."

"I thought he was going to kill *you*." She spun away,

paced the length of three stalls, and back again, battling to control her flash-fire temper.

Jaret's gaze flicked down to her toes and back. "I can take care of myself. I don't need rescuing by a half-dressed woman who races under the hooves of a crazed stallion. Were you trying to distract the horse or do you make a habit of running around showing yourself to the hired help?"

At the mention of her clothing, embarrassment rapidly doused her temper. Whirling around, Isabel showed him her back while she fumbled with the hooks to close her bodice. Most were torn and she was left holding the two sides together. She felt Jaret come up behind her and tried to shrug away when his hands settled on her shoulders. He ignored her, stroking the skin exposed by her modest neckline with his thumbs.

"Damn it, woman, you scared me half to death." His voice was softer, but still rough with anger. "I won't kill the cowboy that opened the gate for you, but I still might beat some sense into him."

Isabel crushed the front of her dress closed as she faced him. "Mr. Walker, this is my ranch and the men know my capabilities far better than you. I raised Lucifer, and despite my best efforts, Manuel and I are still the only ones who can touch him." She frowned as she realized that wasn't true any longer. Jaret had not only touched the horse, he'd succeeded in calming him down enough to reason with.

Isabel closed her eyes. Lucifer whickered and nudged her shoulder. "None of the hands go near this horse, let alone climb into the corral with him, unless I'm there. I was watching from my bedroom window when Lucifer reared. My only concern was to get you out of danger."

Jaret didn't look convinced. He just stood there, silent, still, staring at her as if she had grown a second head.

"I'm sorry if I offended you. I thought I'd fastened my dress as I left my room, but I was obviously unsuccessful. I have never appeared before the men on this ranch in such a state, and I wouldn't have this time if I hadn't been so worried about you."

Her voice rose and she slapped her fists onto her hips in frustration. Her dress gapped open again. With a gasp of dismay, she yanked the edges together and turned her back.

She felt Jaret move, though he didn't make a sound. "I've been taking care of myself since I was six years old, Miss Bennett. Save your worry for someone who needs it."

Before she could reply, he jammed his battered hat on his head, spun on his heal and strode from the barn. He was silhouetted, tall and impressive, against the brilliant sunlight for a moment as he opened the far door, then he was gone.

The slamming of the door brought Isabel back to the present. Muttering about hardheaded men, she turned her attention to Lucifer. At least she could have a civil conversation with one male on the ranch, she thought with a smile.

Jaret hoped the hours before dinner would give his temper time to cool, but riding among the horses hadn't helped. The woman infuriated him one minute and tempted him to kiss her senseless the next. For his own sanity, he ought to just mount up and ride out of here. Someone else could come and protect the spitfire.

The sun was close to setting when he turned his horse over to the boy in the stable and strolled around the back of the house. The ranch was impressive. Now that he'd seen more of it, he had to admit Two Roses truly was a fine legacy. The Bennetts were lucky to have it, although luck didn't keep it going. That took hard work, planning, and sheer grit, something Isabel seemed to have in abundance. All Jaret had to do was keep her alive long enough for Nick to figure out who wanted to steal it from them.

He heard Isabel before he saw her. She was walking in the garden behind the house, singing softly to herself. The basket she carried overflowed with roses in a dozen different shades, but she still wandered among the blossoms.

The woman had been quite a surprise. He'd expected a quiet, proper wallflower, as blond as her brother. Instead she was a high-spirited, black-haired beauty, tall and graceful, curvy in all the right places, with the regal bearing of the Spanish aristocracy whose blood flowed through her veins.

The woman carried herself with confidence. She had a big job running this ranch, and from what he'd heard from the men today, she took her responsibilities very seriously. After more than a month on the trail with Nick Bennett, Jaret was certain that serious wasn't a word used to describe him.

Isabel shared little of her brother's easygoing attitude. Nick always seemed to be laughing, a bright burst of light in a dank, murky place.

The night he'd met Nick Bennett in a saloon in Galveston, he remembered thinking, for one brief moment, this was a man he might have come to call friend. But Jaret was a gun for hire, and he'd been paid to capture Bennett and deliver him to Perote Prison, deep inside Mexico, not make friends.

Now Nick was recovering after the bullet meant to silence Jaret had nearly killed him instead. He owed Bennett, and Jaret Walker always paid his debts.

Jaret watched Isabel wander through the flowers, gently touching one, inhaling the sweet fragrance of another. She had changed her dress. This one was a green that reminded him of the hills back east. Its softness made her seem almost delicate.

With a rush of heat he recalled that afternoon, when she'd been so angry with him that she'd forgotten her dress no longer covered her. The memory of the creamy flesh he'd glimpsed through the torn gown made his fingers itch to touch her, to see if she was as soft as he imagined.

He cursed under his breath at his body's response. He was still furious with her for taking such a risk, but his body was entertaining ideas of a nature that had nothing to do with anger. Disgusted with himself for losing even that much control, he turned around, not wanting her to see how she affected him. She spotted him before he could get out of sight.

"Mr. Walker, I didn't know you were there."

"I didn't want to intrude, ma'am. You seemed to be enjoying yourself."

She looked away, a bloom of pink coloring her cheeks. "I love this garden. So much of my mother remains here. The flowers were her greatest joy. My parents came to live here soon after they were married, and Papa told Mama she could have anything she wanted. She wanted roses. So my father planted two rosebushes under that tree the day they arrived. Each year after that, on their anniversary, he planted two more. Nick and I continued the tradition."

Isabel joined him and they strolled toward the house. "That's where the name of the ranch came from, according to my mother. My father insisted he named it for my mother and me."

Jaret took her elbow as they climbed the three steps onto the back porch. The gesture was so natural that he didn't think about it. But it brought them close together, and he saw for the first time that her dark eyes were rimmed with gold, and she had a sprinkling of honey-colored freckles across her nose. They softened her somehow.

He had a sudden urge to kiss the tip of that aristocratic nose. Instead, he released her arm and stepped back, needing to put some distance between them. With a nod, Jaret tipped his hat and walked away.

Isabel stood watching him, confused by his sudden departure. They'd been talking—no, *she'd* been talking. Isabel shook her head, frustrated. She'd managed to scare off the first man she'd ever met who truly interested her.

She could still feel the warmth of his hand on her arm. Jaret Walker stirred up all her girlish fantasies of husband and family, things she thought she'd given up on. It was probably foolish, but she wanted to know what it felt like to be kissed by a man like him. No, she corrected, refusing to lie to herself. She wanted to be kissed by *him*.

Shaking off her disappointment at chasing him away, she went into the house to check on dinner. She heard Uncle Enrique railing at the cook as she opened the door.

"Damn it, woman. Can't you even make a proper meal?"

"Of course she can, Uncle. What is it you expected to have this evening?"

He swung around to face Isabel, and swayed on his feet as he worked to focus on her. She sighed quietly and set the basket of roses on the table. Dinner was going to be a difficult affair with him in this state. And a small part of her wanted it to be special, because Jaret would be there.

"Listen, little girl, I've tried to be patient. But this has gone on long enough. If you would tend to your duties instead of pretending to be a man . . ."

He paused for breathe and Isabel braced herself for another argument about her unmarried state. But before her uncle could launch into his speech, the door opened behind her.

"Excuse me, Miss Isabel." Manuel, the dear old man

who had been foreman on the ranch since before she was born, stepped into the kitchen.

"What is it, Manuel?" Isabel spoke, but didn't turn away from her uncle. Experience had taught her to be wary of his temper when he'd been drinking.

"It's Lucifer."

She spun to face him, no longer concerned about her uncle's wrath. "What's wrong?"

"Nothing terrible, *pequeña*. He needs to be groomed, but he is in a difficult mood."

She relaxed a little. "I'll be there in a few minutes."

Manuel left without answering, but she knew everything would be ready for her. Reminding herself to be patient with her uncle, she turned back to find him weaving his way out of the kitchen, muttering about horses, women, and whiskey. She prayed he would be unconscious before dinner and followed it with a prayer for forgiveness for having such thoughts. Then she hurried to change her clothes. Lucifer wouldn't be as patient with her as she tried to be with her mother's only brother.

Jaret waited until Isabel was busy with her horse before returning to the house. Nick had told him there were two people on the ranch besides Isabel he could trust completely. While her brother thought she should be told the truth, Jaret still wasn't convinced. He no longer thought she was the one trying to make Nick disappear, but someone wanted the man dead and Jaret suspected there were accomplices on the ranch watching Isabel. He didn't want to tip his hand.

Jaret had cornered Manuel after he left Isabel on the porch. The old vaquero had been tight-lipped until Jaret gave him Nick's message. Something in the words he'd carefully repeated had convinced the old man Jaret was telling the truth.

"Is he well?" Manuel had continued to groom the young colt tethered in front of him.

"As well as can be expected. He's not strong enough to travel yet or he'd have come himself."

The old man limped around the horse he was grooming to brush the other flank. "Nicolas is right, Mr. Walker. Something is going on here, but I can't discover what. I fear for Isabel, but what am I to do? She is strong-willed, that one. She will stay and fight rather than leave the ranch to save herself."

"That's why I'm here. Nick wants her protected. I can manage it on my own, but I'd rather have your help." When Manuel nodded his agreement, Jaret glanced around to assure himself they were alone. "Let me tell you what I have in mind."

With Manuel's cooperation gained, Jaret went in search of the only other person he would confide in. Climbing the stairs, he spotted Lydia going into a room across the hall from his own. Making sure they were alone, he followed.

The room was light and airy. The walls were a soft white and the numerous windows were framed by draperies of a rich ivory fabric that glowed in the early evening light. Above the fireplace hung a painting of Isabel, but it didn't look quite right. Her mother, he decided, and knew without a doubt where Isabel had gotten her dark Spanish beauty.

A simple kneeling bench of ancient mahogany sat in the far corner. On the burnished wooden shelf beneath an old, beautiful icon of the Virgin and Christ Child, three small candles waited to be lit for prayers.

On the wall opposite the fireplace hung a large gilded mirror. It reflected the feminine furnishings. The room was simple and elegant, not filled with the girlish excesses he'd expected. But it held her scent. A light mix of roses and female filled the air. Her perfume had distracted him more than once since they'd met. Now he wondered if he'd ever again smell the scent of roses without thinking of Isabel Bennett.

Lydia moved through the room, folding this, straightening that. She was short, barely reaching Jaret's chest, and her rather round body gave the impression of someone who moved slowly through life. From what Jaret had seen, the notion couldn't be more wrong. This woman was a force to be reckoned with. He made a slight noise to gain Lydia's attention.

She straightened from the bureau. "*Señor,* your room is across the hall."

"Yes, Mama Lydia, I know."

He called her by the nickname he'd been told only Nick Bennett used. The effect was immediate. The old woman stared at him in shock. Then her round black eyes filled with tears. Jaret read the surprise and the worry shining in their dark depths. He was sure she had questions, but she didn't say a word.

"He's all right," Jaret assured her. "Sick and worn nearly to the bone, but he will live for a long time yet."

Her shoulders dropped slightly in relief, then straightened with annoyance. "Then why doesn't he come home where I can make him well again?"

Jaret glanced into the hall to be certain no one was nearby, then closed the door before answering. "He's too weak to travel. The bullet he took nearly killed him."

"He was shot?" Lydia hurried forward. "I must go to him."

"No."

She took a step back at the command in his voice, and he cursed under his breath. It wouldn't do any good to frighten the woman. He gentled his tone. "He's on the mend and will be here as soon as he is strong enough to travel. Then he'll take all the nursing and fussing you have in you. But for now, he needs your help. So does Isabel."

Lydia frowned and nodded slowly, never looking away from him. Jaret hoped his friend was right about the fierce loyalty this woman had toward the children she'd helped raise.

"I'm taking Isabel away from here."

He waited as Lydia choked back an instant denial. She had something to say, but she remained silent, waiting for him to finish.

"Nick is afraid for her safety if she remains here. I have a plan to get her off the ranch, but I need your help to do it."

Lydia wandered to the tiny altar and stared at the painted image of salvation for a long moment. Then she turned to him. "What does Nicolas say I am to do?"

The plan to kidnap her mistress was his, not Nick's, but Jaret didn't bother correcting her. For now, gaining the woman's agreement to help was all that mattered.

"I will ride out in a couple of days. That same night, I'll return and take her with me. Manuel agreed to help me. I need you to conceal the fact that she's missing for as long as possible. Tell anyone who asks she's ill and keep everyone, including her uncle, away from this room. Can you do that?"

"*Sí.* Of course. But how will you do this thing?"

Jaret shook his head. "The less you know, the less you may have to lie about." And the less chance of giving him away.

"Then you'll want to know that she checks on that devil horse every night just before retiring."

He allowed a rare smile to show, his mind assimilating the new information. "Go on."

"Long after dinner, Miss Isabel goes out to the barn to say good night to the horse. The ranch hands are already at their own dinner or card playing, so she is always alone. She says it's the way she likes it."

"Thank you, Lydia. I swear to you I'll keep her safe." Jaret checked once more that the hallway was empty, then he walked across it and into his own room. His step was a little lighter. If Don Enrique was drunk by nightfall every night, as Jaret suspected, getting Isabel off the ranch might not be hard after all. For the first time since he'd ridden in, he felt his plan had a chance of success.

Dinner was not as difficult as Isabel had feared. Her uncle had requested his meal be served in his room, saints be praised. With him unconscious upstairs from the whiskey and wine he'd consumed, she had only her guest to entertain. Though he was a very contained man, Jaret Walker was intelligent and a good conversationalist, once she'd prodded him into talking.

"I understand you rode over quite a lot of the ranch this afternoon, Mr. Walker. Did you find anything of interest?"

He hesitated over the bite on his fork before nodding. "It's an impressive place. Your father put together quite a spread here."

"Thank you." She smiled. Pleasure and pride filled her heart. "We're very proud of Two Roses."

"I saw a couple of dams I liked the looks of, but I want to spend more time with the horses tomorrow before I make any decisions. When Nick gets back, I should be ready to bargain on a price."

"There is no need to wait for my brother to return. I can handle the sale, whenever it's convenient for you."

She waited for him to make a remark about how a woman

has no head for ranching or horse trading, but he didn't. Instead he nodded.

"Then I'll let you know once I've made my final choices."

She knew her smile was too big, but she couldn't help it. She'd been running Two Roses since her father died, and this was the first time a man other than her brother had accepted that she was in charge.

Unfortunately, the hands weren't so quick to change. She was gradually bringing around the men who'd been here under her father, but those that Uncle Enrique had hired were unlikely ever to be swayed, including Hank Hardin, his new foreman. But if a man like Jaret Walker didn't mind conducting business with her, she might still have a chance to win over the rest of them.

"Thank you, Mr. Walker."

He looked up, his surprise evident.

"Most men have difficulty with a woman being in charge."

The look he pinned her with was sharp and direct. "I'm not most men."

She glanced down at her half-finished meal and smiled. But her smile faltered when he continued speaking.

"Have you been running the place since your brother left?"

So much for accepting her role as owner of the ranch. "I've been in charge since the death of our father."

"Doesn't the land usually go to the eldest?"

She took a deep, calming breath. She'd had this same conversation with several other men—not that they'd believed her explanation. But she could go through it once more for him.

"I *am* the eldest and Nicolas the youngest. Two brothers were born between us. The first died within a month of his birth. And our brother, Warren, was trampled by Lucifer's dam when he was four."

If she allowed herself, she could still hear her mother's screams of anguish and despair. There were times when the grief was almost alive within the house, like black wings beating at the windows. Isabel shook off the image and concentrated on her story. She wouldn't give in to the memories tonight.

"Nicolas was born just after Warren was killed. Mother never really recovered. She died a few weeks later."

Jaret laid a hand over hers where it was fisted on the table. The warmth of the simple touch swept through her.

"I'm sorry. I didn't mean to bring back your grief."

She slipped her hand from under his and stood. Jaret rose with her. As she led the way into the parlor, she wondered what had gotten into her. She'd never shared such intimate information with a stranger before. What was it about this man that made her say and do things that were so unlike her?

"Forgive me. It wasn't necessary to burden you with my family's history."

"I don't count it as a burden, ma'am. I consider your brother a friend. I'm interested to know more about him."

She brought herself back to the issue at hand. "My father never felt that my being female was an obstacle to running the ranch. He taught me as he would have taught Warren. Nicolas and I learned together."

Jaret declined her offer of brandy. She replaced the crystal decanter on the side table, secretly pleased he didn't take advantage of every opportunity to drink, as her uncle did.

"My father died when I was twenty-one, and I was left to run the ranch and raise a brother who was not yet sixteen. Nicolas made it clear he preferred to breed and sell horses, not fret over payroll and winter supplies, so he worries about the stock and I manage the operations of the ranch. It has proven to be a good arrangement for both of us."

Jaret watched her intently, but his eyes gave no indication of his thoughts. She forced herself not to fidget, waiting for his decision with outward calm.

"Then, in a day or two, we'll have business to discuss."

He bid her good night, but Isabel barely noticed. She danced in a circle, too elated to stand still. Finally she had been accepted as the owner of this ranch. For the first time, someone was willing to transact business with her instead of insisting on speaking with her brother or her uncle.

It had taken a long time, but at last she was regaining control of her home. Walking slowly, she headed to the barn to say good night to Lucifer. It wasn't necessary, since she knew Manuel would already have him settled, but it had become a ritual both she and the horse enjoyed. Since Nicolas's disappearance, it was about the only thing on the ranch that never changed.

When her father died, her world had collapsed. Everything comfortable had been torn away from her. She was suddenly in charge of a large ranch and a younger brother who, at fifteen, was already beginning to strain against the rules and expectations set down for him. These three years hadn't been easy but they'd survived and even begun to enjoy life again. Then Nicolas disappeared.

Enrique de la Rosa arrived the day after her brother left, offering his assistance in taking care of the ranch. Very quickly, he and Hank Hardin began to take over.

She had been too wrapped in fear to realize what was happening until it was nearly too late. Manuel had been the foreman for as long as she could remember, but he was pushed aside by her uncle and Mr. Hardin put in charge. Within a month, they'd hired ten new hands to work near the house and sent all the men who were loyal to her out onto the range, strengthening Hardin's control.

As if thinking of the foreman had conjured him out of thin air, Hardin stepped into her path. "Evenin', Isabel." His blond hair hung almost to the collar of his wrinkled blue shirt and his light brown eyes glinted hard in the moonlight. She supposed he would be considered handsome by most women, but to her he seemed ugly to his soul. He was tall enough that she had to look up and even that small advantage over her felt threatening.

"Excuse me." Isabel veered around him, but Hardin grabbed her arm and pulled her against his thick chest. "Let go of me, Mr. Hardin. Now."

Instead of complying, he tightened his grip and stroked a finger down her cheek and throat. "What's your hurry? Isn't a man allowed to spend time with the woman he's going to marry?"

"Marry!" She leaned away from his touch and managed to put a little space between them. "We've had this discussion before. I am not going to marry you."

"Sure you are. You just need a little time to get used to the idea. A beautiful woman like you ought to have a man around to see to your needs." He wrapped one big hand around the back of her neck. "And I've got all kinds of ways to convince you I'm just the man for the job."

Hardin dragged her closer until her breasts were flattened against him, his cold eyes staring at her lips. Isabel bent back and twisted her head, trying to avoid the kiss she knew was coming, but she couldn't break free of his grip.

"Let her go, Hardin." The command whipped out of the darkness near the barn.

"Stay out of it, Walker. This is between Isabel and me."

Jaret stepped between them, forcing Hardin to release

Isabel and take a step back. "From where I'm standing, Miss Bennett seems to disagree."

Hardin glared at Jaret and Isabel wondered if it would come to blows before the foreman backed down.

"Looks like you're safe for the time being, Isabel," he whispered. "I'll collect that kiss later." Hardin sauntered away, never sparing a glance at Jaret.

"Are you all right?" Jaret stayed between her and Hardin until the man disappeared into the darkness.

She took a hidden breath and concentrated on slowing her racing heart. "I'm fine. He didn't hurt me. I think he just wanted to intimidate me a little."

Jaret cursed under his breath. "I'm sorry I didn't get here sooner."

Isabel bit back a laugh when she realized he was serious. "You aren't responsible for my protection, Mr. Walker. Mr. Hardin is under the impression I'm going to marry him. That will never happen and he's going to have to learn to accept the disappointment."

Jaret glanced at her, humor sparking in his light blue eyes. "He isn't the only one who will be unhappy. Your uncle mentioned it three times when I ran into him this afternoon."

"He didn't!" When Jaret raised an eyebrow at her denial, she felt her face flame. "I'm so sorry. My uncle had no right to embarrass you like that. He refuses to accept that I won't get married and move away from Two Roses."

"Why not marry and stay on at the ranch? That would ruin his plans."

Isabel laughed. "True, but everything I have would belong to my husband the moment we speak our vows. And since I refuse to give up my ranch to anyone, I've decided never to marry."

Leaving Jaret to ponder that announcement, Isabel

hurried into the barn through the small side door. Lighting the lantern that hung on a peg just inside, she made her way toward Lucifer, pausing to stroke the nose of an old mare as she passed.

She inhaled the familiar scents around her and felt peace steal into her soul. The ranch was all that mattered. She didn't really want to give up her dreams of having children of her own and a love like her parents had shared, but she'd shrivel up and die if she had to leave Two Roses.

Jaret's face filled her mind, and she shook her head to scatter the vision. She wouldn't be foolish enough to build any dreams around that man, no matter how much he appealed to her. She had to stay firm in her decision to manage alone. She comforted herself with the knowledge that she was in charge of her own future, her destiny.

She smiled when Lucifer stuck his nose over the stall door and whickered a greeting. It would have to be enough.

Chapter Three

Jaret slipped into the barn and watched from the shadows as Isabel talked to her stallion. No one else was around. If it was like this every night, he should be able to grab her with even less trouble than it had taken to get her brother.

Her vulnerability should have made him angry, but under the circumstances, he was grateful. It would make his task easier and he'd take any break that came his way, since Isabel wasn't likely to cooperate. After her declaration that nothing would take Two Roses away from her, he doubted he would be able to convince her that leaving the ranch was necessary to keep her alive. If they were caught before he got her to Nick, he'd probably hang for kidnapping, a possibility he didn't care to dwell on.

While Isabel spoke in a soft voice to her horse, Jaret stayed alert for any sign of Hardin or one of the ranch hands returning to the barn. All he heard were the distant sounds of laughter from the bunkhouse and her quiet words. He knew he should slip out before he was spotted, but he found himself creeping closer and listening to her instead.

She stood inside the stall brushing Lucifer and carrying on a one-sided conversation. "Don't you look handsome tonight?" She ducked under the horse's head to the side near Jaret. "I'm so proud of you for not stomping Mr. Walker into the dust this afternoon." Lucifer tossed his head and whinnied. "I know, he should never have come into the corral, but he couldn't know that, and Hardin didn't tell him no one dared get close to you. I wonder if that was intentional on the part of our most unpleasant foreman. Regardless, Lucifer, I appreciate you not hurting my guest."

While Jaret was glad he hadn't been crushed beneath the flailing hooves, he figured it was more because he'd been able to get out of the way than any control exhibited by the horse.

Jaret decided on a change of plans. He'd never yet met a horse he couldn't handle. He could show her that her devil horse wasn't so tough after all and solve the problem of what mount she was going to ride on the long trip back to where her brother waited, all at the same time.

Jaret slipped out of the barn, checking the watch in his vest pocket to see how long she'd been inside. No one else was nearby. He waited a full minute before strolling back into the barn, closing the door with a loud *thump.*

She called out softly from the stall. "It's all right, Manuel. I'll settle Lucifer for the night."

"I'm not Manuel."

He crossed to the stall and leaned against the gate before she could escape. Lucifer tossed his head at the unfamiliar voice. Isabel soothed him and scratched his ear.

"Mr. Walker, I didn't expect to see you again."

"It's a nice evening. I thought I'd enjoy the air for a few minutes and make sure Hardin didn't follow you in here."

"He wouldn't dare." She tossed her long black hair over her shoulder, the move reminiscent of the proud horse behind her.

"Working with your devil horse, I see."

Her eyes flashed hot and he recognized the annoyance even in the flickering light of the lantern.

"He is not a devil, Mr. Walker."

"Sure looked like it from where I was this afternoon. But then, it's hard to tell the heart of a horse until you get to know him a bit."

Jaret kept his face impassive while he watched indecision race across hers. When she reached for the lantern he thought he'd lost the gamble, but she only turned up the flame.

"Give me your hand."

"Ma'am?"

Her eyes flashed sparks of gold in the twisting light.

"I doubt if he will allow it tonight, but if you truly want to get to know Lucifer, it's the best way. Come into the stall and give me your hand."

He quietly opened the gate and stepped inside, taking care not to make any sudden movements that would spook the massive animal. In spite of the control she demonstrated with the horse, he wouldn't risk her being crushed against the boards of the stall. Holding out his hand, he waited to see what she would do.

Talking softly to Lucifer, telling him what she was doing, Isabel took Jaret's outstretched hand and laid it on top of hers, much as he had done that afternoon in the corral. The jolt he felt at her touch caused his blood to heat, but Isabel gave no indication that she felt it. Very gently she began petting the horse's neck with long sweeping strokes.

She was so intent on the horse that Jaret was sure she didn't realize how close he was standing. He could feel the fabric of her skirt brush and tangle around his legs. He tried to concentrate, but the scent of roses clinging to her hair kept distracting him.

"Now keep the motion going and I'll move my hand out

of the way." She slipped her fingers from beneath his and he felt with amazing clarity the softness of her skin as it slid against his work-roughened palm.

She must have noticed it, too, because she took a sudden step back, treading on his boot. She didn't make a sound as she lost her balance. Jaret snaked an arm around her waist to keep her from toppling over and spooking Lucifer.

He held her for a long minute, inhaling roses and woman. The instant hardening of his body was natural, he reasoned, just the result of holding a beautiful woman in his arms. So he couldn't remember ever having feelings this sharp, this intense. That didn't mean Isabel was getting under his skin.

Jaret shifted a little so Isabel wouldn't bump into the effect she was having on him. He wouldn't mind standing here all night, but he doubted she'd take to that idea. He loosened his grip gradually until she stood on her own, all the while keeping up the sweeping strokes on the horse's long neck.

He half expected her to call a halt to the whole thing, but she remained where she was, trapped between his body and Lucifer.

They stood together for some time, both of them murmuring nonsense to the huge animal. When Isabel shifted, Jaret moved back a few inches to give her the space she wanted. She glanced up at him and the lantern light glowed in her dark eyes. When she moistened her lips with the tip of her tongue, Jaret nearly groaned aloud. What would those lips taste like? Isabel stepped to one side to allow Jaret more access to Lucifer and the moment was gone.

The horse shied when she moved, bringing Jaret's attention back to the animal. He spoke to Lucifer in a low voice, calming him, until the horse decided the stroking felt too good to worry about who was providing it and settled down once more.

Jaret extended the contact, gently scratching around the ears, then moving to the silky mane and long nose, making sure the horse would remember his scent. Finally he gave Lucifer a pat on the neck, praised his patience and good temper, snagged the lantern, and stepped out of the stall to join Isabel.

As he closed the stall door, he motioned for her to lead the way out of the barn. She walked ahead of him within the circle of light the lantern threw. He enjoyed watching her long skirt sway with her steps, the motion gentle, feminine. When his body jumped to attention again, he looked away, concentrating on anything but her.

Isabel waited while Jaret secured the door behind them. In the moonlight, she could see the stretch and play of muscle beneath his shirt as he blew out the lantern and returned it to its peg. She wanted to touch him, to see if he was as strong as he seemed when she'd fallen against him in Lucifer's stall. The desire was so overpowering, she had to clasp her fingers together to keep from reaching out.

When he offered his arm to escort her back to the house, giving her the excuse she needed to feel the muscles hidden by black cloth, she hesitated. She didn't understand what she'd felt earlier, the jolt that went through her each time she took his hand. The little ripple of anticipation that raced through her at the brush of Jaret's skin against hers unnerved her.

He'd done nothing improper, while he held her close in Lucifer's stall. She may be innocent, but she knew what the change in his body meant. She'd grown up on a breeding ranch, for heaven's sake. And she'd gained some personal experience the year before when a new ranch hand trapped her against the barn wall. His body had been hard like that, but his touch hadn't made her curious to know more. She was definitely curious now. Gathering her courage, she tucked her hand in the curve of Jaret's arm.

"It's a nice night." His deep voice broke the silence that settled between them, raising goose flesh all over her skin.

"Yes, it is." Isabel struggled to sound normal, but she couldn't think of a thing to say.

He guided her away from the front porch and strolled around the house toward the rose garden. "Do you like living out here?"

She smiled at the question. "I love it. I can't imagine living anywhere else."

"It must be kind of lonely, being surrounded by nothing but dust and ranch hands."

She looked up to find him watching her closely. "I've always had my brother. And the ranch employs nearly one hundred men *and* women. It's hard to find time to myself, let alone be lonely." She smiled at his sound of agreement. "And I have the children and my school."

Jaret glanced her way with a question in his eyes.

"A few years after Mama died, I started a school to teach the children of the ranch hands to read and write in English and in Spanish. I wasn't old enough to take on most of the work with the horses and I needed something to keep me busy. I found I love working with the children."

He slowed the pace as they strolled among the roses.

"I can't end the feelings of hatred and mistrust most settlers in these parts still feel toward the Mexicans who share this land, but those living on Two Roses are my family. I want to be certain the children who grow up here are able to make their way in either world should they ever choose to leave."

"How do you manage to teach school and run a ranch as large as this?"

"Since Nick disappeared, I've hardly had time for the lessons, but I just can't give it up. When I'm with the children, I don't . . ." Her words trailed off as she realized she was once again telling a man she hardly knew things even her own brother had never guessed.

"You don't what?"

She looked into Jaret eyes. Something in their blue depths dared her to share her greatest fear. "I don't worry so much about failing."

She let him lead her to a small stone bench set among the roses. How would she explain what that revelation meant? She waited for him to question her but he didn't ask.

"What about a husband and family? Or doesn't the thought of raising a family of your own interest you?"

She fussed with the folds of her skirt, suddenly unsure of what to say. He seemed to dip into her mind and pull out the very dream she tried so hard to give up. When she looked up again Jaret was waiting, his eyes shadowed and unreadable.

"Of course it does, but the men who've come calling have been more interested in having the ranch than marrying me. I won't marry a man who doesn't love me, not even to have a family. I would rather be alone than give up Two Roses."

Jaret sat next to her on the bench. "I can understand that. It's beautiful here."

His voice rumbled in her ears. In the darkness of the garden it seemed to caress her, like hidden fingers.

"Are you cold?"

"No, not at all." She caught herself rubbing her arms, and dropped her hands to her lap. "I'm fine."

"You're shivering."

She turned her head and found she was looking directly at his lips. She stared at them, wondering what they would feel like pressed against hers. All she had to do was lean forward, just a little. And why shouldn't she? After all, she'd decided not to marry. Why not have a taste of the fruit forbidden to a young woman saving herself for her husband? As she stared, his lips tilted upward in a slight smile.

Without a thought to the consequences, Isabel swayed toward him. He lowered his head to meet her.

Soft. It was the only thought her muddled mind could form. The kiss was as gentle as a warm spring breeze. She breathed in the mixture of his scent and roses and the combination made her light-headed. With a sigh, she leaned closer, putting her hands on his broad chest to keep her balance.

Jaret's arms came around her, gentle at first, tightening as he deepened the kiss. When she felt the tip of his tongue stroke the seam of her lips, she gave him access and soared with him to places she hadn't known existed.

She never wanted to stop. She wanted him to go on kissing her forever. He lifted his lips from hers and trailed kisses along her cheek and into her hair. She thought he whispered her name, but she couldn't be sure. The blood rushing through her veins drowned out every sound. She slipped her arms up to his shoulders, then around his neck, pulling him closer.

She could feel him, neck to hips, and she liked it very much. Hoping he would kiss her again, Isabel pressed swollen lips to his neck, tasting the skin above his collar with her lips, then hesitantly with her tongue. She felt his hands fist in her hair before he pulled her head back and found her mouth again.

This kiss was very different. Gone was the gentle breeze. It had been replaced by a whirlwind of feeling. He crushed her to him until she couldn't draw a breath. She heard a moan and realized with surprise that it came from her. She felt herself being lifted as Jaret settled her across his lap, never breaking the kiss.

Alarm began to weave into the fabric of desire. Dimly she realized she was lying in the arms of a man she barely knew. Old lessons surfaced to dampen her enjoyment. She stiffened only slightly, but it was enough.

With a groan, Jaret tore his lips from hers, but didn't release her. Isabel dropped her head to his shoulder, blushing as she realized she was holding him as closely as she was held.

Jaret rested his chin against her hair as his chest rose and fell under her cheek. Over the pounding of her heart, Isabel could hear his harsh breathing. What was she doing? Suddenly aware of where she was, and how she'd come to be there, embarrassment heated her already warm cheeks.

Isabel snatched her arms from around his neck and tried to put some space between her body and his, but found she couldn't without being dumped into the grass at his feet. She didn't want to struggle, but anyone in the house could look out a window and see them. So she began to wiggle, trying to turn enough to get her feet on the ground.

"What the hell are you doing?"

The rough edge to his voice made her tremble.

"I . . . we shouldn't . . . someone might see us," she managed.

With a soft laugh, he lifted her and set her back on the bench beside him. She immediately shifted away, but not before his hand trailed through her disheveled hair, brushing it out of her eyes. "It's kind of late to think of that, Princess."

"Don't call me that. You have no right to be so familiar."

"We were just tangled up on a garden bench in plain view of God and everybody. I think that gives me the right."

"I decide what liberties I allow a man to take. You have no say in the matter."

All softness disappeared. His face went hard and his eyes glinted like ice from beneath narrowed lids. When he spoke, his voice was cutting.

"Then let me be sure I understand where you've put the fence."

Without warning, he dragged her against him and crushed his mouth on hers, all gentleness gone. He mastered her struggles easily and took what he wanted. Her mind hazed and thoughts of fighting him faded away. Abruptly, he ended the kiss and released her. Before she could regain her balance, he stood and strode away without looking back.

Damn, how stupid could he be? Jaret railed at himself as he walked into the darkness, trying to regain the control he'd always taken for granted. He was a fool, kissing her like a common cowboy. *But that's what you are,* his conscience taunted. *Just a common, useless cowboy, the son of a bastard gambler. With dreams that are way too big for you.*

He tried to forget her taste, and how right she felt in his arms, but his mind refused to let go. He wasn't paying attention when he came around the house or he would have noticed the men waiting in the shadows.

"Walker."

Jaret's head snapped up as Hardin spoke from the darkness. He reached for his belt gun automatically, but froze at the sound of a cocking pistol. He held his hands away from his sides, in plain view.

"Go ahead." The foreman's voice dripped with malice and threat. "Draw. It'd be fine with me if I could just kill you now and be done with it."

Jaret didn't move.

"Pull it out slowly and toss it over there." He indicated the direction with a jerk of his head. Jaret did as he was told, except he tossed the gun behind him, toward the garden and away from Hardin.

A second man stepped into the moonlight on his left. Jaret hoped there were no more waiting in the shadows, but decided to concentrate on the ones he could see. He faced Hardin, keeping his body relaxed, ready for the attack. By the fury he read on the man's face, it wouldn't be long coming.

"What do you want, Hardin?"

Without taking his eyes off the foreman, Jaret followed the progress of the second man as he took up position. He was boxed in, with the house at his back.

Hardin took a step forward. "I'm sure you didn't realize it, but the woman is mine. And I don't allow poaching on my territory."

"What woman would that be?"

Hardin laughed, but it was an empty sound. "Now how many women have you seen on this ranch? Miss Isabel is promised to me. Part of my contract, you might say. You shouldn't have interrupted us before and you sure as hell shouldn't have gone walking with her. Guess you need to be taught to respect another man's property."

Jaret wondered if Hardin knew they'd done more that walk in the moonlight. When the man's fist connected with his jaw, he figured he had.

He sensed the other man moving in to join in the fray and braced himself to take on both of them, but the attack never came. When Hardin took a second swing at him, Jaret ducked and delivered three punches in rapid succession. Hardin grunted but didn't fall. Instead he threw his arms wide and rushed Jaret, sweeping him to the ground.

The dust that boiled up nearly blinded him and Hardin took full advantage of it. Jaret felt his lip split when the big man landed a punch. As Hardin pulled back to hit him again, Jaret surged upward to throw him off, then rolled to his feet.

When Hardin tried to stand, Jaret kicked his legs from under him, but the foreman didn't stay down for long. Jaret staggered backward when Hardin came off the ground and slammed a shoulder into him.

Fists flew, flesh connected with flesh with damaging results to both men. They were equally matched. Finally Hardin made a mistake. Jaret ducked a wild punch and delivered a double-fisted blow to the back of the foreman's head. Hardin went down without a sound and stayed there.

Jaret spun to face the second man, but found him flat out in the dust at Isabel's feet, his hands clasped behind his head and Jaret's pistol pointed at his back.

"Thank you, Miss Bennett." Jaret dragged the back of his hand across his mouth and winced at the stinging pain. Hardin had gotten in a couple of good licks. He leaned forward with his hands on his knees for a few seconds, trying to catch his breath. He took a quick inventory of his injuries. No bones were broken, but he'd be plenty sore in the morning. He dropped his head to his chest and let some of the adrenaline drain away before he straightened. "I can take care of him now."

"I'm still deciding if I want to shoot him."

Jaret saw the man pale at her words. "Do you think that's necessary?"

"Probably not." She stepped back and pointed the barrel of the gun at the dust. "He's a sorry excuse for a man, ganging up on a guest of mine, but he's not worth shooting." She walked around until she stood in front of the shaking man. "You're fired, Mr. Baker. I'll have your pay ready at first light. If I see your face on my land again after that, I'll shoot you for trespassing."

The ranch hand didn't waste a second getting out of sight.

Hardin groaned and stirred behind them. Moving faster than Jaret expected, Isabel spun around and pointed the weapon at her next target. The foreman lifted his head and focused on the shiny silver barrel aimed in his direction.

"Explain yourself, Mr. Hardin." Her words were said in a quiet, polite tone, but she was shaking with fury.

Hardin didn't cower in the dirt like the other man. He pushed to his feet and knocked some of the dust from his shirt before facing Isabel with an insolent smile.

"Just doing my job, Isabel. Your uncle told me to keep an eye on you. I didn't like what I saw, so I *explained* the situation to Walker. It's nothing to concern yourself with."

"You're wrong, Mr. Hardin. Everything on my ranch concerns me. I don't want you on my land any longer. You're fired."

The man laughed in her face. "Now, missy, we both know you can't do that. Only Mr. de la Rosa can fire me. Why don't you hand me that revolver and go on into the house like a good girl, so I can finish what I started?"

Jaret took a step toward the insolent man, but Isabel was quicker. She shifted the gun to point at Hardin's chest.

"Get out of my sight," she hissed. "Now!"

Hardin looked like he might argue then decided against it. With a glare at Jaret that promised it wasn't over, he turned his back on them both and sauntered into the night.

Jaret watched until the man went inside the bunkhouse before turning to Isabel. She was staring after Hardin, but he doubted she saw anything past the tears pouring down her face.

"Come on, honey, he isn't worth getting this upset about." When she didn't respond, he took the gun from her hands, eased the hammer forward and holstered the weapon. Then he led her around the front of the house and into the parlor. Leaving her for a moment, he searched until he located a lamp and some matches. Once he had light, he urged her into a chair and went looking for some whiskey.

When he returned, her tears had stopped, but Isabel didn't take the glass when he held it out to her. Dropping to one knee in front of her, he lifted it to her lips. "Come on, honey. Drink some of this. You'll feel better." He coaxed her to take a sip, then another, until she finally took the glass from him and drank on her own.

Jaret glanced in the mirror that hung over the mantel and grimaced. He was a mess, but he didn't want to leave her alone. Instead he poured a healthy shot of whiskey for himself, tossed it back, and waited for her to come out of it.

"He's right, you know. There's nothing I can do. It's my ranch, but I'm powerless."

Her voice wasn't much more than a whisper, but Jaret heard the defeat. "There's no such word, to my way of thinking."

"I can't fire him. I own the ranch, but I don't have the power to throw him or any of the other hands my uncle hired off the ranch. Except for the few men who were here when he arrived, my uncle has taken control." Isabel fidgeted in her chair, clenching and unclenching her fists.

"Then why not marry? You might have to share the place with your husband, but at least you'll keep your uncle and Hardin from taking the ranch away completely."

"I have no intention of marrying, ever."

Jaret doubted she was serious. "You're too young to make a choice like that."

"Well, I've made it." In a gesture of defiance, Isabel gulped down the last of the whiskey and began to cough as it seared a path down her throat. Tears welled, but this time it was from the burning of the liquid.

Jaret took the glass from her hand before she dropped it. There was nothing he could do but wait her out, so he patted her back in sympathy.

When the coughing subsided, Isabel looked up. “You’re bleeding!”

Jaret stared in confusion at her abrupt mood swing. He shrugged. “It’s happened before. Nothing I won’t get over.”

She sprang to her feet and grabbed his wrist. “Nothing, he says.” She huffed, and started to the kitchen with him in tow. “Blood running down his cheek and threatening to drip on my furniture, but it’s nothing,” she mocked. “Hard-headed cowboy.”

“Thank you, ma’am. I didn’t think you’d noticed.”

Muttering to herself about men in general and him in particular, she pointed Jaret toward a chair and went to the hearth for hot water.

“Look, Miss Bennett, this isn’t necessary. I’ll manage on my own.”

“Sit down, Mr. Walker.”

Wishing he’d thought to grab the whiskey, Jaret did as he was told. That surprised him. The last time he’d done what he was told without arguing was probably before he’d left home. Except for following his many bosses’ orders, of course, but he didn’t think that counted here.

He raised an eyebrow at the pan of water and pile of clean cloths Isabel set beside him on the table, but he didn’t comment.

She went to work cleaning up the cuts and scrapes Hardin had inflicted. He broke the silence once or twice with a hissed curse, but Isabel didn’t stop until the job was completed. At last, she handed him a clean, damp cloth and stepped back. “Keep that on your lip, Mr. Walker. I’ll be right back.”

When she left the room, Jaret dragged air into his lungs.

It'd been hard to breathe ever since she'd stepped between his knees and started on his face. He knew how soft her skin was, and her scent clouded his mind. It had taken more control than he thought he possessed to keep his hands from reaching for her. More than once, he'd opened his mouth to tell her to go away, but he hadn't been able to do it. He found he liked having her fuss over him.

That was another surprise, since he'd never allowed a woman to worry with the minor bruises life put on him. Even his mother had given up. After his good-for-nothing father had taken off and he'd become the man of the family, Jaret had turned away her concerns and kisses with half-man bravado, even while the boy inside him longed for the attention. When she hadn't looked beyond the bravado, he'd convinced himself he didn't want the attention anyway.

Isabel returned, carrying the whiskey bottle and a glass. Jaret nearly kissed her hand in gratitude, but doubted that he'd be able to stop with her hand. He thanked her with a nod.

She sat across the table from him while he took a healthy swallow, welcoming the burn of the liquor on his busted lip. It reminded him that coddling and mothering were two things he no longer needed.

"I'm sorry, Mr. Walker."

He looked up, but Isabel was staring at the floor. "You have nothing to apologize for."

That brought her head up. "I should've realized that Mr. Hardin would assume you were a suitor. I could have set the matter straight and there would have been no reason for this outrageous attack."

Her eyebrows lifted at his hissed response to that bit of nonsense, but he didn't care. "You were only the excuse. He didn't jump me because I was poaching on his intended bride. He was worried I might beat him to the land through you. Hardin would marry a mule if he thought it would get him what he's after." He slammed back the whiskey and stood.

"Is that why you kissed me, Mr. Walker? Because it might help you get my ranch?"

"No! I—" Before he could finish she stormed to her feet and whirled through the room, her skirts snapping at her heels.

"I thought you were already building a ranch of your own. Why do you want mine?"

Jaret grabbed her arm as she stalked past. "Let's get one thing straight. I didn't kiss you to get at your land. I kissed you because I wanted to. One has nothing to do with the other. And don't ever compare me to Hardin again."

Chapter Four

"Morning, Miss Bennett."

She waved at the cowboy coming out of the bunkhouse and nearly tripped over the dogs that tumbled over one another in their race to greet her. She leaned down to pet them and laughed as a cold nose bumped her chin. "Go on, now." She straightened and shooed them away. "Go find your breakfast, you silly pups."

A light breeze ruffled her hair and she closed her eyes to inhale the sweet scent of morning. Though the sky was barely light, the ranch was already humming with activity. Men and women alike were at their chores long before the sun made an appearance. Even the children were up, though not quite awake.

She grinned as three boys under the age of ten went running past, racing to answer the bell that called everyone to breakfast. Marta's youngest son, Miguel, waved as he dashed by, followed closely by the half-grown puppy he'd been given for his eighth birthday.

When Isabel headed for Lucifer's stall, the puppy bounded after her, nearly tripping on its long ears. She rubbed its head and received a tongue-bath in return. Grinning, she sent the dog back to Miguel.

Lucifer voiced his opinion of her the moment she came within reach, giving her an equine lecture for ignoring him to play with a mere dog. She tried to sooth his displeasure with grain and fresh water, but Lucifer refused to settle down. Finally she gave up and led him out of the stall. He nearly stepped on her in his eagerness to get out.

"What is the matter with you this morning, Lucifer?"

"Problem?"

Isabel jumped when Jaret spoke from right behind her, causing the horse to dance away to the end of his lead. She held on tightly until he calmed a little.

Jaret put out a hand for the horse to sniff, then took hold of his halter while Isabel secured the leather lead to a nearby post. "Sorry, I didn't mean to startle either of you."

"It's all right. I get caught up in what I'm doing and forget I'm not the only one in the barn." She patted Lucifer's neck. "What are you doing in here?"

"Just checking on Sand Dune."

"Sand dune?"

"My horse."

"Of course, the buckskin mare." Isabel pushed Lucifer away when he nibbled at her pocket looking for a treat. "She's a beautiful horse."

"She's got a heart of gold, and she puts up with me, which is all I can ask."

He stroked long fingers along Lucifer's nose and jaw. Something was definitely on the man's mind.

"I owe you an apology for last night." He pulled his mangled hat off and ran impatient fingers through his hair. The bruise around his eye and the split lip showed up well in the sunlight. "I lost my temper and behaved as badly as Hardin."

For an instant, Isabel considered pretending she didn't understand, but the stiffness of his manner and the muscle jumping in his clenched jaw hinted that an apology didn't come easily for him.

"Apology accepted. Neither of us was thinking very clearly last night. Let's forget it happened."

Jaret settled his hat back in place. "That won't be easy with a shiner like this for everyone to see."

She reached to sooth his scraped cheek, snatching her hand back when she realized what she was doing.

Jaret didn't comment. Instead, he shoved his hat back a little and hooked a boot heel over a low board of a nearby stall. "Lucifer seems a little spooked this morning."

Grateful for the change of subject, Isabel focused on the horse. "He is, and I don't understand why. Normally he loves the attention, but today he doesn't want to settle down." She patted the horse's neck and went to the small area next to the stall to retrieve Lucifer's saddle. Jaret followed to help. When she saw a blanket on the floor she frowned again. "What is this doing here? I'll have to speak with Manuel. The men should be more careful." She grabbed a corner of the heavy wool.

Isabel heard the warning rattle the instant she touched the blanket. She jumped back with a scream but Jaret moved faster. Wrapping one arm around her waist, he yanked her away and drew his gun, watching carefully for any sign of the rattlesnake.

"Don't shoot yet," Isabel whispered, breathless from the scare. "You'll spook the horses. I don't want them hurt."

Jaret nodded slightly and released her, never looking away from the snake's hiding place.

Isabel turned to the men who'd come running when she screamed. "We've got a rattlesnake in here. Move all the horses out into the corral. If we have to shoot it, I don't want any animals panicking and hurting themselves or one of you."

Several of the men started to argue about her staying when one of them could do it, but she cut them off. "I'll be fine. You worry about the horses. Take the dogs, too," she added when one of them stalked forward on stiff legs to investigate, a low growl rumbling in its throat.

The men scattered to do as she'd asked. Once the barn was empty of everyone else, she turned to Jaret. "I'll move the blanket aside and—"

"You'll stay the hell out of the way," he snapped.

Her temper flared. "Mr. Walker, I give the orders here."

"Not this time. Hand me that pitchfork and get back."

Isabel stayed where she was for one stubborn instant before doing as she'd been told. There was nothing to be gained by arguing with the man until the snake was disposed of. Then she would give him a piece of her mind.

Jaret tested the balance of the pitchfork until he was satisfied. When he shifted the blanket again, this time using the pitchfork, the snake rattled another ominous warning. Jaret remained still, only turning his head like a wild animal focusing in on its prey. Then, in a move so sudden it shocked her even when she was expecting it, he threw the blanket aside and fired his pistol twice in rapid succession. Using the pitchfork, he prodded the carcass of the rattlesnake a few times, then holstered his gun.

The dogs set up a ruckus outside the barn, and shouts came from some of the men. Isabel stomped to the large doors of the main entrance and heaved one open, spending some of her anger on the heavy wood. The dogs leaped into the barn, circled her twice and then raced toward Jaret. Miguel's puppy rolled along in their wake. A sharp command from Jaret had them dropping back with a whine, their bodies vibrating with barely contained excitement.

Manuel was the first man in, followed closely by Miguel. The rest of the ranch hands and a good number of the children crowded inside behind them, all talking at once. "Are you all right?" "What the hell was the shooting about?" "Can I see the snake, Miss Bennett?"

Isabel focused on the last question because it was easier to answer without the risk of losing the grip on her temper. "Yes, Miguel, you may, if Mr. Walker says it's safe." She recognized the sarcasm in her tone as she said his name, but she couldn't help it.

Men and boys alike fell silent as Jaret approached with the snake dangling from the tines of the pitchfork. It was at least six feet long, with an impressive number of rings to its rattle. A bite from it would probably have been fatal, a slow, agonizing way to die. Isabel swallowed hard when she realized how close she'd come to finding out. She forced herself to look up, intending to offer an apology. The words backed up in her throat when she saw the icy fury smoldering in his cobalt eyes.

Miguel couldn't wait to take a closer look. He bounced forward, staring wide-eyed at the snake. Jaret stopped him from touching it with a sharp look. "Take it outside." He held out the pitchfork. "Skin it if you want to, but keep the dogs away."

Manuel called the dogs and one of the men scooped up the puppy as Miguel passed carrying his prize. The combined weight of the pitchfork and the large snake was almost more than he could manage, but he tightened his grip on the wooden handle and marched proudly out of the barn, followed closely by two other boys, both asking if they could help carry it. After a few more questions and comments, the men went back to their morning routines.

"Miss Bennett." Jaret's voice was cold and commanding.

Isabel spun to face him, her anger flaring back to life. "How dare you question me! I give the orders here."

"Then give intelligent ones," he fired back. "Nobody

with any sense would just walk up to a cornered snake and try to force it into the open." He slammed the door of the nearest stall, rattling it on its hinges. "Or did you figure it was a gentleman snake and wouldn't dare bite a woman?"

"I had no intention of getting that close. You aren't the only one here capable of rational thought. I would have used something to pick up the blanket." But she had to admit, at least to herself, that she hadn't considered how to stay a safe distance from the snake when she'd made the suggestion to move the blanket.

She tossed her head and pushed past him, but he grabbed her arm and dragged her to a halt. She rounded on him and found herself standing so close she could feel the heat radiating from his hard body.

"Let go of me. I need to see to Lucifer."

"Not until this is settled."

She yanked from his grip. "There is nothing to settle." She spun around and stomped off.

"How did that snake get in here?"

His soft words stopped her in her tracks. She didn't face him, but she was listening. "There are rattlesnakes everywhere in this country, Mr. Walker. It's not inconceivable that one would find its way into my barn."

"Then how did it happen to end up all the way down here instead of in the first dark corner it found? Lucifer's the one horse in here that won't tolerate anything or anyone remotely unfamiliar near him, yet he lets a six foot rattlesnake slither in and curl up next to him without making a sound?"

Jaret crossed to stand in front of her. "From what I've seen, everyone here is very careful about these horses. I find it hard to believe anything as large as that snake could have gotten in and crossed the barn without anyone seeing a sign of it. Even if the hands missed it, the dogs shouldn't have."

Isabel looked over her shoulder toward Lucifer. "It doesn't seem likely, I'll admit."

"And I guess it was just your bad luck that a blanket happened to slide off the rail and land on top of the snake, keeping it from moving until you came along to uncover it."

Possibilities raced through Isabel's mind, but they all led back to the same conclusion. "You think someone put that snake in Lucifer's stall for me to find."

Jaret didn't reply. He didn't have to.

"Why would anyone go to all this trouble?"

Before he could say anything, two of the men walked in with the dogs on short leads.

Isabel's brows drew together. "What's going on?"

Manuel pointed the other man toward the left. "I want to be sure there aren't any more surprises waiting before we bring the horses back inside."

Isabel stared at the blanket still crumpled in the dust, her mind racing ahead with gruesome images of what might have happened. What if Jaret hadn't been there to pull her to safety? Her hand went to her throat, finding it difficult to draw a breath. She jumped in fright when Jaret touched her shoulder.

"Are you all right?" His soft question undid her.

She took a step back. She had to get out of here. "Manuel, please take care of Lucifer."

The barn walls were beginning to close in on her. She needed to be outside for a while. She walked toward the door and sunlight, fighting the urge to run, forcing herself to at least appear calm.

"Isabel, wait."

She kept going, suddenly desperate to get out of the barn. Once through the door she walked faster, trying to leave behind the fear and worry that was plaguing her.

"Damn it, woman, where are you going?"

She finally stopped in the shade of a huge live oak tree. Its small green leaves rustled in the wind, and she closed her eyes to absorb the soothing sound.

Jaret followed close on her heels. “Isabel, what’s wrong? Talk to me.”

She shook her head, not trusting her voice to be steady.

“Easy, sweetheart. Just take a deep breath. Everything will be all right.”

Her breath hitched and she felt tears sting her eyes. She fought to keep them from falling. Tears made her appear weak and feminine, and she couldn’t afford to be either if she wanted to be accepted as the one in charge. When Jaret put a hand on her shoulder, she flinched before accepting the simple comfort he offered.

She concentrated on the weight and warmth of his hand. When she was sure she could speak without sobbing, she opened her eyes. Jaret stood between her and the barn, blocking her from view of the people gathered around. “I just needed some air. I suddenly realized how very close I’d come to that snake.” She dragged the warm morning air into her lungs. “I hate snakes.”

“Well, at least you’ve got the sense to be scared.”

She knocked the hand off her shoulder. “I didn’t say I was scared. I was only a little . . . unnerved.”

“Then I take it back. You don’t seem to have much sense after all.”

“Oh.” She balled her hands into fists. “I swear, Jaret Walker, if you weren’t a friend of my brother’s, I would—”

She broke off when something flashed in the sunlight, drawing her attention. She stared hard at the three approaching riders. One of them seemed familiar, but they were too far away for her to see clearly.

“Expecting company?”

She shot him what she hoped was a discouraging glare.

"No, but that doesn't mean no one will show up. Sometimes people send letters that never get here." She aimed a falsely sweet smile at him and went to meet the riders.

She was halfway across the yard when her uncle came out of the house. He was dressed in his best suit, and his thinning hair was slicked back with oil. A feeling of dread settled in the pit of her stomach. "No, it can't be." She glanced toward the riders, then glared at her uncle. "He wouldn't dare."

"Who are they?"

She jumped when Jaret spoke. "Stop sneaking up on me! And who they are doesn't concern you." She stomped off a few feet in the direction of the riders, then changed her mind and headed for the house, leaving Jaret behind. Her uncle was going to get a piece of her mind before they made it to the yard.

"Isabel, there you are. Go change into an appropriate gown, my dear. You have company."

"What are they doing here?" She stopped on the stairs in front of him, eye to eye with his less than impressive height.

He harrumphed once, then cleared his throat. "I invited them. Now you go get yourself cleaned up. There's no need to shame me by looking like a common ranch hand."

Isabel could feel her temper rising. Her uncle had never seen her full Spanish fury before, but a demonstration might be in order. Before she could open her mouth, a shout from the barn let her know the riders had been spotted.

"This won't work, Uncle. I'm not going to marry him."

"Nonsense, girl. It's past time you found a husband. Silas Williams has done very well for himself. He's a fine catch, and he'll leave you a wealthy woman when he dies."

Isabel gave in to temptation and stomped her foot. "Then *you* marry him! How dare you invite them here without asking me? I'm not a horse to be sold to the highest bidder."

"That is quite enough, young lady. You refuse to understand my responsibilities in this matter. Without your father here to care for you, it falls to me to make you see reason. Now go inside and change."

Isabel lifted her chin and arched a brow. She might have to offer hospitality to them, but she didn't have to dress up to do it. Pasting a smile on her lips, she waited for the riders to reach the house.

"Mr. Williams, what a surprise. I wasn't expecting visitors."

The older man glanced over at her uncle with a frown, but recovered quickly. "Good afternoon, Miss Bennett. When I got Mr. de la Rosa's invitation, I rounded up my boys and left the ranch as quick as I could. We certainly wouldn't want to keep a lady waitin' at a time like this."

What exactly her uncle had put into that letter? She shot a glance over her shoulder, staring daggers at the infuriating man, letting him know she wasn't finished with him.

The other two riders flanked Silas. "Isabel . . . You don't mind if I call you Isabel, do ya? After all, we're practically family now." He cackled at the statement, as if it was some grand joke. "Now then, Isabel, I don't believe you've met my boys. This here's Jacob."

He motioned to his right with a knobby left hand. "He's the oldest. Not much to look at, but he's a decent enough boy and he's turning into a fine rancher." Jacob shared his father's dark coloring, but looked to be better groomed. He glared at his father as he touched the brim of his hat in greeting.

Silas shifted his hat into his left hand to motion with the right one. "That one's Eli. Got his mama's looks, God rest her, but not much of a head for business." Eli swept off an expensive-looking hat to reveal a thatch of curly yellow hair that brushed his collar. In another situation, he might have struck her as handsome, but right now she could only think about how long the day was going to be.

She didn't let her thoughts show on her face or in her voice. "Welcome to Two Roses, gentlemen. Won't you come inside?"

"Thanks, ma'am," Jacob replied, "but I'd like to see the stock first, if it's all the same to you."

"The stock?" She was confused. "Are you here to buy horses?"

Silas Williams laughed. "Well, hell—I mean, uh, shoot no, Isabel. The boy just wants to see what sort of animals he'd be bringing to our place when you two get hitched. That is if you choose him over me or Eli, of course."

Isabel knew her mouth was hanging open, but she couldn't help it. If she understood the man, her uncle had offered her to all three. All she had to do was pick one. She turned very slowly on her heel to find her uncle had disappeared inside the house. "Coward," she muttered.

"Pardon, ma'am?" Eli moved close, too close to Isabel's way of thinking. She eased back a little, but he followed. She took another step away and bumped into a warm, hard body. She glanced over her shoulder at Jaret. *Wonderful,* she thought. *Another one.*

Eli's eyes took on a predatory gleam as he sized up his assumed rival. Jaret was so close she felt him stiffen before he eased her to his left side, caressing her shoulder before releasing her. Isabel considered letting them work it out among themselves, but let the impulse pass. She resented having to give any explanations, but when the three Williams men closed ranks to face Jaret, she knew she had to do something before their territorial displays got out of hand. Pasting a smile on her lips, she stepped between them.

"Mr. Williams, this is Jaret Walker, a rancher from over near Galveston. He came to see Nicolas about buying some horses." She glanced over her shoulder. "Mr. Walker, these are our nearest neighbors, Silas, Jacob, and Eli Williams."

Silas's brows furrowed for an instant as he stared at Jaret. The anger that flashed through them surprised her, but it was gone so quickly she wondered if she'd imagined it. Jacob and Eli were as easy to read as a picture book. The instant she mentioned business, they both relaxed.

Silas stuck out his hand. "Welcome to our part of the world, Walker. What happened to your face?"

"Just a *discussion* I had last night." Jaret shook Silas's hand. Jacob raised his chin in a perfunctory nod and headed for the corral. Silas struck up a conversation about ranching in general and this ranch in particular, while Eli resumed sniffing around her like a dog after a potential mate.

Only Jaret's reaction remained a mystery. His eyes were shaded beneath his hat, and his mouth seemed relaxed as he made small talk with Silas. Only the muscle jumping in his jaw gave her any indication of his mood. Deciding it was more than she wanted to contend with, she excused herself and went to see Marta about lunch.

Isabel finally gave in to her uncle's badgering and changed into a soft blue muslin dress for the meal. When she walked into the room, the three Williams men jumped to their feet. Jaret straightened more slowly, his eyes moving over her in a quick appraisal of her appearance before looking away.

It annoyed her that he didn't seem to notice that she'd taken the time to put on far too many clothes for the occasion. She'd even let Lydia convince her to wear a corset, though she was already regretting it. The thing was so tight it was difficult to breathe. She'd probably suffocate, if she didn't melt away from the heat first.

Silas Williams led her to the seat beside him. At least he'd bathed recently. The last time he'd visited he'd reeked of sweat and horses and some rancid cologne he'd used liberally to try and cover up the evidence.

She perched on the very edge of the settee, the extent of movement the corset allowed, and tried to concentrate on what Silas was saying.

"Walker here was just tellin' us yer pretty good at handlin' the ranch all on your own."

She shot a surprised glance at Jaret where he leaned against the mantel. He raised one eyebrow in acknowledgment.

"Of course," Silas continued, "I don't think you should be worrying about such things, not when there's bread to be baked."

Her uncle answered from his customary seat near the whiskey. "I quite agree, Silas. The running of a ranch is not the realm of a woman. My late brother-in-law was rather indulgent and allowed Isabel to do as she pleased. Though, I must admit, she seems to show some talent with the animals."

"My father didn't feel that being female made me incapable or stupid," Isabel countered, trying to rein in her anger. "He taught me as he taught my brother."

"We ain't sayin' yer not smart enough, girl," Silas placated her. "Just that it ain't necessary."

"No woman is gonna run my ranch." It was the first time Jacob had spoken since his father's embarrassing introduction in the yard. Of course, Silas barely paused in his diatribe even to breathe, making it difficult for anyone else to get a word in edgewise.

"Yeah," the second brother chimed in. "My woman will

be too busy making sons to worry about raising horses." Eli and his brother laughed heartily, while Silas edge a little closer to Isabel on the settee. When he brushed her thigh with a bony hand she sprang out of her seat.

"Excuse me. I need to check on lunch." She caught Jaret's eye as she turned and thought she saw him mouth the word *coward.* Temper and humor warred inside her. The humor won out and her lips twitched. The entire situation was absurd. Glad to find something to smile about, Isabel headed for the door and freedom.

Only the manners Lydia had ingrained in her kept Isabel from howling in frustration when Lydia opened the door before she reached it. Was it too much to ask that she have a few minutes alone? She forced a smile and turned back to her guests. "I believe lunch is ready, gentlemen."

Isabel barely got out of the way before the brothers crashed into the doorway, each trying to be the first one through. Jacob shouldered into the lead and beat his brother into the dining room. Eli sulked all the way to the table.

Isabel lowered herself into the chair Jacob held for her, trying not to show how much she was dreading the meal. She was already miserable, and the afternoon had barely started. Jacob slid into the seat on one side of her, and Eli dropped into the other. Her uncle took his place at the head of the table and invited Silas to sit at the foot, which left Jaret to take the chair directly opposite hers.

Isabel glanced up to find Jaret watching her closely. A small grin kicked up one corner of his mouth. She forced herself to smile instead of sticking out her tongue. His grin widened, as if he knew what she was thinking. She straightened in her chair and aimed her most brilliant smile at Eli, hoping to wipe the grin off Jaret's face.

It was a mistake. Eli took her expression as encouragement to move his chair a bit closer. Not to be outdone,

Jacob pulled his in, too, until Isabel couldn't move either arm without brushing a brother. When Jaret passed the platter of meat across the table, she had no choice but to let Eli serve her.

"Boys," Silas bellowed, making Isabel cringe. "Give her some elbow room. No need to press your case at the dinner table." Eli and Jacob shifted enough for her to get fork to mouth, but not nearly enough for her comfort. Only when Lydia entered and stood glowering at them did Eli and Jacob finally move their chairs away and concentrate on their food.

Jaret joined in the conversation with ease. He seemed interested in Silas's opinion of water availability for the herds and about the Spanish and Mexican governments' attempts to regain lands sold to Americans. Isabel was impressed by his knowledge, then remembered he was a rancher, too, and would, of course, be versed in the issues of the day.

She managed to eat a little, but, with the layers of clothing she wore, it was too warm in the room to enjoy the meal. The heat didn't seem to affect the men as they dug into everything Lydia served. Food disappeared with amazing speed.

Isabel breathed a sigh of relief when her uncle finally stood to signal an end to the meal. Nearly dumped out of her chair when both Jacob and Eli tried to help her stand, she was stunned speechless when Jacob suggested they go take a look at the horses. She opened her mouth to decline, since there wasn't a single cloud to offer respite from the sun, but he gripped her elbow and hustled her from the room before she could protest.

Lydia handed Isabel a parasol to ward off the sun as she was dragged out the door, but it offered no protection from the heat. Jacob dragged her down the steps and across the yard. They made three trips through the barn and around the corral, with Jacob doing no more than grunting when she attempted conversation. "Mr. Williams"—she finally dug in her heels in the shade of the barn—"you obviously don't care what I have to say about the horses. What are we doing out here?"

He looked at her as if she was daft. "Because it's my turn to court you and this is what a man does."

Isabel blinked in confusion, which he obviously took as a sign she was flirting and wrapped an arm around her shoulders. She shrugged away and faced him, using the umbrella as a weapon to force Jacob to keep his distance. "What do you mean, *what a man does?*"

"A man courts a woman by taking her on walks alone in the sunshine." He said it in a flat voice, as if quoting from a book. "Personally, I think it's too damn hot for walking, but this is what I've got to do, and I'll do it, damn it."

Isabel bit her tongue against an unladylike curse. "Thank you for explaining. You've done your duty admirably, Mr. Williams. Why don't we go back inside?"

"Fine with me." Jacob set off at a pace that had Isabel almost running to keep up. She nearly wilted with relief when they stepped inside the house. She followed Jacob into the parlor and dropped gratefully into a seat, fanning her face with one hand while she reached for the glass of water Lydia brought. She managed only one sip of water before Eli offered his arm and asked her to walk in the rose garden.

Had the whole world had gone mad? Jaret stood across the room, in his customary spot by the mantel. When she looked at him, he arched an eyebrow and one corner of his mouth curved. He looked like he was enjoying her discomfort. Temper threatened again, but it was short-lived. Before she could protest, Eli grabbed her wrist, hauled her from her seat, and hustled her out the door. There wasn't even time to snag the parasol.

Evidently the youngest of the Williams clan was also a man of few words and he wasted none of them as he dragged her out the back door to the garden. At least it was cooler here than walking around the corral. Isabel aimed for a bench under the nearest tree offering shade. Unfortunately, Eli took her eagerness to mean that she couldn't wait to be alone with him.

She'd no more than sat down when he pounced on her, wrapping his arms tightly around her and planting open-mouthed kisses on her face and neck while she struggled to free herself.

"Eli, please stop this. We can't . . . You mustn't . . . Stop it!"

Her shout finally got through to him. He loosened his hold in surprise and she gave him a shove backward. When he toppled off the bench, she jumped to her feet and stomped back inside.

Silas was waiting for her. She wondered if they'd drawn lots to decide in what order they were going to accost her, and now it was his turn. She opened her mouth to ask but words failed when he took her elbow and led her into the empty parlor.

"Come in here, girl, and join me."

Isabel glanced around nervously, praying to see her uncle. She'd even be glad to see Jaret, she decided, just so she wouldn't be alone with Silas.

At least the older man moved somewhat slower than his energetic offspring. He acted like a perfect gentleman as he seated her with her back to the door. Her glass of water still sat on the table by her elbow, so she lifted it and took a healthy swallow, then nearly choked on it when she heard the door close behind her. Before she could get to her feet, Silas joined her on the tiny sofa.

"Miss Isabel," he began in a gracious tone of voice. "I hope we haven't overwhelmed you, my boys and me."

Isabel looked away and dabbed at a bead of perspiration that was threatening to run into her eye.

"Now, girl, don't get all weepy on me."

She turned her face back to him in disbelief and found him much closer than he'd been a moment before.

"I know women have a soft spot for pretty words, but I don't have many of them in me."

Silas laid his hand on her knee and began a rapid journey up her thigh. She clamped onto his wrist and struggled to hold him off.

"Mr. Williams, stop that immediately."

Unlike his youngest son, she didn't catch him by surprise. He just tried another tack. Grabbing her shoulder, he pulled her close. Dear God, he was going to kiss her.

That was the last straw. She struck out with her free hand, catching him under the chin. His head snapped back and she lunged from the settee, but he dragged her back and gave her a sloppy kiss that tasted of roasted beef and whiskey. She struggled with him and managed to avoid his mouth the second time. She wasn't as successful at stopping his roving hands. Finally she gave up trying to act like a lady, fisted her right hand and smashed it with all her might into his belly. "Let *go!*"

The breath left him in a whoosh. Isabel leaped to her feet and headed for the door, Silas right on her heels.

"Now, Miss Isabel, I'm sorry if I came on too strong. It's only that my boys and me, we wanted you to have a chance to get to know us all before you made your choice."

Isabel flung open the door and came face-to-face with Eli and Jacob. The younger man leered at her while his brother stared accusingly at his father.

"What the hell did you do, old man? I had her all primed to say yes and you had to go and ruin everything."

Isabel squared off with him. She had to lace her fingers together tightly to keep from giving in to temptation and belting him, too. "Listen very carefully, all of you. I will not marry any of you," she hissed. "Ever!"

She shoved past Eli and Jacob, her skirts snapping in indignation. She was ready to scream for help if any of them followed, but spotted Jaret standing at the foot on the stairs. Relief made her a little light-headed. At least someone realized she needed protection from these madmen. Then she saw his lips twitch as he fought not to laugh and her gratitude exploded into furious embarrassment. "That includes you, Jaret Walker!"

Sweeping past him, she stomped up the stairs and slammed the door of her room.

Chapter Five

Isabel stayed in her room for the rest of the day. She didn't care how inhospitable it seemed, she refused to come out while Silas and his sons remained in the house. After sunset, her uncle sent word that she was to appear for dinner. "You can tell that yellow-bellied matchmaker he can entertain his own guests. I didn't invite them and nothing will force me back into the company of those devil-spawned snakes!"

Lydia muttered at her in disapproval, but went away and left her alone.

When Isabel came down the next morning, Silas, Jacob, and Eli were gone. She'd watched them ride away at dawn from behind her drawn curtains. A wave of disappointment swept through her when Lydia told her Jaret intended to leave as well. She enjoyed his company, even if all they seemed to do was argue. In spite of her denials, she did get lonely sometimes. And she hadn't asked him all the questions she had about Nicolas. Instead she'd wasted time with that ridiculous disagreement about Hardin, then practically accused him of trying to court her to get at the ranch, when he'd done nothing more than stay out of her way.

She glanced down at the hat she carried. The black felt brim was wide and flat. The low crown rose straight up from the center and was ringed by a thin silver hatband. The hat had belonged to her father, one of several personal items she hadn't been able to part with. But she thought it might fit Jaret and could serve as a replacement for the one Lucifer destroyed. If it looked a little like a peace offering, so be it.

She searched through the rooms quickly, but Jaret wasn't in the house. He couldn't already be gone. He'd promised they would discuss business before he left. She started out the door to find him, then changed her mind. Jaret Walker was a man of his word; he'd find her when he was ready to talk.

She plopped the hat on her head and faced the mirror over the hall table. As a little girl, she'd loved putting on her father's hats, only they used to drop past her ears. This one was still a little too large for her, but the knot of hair on top of her head kept it from falling over her eyes. Shaking her head at her foolishness, she headed toward her father's library and a pile of neglected correspondence.

Less that an hour later she heard the front door open and spurs ring out on the floor. She snatched her reading spectacles off her nose and hid them in a desk drawer just as Jaret entered the room. He was dressed all in black again, and looked tall and rather dangerous standing in the doorway. Evidence of his fight with Hardin still darkened the skin around one eye.

"Good morning, Mr. Walker." Isabel began to fuss with the papers on the desk, then stopped and laid both hands on the desk. It wouldn't help to let him see how nervous she was. "Won't you sit down?"

"That depends. Are you planning to take a swing at me when I get close enough?"

Isabel stared at her hands, vaguely surprised to see they were clenched into fists. She relaxed them, one finger at a time, then laughed at herself. "I apologize for my behavior yesterday. I have an awful temper. I can usually control it, but I hate to be pawed by men in whom I have no interest just because they refuse to take no for an answer."

The memory of Jaret's kisses in the moonlight filled her mind. She felt a blush flame her face. The look in his eyes told her he was remembering their walk in the garden, too. She couldn't have made it more obvious that she didn't include him in the grouping of men who didn't interest her.

She gave in to her nerves and straightened her papers into neat piles. Jaret crossed the room to the desk and dropped into the leather chair on the opposite side. She bit back a sigh of relief that he wasn't going to pursue it any further. She held her father's hat out to him. "I have a gift for you."

"What's this for?" He accepted the hat and brushed a finger along the crown.

"Consider it a replacement. Lucifer and I owe you a hat."

He shook his head, but didn't refuse her gift. "Whose is it? Your brother's?"

"No." She reached out and brushed a spec of dust from the brim. "It belonged to my father."

Jaret's eyes showed surprise as he studied her face. "Are you sure you want to part with it?"

"It's senseless to leave it gathering dust on a shelf. A hat should be worn. If it fits, it's yours."

Jaret settled the black felt into place. It looked as if it had been made for him. "Miss Bennett, I know how much your father meant to you." He took the hat off and smoothed his fingers around the brim. "This is a fine gift. I appreciate you entrusting it to me."

Isabel looked away, battling tears. Jaret sat in silence,

waiting until she had herself under control again. "Did you find any horses you're interested in?"

He crossed one booted foot over the other and balanced the hat on his raised knee. His dark sable hair gleamed in the sunlight coming through the windows. She had to force herself to concentrate on what Jaret was saying.

"You have a fine herd to choose from. I can see why you're so proud of them. A couple of stallions caught my eye, but I'm not quite ready to commit to one of them. There are two mares I'd like to discuss, though. One of them is still nursing, so I'll have to wait until the colt is weaned, unless we can agree on a price that includes it."

"I'm sure we can come to an agreement. Which mares interested you?" Their business went smoothly. They discussed the animals and haggled over the price and in the end both were satisfied. She signed her name beside his on the bill of sale and blotted the ink carefully.

It was done. He walked away with two of her finest mares and a newborn colt, and she'd concluded her first sale since taking over the ranch. With a wide smile, Isabel stood and offered her hand. "Thank you, Mr. Walker. I enjoyed doing business with you."

Jaret shook her hand, but instead of releasing it, tightened his grip and drew her around the desk to stand close in front of him.

"Good-bye, Miss Bennett. I'll be back as soon as I can make some arrangements."

"We'll take good care of your horses until then."

He stared at her for so long she thought he would say more, but he released her hand and walked out of the room without looking back. He was already on his horse by the time she gathered her scattered wits and got to the front door.

"Go with God, Mr. Walker."

Jaret turned in the saddle, his eyes glinting like the sunlit sea. Then he touched the brim of her father's hat with two fingers and rode away.

Isabel started back inside, but caught sight of Hank Hardin and decided to make a clean sweep of the business of the morning. She stepped off the porch and walked over to where he stood leaning against a fence rail. The sun was climbing over the barn and the morning breeze mixed the scents of roses and wildflowers with dust and horses.

"Mr. Hardin, I want a word with you." She stopped in front of him, but not within reach. She wasn't a fool.

Hardin's gaze traveled from her head to her boots and back again, lingering long enough below her chin to make her nervous. She bore his insolence in silence, refusing to let him see her discomfort.

"What can I do for you, Miss Isabel?"

"Is the hand I fired yesterday ready to leave?"

He nodded. "He was too stupid to be of any use to me anyway. He left at first light."

"What about his pay?"

"I paid him."

"With what?"

He smiled and she took a step back. "Mr. de la Rosa has given me access to the funds I need to take care of my men."

Isabel stared at him, anger mounting. "*Your* men? The men on this ranch work for me. I decide whom to pay and when, not you."

"I don't see it that way. If you don't like the arrangement we made, go talk to your uncle. I've got work to do." Hardin gave her a suggestive wink and strutted off toward the barn.

It wasn't possible. Her uncle wouldn't have given him access to the gold and silver she kept on the ranch. He wouldn't have the nerve.

"Uncle Enrique?" she called out the instant she opened the door. Her uncle must be up already, she decided, and had taken the necessary funds from the safe. But as she went from room to room and found no sign of her uncle, she had a sinking feeling the foreman told the truth.

Locking the door to the library behind her, Isabel lit a lamp and drew the curtains against curious eyes. The wall safe was well hidden and she wanted to keep it that way. But when she reached to move aside the small cabinet that concealed it, she realized it had been moved recently. The signs were obvious in the fine layer of dust that had blown in through the open windows. Her hands shook as she searched for the key and opened the safe.

"At least there is something left," she whispered when she saw the bags of coins inside. But how much had been removed without her knowledge? Isabel carried the contents to the desk. She moved everything aside and set her ledger in the middle. She kept meticulous records of the monies spent in the upkeep of the ranch and knew how much should be here. She counted the coins quickly, then counted again. With a cry of dismay, she sank into the chair.

It was true. Someone had been taking money from the safe without her knowledge, quite a lot of money. The amount wouldn't bankrupt the ranch, but it would limit the winter supplies they could afford. Isabel checked her figures again, but they didn't change. She didn't want to believe it was Hardin, but she had no reason to doubt.

Forcing herself to remain calm, she recorded the amount of cash that was left and noted how much was missing. She ignored the fear growing inside her and gathered up the remaining money and carried it out of the room. She'd find a hiding place her uncle and Hardin didn't know about. Then she would order another lock for the safe and keep the key on a chain around her neck. No one else would have access to it again.

She spent the next couple of hours on the ledgers, trying to juggle accounts to make up for the loss.

"Isabel!"

She flinched at her uncle's voice. The morning was nearly gone and he was just getting out of bed, though he sounded like he'd been at the whiskey bottle since dawn. She squared her shoulders and went to meet him.

"Yes, Uncle?" Even to her ears her voice sounded falsely sweet. She took a deep breath to calm the anger that had been building all morning.

"Where is it?"

Isabel stopped where she was. He couldn't know about the money. He hadn't been in the library yet. She hurried toward the sound of his voice and found him in the kitchen. "Where is what, Uncle?"

"Don't play games with me, young lady. Where the hell is my whiskey?" He stumbled through the room, shoving aside chairs and banging open cupboards. "Where have you hidden it?"

"I don't have any idea what you're talking about, Uncle. I haven't touched your whiskey." She watched his tirade for a minute more before stepping in front of him.

"Uncle, it isn't even noon. You don't need alcohol."

He shoved her aside. "Don't tell me what I need, girl."

Isabel stumbled and caught herself on a chair. She stayed out of the way, ignoring the curses he hurled about meddling females. But when he began to blame the cook, she stopped him.

"That's enough. Marta would never touch your whiskey. If you'll go into the parlor, I'll see if I can find it for you. Please, Uncle," she placated when he rounded on her to argue some more. Finally he gave in and stumbled down the hallway.

Isabel waited until he was gone, then went to the large pantry off the kitchen and pulled a set of keys from a hook behind the door. Checking to be sure her uncle hadn't returned she climbed onto a stool and reached to unlock a small, high cabinet. Inside was the last of her father's whiskey. Six bottles sat side by side behind three bags of sugar, out of sight should anyone wander in while Marta was in the pantry. She wondered what would happen when he'd drained the last of it.

She pulled down one bottle and carefully hid the rest again before locking the cabinet. For an instant she considered taking the keys with her. The recent discovery of the missing money had destroyed her trust. With a sound of frustration, she replaced them on the hook and closed the pantry door. Now wasn't the time to make a choice like that.

She searched until she found a suitable glass and splashed a small amount of whiskey into it, then added a little more. Setting the bottle out of sight, she headed for the parlor and her uncle.

"Where the hell is the rest of it, girl?" Her uncle sat slumped in his usual chair in the darkened room.

"This is sufficient for now, Uncle Enrique. I'll ask Marta to serve lunch a little early."

The older man harrumphed and swallowed most of the contents in the glass. His eyes watered, but he grunted with contentment. "That's better." He coughed. "Much better. I couldn't seem to get started today without a little help."

Isabel said a silent prayer for courage and lowered herself into the chair opposite him. "Uncle, did you give Mr. Hardin some money this morning?"

"What?" He looked at her through bloodshot eyes. "Money?

I didn't leave my room until ten minutes ago, girl. I haven't given anyone anything."

"But Mr. Hardin said he already paid one of the men, and I thought perhaps you'd given him the silver."

The man took another drink of whiskey. "It isn't necessary for me to give Mr. Hardin funds. I granted him access to the safe some time ago."

"Why?" Fear and frustration battled inside her. "Why would you give anyone access to our money?"

"Because, child." He spoke to her as if he were lecturing a little girl. "The man needs to be able to run the estate. I haven't the time to be concerned with details like the salaries of the employees."

"The men that work on this ranch are *my* responsibility, not yours and certainly not Mr. Hardin's." She rose to pace the room. "Far more money is missing from the safe than is needed to pay the men. What else did you give Mr. Hardin permission to take care of?"

He mumbled something about provisions and comforts but didn't make much sense.

Furious, she yanked open the curtains, flooding the room with sunlight. Her uncle yelped in pain. She crossed to stand in front of him and leaned down until her eyes were level with his, forcing him to look at her.

"Understand this, Uncle Enrique. This ranch is mine. I'm not a child that needs tending by you or anyone else."

"Young lady, you should be concerned with finding a husband, not trying to run an estate that is far too much for you to handle."

Isabel wanted to stomp her foot in frustration, but refused to act like the child her uncle seemed to think she was. "I'm not looking for a husband, Uncle Enrique. And as long as Mr. Hardin is on this ranch, I won't change my mind. Fire him and I'll think about finding a rich husband for you."

"*I* don't need a husband, you daft girl. You're the one who must marry. And I can't fire Hank Hardin. Who would run this place if he wasn't here?"

She nearly screamed at him that *she* could, but she'd be wasting her words. Instead, Isabel stomped up the stairs to change into riding clothes. She would saddle Lucifer and ride for a while. She needed to be alone.

When she passed the room that Jaret had used, she paused in the doorway. He was the first man since her father who'd taken her seriously as a businesswoman. She wandered into the room, and even though it had already been cleaned and straightened, she could smell his scent of leather and soap.

Her father would have liked him, she thought. And Nicolas *did* like him.

Her mood plunged again when she thought of her brother. Where was he? Even though Jaret had been unable to provide much information, at least he'd seen Nicolas. She had to believe he was still alive, but it was hard. If he couldn't come home, why didn't he at least send word? Isabel crossed to the window to stare out over the land that was so important to her brother's future.

What would she do if her uncle was right and Nicolas never returned? That was the question she'd been avoiding all these long months. If something had happened to her brother, how would she go on?

Isabel squared her shoulders. She would survive, like she had when her mother died, and after her father had passed on to join her. She loved this ranch, and if she had to, she'd do everything herself.

* * *

The sun was setting when Isabel slowed Lucifer's pace as they neared the house. It had been a nice ride and she dreaded going back inside.

Marta saw her first and called out to someone. A moment later, Manuel limped onto the porch to take the reins.

"Is your leg bothering you today, Manuel?"

The old man shrugged away her concern and led Lucifer toward the barn. She didn't follow. He would see to the horse for her.

"Is something wrong, Marta?" Isabel climbed the steps to the woman's side.

"I was only worried that I hadn't seen you all day. But now you are here. Dinner is ready when you wish to eat."

Isabel started up the back stairs to dress for dinner.

"Your uncle will not be joining you," Marta called after her. "He has already eaten."

A true smile spread across Isabel's face. A quiet dinner alone. How marvelous. She cleaned up and slipped into the dress Lydia had laid out for her. It was one of her favorites, made of dark blue muslin that was soft and comfortable.

She brushed her hair until it shone and twisted it into a soft knot in the back and went down to dinner.

Clouds obscured the moon when Isabel walked to the barn for her nightly visit to Lucifer. The lantern wasn't in its place by the door. Frowning, she slipped inside. Though she didn't much care for the dark, she certainly didn't need a lantern to find her way to Lucifer's stall. As she worked her way down the stalls by feel, Isabel called softly to the stallion. He whickered a greeting, but it came from the opposite side of the barn. Before she could turn toward the sound, hands snaked out of the darkness.

Chapter Six

Strong hands clamped her to a hard male body and covered her mouth firmly. She struggled against her captor, trying to scream for help, but she was no match for his strength. In a quick move, he replaced his gloved hand with a strip of cloth, ensuring her silence. Though she fought to get free, he lifted her with ease, tossed her onto the back of a tall horse and vaulted up behind her before she recovered her balance. Holding her in place, he turned the horse toward the desert, leaving the ranch behind.

Panic rose up, making it hard to breathe. This couldn't be happening. She continued to struggle in his arms until she nearly unseated them both.

"Stop it, or I'll truss you up like a chicken and toss you over the back of the saddle." The voice was soft and close, but she didn't recognize the rough whisper.

She tried to turn and see the face of the man who held her, but she only managed to twist loose from his hold. When she started to slip from the horse face-first toward the dust, she screamed in fear.

"Stop it," the man hissed. "Are you trying to kill yourself?" She was hauled back roughly but didn't complain.

She stayed very still until her captor held her securely again.

Isabel studied her surroundings. They were heading northeast, angling away from the stream. The horse they rode was a rich tan with a dark mane. The arch of the elegant neck seemed familiar somehow. Another horse followed them, close enough to hear but not to see. Since the man didn't seem concerned, she assumed he knew who it was.

After what seemed like forever, her kidnapper slowed his horse to a walk, allowing it to rest a little. She wondered if he'd stop now, but he only lifted her and settled her astride the saddle. He removed the gag, but before she could thank him, he grabbed both of her hands and bound them in front of her. Though his hold was gentle, she couldn't pull free.

"Who are you? Why are you doing this?"

She didn't really expect an answer. Twisting around, she managed to turn enough to see him. A black cloth, tied across his nose and mouth, hid most of his face. Only his blue eyes were visible in the darkness. Staring into their dark depths, Isabel realized why she wasn't frightened. Somewhere deep inside she must have recognized his voice. The scent and feel of this man had haunted her all through the previous night.

"Jaret?"

The man stared at her for a long moment, then released her long enough to pull the cloth from his face.

"Evening, ma'am."

She swung her bound hands in the general direction of his chin. Jaret barely managed to keep them both from pitching to the ground. "Stop it, Isabel. I don't want to hurt you."

"Don't want—" She swung again and he caught her fists easily. She tugged free and glared at him. "You grab me out of the dark, throw me onto a horse, gallop hell-bent across the countryside, and you say you don't want to hurt me?"

He shook his head, a smile lurking at the corners of his mouth. "That's impressive. You turned yourself into a princess with no effort at all. I don't know whether to laugh or bow."

"Why are you doing this?" Isabel hated that her voice shook, but she couldn't help it.

Jaret hesitated over his answer. "Because I was asked to."

She stared at him in shock. "Why would anyone want you to kidnap me?" A nasty thought crept in. "You're working for someone who wants my ranch, aren't you? Does the worm plan on demanding ransom? Or is there a priest waiting at the end of this ride? You're just like Hardin. All you care about is land."

Jaret pinned her with a furious look, his blue eyes icy in the moonlight. "I told you before not to compare me to Hardin."

He turned to check their back trail. "Let's walk for a while and rest Sand Dune."

Without waiting for a response, he swung out of the saddle and lifted her down. He held her close until her legs steadied, then released her and started walking.

Isabel turned to follow, but was bumped in the shoulder from behind and nearly pitched headfirst into the dust. Her muffled scream changed into a gasp of delight. "Lucifer! What are you doing here?"

Jaret replied from the darkness ahead. "I invited him."

"But he won't allow anyone near him except me or Manuel."

"You just have to know how to talk to him. I explained that you were going on a trip, and how I thought he'd want to come along. He practically put the saddle on himself."

Isabel kept one hand on Lucifer's neck as she picked her way along in the dark. "Why bring him?"

"You need a mount, and I knew you'd worry if we left him behind for that useless bunch of cowboys you call ranch hands to take care of."

She hurried to catch up to him, incensed. "Manuel is not useless."

Jaret nodded his agreement. "I wasn't talking about him. He's one of the few bright spots around the place. But he won't be there long once they figure out you're gone."

Fear gripped her, not for herself but for her friend. "Then we have to go back. I can't let them hurt Manuel."

He kept walking.

"Jaret, please take me back." When he still didn't respond, Isabel turned toward Lucifer. She wasn't sure she could mount with her hands tied, but she was going to try. Jaret grabbed her before she reached for the saddle.

"No." He remained silent until she took a breath to argue again. "Hardin won't have a chance to hurt anyone." He prodded her forward, setting a quick pace over the rough terrain.

"What do you mean?"

Jaret steadied her when she tripped on a small rock. "Because he'll be too busy trying to cut sign on a trail that goes nowhere."

"I don't understand."

Jaret's smile sliced the darkness. "Manuel is going to lead the posse in the opposite direction. That should keep us ahead of them for a while."

Isabel was stunned. The man she'd known all her life, a man she considered her second father, was working with Jaret. She held onto Lucifer as her mind whirled. It didn't make sense. Manuel would never do anything to hurt her, but if he had helped Jaret kidnap her, did she really know him at all?

"Don't think badly of Manuel." Jaret seemed to read her thoughts. "He understands what's at stake here and wants to keep you safe."

"How does dragging me into the desert in the middle of the night accomplish that? At home, I was safe."

"No, Princess, you weren't," Jaret scoffed. "You have no idea the danger you were in."

"Then explain it to me."

"I will, but not yet. When we get where we're going, you'll understand."

Jaret tightened the cinch on Lucifer's saddle, lifted her with ease and settled her into place. After checking to be sure she was stable, he took her reins, swung onto his own horse and set off again.

It seemed like hours before Jaret slowed the pace. Isabel looked around but didn't recognize the terrain in the darkness. She looked up at the moon. It gave off plenty of light to ride by, but it made the surrounding desert look white, almost snow-covered.

She searched again for familiar landmarks, but she was so confused she couldn't even be certain in which direction they were riding. Frustration warred with fatigue. When Jaret kicked up the speed again, Lucifer followed, causing Isabel to lose her balance. Grabbing at the saddle horn, she decided to concentrate on riding and worry about getting home later.

Finally, they slowed to give the horses a rest. Jaret let the animals walk while he uncapped a canteen and held it out to her. When Isabel refused to take it, he urged his horse closer.

"Drink some. We can't stop to eat yet, but you need water.

It won't help if you crack your skull on the rocks when you faint and fall out of the saddle."

She wondered if he'd seen her lose her balance earlier, then realized he must have. Jaret didn't miss much. She snatched the canteen from his hands and took a sip, embarrassed that she'd been caught not paying attention. The water tasted good. With a sigh of pleasure she took a longer drink. The cool liquid felt good on her dry throat.

"That's enough, Princess. Save some for later." He pulled the canteen from her hands and lifted it to his own lips, swallowing twice before he replaced the cap.

"Didn't you bring sufficient water for us?"

"Enough so we don't have to stick too close to the stream. That'll be the first place they look."

"But I thought Manuel was going to lead the others in the opposite direction?"

He ignored her taunt and studied the horizon. "We don't have much farther to go tonight."

Isabel looked around, but couldn't see anything that would indicate they were near a dwelling.

Jaret didn't answer, just urged his mount into a canter. She settled back into the rhythm of the horse beneath her. When he increased the speed slightly, Isabel tried to lift herself off the saddle to spare Lucifer, but her legs were too tired. She considered asking Jaret to slow down again, but couldn't form the words. He wasn't a cruel man. If he kept up the pace, it must be for a good reason. All she could do was concentrate on staying atop her horse.

Some time later he pulled his mount to a stop, and waited for Lucifer to walk the last few feet to his side. "We go on foot from here."

She bit back a groan and moved to dismount, but Jaret was there to lift her from the saddle before she could take her foot from the stirrup. He set her on the ground and held her close, like before, watching her face.

"I'm fine. You can let go now," Isabel snapped.

He made a sound of agreement, but didn't release her. When she looked at him, he was staring at her lips. Self-conscious, she moistened them with a quick motion of her tongue, and his eyes narrowed. Memories of kisses in the moonlight swept through her and she swayed toward him. Abruptly he released her and stepped back.

"Can you walk or do you need help?" The impersonal tone of her kidnapper was back, and Isabel's shoulders sagged with disappointment. Instantly she straightened them. What was the matter with her? This man had grabbed her from her home, tossed her onto a horse, and taken her on a dangerous ride across the dark landscape. Why would she want to kiss him after the night she'd been through? Since she didn't like the answer that came immediately to mind, she started walking.

The terrain became rocky and rough. There was very little dirt to hold tracks, and what there was blew around in the wind. Jaret had chosen their route well. It would take an experienced tracker to follow them, and except for Manuel she doubted any man at the ranch was up to the task. If Jaret was telling the truth and Manuel was in on her kidnapping, then she wouldn't be rescued by anyone from home. She'd have to find a way to escape on her own.

Isabel was so lost in thought she bumped into Jaret before she realized he'd stopped. He moved quickly to keep her from falling, and released her almost as fast. Before she could turn away, he took her hands and removed the cloth that bound them. She saw a flash of regret in his eyes when he spotted the red flesh of her wrists, rubbed raw by the binding.

"I'm sorry, Isabel. I really didn't intend to hurt you."

She stared at him, refusing to accept the apology. "You've dragged me halfway across the territory in the dead of night with no explanation. Pardon me if I don't believe you."

"Believe what you want. We'll rest here for a few hours."

Isabel started toward the small overhang he indicated. She could hear water running nearby, but even the prospect of removing the dust from her skin didn't interest her. She had to stoop a little to enter the shallow indent in the rock. The ground had been swept clean by the wind, leaving a mostly level area large enough for two. She moved to one side and dropped to the ground. Stretching out on her back, she closed her eyes.

Isabel awoke to the light of dawn. She lay still and stared at the rock over her head and the scraggly grass under her fingertips. Had it all been a dream? Had she slept through the night out on the range? Lydia would be frantic.

She didn't recognize the terrain, but that fact didn't concern her. If she was tired enough to sleep this long, she wasn't surprised that she couldn't remember where she'd stopped to rest. She rolled to her knees and stood, ignoring the small aches that sleeping on the ground left behind. She folded the blanket that had been wrapped around her and draped it over her arm. When she reached for her saddle, she realized there was another one nearby.

Only then did she notice other things, like the tiny fire that burned a few feet away, the two horses cropping grass downstream, and the man crouching at the water's edge. She took an involuntary step backward before she realized who it was.

Though he had his back to her, she recognized Jaret, and her panic subsided. It hadn't been a dream, but neither was it a nightmare. Isabel approached him without making a sound, unsure whether or not she was glad to see him.

"Did you sleep well?"

She hesitated a moment when he spoke, then continued toward the stream. She should have known she couldn't approach him unnoticed. Kneeling in the grass beside him, she tugged a handkerchief from her pocket, wet it in the stream and rinsed the previous night's ride off her skin.

The gurgling creek was clear and cool, and she was in no hurry to finish. It was several minutes before she answered him. "Reasonably well, given the circumstances." She twisted the cloth until most of the water was out of it, then snapped it straight and laid it on the grass to dry.

"My apologies for the accommodations, Princess, but you were asleep before you hit the ground. I considered making a pallet of grass for you, but you didn't seem to need it, so I wrapped the blanket around you, propped your head on your saddle and let you sleep." He stood in a fluid motion and offered her a hand up. When she didn't take it, he dropped it to his side and watched her silently.

"Why am I here?"

When Jaret didn't answer, she pushed to her feet and faced him squarely. "It's a simple question. Why have you done this?"

Jaret turned away and crossed to the fire. A pot of coffee simmered near the heat and he poured two cups. The control in every movement he made drew Isabel, but she fought the attraction. She was here for a reason and she wanted—needed—to know what it was.

Instead of answering, he offered her a cup of coffee. She sipped the scalding brew, shuddering at the bitter taste.

Jaret chuckled. "Sorry. I can make it hot and strong, but I don't know much about making it good."

Biting back her own laughter, she returned to the stream to add a splash of cold water. It didn't improve the flavor, but at least she could finish it faster.

She accepted his offer of cheese and bread, then settled back to watch the morning sun creep over the horizon. "Will you answer my question now?"

Jaret tore a chuck off the bread. "The man who sent me believes you're in danger. I think he's right." He rose, cutting off her next question. "We need to get moving."

Isabel didn't argue. This time she accepted his help up, then bent to retrieve the tin cups. As she rinsed them in the stream, she considered his words. Who thought she was in so much danger they would send Jaret? No one but Nicolas would care. But if her brother sent him, why didn't Jaret just say so?

She kept her back to Jaret, afraid he might read her thoughts on her face. She wasn't going to go along with this like a lamb being led to slaughter. Making plans, Isabel joined Jaret, watching as he packed the last of their gear in the saddlebags.

Jaret boosted her onto Lucifer's back and she settled into the saddle with ease. When he touched her knee, she lifted her gaze to meet his.

"I'm sorry I can't let you rest longer, but I don't want to risk getting caught."

She didn't respond, only extended her hands, wrists together, in his direction. When he did no more that raise an eyebrow, she explained. "I'm your captive. Aren't you going to tie me up again? After all, I know this land better than you do. I might ride away before you can stop me."

Isabel gained a small amount of satisfaction from the muscle that jumped in his jaw, then did exactly as she'd warned. Shoving a boot into his chest, she kicked Lucifer into a gallop and raced up the small hill, heading upstream.

She knew this creek had to be the same one that ran near the house. There wasn't any other source of water for a hundred miles. All she had to do was follow it home, provided she could outrun Jaret.

She crested the next rise and reined in Lucifer. She wanted to get away, but she wouldn't risk him stepping into a hidden hole and breaking his leg. She glanced back in the direction she'd come from, but didn't see Jaret anywhere. Her smile was triumphant. It had been so much easier than she'd expected. Or maybe he'd had an attack of conscience and decided to let her get away.

She was still congratulating herself when she rode around an outcropping of rock and straight into Jaret's arms. He swept her from Lucifer's saddle with ease, and settled her across his knees. Other than a squeal of surprise, she didn't bother screaming. It would only have wasted her breath, and she didn't have much to spare after changing horses so unexpectedly.

"Let's have them."

She stared at Jaret, confused, then saw the cloth bindings he held in his hand.

She considered arguing, struggling, pleading with him, but rejected them all. He wouldn't listen, and she'd still be tied up and riding in front of him in the end. Beaten, she held out her hands, and let him bind her wrists.

With a soft whistle that brought Lucifer to his side, Jaret turned his horse downstream and retraced her route. She stared at him. "When did you have the time to train Lucifer like that?" He ignored her. No surprise there. From the look on his face, Jaret wasn't in the mood for conversation. They crossed the stream and he picked up the pace, tightening his arm around her waist to hold her in place.

"I can ride, Jaret." When she repeated it, he gave a snort

of disbelief. "You have my word. I won't try to escape again."

At that he laughed. "Sorry, Isabel, but I don't believe you, and I don't have time to take the chance."

They rode most of the morning, only stopping when the horses needed rest. The heat increased until they were both sweltering and Sand Dune was beginning to show the strain of carrying two riders. Isabel was feeling light-headed, but she refused to ask Jaret to stop.

When the sun was nearly overhead, Jaret pulled up near a group of mesquite trees, dismounted, and lifted her from the saddle. Instead of setting her on her feet, he carried her into the shade, laid her on a tiny patch of grass, and removed the cloth binding her wrists.

The midday sun was hot and bright, reflecting blinding flashes off the tiny trickle of water that remained of the stream they'd been following all day. When he returned from unsaddling the horses, she closed her eyes and feigned sleep.

"Quit fooling around and eat." She opened her eyes and took the jerky he offered. She tore off a piece and popped it into her mouth. It was very dry, with a smoky, almost sour flavor that wasn't altogether pleasant. She washed it down with a swallow of water.

Jaret settled into the grass beside her. "It's too hot to keep riding. We'll rest here until the sun goes down some. With any luck, we'll make our destination by this time tomorrow."

When he stood and whistled for the horses, Isabel pushed to her feet. Jaret motioned her back.

"I'll take care of Lucifer. You rest." He drew one of his belt guns and put it beside the saddle. "Keep this close, just in case."

Without a word, she lay back in the grass, closed her eyes and fell asleep.

Jaret watched her for several long minutes before he went to tend the horses. She kept surprising him. He'd expected her to drive him crazy with questions about where they were going and who had sent him in the first place. Any other woman would have been verbally beating him about the head and shoulders for dragging her around the countryside, but Isabel didn't complain. Even when she was so tired she could barely stay upright in the saddle, she hadn't asked him to stop.

It was possible she was only pretending to go along with him until she could try and escape again, but he didn't think so. She seemed to be a woman who faced life head-on, without pretense. And she'd given her word. She was one of the few people he'd met who he believed would keep it. Besides, it was easy enough to read her, since her thoughts and emotions were always written on her very lovely face.

Caught off guard by the direction of his thoughts, he stopped grooming Lucifer to look over at Isabel. It was the simple truth. She was beautiful, and kissing her in the moonlit garden had given him a lot of pleasure and more than a couple of restless nights.

Nick Bennett had told Jaret all about his sister, from the fact that she'd raised him after their mother died to how she'd gotten in the way so much around the ranch their father finally agreed to teach her to run the spread. Nick had easily admitted he was only interested in the horses, breeding them, raising them, selling those and raising more. It was Isabel who kept the ranch running. And she was doing it well, in spite of the interference from their uncle and his hired henchmen.

Jaret left the horses tied to a scrubby bush and scouted

back along the route they'd taken. Maybe Hardin and his men wouldn't chase them for long. They didn't need a body to declare her dead and take over the ranch. Still, it was a chance he couldn't take.

He studied the surrounding desert for any sign of other riders. Nothing moved that he could see. Exhaustion pulled at him until he gave in and returned to where Isabel slept with her back to the desert. Trying not to wake her, Jaret crept into the shade behind her. As he settled onto his knees, she rolled over and cocked the pistol she held. Almost immediately, she pointed the barrel away.

"Sorry." She eased the hammer forward and laid the revolver within reach.

"Thanks for not pulling the trigger."

She grinned up at him, squinting a little against the light. "You're not half bad to have around. Besides, if I'm really in danger, I shouldn't shoot the one protecting me."

Jaret stretched out beside her and pulled his hat over his eyes. "You believe me, then?"

"I've thought about it and, yes, I believe you want to protect me. I also think my brother sent you here." She rolled to her side and pulled the hat from his face. "Did he?"

There was no reason not to tell her. He nodded. "Nick asked me to come in his place."

"See? That wasn't so hard, was it?" She gave him a smacking kiss on the cheek.

"Aren't you going to ask me why?"

She smiled. "I imagine you'll tell me when you're ready." Isabel untied the ribbon from around her long hair and combed her fingers through it a few times before she lay back down. Jaret watched the sun shimmer in the black strands. Unable to resist, he rolled to his side so he could bury his fingers in the heavy silk, enjoying the feel of it running across his hand. He twisted his wrist once, twice, until they were bound together by her hair.

She stared up at him, her black eyes wide. "Jaret?"

"Shh." He leaned over her, wanting a taste of her, needing it. He nearly groaned aloud when her tongue darted out to moisten her lips. Moving slowly, giving her a chance to object, he settled his mouth over hers.

Isabel raised a hand to his chest, but not to push him away. Instead, she traced a path along his collar and around his neck. When her nails scraped his skin, he deepened the kiss. She went with him, tasting as he did, pulling him under her spell.

Jaret shifted, wanting to feel her stretched out beneath him, neck to knees. As he moved, his elbow bumped the revolver, bringing him back to reality. What the hell was he doing, taking advantage of her with who knew how many men tracking them?

Her protest as he ended the kiss nearly destroyed his resolve, but he eased away from her and watched her beautiful eyes, liquid with desire, begin to focus.

"What's wrong?"

He pulled her hand from his neck and placed a kiss in the center of her palm. "This is." She stiffened and tried to push him away. "Not kissing you, honey, but kissing you here. Now." He rubbed his lips across her fingers. "I should be standing guard, not thinking about all the things I'd rather be doing."

She smiled and tugged her hand free to explore his jaw with her fingers. "What things?" She traced his lips, making him sorry he'd stopped. "Care to share some of them?"

Jaret wanted to do more than tell her, he wanted to demonstrate. His body hardened as the blood left his head for points south. Before he lost all control, he rolled away and shoved to his feet. Isabel sat up, her hair falling like a curtain around her shoulders.

He clenched his hands into fists and took a step back to keep from reaching for her. "God, woman, you do tempt me."

"Good. I'd hate to be the only one." Combing her fingers through her hair, Isabel tamed it with the ribbon once more. "Go on. Do what you need to. I'll be fine." She patted the revolver once, then stretched out in the grass again.

Jaret forced himself into the sun, away from her. He repeated a pattern of checking on Isabel and watching their back trail. An hour before sundown, he spotted a dust cloud on the horizon. It might just be the wind, or it could be men and horses. He didn't wait to see which one. They had to get moving.

Isabel opened her eyes to find Jaret saddling their horses. Muscles bunched and shifted under his shirt as he lifted the heavy leather. He was certainly good to look at.

"I hope that smile means you're ready to ride."

Jaret spoke in a whisper, his tension palpable.

Something was wrong. Had Hardin found them? She accepted Jaret's hand up and followed him to the horses. When he stopped beside Lucifer, her surprise must have shown on her face.

"We'll make better time if you ride alone."

He helped her mount, then vaulted into his own saddle. "Stay close," he admonished and kicked Sand Dune into a gallop.

Twice she felt as if they were being followed, and once she thought she saw something in the distance. Jaret pushed on at a pace just short of suicidal, negotiating the narrow strip of ground between the scrubby trees and the open land.

The moon hadn't risen yet when the light from the sun finally bled away. Jaret pulled up and waited for her to come alongside.

"Stay in the saddle and don't let Lucifer wander."

Before she could respond, he disappeared into the darkness in the direction they'd come from. She held Lucifer still until Jaret returned a few minutes later.

"It looks like I was wrong."

"There's nobody behind us?"

Jaret's head whipped around. "What did you see?"

"I didn't *see* anything. It's more a feeling we're being followed."

He nodded. "I felt it, too."

"Friend or foe?"

"I don't know." He looked over his shoulder. "Whoever it is, I haven't been able to spot them. Let's walk the horses for a while."

Isabel dismounted and looped the reins around the saddle horn, knowing Lucifer would follow without being led. Walking fast, she joined Jaret and matched her steps to his.

They walked in silence, their footsteps and those of the horses the only sounds she could hear. He kept the pace steady, but not fast, until the moon rose. Once the silvery white light spread across the ground, he moved faster and Isabel had to work to keep up.

She jumped and edged closer to Jaret when a scrabbling sound came from nearby. When he didn't react to the noise, she realized it was only a desert mouse, or some other small creature. She shook her head and laughed softly.

"The quiet doesn't usually get to me like this." She kept her voice just above a whisper. "Is it all right if we talk?" Jaret shrugged, which she took as a yes. She needed some kind of sound or she'd go crazy in all this darkness. "Tell me about yourself? Where did you grow up?"

He stared down at her so long she thought he wouldn't

answer. She looked away and resigned herself to coping with her fears in silence.

"I was born in Virginia." Jaret again checked their back trail. "We lived in a busted-down shack on the edge of a dying town. My father didn't stick around long enough to be of any use. After Mama died, I was passed from family to family, living on the charity of others. As soon as I was old enough, I left."

She waited while he looked around for signs they were being followed. "Where did you go?"

"Here and there. I worked for a farmer for a while, caring for his horses. Learned to plow a straight row and milk a cow."

He turned around again, his eyes constantly moving as he searched the landscape. She looked forward, trying to figure out where they were, but could determine only that they were heading south. She knew they'd started out going northeast.

She started to ask him about their change in direction, but he stopped her with a small movement of his hand. He stared along their back trail, watching the darkness. She couldn't see anything but him and their horses, and a dozen feet of the tracks they'd left as they walked.

Suddenly he hissed a curse. Reaching for her, he tossed her up into Lucifer's saddle. "Riders, and they're coming on fast." Vaulting onto his own mount, he scooped up both sets of reins and kicked the horses into a gallop.

She had no breath to ask questions as Jaret set a punishing pace. They galloped over the uneven ground, hooves ringing on the rocks. Without warning, he spun the horses in a tight circle and started back the way they'd come.

Jaret pulled the horses to a sliding halt and vaulted from the saddle. He pulled her down and hustled her into some heavy scrub. Both animals followed, but there wasn't enough cover. Jaret surged to his feet and dragged her a little farther, until he found a spot in a small ravine that would hide them all.

"Stay here." He ripped one of the scraggly bushes out by the roots and began brushing out their tracks. She watched until he disappeared into the night.

Isabel dragged air into her lungs and battled to quiet her breathing. Minutes ticked by with no sign of Jaret. Fear for him overwhelmed her. She started to crawl away from the hiding place, needing to find him, when a hand grabbed her ankle.

"Stay put," he hissed. "If we're quiet, they might pass by. I'm hoping when they lose the trail they'll assume it's too rocky to hold tracks and keep going."

Seconds later she heard horses, at least a dozen, running hard. They passed very close to where she and Jaret hid. She thought of their own mounts, and prayed they would stay quiet.

When the thunder of so many hooves finally faded into the night, Jaret rolled to his feet and pulled her up with him. Holding her arm to keep her from falling, he hustled her away from the path the posse had taken, down the shallow ravine to where the horses were tied. He tossed her into the saddle, then mounted and started riding hard.

He left her no choice but to follow. She knew it was possible the men from the ranch were still tracking them, but it was equally possible the eyes in the dark were those of Indians or Mexican renegades.

The moon slipped behind clouds, slowing them down but also making it more difficult to be seen. Jaret checked the back trail once more before he pulled up beside her.

"Who was it?" She didn't want to know, but the tension was beginning to get to her and she had to talk about something.

"I'm not sure. I didn't see any evidence of renegades when

I scouted the ranch, but that doesn't mean they aren't around." He looked up at the sky and watched the moon slip in and out of the thinning clouds. "It may be just a bunch of cowboys riding at night to stay out of the sun."

She couldn't imagine anyone riding at that pace unless they were chasing or being chased. Jaret didn't seem any more relaxed, either, but for now they were alone. Then the wind shifted and brought with it the sound of horses.

Jaret spurred Sand Dune back to a gallop. Isabel clung to Lucifer with all her strength and kept pace, not wanting to lose Jaret in the dark. She only hoped they were able to get over the next rise before they were spotted.

Before they could put much distance between themselves and their pursuers, their luck ran out. The moon ended its dance with the clouds and flooded the land with light. They were exposed, and it wasn't long before the sounds of horses and men began to grow louder.

Jaret pushed on, but she knew it was too late. She heard the shout that meant they'd been spotted. Jaret slowed his horse until Lucifer came alongside.

"Be very careful, Isabel. There's more going on here than you know. Most of these men don't have your safety in mind. They only want the ranch."

The posse encircled them and Isabel recognized Hank Hardin's voice as he called out orders to the men. The sound of pistols and shotguns being cocked carried well in the night air as a dozen barrels were trained on Jaret.

Chapter Seven

Jaret studied the men surrounding them. Anger and frustration roiled in his gut. He'd taken this job knowing the risks, and he'd nearly made it. But he hated to fail, and this time he'd done it in a big way—a fatal way. He only hoped he hadn't put Isabel in more danger than she was in already.

"Jaret Walker. I should have guessed." Hank Hardin separated from the others and moved into the center of the circle. "You led us on quite a chase. I figured you'd head for Mexico. Imagine my surprise when I realized you were cutting a wide circle around the ranch. Where were you going, anyway?"

Hardin paused, but Jaret remained silent. He wasn't going to supply any information the man didn't already have. There was no way Hardin could know Nick Bennett was alive, and Jaret wasn't going to help them finish the job they'd started.

"You know, Walker, you probably would have made it if one of my men hadn't seen you grab her." He jerked his head toward Manuel, who'd ridden in with them but had stayed outside the ring of men. "The old man tried hard to steer us the wrong way, but it didn't work for long. How long has he been working for you?" He stopped again, but Jaret didn't answer. Hardin shrugged. "Doesn't matter. I'll deal with him later, in my own way. Move away from the lady, cowboy."

He spurred his horse forward with the air of a triumphant conqueror and tried to ride between Jaret and Isabel. When Hardin grabbed for Lucifer's reins, Isabel pulled back on them slightly and the horse danced out of reach.

"Take it easy, woman."

"What is the meaning of this, Mr. Hardin?"

The man looked confused for a moment. "Meaning? He's a horse thief. He stole the most valuable animal on the ranch, and kidnapped you, too, of course, probably to demand money for your safe return. Now he'll hang for it." A rumble of agreement and glee came from the ring of riders. "Get his gun, Jeffers."

One cowboy separated from the rest and urged his horse forward to meet Hardin. Another followed with a length of rope. Jaret was glad it wasn't long enough for a noose, but if they bound his hands, getting Isabel away from them was going to be impossible. He tensed, but didn't move when the two men reached for him.

"He didn't kidnap me."

Stunned silence descended on the ring of men when Isabel spoke. Jaret turned in the saddle to stare at her. What was she up to?

"Of course he did." Hardin dismissed her. "He dragged you on to a horse and tried to escape with Lucifer running along behind. My man saw it all."

"Exactly what did your man see, Mr. Hardin?"

The foreman stared at her as if her mind was slipping. "Well, *Miss Isabel,* he saw Walker ride off the property with Lucifer on a long lead and you in front of him, fighting and clawing to get away."

Amazingly, she laughed. Jaret wished he knew what she was planning.

"Perhaps it looked that way to your spy, but I assure you I wasn't fighting to get away. I was trying to get closer."

Hardin thumbed his hat back on his head and leaned one arm on the horn of his saddle.

"Are you saying this man didn't kidnap you?"

"It isn't kidnapping if I left willingly."

Jaret was as surprised as the rest. He had the bruises to prove it hadn't been a willing departure. Harding didn't buy it, either.

"What the hell are you saying?"

Isabel straightened in the saddle and aimed a haughty glare at the foreman. "Watch your language, Mr. Hardin."

Jaret bit back a laugh. Her royal Spanish blood looked good on her. When she nudged Lucifer closer, he took the hand she held out to him.

"Are you all right, Isabel?" Jaret searched her eyes for a clue to her intentions, but in the moonlight he couldn't tell.

"I'm fine, my love."

Her words sent a ripple through him that he had to work to ignore. He felt her squeeze his hand slightly, and realized she wanted him to go along with her. Whatever she had in mind had better be good. He could almost feel the rope tightening around his neck.

Hardin moved his horse closer to Isabel. "Would you tell me what the hell you're talking about?"

She faced him with an icy stare. "I believe it is you who should explain, Mr. Hardin. Why have you pursued us as if we are common thieves?"

"Because he is." Exasperation was evident in Hardin's voice.

"He's not a thief. He's my husband."

Jaret thought he knew what she was up to, but even he

was speechless. Husband? He tried to cover his shock and play along, but it was difficult when he didn't know the rules.

"Mr. Walker and I exchanged promises tonight, Mr. Hardin." Isabel shifted a little closer to Jaret. If she was nervous she hid it well. "Not being from this territory, you may not be aware of our customs. When no priest is available, two people can make a promise of marriage to each other. Once the words are spoken, it is as binding as a ceremony in a church. We'll say our vows again and solemnize the union before Father Perez the next time he visits the ranch, but make no mistake. We are married."

Isabel turned toward Jaret with a bit of the devil and a naked plea in her eyes. He lifted her hand to his lips without looking away. "And you've made me a very happy man, Mrs. Walker."

Jaret squeezed her fingers in reassurance before facing the men. "Put away your guns, gentlemen. This should be a celebration, not a lynching."

The sounds of hammers being eased forward and guns sliding into holsters went a long way toward relieving his tension. Jaret watched carefully, noting the men who were slow to respond. Those would be the first he'd check out. Jeffers returned Jaret's revolver, then backed his horse away. There was some grumbling and a little laughter among the men, but finally every gun but one in the deadly circle was holstered. Only Hardin didn't follow Jaret's orders.

"You're lying." His bellow of outrage rang out among the group, startling Lucifer into shying. Isabel gasped as the sudden movement nearly tossed her from the saddle. Jaret tugged her upright and grabbed the reins to bring the horse under control.

"Hardin." Jaret watched Isabel as she reached down to

sooth her mount. Satisfied she wasn't hurt, he turned all his attention on Hardin. "You'll apologize to my wife, then you'll ride out of here. I want you off the ranch before we get back to the house."

"You can't fire me." Hardin urged his horse a step closer.

"The hell I can't," Jaret shot back. "The moment Isabel said 'I do' the ranch became mine. Any contract you had with de la Rosa is no longer valid. I'm in charge and you're fired."

Jaret laid his hand on his belt gun. "Manuel. Henderson." He singled out two of the men he knew were loyal to Isabel and her brother. They separated from the others and rode closer. "Escort Hardin back to the ranch. Help him pack his gear and get him off our property before we get there. I'll send a rider after you with his pay."

Isabel edged Lucifer forward, drawing all eyes to her. "That won't be necessary. The money he stole from the safe will more than cover the wages he's owed."

Jaret glanced at her. She sat her horse stiffly, her face pale and set. She didn't look much like a blushing bride to him. He could only hope she could see the charade through.

"You heard the lady. Now get him out of my sight, Manuel."

"*Sí,* Mr. Walker."

"And check his gear before he leaves. Make sure he doesn't take anything else that isn't his."

When the three men had ridden off, Jaret faced the rest. He turned his horse in a slow circle, silently studying each man. A few were grinning at Isabel, obviously happy at the outcome. Others were watching him, some defiant and some apprehensive. His first task would be to weed out those loyal to Hardin and send them packing. Then he'd know how many men Isabel had left to guard the ranch.

"Those of you who won't work for me say so now. If I find out anyone is helping Hardin steal anything else around here, the man will find himself watching a hanging from the wrong side of the noose. But if you want to help me give Mrs. Walker the ranch she dreams about, I'll try to make it worth your while. Anyone want out?"

Jaret waited for a full minute. When no one spoke up, he nodded. "Good. Then let's head back to the house. We have a wedding to celebrate."

A cheer went up from the men. Jaret wheeled around and cantered back to Isabel. "Are you all right?" The sound of horses on the move kept anyone else from hearing his question.

She looked tired, but there was still steel in her voice. "I want to know about my brother."

Jaret rode close and plucked her from the saddle. He ignored her protest and settled her sidesaddle across his knees. "Hush. We can talk easier this way." She seemed to consider his words carefully before relaxing against him. He wrapped an arm around her waist to keep her safely in place.

"Nick is fine. Or at least he was a week ago."

"Where is he? Why didn't he come with—"

Jaret silenced her questions with a kiss.

"Stop that." She turned her head away.

"I didn't have a chance to kiss the bride." He grinned at the anger that snapped in her eyes. "I have to admit, you surprised me. Not that I'm ungrateful," he added. "I didn't much like the idea of swinging from the barn rafters at sunup."

Isabel shivered in his arms. "I couldn't let them harm you," she whispered.

He held her a little closer. "I'm in your debt, Isabel. And I'll do everything I can to keep you safe and get your ranch back. You have my word on it."

She lapsed into silence. Exhaustion was etched on her face and in the slump of her shoulders. He urged her closer until she laid her head on his chest. "Rest. I promise to answer your questions when we get home."

The change in motion woke her. Disoriented, Isabel opened her eyes to a beautiful sunrise. She yawned and breathed deeply, inhaling the sweet morning air. She loved this time of day. Glancing around, the smile faded from her lips and she went completely still. She was sitting on top of a horse, nestled in Jaret's arms while more than a dozen people stared up at her.

The previous night came rushing back. She remembered the wild ride into the desert, and her plan to save Jaret. Flustered and embarrassed, she tried to sit up, but Jaret's arms tightened and held her in place.

She felt his laugh before she heard it. It rumbled through him and into her, filling her with unexpected longing. When he kissed her, first on the forehead, then full on the lips, she didn't think to object. Instead, she slipped a hand around his neck and kissed him back. The cheers and laughter from their audience brought her back to reality.

This time when she sat up, Jaret helped. He lifted her easily and passed her down to one of the ranch hands. The instant her feet touched the ground, Lydia wrapped her in a hug.

"I am so happy for you, *niña*. You chose very well. Your mama and papa would have been pleased."

Isabel let herself be gathered into Lydia's arms. She

hated lying, but it wasn't possible to tell her the truth in front of all these other people. So Isabel took a deep breath and played the role she had chosen.

"Thank you, Lydia." She glanced around but didn't see her old foreman. "Isn't Manuel here?"

Lydia's eyes hardened. "He and Jim Henderson are following that man to make certain he leaves the ranch."

Isabel started to ask which man, then realized Lydia was referring to Hank Hardin.

"Where is Uncle Enrique?"

The old woman looked past Isabel toward the house. Without turning around, she knew her uncle was there. As she steeled herself to face him, Jaret joined her. Together they climbed the steps to the porch where Enrique de la Rosa waited.

"Well, you certainly changed your mind quickly, young lady. Just yesterday you swore never to marry, and then you go sneaking off into the desert with a man you barely know. I wonder that *true love* could come so quickly. But then, it isn't always love that lures the innocent."

His implication was obvious. Isabel recoiled from the censure in his eyes. Before she could find her voice, Jaret stepped forward, partially shielding her from the man.

"Isabel made her choice and that's all you need to know."

She was impressed. Jaret had put the man in his place without telling a single lie. Of course, there were shades of truths, but that was to be expected. Jaret could hardly tell her uncle she'd spoken in haste to keep him from being hanged as a kidnapper and horse thief.

When Jaret slipped a supporting arm around her waist, she leaned into him. He turned her toward the yard and the people gathered there.

"We appreciate your good wishes. Give us some time

to rest and clean up. Then you're all invited to a wedding feast at sundown." His announcement was met with more cheers. Jaret led her into the house and up the stairs before releasing her to Lydia's care. She turned to thank him and found him entering the adjoining bedroom.

"Jaret?"

His answer was a wicked tilting of his lips and a shrug of his shoulders before he disappeared inside.

"Lydia, why is Mr. Walker going into my father's room?"

The old woman bustled around, pouring water into the washbasin and setting out fresh clothes for her. "Because that is the master's room and he is now the master."

"Oh, God, what have I done?"

"What do you mean, little one?" Lydia turned her around and started unfastening her dress.

"Lydia, you deserve the truth. Jaret and I didn't exchange promises."

Lydia kept at her task.

"Did you hear me?" Isabel turned to face the woman who had raised her. "We aren't married."

"I suspected as much." Lydia took her by the shoulders and gently turned her around again. "Mr. Walker told me he would find a way to keep you safe. I trust him to know what is best."

Movement in the bathing chamber next door brought her gaze to the door. Isabel didn't know whether to curse or pray.

Everyone would think they . . . that she and he would . . . Isabel sank into a chair as the implications of her choice became obvious.

She had not only saved Jaret from hanging, but she'd handed over her ranch as well. Or at least she'd given him the right to run it until this farce was over. Last night, she'd thought only of saving his life. When he'd given orders to the men, she'd accepted that he had to create the impression of being in charge. At the time, she'd thought it would work out. Now she wasn't so sure.

If everyone on the ranch accepted that they were married, it was no better than letting Hardin and her uncle take over.

Isabel turned away from the window. She'd spent the last several hours sitting there, staring at the land, trying to come to grips with what she'd done. She didn't regret saving Jaret, but losing control of her ranch was almost unbearable. She could only hope it was for a good reason.

She needed to find Jaret. Last night, he'd avoided answering her questions and then kissed her until she couldn't remember what she'd asked. She wouldn't fall for that again.

Halfway across the room she realized there was someone in the bathing closet that separated the two large bedrooms. The distinct sounds of splashing water came from the large copper tub kept there. Jaret must be inside.

The image of her almost-husband naked in the tub held her motionless. Before she was aware of moving, Isabel had crossed the room and was reaching for the latch. She snatched her hand back and paced to the far window.

What was wrong with her? Inventing a fairy-tale marriage under a full moon didn't give her the right to intrude on his bath. Her imagination filled in the details of Jaret, sitting in a tub that was large enough for her to stretch out fully. He'd have to bend his knees, but even Jaret should be comfortable.

She imagined the breeze from the open window ruffling his dark hair, the water running off his shoulders and arms. Abruptly she snapped back the curtains and lifted the window further. She breathed in the air and let the wind cool her burning cheeks.

The clouds that had obscured the moon the night before had returned, and the thick white mass floated overhead, blocking the sun. It wasn't going to rain until much later tonight, but the shade gave the parched ground some relief. The sounds of the day floated up to her from the yard below. Horses stamped and snorted, men shouted greetings and questions across the space from barn to bunkhouse.

How could everything around her be normal and she so different? Before Jaret, she'd never have dared to imagine such things. She stared through the glass at the distant horizon, but didn't really see it. The image she'd conjured refused to be banished. She could almost see Jaret rising from the tub, water running down the long length of his arms and legs. In her mind he wrapped a cloth around his lean hips and turned toward her door instead of his own.

Isabel jumped when a soft knock sounded on her door. Heat flared in her cheeks and she took a moment to collect herself before going to answer it. Miguel stood on the other side, shifting impatiently from one foot to the other, a bunch of wildflowers clutched in his hands.

"These are for you, Miss Bennett—I mean Mrs. Walker. He asked me to find you the very best ones," he finished in a rush, jerking his head toward Jaret's door.

"Thank you, Miguel. They're perfect."

The boy's grin lit up the darkened hallway. She watched him race away, taking the stairs two at a time and swinging around the newel post at the bottom to head toward the kitchen. Isabel shook her head at the energy of youth. She was still smiling when she turned around and found Jaret standing in the doorway from the connecting bath.

He was wearing a shirt and trousers, rather than the towel she'd imagined, but he hadn't bothered to completely button either one. His hair was still wet, making the sable color even darker. The grin that spread across his face reminded her of Miguel, just boyish enough to make her respond in kind.

She looked down at the bouquet of tiny rosebuds and wild anemones, trying desperately to stop thinking of him in the bath. Burying her face in the blossoms, she inhaled their sweet scents. No one had ever given her flowers before.

"Thank you," she managed around the unexpected tears tightening her throat.

"Hey, what's this?" Jaret crossed to her and lifted her chin with a gentle finger. He brushed at moisture that flowed down her cheek. "The flowers are supposed to make you happy."

"They do." She sniffed back more tears as self-pity warred with pleasure. "Truly. They're lovely."

"Not as lovely as you are."

She stared at him over the top of the flowers, suddenly unsure of herself. She'd been complimented before, by her brother and by some of the suitors who'd visited, but never by Jaret. She told herself a few pretty words shouldn't turn her head, but it was impossible to stop the spread of pleasure.

When warmth stole into her cheeks again, she lowered her gaze and found herself staring at his chest where the two sides of his shirt didn't meet. His skin was lightly furred with sable hair and tanned, as if he often worked outside without a shirt. The images she'd so recently conjured of him in the tub flashed through her mind. The warmth flared to a slow burn.

Jaret watched her closely, one eyebrow arched at her obvious embarrassment. "What's that for?"

Though she would have sworn it was impossible, Isabel

felt her cheeks heat even more. "Nothing," she mumbled. "Thank you again for the flowers."

She managed to smile, hoping to change the subject. She went still when Jaret reached up to gently trace her lower lip with his thumb.

"Just as I thought. Your smile is as soft as it looks."

Isabel laughed. "Don't let it fool you. The men around here will tell you I can chew on iron and spit out nails."

He laughed with her. "I'll keep that in mind."

Isabel crossed to her dressing table, inhaling the scent from a tiny pink rose as she went. It was cut from her favorite bush, the one her father had planted when Nicolas was born, hoping to give Mama a reason to recover and live. Unanswered questions filled her mind at the thought of her brother. She glanced at him in the mirror over the vanity.

"Jaret, where is Nicolas?"

His laughter faded and his eyes hardened. "Recovering."

She spun to face him, worry crowding out her pleasure in the flowers. "From what? Is he ill?"

A knock on the door interrupted them. Isabel wanted to scream. "Tell them to go away."

"Tonight," Jaret promised instead. "I'll explain what I can then." He turned and went through the door that led to the adjoining bath and the bedroom beyond.

Another knock sounded from the hallway door. Lydia bustled in, her arms overflowing with ivory silk and chiffon. Isabel heard the door to Jaret's bedroom open and close, and listened as his footsteps passed her door and faded down the stairs. She crossed to the window and watched until he came out of the house, his stride long and confident. Someone called to him from the barn and he veered in that direction.

He looked every bit the master of his domain. Obviously,

he wasn't having any difficulty with their pretense. She straightened her shoulders and turned away from the window. If he could carry it off, so would she.

Isabel was tying the ribbon at the waist of her gown when a knock sounded on the adjoining door. "Come in."

The door swung in without a sound. Jaret stood in the opening, wearing a white shirt that had been carefully pressed. His black pants were clean and fit him perfectly. She drank in the sight of him for one long, silent moment. "I've never seen you in anything but black," she explained when he lifted a brow.

"I didn't come here planning on a wedding." He set a small box on the fireplace mantel. "It wouldn't have mattered much if I had. This is about as fancied up as I get."

She answered his grin with a small smile. "You fancy up just fine, Mr. Walker." She turned back to the mirror above her wash table.

"You look beautiful."

Familiar warmth stole through her at his compliment. "The dress was my mother's. I'm a little taller than Mama was, but it will do for tonight."

She ran loving fingers across the embroidery at the neck of the ivory silk evening gown. Though the square neckline was lower than she would have liked, a dozen different colors of thread had been plied skillfully, weaving a garland of summer roses to surround her. The same pattern was on the sleeve cuffs, and a bright bouquet had been fashioned on the puff of fabric on each arm. The matching silk fan lay open on her dressing table.

Isabel lifted a silver-backed brush to smooth the last tangles from her hair. For reasons she didn't want to explore, she felt as nervous as a real bride.

Jaret moved close behind her, took the brush from her hand and ran it the length of her hair. Her breath slipped out in a soundless rush when his hand followed the brush, stroking her from the top of her head to her hips. She wondered briefly if she should stop him, but she couldn't think why she would want to. When Jaret lifted her hair to brush underneath, his fingers caressed the nape of her neck, lingering a moment before threading through the long black mass.

"The first time I saw you, standing on the front porch, I thought your hair must be as soft as the silk scarf you were wearing. I was wrong. It's softer."

He lifted her hair aside to place a soft kiss to her neck. His breath whispered across her ear and he feathered kisses along her cheekbone. But when she lifted her lips to meet his, he straightened and stepped back.

Isabel struggled to break free of the spell he wove with only a touch. She tried to steady her world by concentrating on dressing her hair. As she twisted it into a simple knot at the base of her head, he leaned down to kiss her bare shoulder.

"Jaret, this can't happen."

His gaze snared hers in the mirror and he waited in silence for her to continue.

She fussed with her hair and picked up her fan. "What I mean is, we're not married, and we can't act as if we are, at least not in private."

"Go on," he prompted.

"Well, tonight everyone will expect us to . . ." She swallowed again the lump of embarrassment rising in her throat. "They'll all think that we'll . . ."

Jaret didn't even have the good manners to look like he understood. She finished the sentence in one furious rush.

"Everyone thinks we'll share a bed tonight, but we can't

because we aren't really married and it just wouldn't be right."

He stared at her for a long moment while the muscles along his jaw clenched and relaxed. Finally he straightened. "We can keep to that, if it's really what you want, Princess."

"It is. And stop calling me that!"

"Whatever you say."

She rose from her seat and faced him. "Do you promise?"

"Lady, when I give my word I keep it." He stroked her cheek with a work-roughened thumb. "But since there's no way to prove that, you'll just have to trust me."

She batted his hand away, frustration evident in the stiffness of her shoulders. "I don't know you well enough to trust you."

"You don't have much choice. We should go. Everyone is gathering out front."

When she started to ask another question, Jaret pulled her close and kissed her. His lips were soft and persuasive, coaxing her to respond. Isabel resisted for a heartbeat, then melted into him.

She was disappointed when Jaret ended the kiss and stepped back. When she moved forward trying to close the gap between them, he laughed softly. "I guess you do trust me after all."

The haze of desire he'd created vanished, leaving her disoriented and mortified. What was she doing? She'd just lectured him on keeping his distance and with one kiss she was practically throwing herself at him. The flush of embarrassment heated her cheeks as she backed away.

Jaret caught her hand and tugged her across the room. "I have something for you." He held out the box he'd carried in.

It was made of leather, burnished and oiled until it gleamed. A stylized rose was carved into the lid and painted in several shades of yellow. "Manuel told me I needed to give you a bride gift, a *donas,* I think he called it. I know this isn't much in the way of a trousseau, but it's the only thing of value I have besides Sand Dune."

Isabel lifted the lid to find an intricately carved silver pocket watch, nestled in a bed of scarlet satin. The chain was fashioned from dozens of small silver links, hammered and twisted together to reflect light.

"It belonged to my father. I've carried it since he walked out, as a reminder that my word is the most important thing I have to give." He captured her hand and brushed a kiss on her fingers. "I give you my word I'll take care of you and your ranch until your brother returns."

"Jaret," she tugged her hand free and lifted the watch from the box. "I can't accept this. It's too important to you."

He was shaking his head before she finished. "I want you to have it, to remind you."

Isabel fastened the watch to the ribbon at her waist. It was heavy, but she couldn't leave it behind. When she glanced up, his face reflected a longing she'd never seen before. "Remind me of what?"

He looked away and the vulnerability faded as if it had never been. Isabel looked around the room, searching for something to break the sudden tension. "I don't have a gift for you," she blurted.

"It isn't necessary." Jaret caught up his hat.

"We should at least offer the *puesto de flores.* Placing flowers for the Virgin," she explained at his look of confusion. "Usually it is done by the groom's family a few days before the wedding, but I think the Holy Mother will understand, under the circumstances."

Jaret stood close by as she placed a sprig of wildflowers from her bouquet beneath the icon of the Virgin Mary and

Christ child, lit the three candles and kneeled on the padded bench. Making the sign of the cross, Isabel offered a silent prayer for guidance, hoping they were doing the right thing, deceiving everyone like this.

After she made the sign of the cross again and blew out the candles, Jaret slipped a hand beneath her elbow and helped her up. "Come on, honey. They're waiting for us." He chose a single white blossom from the bundle in her hands and tucked it into her hair. Taking her hand, he kissed her softly on the lips and led her from the room.

Cheers greeted the couple as they stepped onto the front porch arm in arm. Tables were set up in long lines in front of the house, each one covered with bright cloths and flowers. The doorway and porch railing were decorated with garlands of twisted wildflowers and roses.

The feast that Lydia, Marta, and the other women had put together was impressive. Every flat surface seemed buried under a layer of food. A side of beef had been spit-roasted, vegetables picked and cooked, and there were more pies and cakes than Isabel would have thought possible in such a short time.

"It's wonderful," she whispered to Jaret. "They went to so much trouble. I hope the rain holds off for a few hours so everyone can enjoy the evening."

Jaret smiled his agreement as he raised a hand to quiet the crowd of well-wishers.

"We appreciate you coming out to celebrate with us, although I suspect Marta's mince pie is as much of the reason as anything else." Laughter rippled through the gathering. "We appreciate all you've done to make this a memorable evening. I realize this morning was a surprise." Jaret squeezed the fingers of her hand as he walked the fine line of truth. "To be honest, it was a surprise to us, too. I'm still having trouble believing she went through with it, but I plan to keep her busy so she won't think to change her mind."

Laughter rang out again and some of the men offered suggestions on how to keep Isabel occupied, causing her cheeks to heat. Isabel glanced up at Jaret. He spoke to the ranch hands like he'd known them for years rather than days. Without Mr. Hardin, the mood was lighter and the smiles easier. Until this moment, she hadn't realized how little laughter there'd been on the ranch lately. That was one more thing to thank Jaret for.

Several seconds passed before she realized he'd stopped talking and was looking at her. His grin widened. "Looks like she's speechless, folks."

That brought more hoots and catcalls. Warmth flooded her face again but she recovered quickly. "When have you ever known me to be totally speechless?" She scanned the faces of the people who had become her family, basking in the love and friendship she could feel radiating from each one of them.

"I'm grateful to all of you for welcoming Jaret in this way. I only wish my brother could have seen it." Tears choked off anything else she might have said. Jaret lifted their joined hands and kissed her fingers, then threaded her arm through his and pulled her to his side.

"Welcome, everyone." With a sweep of his hand, Jaret invited the crowd to the feast.

They stayed on the porch steps accepting congratulations and well-wishes as everyone filed passed. Isabel's uncle waited until last, then stepped around them into the house without saying a word. Jaret started after him, intending to teach the man some manners, but Isabel held him back.

"Let him go. He doesn't matter."

She turned him toward the western horizon, where a

magnificent sunset was setting the clouds on fire. "Isn't it beautiful?"

"Consider it a good omen, honey." Jaret wrapped an arm around her, tucking her close to his side. "Everything is going to work out. Even the heavens are with us."

Together they watched the light drain from the sky, then turned to join the party.

Chapter Eight

The food was plentiful and the mood light. Tables and chairs were set up in a rough square around a flat area of the yard, leaving plenty of room for dancing. A couple of the men plied bow to fiddle for hours. Isabel whirled around the yard in the arms of one man after another while Jaret stood a little apart, watching her closely and taking the measure of the men who partnered her.

He was reasonably certain all of them could be trusted. Only half a dozen men had collected their pay and ridden out first thing this morning, but that couldn't be all of the men loyal to Hardin. There had to be others still on the ranch, and Jaret wanted to smoke out the others as soon as he could. Isabel's safety was at stake.

"Nice party."

Jaret glanced at Manuel. The older man had returned late in the afternoon after taking Hardin to the eastern edge of the ranch. "Sure is."

Manuel nodded sagely. "It's been too long since we had one on the ranch. Miss Isabel hasn't felt much like celebrating since Mr. Bennett passed on. Then with Mr. Nicolas going off and not coming home . . . It's good to have a reason to dance."

Jaret agreed, even if it was based on a lie. He watched Isabel swing past in the arms of one of the younger ranch hands. She was beginning to look a little worse for wear. With a nod to Manuel, he went to cut in on her partner.

The reel ended as Jaret walked up. The young man thanked her and stepped back to allow Jaret to take his place. As the fiddler started into the next tune, he took her hands and led her into the dance. Her smile was tired, but brilliant, and she laughed as they executed a turn.

"You're the prettiest bride I've ever seen, Mrs. Walker."

Isabel missed a step, but Jaret caught her easily and set her back on her feet.

She waited until the dance steps brought him close again. "I wish it wasn't . . ."

Her voice trailed off, but he thought he could guess what she'd been about to say. He wasn't happy about the pretense, either. "I know." He caressed her fingers with his thumb as they stepped through the arch made by the other dancers.

As the dance came to an end, she dipped into a curtsy and looked at him across their joined hands. "Could we rest for a minute?"

Without a word, Jaret led her out of the circle of dancers and into the house. The library was empty and he closed the doors behind them. "That should buy us a couple of minutes before your admirers come looking for you."

She crossed the room and sank into a chair near the window. She eased her feet from her slippers and massaged one arch with the other foot.

"You look tired, Mrs. Walker."

"Don't call me that! At least not when we're alone." She twisted her hands in her lap. "I'm sorry if that seems rude."

He leaned against the wall and crossed his ankles. "You're going to have to get used to it, Isabel."

"I know, and I will eventually, but not when it's only us." She stared at the closed doors, then turned back to the window. "I hate having to lie. Most of these people have been here since before I was born." Her shoulders rose and fell on a sigh. "It just feels wrong."

"It is wrong," Jaret replied. That brought her head up. "I don't like lying to them, either, but it's necessary."

"Is it? You tell me my brother is ill, but you won't let me go to him." She rose and crossed to where he stood leaning against the mantel. "Where is Nicolas? Tell me what happened."

"Not tonight." He reached for her arm as she turned away. "Isabel, you have to trust that I know what I'm doing."

She spun to face him. "Why should I? I don't even know who you are." She wrenched her arm loose and started for the door.

"Hang on a minute." Jaret took her by the shoulders. When she tried to shake him off again, he tightened his grip. "Stop acting like a child."

"I'm not acting like a child," she insisted, then stomped her foot to make a lie of her statement.

Jaret smothered a grin. She was a beautiful woman, but with the flare of temper in her eyes, she was magnificent.

She laid a hand over his, connecting them. "This is my home, Jaret. I'm surrounded by people who love me and will help me cope with whatever you tell me."

"Not everyone on the ranch is looking out for your best interests, honey. And before you ask, telling you any more might put you in even more danger. I won't take that chance."

"What about you? Now that you own my ranch, won't they be after you, too, whoever they are?" She broke away from him to pace to the window and back. "I'm a grown woman and capable of taking care of myself."

"Not this time," he countered. He should never have brought her in here, away from the party. She'd been enjoying herself. He'd seen her smile more in the last few hours than in the past three days combined. He was sorry he'd spoiled it.

"You don't have the right to make this decision, Jaret. Tell me what's going on. Let me participate in my own life."

Before he could decide how much to tell her, someone pounded on the door. Jaret closed the distance between them and pulled Isabel behind him. Holding her in place with his left hand, his right settled lightly on his gun.

"Mr. and Mrs. Walker, are you in there?"

The singsong quality of the question, followed by muffled laughter, told Jaret all he needed to know. The party was coming to them. He relaxed his grip on Isabel, but didn't release her. "Better smile, honey. They found us."

The door opened and a flood of people entered. Before Jaret could protest, they were both gathered up and carried along with the tide, out of the library, down the hall and up the stairs. The ladies opened Isabel's door and urged her inside, while the men good-naturedly shoved Jaret a little farther along to the master's bedroom.

He let them remove his tie and boots, but when one of them reached for his belt buckle, he stopped the antics. With lots of laughter and a few ribald comments, the men dragged him to the connecting door between the rooms.

One of the women opened the door from Isabel's side, and someone gave Jaret a shove. He heard the door close and lock behind him. The women crowded out and turned the key in the lock from the hallway. A final toast for long life and many children was shouted through the closed door and the party broke up, leaving the couple trapped inside.

Jaret didn't see them leave. He couldn't take his eyes off Isabel. She stood halfway across the room, a vision in a nightdress made of lace and not much else. Her hip-length black hair hung loose and glistening over her shoulders, framing her face and hiding her breasts from view.

A few candles burned and a small fire had been lit to take away the chill of the desert night. The flickering light made her seem ethereal, unreal. She clasped and unclasped her hands, then reached for the dressing gown that lay nearby. Unfortunately it was made of the same gossamer fabric as her gown, and did little to cover her.

Gut-deep need burned through him. Running both hands down his face, Jaret reminded himself that this wasn't a real marriage. It was a sham. He didn't have the right to cross the room and take Isabel into his arms.

He shook his head to dispel the images and headed for a bottle of brandy that had been left on a table near the fire. He poured a little for both of them.

In silence, he held out a glass. After a brief hesitation, she crossed to take it.

The instant she stopped in front of him he realized his mistake. Rose petals scented the air around her. He curled his free hand into a fist to keep from reaching for her, but he couldn't stop his body's reaction to her nearness. With a muttered curse, he downed the contents of his glass and grabbed the bottle.

Isabel sipped at the brandy. "They locked us in."

He heard her nerves in the simple statement. "Yeah. Is that a tradition in these parts?"

Isabel shrugged, drawing Jaret's eyes to her breasts rising and falling under the thin material. He forced himself to look somewhere else.

"When do you think they'll let us out?"

It was Jaret's turn to shrug. "I imagine Lydia will unlock the door in the morning."

Isabel looked panic-stricken. "What are we going to do until then?"

He glanced toward the bed across the room, bit back the first response that came to mind and tried hard to think of something else. Isabel kept talking, saving him the trouble.

"I know what they think we're going to do, but we're not. We can't." She glanced at him from under long dark lashes. "I don't even have a deck of cards in this room."

He laughed at her tone. "We'll manage, honey."

"Don't call me that," she snapped. "I'm not your honey. None of this is real. It can't be."

Jaret stared at her abrupt change. "It feels pretty real to me right at the moment."

"You know what I mean." She perched on the edge of a chair for a second, then rose and crossed to her bureau. He knew before she cried out in dismay that it was empty. The women had been thorough.

"Everything's gone. They've taken all my clothes."

Jaret didn't need that image to add to the others. He dropped into the opposite chair with a groan. "I'd say they removed anything they thought might be a deterrent."

"How could Lydia allow this to happen?" Isabel's face gave away her thoughts. "I told her we aren't really married."

Though her words were spoken in barely a whisper, Jaret heard. "Everyone else thinks we are. Lydia has to go along with them. It can't be helped, honey."

Isabel pulled the coverlet from the bed and wrapped it around her shoulders before returning to the fire. "When will that be?"

He couldn't put her off again, and there wouldn't be another timely interruption. Jaret stared at the flames, considering how much to tell her. "I'm not sure, but probably not too much longer. Nick is going to be fine. He's been . . . ill."

"So you said." Isabel turned her face away, treating him to a view of her long, elegant neck. "Was he too ill to write and tell me he's alive?"

Jaret took another long swallow of brandy and let the liquor warm a path down his throat. "Yeah, you could say that."

But she wasn't satisfied. "Then why didn't one of his *friends* write for him?"

He clenched his jaw until he could control the anger her words ignited. "You're aiming at the wrong target, Isabel. I wasn't responsible for his disappearance." He took a slug of brandy to wash away the near lie. Shades of truth. God, how he hated them. "I only really got to know Nick when I pulled him out of a Mexican prison."

"Prison?" The word was barely a whisper.

Jaret nodded. "Your brother spent most of the months he's been gone in Perote Prison."

He watched her struggle to absorb the revelation.

"Why . . ." Her voice broke, and she sipped at her brandy before continuing. "What did he do to be put in prison?"

"Who says he had to do something? You're pretty quick to assume he belonged in there."

"That's not fair," she cried. "What else am I supposed to think? My brother leaves to buy horses and I don't hear from him for months. Now you tell me he's been in prison. If he didn't do anything, why was he in there?"

"Because somebody wants him dead, but they don't want his blood on their hands."

Jaret could still taste the disgust and fury he'd felt when he finally heard Nick Bennett's side of the story. He reached for the brandy bottle, then set it back down. No amount of liquor could change the past.

Isabel stared at the fire for long, silent moments. "Who would want my brother in prison?"

"For a while, I thought you did."

Isabel glared at him, indignant. "I love my brother. I'd never do anything to upset him, let alone put him in a place he'd be lucky to survive."

Jaret nodded. "I know that now. But somebody wanted him out of the way. Not bad enough to murder him and risk involving the authorities, but they didn't want him coming home too soon."

"Hardin." Isabel spat out the name as if it tasted foul.

"He's high on the list."

"But you sent him away." She rounded on Jaret. "What if he goes after my brother? You can't protect him from here."

"Nick is fine where he is."

"You should have brought him home, not left him alone and unprotected in some strange place."

Jaret's temper flared. "He's not unprotected. And he wasn't strong enough to travel."

"Then why didn't you wait for him to get better before coming here?"

"Because Nick is afraid, since he's out of their reach, they'll come after you."

That silenced her, but only for a moment. "Why would he be worried about me? I've been on the ranch the entire time he's been gone. I wanted to look for him myself, but Uncle Enrique forbade me to go. He wouldn't listen to reason."

"That's the first intelligent thing I've heard of him doing. You have no business running around the countryside looking for your brother. You'd only get yourself into trouble."

"I can take care of myself. I've been doing it for most of my life. I don't need some overbearing cowboy to chase away the danger for me."

"Isabel, you have no idea what you're up against."

"And you do?" She arched one eyebrow. "It seems to me you're fishing around in the dark, too."

Jaret absently rubbed the back of his neck, trying to release some of the tension. "You're probably right."

She harrumphed, and pulled the coverlet tighter around her shoulders. Jaret got up and stirred the fire until the flames danced in the hearth. Instead of returning to his chair, he leaned one arm on the mantel and stared at the burning wood.

"Jaret?" Isabel rose and crossed to his side. "I'm sorry. I know you're trying to help me, and I'm grateful, even if I don't seem to be."

He grinned at her. She was just like a rose, all thorns when you grabbed hold, but with a softness and beauty that made him want to hang on in spite of the holes she put in his hide.

"It's confusing and frustrating for both of us, honey, but we'll have to make the best of it. Until I figure out who wanted Nick out of the way, the only way I can be sure you're safe is to keep you close by."

Isabel considered his words carefully. "You're right, of course. I'm just not used to letting anyone take care of me."

"It's okay to let someone else take on part of the load. I'm not asking you to give up anything. Just let me help."

Isabel's hesitant nod sent a lock of her long hair tumbling over her breast. Against his better judgment, Jaret reached out and lifted one of the raven curls. Fascinated by its softness, he slid the strands across his palm, then twined them around and around his fingers, drawing her closer with each turn of his hand, until he could brush her flushed cheekbone.

Jaret lifted her face to his with a gentle touch. Her eyes were liquid in the firelight, reflecting the dancing flames.

Within their depths he saw uncertainty, but there was something else, too. The agreement they'd reached only a few hours ago was getting harder to remember, especially with her looking at him like that. Hoping he was reading her right, he leaned down and brushed a kiss on each eyelid, then skimmed her long, silky lashes with the tip of his tongue.

Taking her silence to mean she didn't object, he released the hair he had wrapped around his fingers and tangled both his hands in the heavy mass, stroking her scalp until she made a tiny sound of pleasure and pushed against his touch. All the while he pressed kisses to her forehead, her cheeks, teasing her by moving toward, but never meeting, her lips.

He contented himself for a long time with only small tastes of her skin, enjoying its velvety softness, while the soft mewling sounds she made nearly drove him over the edge. When he finally covered her lips with his own, it was like a drink of sweet water after a lifetime in the desert. He sank into her, deepening the kiss, and skimmed his hands to her shoulders to draw her closer.

Jaret outlined her lips with his tongue, tracing the crease where they met, coaxing her to give him access. Isabel moved against him, but he doubted she realized what she was doing. Her hands brushed lightly up and down his back before they tightened around his waist.

Isabel whimpered when Jaret moved his hips against hers and her lips parted. Jaret didn't hesitate. He slipped his tongue inside, exploring the softness behind her smile. He fed her awakening passion with practiced strokes, and invited her to join in the dance.

In a haze of desire, Jaret lifted Isabel and crossed the room, never breaking the kiss. He lowered her onto the bed and pushed the coverlet aside so he could see her body. Isabel protested his distance until her arms were free of the blanket. When she raised her hands to his shoulders and pulled him back to her, he went willingly.

Without the quilt between them, Jaret could feel every curve. He shuddered as the heat of her body pressed against his. He swept his hand up her arm and down her side, learning the shape of her breast, the indent of her waist, and the flare of her hip. Her long legs trembled as he traced first the outside, then the inside of her thigh. He hesitated a moment at the point where lush curls beckoned him to touch, then continued his journey up the center of her body, untying satin ribbons on the way, until the filmy dressing gown parted, leaving her covered only in lace and firelight.

His body surged to painful attention. The lace of the nightdress had been cut with skill, allowing only a glimpse of the treasures beneath. He traced the dipping neckline with the tip of his tongue, slipping beneath the fabric to taste the curve of one breast. He smelled roses, on her skin, in her hair. He buried his face at the base of her neck, nipping at her fragrant skin until she moaned.

A flash of lightning and the rumble of thunder announced the arrival of the storm, but the blood racing through Jaret's veins drowned out the sound of rain. His hands trembled when they found her breasts. Struggling to be gentle, he fit his palms around the generous mounds and lifted them to his waiting mouth. His thumb teased one nipple while he licked and suckled the other through the lace of her gown.

Isabel moved under him, arching into his touch. Jaret lifted her enough to slip the dressing gown from under her. Dropping it to the floor, he slid the short sleeves of the lacy nightdress from her shoulders, tasting her skin as it was exposed. His tongue blazed a path down the inside of her arm to her elbow, following the lace until she lay bare to the waist. Leaving the gown tangled around her arms, he returned his attention to her breasts.

Her skin flushed with passion and seemed to glow from within. Jaret wished there were more candles burning so he could see all of her. Letting his hands be his eyes, he skimmed his palm down her length and back up, this time slipping under the hem of her gown to touch her soft skin. When his fingers reached the triangle at the top of her thigh, he didn't resist the lure.

The scent of her arousal was intoxicating, tempting Jaret to plunge into her waiting warmth. He forced himself to slow down. He teased the dark curls before slipping a finger into her moist softness to stoke her desire. Isabel shifted beneath him, restless, her movements allowing him freer access.

When she clutched at his shoulders, he thought passion had taken her over the edge. Then her panicked voice penetrated the haze of desire.

"Stop. Jaret, please, don't do this."

He shook his head hard to try and clear it. "It's all right, sweetheart. Don't be afraid."

As he allowed some space between them, Isabel doubled her frantic struggles, pushing and striking at him until he grabbed both her wrists and pinned her beneath his body. Her chest rose and fell with each ragged breath.

"Isabel, what's wrong?"

"Get off of me."

He stared into her eyes and what he saw confused him. She wasn't frightened, she was furious. "First you tell me what the hell is going on."

He felt her gathering herself to fight again, and rolled to cover her a little more to keep her still.

She huffed out a breath. "We can't do this."

"We were doing just fine until a minute ago."

"I don't want this."

He laughed, a harsh grating sound that echoed through the room. "Honey, your body's telling me something different. Now spit it out."

She glared at him. "We aren't married, and you have no right to force me."

"Force you?" He released one wrist and ran his hand the length of her. He felt her quivering response to his touch and a dark satisfaction filled him. "Believe me, honey, I wouldn't be forcing you."

"Get off me, you arrogant, conceited . . . You already have my ranch. You can't have me as well."

A crash of thunder drowned out the rest of what she hurled at him, but he didn't need to hear the words. Her eyes were spitting more fire than the storm outside. He rolled off her in one smooth motion and stood glaring down at her mostly naked body. Isabel wrapped her arms over her breasts.

"Don't worry, *Miss* Bennett. You want to save yourself for a real husband, that's fine. I doubt you'll find anyone to marry you, buried out here in the wilderness, but that's your business. I'm just thankful it won't be me."

Jaret stormed across the room. When he reached the locked door, he let loose with a string of curses. He considered kicking it down. For one long moment he let himself enjoy the thought of pounding out some of his frustration on the thick wood. But it wouldn't help their cause if the other members of the house found a broken door and him sleeping in another bedroom.

Spinning on his heel, he stalked back to Isabel, yanked a pillow from the bed and went back to the chairs in front of the fire. Dropping into one, he poured himself a hefty amount of brandy, downed it in one swallow and closed his eyes.

Isabel stared across the room for a long time, trying to make her body stop shaking. She could see Jaret every time a flash of lightning illuminated the room. After all he'd put her through in the last two days, his display of temper didn't frighten her. But if she wasn't afraid, why was her heart racing? She took a couple of deep breaths to slow its frantic pounding, but it didn't help.

The room was quiet except for the sound of rain against the windows. The longer she listened, the colder she became. She considered climbing out of bed to coax the fire back to life, then decided against it. She would have to get too close to Jaret and she didn't know how he would react. For that matter, she wasn't certain she wouldn't beg him to come back to the bed and finish what they'd started.

She turned away to straighten her nightgown. When she pulled the sleeves back into place she could almost feel how his work-roughened hands had slid the fabric aside. She gathered the coverlet more tightly around her shoulders and lay on her side to stare out at the storm, remembering Jaret's mouth on her body. Like dry wood on a fire, she'd felt as if she were being consumed by him. His kisses robbed her of coherent thought and his hands made her burn.

She'd never expected to feel like this. Had her parents shared this kind of passion? She'd always known they loved each other. Now she understood why her mother would forget what she was doing when Papa came into the room. When Jaret kissed her, she couldn't breathe, let alone think. Was this longing to be touched the reason Papa used to go out of his way to be near Mama, even if it was just to brush her hand with his fingertips? Why he didn't really care about living after she died?

Isabel's lips were still swollen and sensitive. Memories of Jaret's kisses swept through her. What was happening to her? A few days ago she'd sworn she didn't need a man in her life, then she'd foolishly decided to sample a little of what she was giving up. How could she have known a few kisses in the rose garden would open a whole new world? Jaret stirred feelings inside her that she didn't understand and left her wanting things she couldn't even name.

Why had he come? She dashed away a tear. Until Jaret, she'd been content with her life. Now she wanted what she could never have. And he would take a piece of her with him when he left, something she wasn't sure she could live without.

Turning over again to face the window, she bunched the feather pillow under her cheek. She would survive without him, she vowed. She'd be fine when he left. But the tears on her pillow said otherwise.

Chapter Nine

By the time she woke in the morning, the rain was gone and so was Jaret. A blanket lay in a heap on the chair where he'd spent the night. The connecting door to his room stood open, but Isabel couldn't hear anyone moving on the other side.

She considered burying her head under the covers and pretending it wasn't morning, but that would be childish. Shaking off her weariness, Isabel crawled out of bed and stretched. On her dressing table lay undergarments and working clothes. Lydia had been in and Isabel hadn't heard her. But she hadn't heard Jaret leave, either.

Jaret. She buried her face in the blanket he'd used. It still held his scent. Last night he offered her everything that she had once dreamed of, given her a taste of what her life could have been, and instead of grabbing the chance with both hands, she got scared and sent him away.

Her own confusion set a match to her temper. Snatching up a pillow, she flung it back into place, then did it again, half hoping it would split open and shower the room with feathers. Until Jaret showed up, she'd been content to run the ranch and wait for her brother to continue the family line. It was Jaret's fault she was no longer sure that was what she wanted.

Reining in her anger and scolding herself for her immature behavior, Isabel picked up the pillow, fluffed it gently and put it in place on the bed.

Before doing anything else, she crossed the room to the icon of the Virgin Mary, knelt on the hand-stitched pad and made the sign of the cross. The move was practiced but respectful. Every morning and every evening she came here, asking for guidance, for patience, and for her brother's return. This morning her thoughts were filled with Jaret. She tried to remember the words she should say, but they wouldn't come. She gave up, crossed herself again and stood.

She hurried through her morning ablutions, brushed her hair and tied it back with a brightly colored scarf. She dressed in a long-sleeved white cotton shirt that was much too large and a dark brown split skirt that resembled wide pant legs. A sturdy pair of riding boots completed the outfit.

She was pulling on her second boot when someone knocked on the bedroom door.

"Come in," she called.

"You're awake."

She stiffened, but didn't stop what she was doing. "Good morning, Jaret." She couldn't look at this man who was her husband in the eyes of everyone on the ranch. "I always rise early. There's too much to be done to waste time lying in bed."

She blushed as she thought of all that had gone on in that bed, and what might have this morning if she hadn't . . . Determined not to think about it, she grabbed the coverlet, folded it and returned it to its place at the end of the bed. As she turned, she spotted her dressing gown, lying on the floor.

Memories of last night raced through her, of Jaret's kisses, the feel of his arms around her and his weight pressing her into the mattress. Snatching up the garment, she hid it in her bureau. She would wrap it in tissue later, when Jaret wasn't watching. Finally she ran out of things to do. Squaring her shoulders, she turned to face him.

The rose he held out to her was pure white and still held the dew of morning on its petals. His large hand dwarfed the blossom, and she couldn't avoid brushing his fingers accepting his gift. She could almost feel that hand touching her skin, as it had the night before. She lowered her head to inhale the flower's perfume, hoping Jaret wouldn't guess her thoughts. When she dared to glance up at him, he was watching her closely, his eyes dark and intent.

"Consider it a peace offering. I'm sorry for last night. I give you my word it won't happen again."

His words sent a wave of disappointment through her. She'd done the right thing, turning him away, hadn't she? Taking her courage in both hands, she met his gaze. "You don't need to apologize, Jaret. I knew what I was doing."

His snort of laughter confused her. "You no more knew what to do than any other virgin bride. And I took advantage of that. I'm sorry," he said again.

Had she been that clumsy? Confusion flooded into embarrassment, then flashed over to temper. "Then perhaps I should be the one apologizing. I'm sorry if my *virginal* response was too tame for you."

"I didn't say that," he fired back. "I knew what I was doing and I dragged you along with me. I had no right to touch you at all, let alone like that."

"Maybe I wanted you to touch me," she argued.

"Tossing me out of your bed was a real funny way of showing it, lady."

"What else was I supposed to do? When Nicolas comes back, do you plan on staying around?"

Jaret didn't look away. "You know I can't. I don't belong here."

"What happens when this is all over and you ride out?

Where does that leave me?" Isabel crushed the stem of the rose in her fist, then yelped in pain. She released the flower and shook her hand to relieve the sting. "I forgot about the thorns."

"Yeah." He stared at her. "So did I. Life's just full of them." He left without looking back.

"I'm sorry," Isabel whispered as tears filled her eyes. She buried her nose in the fragrant blossom and let its familiar fragrance calm her. She didn't want to fight with Jaret. The truth was she didn't care about the consequences. Somewhere between last night and this morning she realized she wanted to be with him, to become his wife in every way. But she hadn't a clue how to entice Jaret to try again.

Isabel didn't waste much time in self-pity. She entered the barn only minutes after Jaret. The storms the night before had left behind a cool, clear morning. Once Lucifer was groomed and spoiled, she would turn him out into the home pasture to get some exercise. She rounded a corner and nearly collided with two of the hands.

"Morning, Miss Bennett—I mean *Mrs.* Walker." One spoke and the other tipped his hat back with a gloved finger, but neither bothered to straighten from their position against the wall.

"Good morning, Luke. Wiley. What are you two doing here?"

Luke smiled, an ugly curving of lips beneath an overgrown mustache. "Waiting for you, ma'am, to see what you wanted us to do." The other man snickered softly.

"Really? I'm sure Mr. Walker has given everyone their work assignments. Since no one else is around, I assume the rest of the hands understood what they were to do. I suggest you haul your lazy carcasses away from that wall and get to doing what you were told, or pack your gear and collect your pay."

Watching from the shadows, Jaret thought Isabel Bennett was most beautiful when temper lit her from within. He'd followed her inside in time to overhear the exchange with the two cowboys. They'd been a thorn in Jaret's side all morning, but he hadn't meant for her to handle them.

"Do you boys need me to remind you what you're supposed to be doing?" Isabel jumped when he spoke from behind her, but she didn't turn around.

"No, boss." Both men skulked off into the sunshine. Jaret stopped in front of Isabel.

"Thank you." He saw confusion in her eyes, not the anger he'd half expected.

"You're welcome," she answered automatically. "For what?"

"For not countering my orders to those two. They've been muttering and mumbling behind my back, loud enough for me to know it, but not enough to call them on it."

She glanced in the direction they'd gone. "Hardin's men?"

"Probably." Nothing else needed to be said. Jaret was almost certain they were still working for the man, even though he was no longer on the property.

"I'll fire them if you feel it's necessary, though it will leave us pretty shorthanded."

Jaret didn't tell her he'd already considered it. "I'd rather keep them here where we can watch them. But if it comes to firing, I'll handle it, not you."

Isabel blocked his path when he started to walk away. "This is still my ranch, in spite of what they believe."

"And if we want them to keep believing it, it'll have to be mine for a while. I'll take care of those two." He stepped around her and headed for the patch of sun outside the door. If he stayed much longer, he was going to kiss her.

She called out to him as he reached the opening. "Then what is my assignment, Mr. Walker?"

He ignored the sarcasm and concentrated on the question. "I had Miguel saddle a horse for you. We need to check the water source upstream. The stock is refusing to drink from the creek. Manuel thinks it's been fouled."

Isabel joined him barely fifteen minutes later, riding a slate gray mare with a long black mane. The horse was one of the ranch's prized breeders, according to Manuel. Isabel sat in the saddle looking cool and calm. *Two elegant females,* he thought. Cutting off the useless wishes his mind was forming, he climbed into the saddle and kicked his mount into a mile-eating trot. They followed the creek nearly two miles before they found the problem.

"That's Daisy." Jaret could tell Isabel was fighting back tears as she looked down at the horse lying half in the water. "The poor old dear must have slipped on the muddy bank and broken a leg."

Jaret dismounted and walked to the edge of the water.

"That's what we're supposed to think."

"What do you mean?"

He straightened. "Someone put a bullet through her head. Whether it was before or after she broke her leg, I can't tell. The rain last night washed away any tracks."

She swiped at the track of moisture on her cheek with the back of her gloved hand. "Maybe one of the ranch hands found her and put her out of her misery."

"Would they leave her in the creek?"

"Of course not. Everyone knows this is the only source of fresh water for miles. Who would do such a thing?"

Jaret scanned the surrounding area. Climbing back into

the saddle, he crossed the creek and searched the opposite bank.

"Jaret?"

"Whoever did this must have led old Daisy down to the creek bed. There are prints from two horses, one carrying a rider. The only other tracks I see are too old to have been made last night. My guess is Hardin isn't giving up without a fight."

Temper fired in her eyes. "He's supposed to be off my property. I should take some men and remind him where my property ends."

"Which ones?"

"What?" She turned to him in confusion.

"Which men would you take?" He pulled off his hat and scrubbed his fingers through his sweat-dampened hair. "Can you be sure they're not working for Hardin? Or would you take only the ones you know are loyal to you and leave the ranch guarded by men who will hand it over to him as soon as he rides in?"

She stared into the distance, her hands fisted around the reins. "You're saying there's nothing we can do to stop him."

"It may not be Hardin."

"You believe it is," she shot back.

"But what do I know? I'm just a dumb cowboy, only good for running stock and protecting another man's herd." He slapped the dust out of his hat and jammed it onto his head. "Let's get to work. There's nothing we can do about Hardin right now, and we need to clear this creek."

They worked together in silence, securing ropes around the dead horse and dragging it out of the water. More than a hundred feet from the creek bank, Jaret signaled a stop. He dismounted to untie the animal. Isabel coiled the rope as he released it and secured it to her saddle. But she didn't follow when he turned his horse to ride farther upstream.

"Isabel?" He guided his horse close to hers. Her head was bowed and her eyes closed. He waited until she finished her silent prayer. "Don't be too sad, honey. A lot of animals will survive another day because of old Daisy." Jaret tucked a stray lock of hair behind her ear, wishing he wasn't wearing gloves. He loved touching the silky mass.

"I know. But I'll miss her." She bumped her heels against her mare's ribs and matched Jaret's pace. "Daisy was the first horse that was truly mine. Papa gave her to me when I proved I could care for her. She was already twenty years old or so. I was only seven and so small that I had to pile two crates on top of each other just to reach her withers. The old dear put up with all my clumsy attempts to groom her." She smiled as she remembered. "Every time I washed her, I had to lean on her to keep from falling. I usually ended up with more water on me than her. And she never once complained."

Jaret laughed. "I'm glad you have such good memories."

"What about you? How old were you when your father let you have your first pet?"

The laughter froze inside him. If he were a fanciful man, he'd have sworn the sun went cold.

"Jaret, what's wrong? Is it Hardin?" Isabel stood in the stirrups to look around. "I don't see anything."

"It's not Hardin." He stared at the landscape, but didn't really see it. Even after all the years that had passed, the pain could still catch him unaware. "I don't really remember my father."

"What happened to him?"

"How should I know? He left one day, after yelling about how worthless I was. I never saw him again."

Isabel nudged her horse closer, until she could see his face. "How old were you?"

"Three, maybe four. I don't even remember what he looked like, just the sound of his voice telling my mother she was worse than useless if she couldn't even give him a son who would amount to anything."

"But you were just a baby."

The indignation in her voice soothed the old wound a little. And it infuriated him that he could still feel anything.

"Where was your mother while he was blaming a child?"

"Drowning in a bottle of laudanum. It took her more than five years, but she finally managed to kill herself with it." He let the pain of losing his mother grind through his gut. It never seemed to get easier, remembering her lying in bed, the remainder of her method of escape pouring out of the dark blue bottle to stain her wine red coverlet.

"Come on." He lifted the reins and increased the pace. "We've got a lot of ground to cover."

They rode north and west, tracing the creek toward its source. Jaret called a halt after a couple of hours, and they dismounted at a place where the water widened into a small pool. A few scraggly mesquite trees offered some shade and the patch of grass along the bank looked like an oasis in the desert.

Isabel swung her leg over the saddle and dropped to the ground. A puff of dust rose and settled over her boots. The afternoon was hot and dry despite the rain from the night before. The scent of water rose on the breeze, lending the air a hint of coolness that was deceptive. She followed her horse to the water's edge and loosened the cinch straps while the animal eagerly slaked its thirst.

"That's enough, you greedy thing, or you won't be good for anything more than standing still."

"Let her drink what she wants. We'll have some lunch and rest here for a while." Jaret tossed his saddle blanket over a bush to dry, unsaddled her mare, then joined Isabel upstream from the horses. The only sounds were those of splashing water as they both rinsed the dust from their faces and necks. Isabel laughed when the gelding Jaret rode dropped to its knees and rolled in the creek a few feet downstream, groaning in pleasure

"That looks like it feels good." She giggled as the big horse tossed water into the air with a shake of its head.

"He sure thinks so." Jaret shook his head at the big animal's antics.

"I'm jealous." Isabel sounded tired and a little wistful.

"Go ahead. I won't look." Jaret watched her rise to the bait and actually consider stripping down and wading into the pool. What was the matter with him? He'd spent most of the morning trying to banish the picture of her lying in bed clothed only in candlelight, and now he was daring her to give him another image to add to his collection. He must be crazy. It was the only explanation.

"No, I shouldn't. We still have to ride back and I'll just get hot and dusty all over again." She opened two more buttons on the man's shirt she wore and wiped the newly exposed skin with a wet handkerchief. Then she unbuttoned and rolled up her sleeves, and plunged her arms into the creek to splash the cool water on her face.

Jaret couldn't look away. Her skin was flushed from the heat. The water sparkled in the sunshine, reflecting its dancing light into her hair. As he watched, her eyes closed. He sat so close he could see the glistening droplets clinging to her long, dark lashes and hear her soft sigh of pleasure. Unable to resist, he shifted until he could kiss her cheek and sip the water from the line of her jaw. Isabel stiffened in surprise when he touched her, but almost instantly relaxed, giving him silent permission to explore further.

He tasted the skin beneath her ear and ran a line of kisses down her throat. Her head dropped back and she sagged against the arm he slipped around her shoulders. Using only his tongue, he traced the delicate bones at the base of her throat to the notch in the center, then back up the other side.

Nipping at the sweet skin of her ear, his body tightened at the soft sound of pleasure she made. When she lifted her hand to his face, he opened his eyes to find her watching him. Figuring she'd had enough, and not wanting a repeat of the night before, he turned his head and placed a kiss in the center of her palm before easing back.

Isabel didn't let go. Instead, she tangled her fingers in his hair and pulled him back to begin an exploration of her own. She kissed the corners of his mouth, and her tongue darted out to taste him. The mix of innocence and curiosity was intoxicating.

Jaret held himself still and let her lead the way. When she nipped at the corded muscles of his neck, his arm tightened around her shoulders, drawing her closer. Isabel traced her other hand up his back to tangle her fingers in his hair and his control slipped a little. Wrapping an arm under her hips, he lifted her into his lap and found her mouth with his.

Jaret wanted to hurry, fearing the moment when Isabel would realize what she was doing and pull away. He fought the urge to lay her back on the grass and cover her with his weight. Instead he traced her lips with his tongue, and when they parted on a sigh, he slipped inside. She followed his lead, exploring him even as he searched for her secrets.

Finally Isabel tore her mouth away, breathing hard. Jaret bit back his frustrated denial and forced himself to loosen his grip. But instead of stopping, she shifted in his lap, trying to get closer to him. He knew the moment she felt the hard ridge pressing into her hip. She froze and her gaze snapped to his.

Jaret expected to see fear, but her eyes were luminous with desire. A small smile curved her lips and she pressed herself harder against his erection. Leaning back, she pulled him with her until she lay on the grass with him above, surrounding her. When her hands began to explore inside his open shirt, Jaret's heart hesitated and then took off in a wild rhythm. Shaking his head to clear it, he sat up and grabbed both of her hands, holding her still until her eyes finally focused on his.

"Isabel, do you realize what you're doing?"

In answer, she arched her back to get closer. He allowed her to pull him in for another heated kiss, then tugged her arms from around his neck. He nipped at the inside of each wrist before speaking.

"Sweetheart, last night I swore not to touch you again. If you're going to stop me, do it now while I can still hear what you're saying."

Isabel hesitated, and he wanted to howl in frustration. But he'd given her the choice.

"Jaret, I know exactly what I'm doing. Last night I was . . . frightened and confused. Not all of the fear is gone, but I know now this is what I want."

"You know I won't stay," he continued, wanting to be sure she understood. "I'm not a staying kind of man. As soon as your brother comes back, I'll be heading out."

"I know."

Her eyes burned with desire and he knew she'd spoken the truth. He couldn't believe it, but she wanted him, regardless of the consequences. He made a silent vow to be gentle, to give her an experience she would always remember . . . and make a memory for himself that would have to last a lifetime.

Jaret stretched both her arms above her head, holding them in place with one hand while he untied the scarf restraining her hair with the other. When it was free, he tucked the colorful fabric into his back pocket and combed his fingers through the long midnight strands. Isabel moved against him. He gathered her close, brushing his lips across her cheeks and kissing her eyes closed.

"Jaret, what do I do?"

"Just feel, honey." With the tip of his tongue, he traced her brows and the fringe of dark lashes that feathered across her cheeks. He kissed the warm skin at her hairline and worked his way to her jaw, nipping at the softness there. By the time he found her mouth again, Isabel was twisting beneath him, trying to free her hands from his grip. When he released them, she slipped both inside his open shirt and around his back, exploring his skin and drawing him closer.

Jaret felt the breeze on his back and realized Isabel had managed to pull his shirt free. Moving slowly, he shifted until he was stretched alongside her and had access to the row of buttons down the front of her shirt. Taking advantage of the ones she'd opened earlier, he worked his way toward the twin mounds of her breasts. Wrapping one leg around hers, he pulled her into the notch between his thighs with one booted foot, then turned his attention to exposing more of her to his exploration.

He tugged on the first button and frowned when it didn't come loose. Isabel's giggle broke his concentration and he looked up to find her watching him.

"Don't laugh, woman. I've never unbuttoned a man's shirt from this side before." Her lips curved even more, and he abandoned the buttons for a moment to taste her smile.

He'd just caught a glimpse of soft flesh rising from the lace of her shift when the sound of hoofbeats rose on the breeze. Jaret rolled away and on to his feet, pulling his revolver from its holster in one smooth motion. Lifting Isabel with his other hand, he was pleased to see her go for her shotgun before worrying about her open buttons and loose hair. Crouching back-to-back in the protection of the mesquite trees, they scanned the landscape until she spotted the riders.

"Two of them, coming in from the northwest," she whispered.

Jaret turned on his heels. "I don't see any others. Better straighten your clothes, honey. We'll have company in a minute."

When she flushed at his reminder of her state of undress, he hauled her close for a kiss. "Don't forget where I stopped. Once we get rid of the interruption, I want to pick up where we left off."

Her smile went straight to his gut, loosening the tension he hadn't known was there. He'd been afraid she would come to her senses and realize she'd nearly given herself to a cowboy with nothing but a good name. But the look in her eyes said she was caught in the same madness he was, and he was glad to have her company.

Isabel laid her gun in the grass and reached for the scarf that he'd pulled from her hair, pushing her fingers deep into his pocket as she retrieved it. With a groan of frustration, Jaret returned his attention to the approaching riders. He knew they'd been spotted when the horses angled toward where he and Isabel were hiding. Then again, it could be the water and grass they were aiming for.

Jaret gauged the distance until the riders reached the tiny patch of green. "Stay here and keep an eye on them. I'm going to saddle the horses."

"I'll help," Isabel replied, and started to stand.

He yanked her back. "What's wrong with you? You want to make yourself a target?"

"It's just two strangers making their way south along the only water source there is. I doubt they're here to kill me."

"I won't take that chance."

His stark statement stopped her. Without another word, she returned to watching the men while Jaret whistled the horses close. Keeping his head low, he quickly saddled both animals and led them into the shade where she waited.

"Mount up and stay behind me." He pulled Isabel to her feet and into his arms for one more kiss. Forcing himself to stop, he lifted her into the saddle. As soon as he was mounted, Jaret urged his horse closer so he could take her hand and kiss her fingers. "How do you get to me so fast? You make me forget everything, even when we're not alone."

"Jaret, I . . ."

She didn't continue, but he thought he knew what she was going to say. Flashing her a cocky wink, he lifted the reins and moved into the sunlight and the path of the approaching riders.

"Afternoon, gentlemen." Jaret was careful to keep himself between Isabel and the strangers, blocking her as best he could. He'd considered telling her to ride for the house, but preferred to keep her close. If there was any protecting to be done, he wanted to be the one to do it. He didn't trust anyone else.

He was only a little relieved when the strangers stopped on the far side of the creek.

"Howdy, mister. Ma'am." The first rider did the talking; the second only nodded his head in silent greeting. The riders looked from Jaret to Isabel, and the shotgun she held.

"Sorry if we surprised you, riding up out of nowhere like this. Mind if we share some of the water?"

Jaret nodded and pulled back on the reins to move his horse out of reach. Isabel copied his movements without question. Both men climbed out of their saddles with easy motions and set their hats beside them in the grass. There was no layer of dust on the felt. Wherever they came from, they hadn't been riding long.

"What brings you way out here?" Jaret kept his voice polite and his hand close to the gun at his hip.

"Heard tell there's a ranch up ahead, along this creek. We left San Antonio yesterday, hoping to find some work. Name's Jedediah Wilson. This here's Harris. He don't say much."

Isabel spoke up. "You're on the right track. Just keep following the creek and you'll come to the Two Roses."

Jaret glanced over his shoulder to where she sat her horse, tall and beautiful, with a loaded shotgun in her lap. She was one hell of a woman.

"You heard the lady." He directed his attention back to the two men. "Ride ahead and ask for Manuel."

"Manuel? Sounds like a Mexican name."

Jaret pinned Wilson with a stare. "If you have a problem with that, keep on riding. If not, he'll get you sorted out. We'll discuss employment when I get back."

"I'd heard there was a woman in charge. You the new foreman?"

"I'm the new owner."

Jaret saw Isabel flinch at the statement, but she didn't argue. He was relieved to see the man was smart enough to figure out Jaret had no patience left for more questions. Both riders checked their gear, then mounted up and turned their horses southeast, toward the ranch.

Isabel and Jaret didn't move until the men were well away from the tiny oasis. Finally she heaved a sigh and eased the hammer forward on the shotgun. "I'm not certain I like that man."

"Which one?" Jaret bumped his horse with his knees and started forward. With strangers heading for the house, he knew Isabel would want to be there.

She slid the shotgun into its scabbard and followed him. "Take your pick."

Jaret laughed. "Then we'll tell them to move on."

"I'd like to, but we could use the help. We should have more than a dozen mares foaling in the next month. Since six men left with Hardin, we need the extra hands to find pregnant mares and bring them into the home pasture."

"It doesn't matter. If you don't trust these two, we'll get along without them." Jaret guided his mount across the creek and turned toward home. "I know they weren't telling the truth."

"What do you mean?"

He waited for her to catch up. "San Antonio is more than a hundred miles from here. Their horses showed no signs of having been ridden hard for a day and a half. More than likely, they've been pacing us, waiting for the right moment to show up."

Her stomach rolled in protest at the thought of the men watching when she and Jaret were . . . Isabel rode beside him in silence for a while. "We should talk to them again before making a decision. They may have a perfectly good explanation." She glanced away before continuing. "I still don't think I'll like them, but it's mostly because they interrupted our afternoon."

When Jaret smiled at her, she flushed a pretty shade of pink. "Honey, you are just too easy to embarrass."

Anything else he'd been going to say was forgotten when he spotted riders coming at them fast from the direction of the ranch.

"That's Miguel in the lead." Isabel started forward. "And Matt Richards. Something's wrong."

Jaret lifted the reins and followed her.

"Miss Isabel. Mr. Walker," Miguel called. "You have to come. The barn." The boy was breathing so hard he was difficult to understand.

"Slow down, Miguel. Catch your breath, then tell me again." Isabel spoke softly to soothe him, but she didn't stop moving. Jaret caught the reins of the exhausted horse and turned it back in the direction of the ranch.

"The barn, Miss Isabel. It's on fire."

Chapter Ten

Isabel stood in the stirrups, trying to make out the ranch in the distance, but they'd ridden too far. Matt Richards caught up with them.

"We'll ride ahead. The creek is just over that rise. You can rest your horses there. Follow us as soon as you can."

"But *Señor* Walker," Miguel objected.

"You heard me, Miguel. You won't be any use to Miss Isabel if you kill your horse trying to ride back now."

Isabel could see the boy was torn. He wanted to follow orders, but he didn't want to miss anything at the ranch.

"I'll take care of him, Mr. Walker," Matt promised.

The youth's back straightened and his chest puffed with importance. "I know what to do."

"Good." Jaret settled his hat low on his brow and faced Matt Richards. "Stay alert. We just spoke with a couple of strangers. There may be more hanging around."

"We'll be careful." The cowboy reined his horse around and followed Miguel toward the creek.

"Let's ride." Jaret lifted the reins and urged his mount into a trot. Any faster would have been dangerous, any slower and she would have gone mad. Still, it seemed an eternity before the ranch came into sight.

From a distance the ranch seemed to be in chaos, but as they rode closer Isabel could see the order within the mess. The horses that were normally in the barn and the adjoining corral had been tethered behind the bunkhouse, well out of the wind and smoke. People moved from the barn to the creek and back, throwing water on the remains of the fire. A few carried whatever could be salvaged into the yard.

The structure still stood, but even from here she could see the damage. Flames still licked at the wood in places. The charred back wall looked close to collapsing. Most of the remaining surface was gray with soot and smoke. Jaret headed for the knot of men gathered to one side of the yard. She angled her horse toward the house where her uncle stood watching from the porch.

"What happened?" She swung off the mare and tethered her horse to the porch railing.

"I have no idea," he replied, sounding bored. "I was napping in my room when I heard the noise. By the time I came downstairs, the men seemed to have it in hand. There was little for me to do." He lifted his nose an inch to look down at her. "Doesn't your new husband know? I would have thought he would have his property better in hand by now."

Isabel resisted the urge to tell her uncle what she thought of him. Biting her tongue, she joined Manuel and Jaret.

"It started in the back, I think," Manuel pointed. "Near the place where the hay is kept."

"They picked the spot least likely to be noticed until it was too late," Jaret noted.

"*Sí.* None of the horses were lost, but most of the hay we had stored is gone."

Isabel watched the activity around her. "Was anyone hurt?"

"Nothing serious," Manuel assured her. "A few have

scratches and one man is a little burned, but that is all. Lydia took care of them."

She turned to look over the barn. In the late afternoon light, the damage didn't look too bad. But the smell of burned wood and leather hung heavy in the air.

Jaret took off his hat and ran his fingers through his hair. Slapping it back on his head, he started for the barn. "Let's take a look."

Following Jaret and Manuel, she tried to prepare herself. Once inside the main doors she stopped and stared, her eyes stinging from more than the acrid smoke.

There was nothing left of the back half of the structure. The floor of the hay loft had caved in, leaving a broken, jagged scar in its place. Where there should have been a wall, there was only a gaping hole. Pieces of leather tack were strewn about, charred beyond repair. Stall doors stood open, left that way after the occupants were released. It looked rather like a prison after all the inmates had broken free.

Nicolas, she mourned. He would be so worried about his horses when he found out what happened. Her tiny sound of distress brought Jaret to her side.

"It'll be okay, sweetheart."

Isabel shook her head, but she couldn't reply. Memories crowded close, making her throat tight. When Jaret pulled her into his arms, she leaned into his strength. "All these open stalls made me think of my brother. He wouldn't care about the burned wood, but he'd be so worried about his horses." Her voice broke on a sob.

"It's all over now. Nick is safe. He'll be home in time to help rebuild the barn."

She nodded again, then stepped away to stand on her own. "You're going to need Manuel here for a while. I'll go see to Lucifer." Standing on her toes and balancing with one hand on his chest, Isabel kissed his cheek. To anyone watching it looked innocent enough, but her tongue darted out to caress the corner of his mouth. Her fingers curled into his shirt for a brief second before she dropped back onto her heels and walked away.

Isabel resisted the urge to turn back to Jaret and fling herself into his arms. She wished they could go back to the spot by the creek. She wanted to hide from the destruction of her barn and let him take care of her. But the ranch was her responsibility. When she passed the bunkhouse, she recognized the two men who'd interrupted them out on the plain. Both were already dripping with sweat and their clothes were smudged with soot. Obviously they hadn't hesitated to lend a hand. For that she was grateful. Perhaps she'd been wrong after all.

She forgot all about the men when she came around the corner of the building. Lucifer stood with his head down, squaring off with the unfortunate man who'd been given the task of moving him out of harm's way. The ranch hand stood with his weight balanced on both feet, waiting for the horse to make the next move. The dust on his pants and shirt told her he'd already had to dodge the angry animal more than once.

Isabel stepped between them without hesitation. "Get out of sight, Adam. I'll take over." Though Lucifer had never lived in the wild, the stallion's survival instincts were strong and being trapped in a burning building, even briefly, had whipped him into a frenzy. When her movement caught Lucifer's attention he bared his teeth and charged.

Stunned, Isabel threw herself to one side, narrowly avoiding the horse's slashing front hooves. Rolling away, she clambered to her feet. Lucifer screamed out his fury and came at her again.

She managed to escape a second time, but her riding skirt tangled around her legs, hampering her movements. The huge horse pounded the ground around her. He struck her shoulder with a massive hoof and landed a glancing blow to her hip.

Someone shouted her name, distracting Lucifer long enough for her to get out of the way. When he pawed the dirt and lowered his head for a third try, she dragged herself out of the dust. Diving away again, she called his name over and over, trying to get the half-crazed animal to recognize her.

This time, when she came to her feet, she found herself boxed in against the bunkhouse. There was nowhere to go. Still talking to Lucifer, she kept her eyes focused on his. She knew there were people gathering behind the horse, but she couldn't see what they were doing. Moving slowly, still calling his name, Isabel stretched out her arms and felt around for a door or window she could get through.

Finally Lucifer brought one ear forward, flicking it toward her. She kept talking, praising him and working to sooth his temper. It took long, painful minutes, but at last the wild look in his eyes began to fade. When she took a step forward the animal flared his nostrils and tossed his massive head, but didn't challenge her.

Though his ears were in constant motion, swiveling back and forth as he followed the sounds of the men gathered nearby, Lucifer allowed Isabel to lay a hand on his neck. He flinched slightly and jerked away when she touched him, but she called his name again, until gradually his muscles relaxed and he dropped his huge head over her shoulder.

She winced in pain when she reached to pick up the rope lead that dangled from around the horse's neck. Keeping her voice low, Isabel spoke softly to those gathered around.

"It's all right now. He's fine. Everyone go back to what you were doing. The less people close by, the better off he'll be." She never looked away from Lucifer, but she could hear the sounds of people moving. When everyone was gone, she gave a gentle tug on the lead and turned him away from the bunkhouse wall.

It was then that she saw Jaret, standing motionless a few feet away, with a rifle aimed at Lucifer's head. She stumbled and Lucifer shied, yanking the rope she held. She could see Jaret's finger tighten on the trigger. She wanted to scream at him to stop, but any loud noise would only frighten the horse more. Returning her attention to Lucifer, she spoke quietly until he calmed again. When he bumped her shoulder, she smiled. "Now you want to be petted, after you've stomped on my patience a few times." She rubbed Lucifer's nose and let him nibble on a strand of hair. When he snuffled near her ear, she knew the danger had passed. "Welcome back, you stubborn mule."

Jaret didn't lower the shotgun until she had Lucifer turned and walking calmly by his lead. He kept the weapon ready but pointed the muzzle into the dirt. When Isabel led Lucifer past, he fell in step a few yards behind, following them away from the bunkhouse toward one of the two temporary rope corrals that had been strung between some of the smaller houses nearby.

Long nails had been driven into the wood in the front and back of both structures, then bent until they resembled hooks. Ropes were knotted around them at three heights. There was sufficient space between the ropes for humans to slip through, but the animals were safely confined.

Isabel led Lucifer to a small empty enclosure. Talking constantly, she lifted the knots from their hooks at one corner of the corral and urged the horse inside. He shied a little, bumping her injured arm. Her cry brought Jaret to her side.

"I'm all right."

Jaret ignored her. He took Lucifer's lead and coaxed the big horse into the corral. While he removed the restraint from the horse, Isabel secured the ropes. Then Jaret slipped out of the corral.

Now that the danger was passed, her legs began to tremble. Before she could find a place to sit down, Jaret scooped her into his arms and headed for the house.

"Jaret, put me down. I just need to catch my breath."

He didn't reply. Crossing the yard in long strides, he didn't slow his pace until they entered her bedroom. Easing her gently to the floor, he steadied her until her legs held her.

She was struggling with the buttons on her shirt when a glass of amber liquid appeared under her nose. "No, thank you. I just want to change my clothes." She yanked at the row of stubborn discs in frustration. "Jaret, would you see if Lydia can come up here for a moment? I hate to bother her, but my left arm doesn't want to cooperate."

"Damn it, woman, you could have been killed and you're worried about a few buttons." He set the glass of brandy on a nearby table, grabbed the collar of her shirt with both hands and ripped it open, scattering buttons everywhere.

Isabel clutched at the edges of her ruined shirt and stared at him, shocked by his outburst. Only then did she see the fury and fear in his eyes. His chest rose and fell with his rapid breaths. Without a word she took the brandy from the table and held it out to him. "I think you need this more than I do."

Jaret took the glass from her hand. For a second, Isabel thought he was going to smash it against the wall, but he downed the contents in one gulp and shuddered. The simple physical reaction seemed to calm his temper.

"Damn, I hate that stuff."

Isabel looked away and giggled. She couldn't help it. "So do I. I replaced it with whiskey a few times, but Lydia would always take it away and bring back the brandy. I finally gave up and let it sit there. I'll tell her you prefer the whiskey. Maybe then she'll leave it alone."

When Jaret didn't say anything, she glanced up to find him watching her. She shivered, wanting to see the warmth that had been in his eyes when they were out by the creek.

"Let me help you get your shirt off. We need to clean up that cut."

Isabel's shock at his offer rendered her speechless. Before she could think of what to say, he had slipped the torn cloth off her right shoulder. She grabbed at it, trying in vain to stop him. "Just call Lydia. She can help me."

"Lydia has her hands full right now. She has a couple dozen hungry, tired people to feed. Now stop arguing."

He stripped the shirt from her right arm. His hands gentled when he touched her left shoulder. "This is going to hurt, honey, and I'm sorry for it."

Isabel didn't argue because it hurt already. Without a word, she relinquished the shirt and her modesty. He eased the cloth off and let it drop to the floor at their feet. She stared openmouthed at the pile of torn and bloody cotton. Her vision grew hazy and the room darkened. She tried to say Jaret's name, but nothing came out. Without warning, everything went black.

Jaret caught her when her legs buckled and carried her to the bed. Trying not to hurt her more, he laid her on her stomach on the edge of the feather mattress and removed what remained of her skirt and shift. The damage beneath wasn't as bad as he'd feared. The skin was abraded and raw, but there wasn't a deep cut. Leaving her alone for a few minutes he went to gather what he needed.

When he returned, Isabel still lay motionless on the bed, her face turned away. From the doorway he could see the black and blue marks spreading beneath the porcelain skin of her back. The angry gash on her shoulder stood out in stark relief. Jaret swore steadily as he knelt beside her and cleaned the wounds. Every whimper she made stabbed into his gut.

Isabel remained blessedly unconscious throughout his ministrations and for that Jaret was thankful. He knew he wasn't as gentle as one of the women would have been, and he hated hurting her any more. Applying a smelly salve that Lydia had given him, he covered the wound and wrapped bands of clean linen around and under Isabel. After what felt like hours, he tied the last end to hold it in place and sat back on his heels, rubbing a shaky hand across his eyes.

He'd let this happen. That thought kept clawing at his mind. He'd sworn to keep her safe and she'd nearly gotten killed anyway. A red haze blinded him as fury rose through him. He surged to his feet, intent on killing that devil horse before it got another chance to hurt her.

"Jaret?"

He spun back when Isabel whispered his name. "I'm right here, honey." He dropped back on his heels beside her. "Don't move around too much."

"How bad is it?" Her words were muffled by the mattress ticking but he understood.

"Not too bad. You're going to turn some interesting colors before it's done, but you'll be all right."

Jaret stared at the band of cloth across her back and started to shake. Without a word, he crossed to the whiskey bottle he'd brought back with him. He didn't bother with a glass, just pulled the cork and took a long swallow. When he turned back to Isabel, he found her struggling to sit up.

"What the hell do you think you're doing?" He set the bottle on the table with a sharp crack and returned to her side. The bandage he'd used was long and wide, but he wished there'd been more of it. It covered her wound, but not much else. When he put a hand on her shoulder to hold her in place, it felt as if her skin burned against his palm. Swallowing hard, he tugged the blanket close so she could cover up.

Isabel tried to stand, but abandoned her attempts when he refused to help. Sitting on the bed, naked except for the quilt, with her hair tumbling around her bare shoulders, it was all he could do not to lean down and kiss her. "You going somewhere, honey?"

"Lying like that makes my shoulder throb. I think sitting up might help. Would you hand me my robe, please? It's hanging in the armoire over there."

Jaret started to argue, then changed his mind. "If sitting in a chair is better, then I'll get you there. Just give me a minute."

"I can walk."

"Give me a minute," he repeated with more force than was necessary. Her eyes widened before she looked away.

He was silent as he helped her into the robe. He convinced her to leave her left arm beneath the cloth rather than trying to get it into the sleeve. Scooping her up, he carried her to a chair near the fireplace, then went back for the blanket to cover her. Finally he picked up the whiskey bottle and both glasses. Splashing a generous amount of liquid into each, he handed her one and carried the other to the mantel. He stared down into the cold ashes and thought of everything that could have happened.

"Thank you." Her words interrupted his gruesome imaginings.

"For what? Nearly getting you killed?"

"Don't be silly. You didn't do anything."

He gulped the whiskey to wash the lump from his throat. "You're right. That devil of a horse could have killed you, and there was nothing I could do to stop him."

"Jaret, it's my own fault that I got hurt. I didn't stop to think about what the smell of smoke would have done to Lucifer. I just wanted to get Adam out of harm's way."

Jaret thought of the ranch hand that had been Lucifer's target until Isabel stepped in. "His hide could have taken the pounding better than yours."

"But Adam wouldn't have been able to get through to Lucifer. I knew I could."

"You damn near didn't!" He needed to shout. He wanted to break something. The rage he'd carried since his mother had chosen death over her son was like acid in his throat, threatening to choke him. He hadn't been able to do anything then, either.

"I need to get back to work." He downed the remaining whiskey in his glass. "You stay here. If I see you outside this room before I say it's okay, I swear I'll tie you to that bed."

Anger snapped in her eyes. "That's ridiculous. This is my ranch, and you can't—"

"Not this time. I mean it, Isabel. I'll take every stitch of clothes you own out of here if I have to."

She surged to her feet to argue, then sank back with a gasp. Jaret dropped to his knees beside her.

"Take it easy, honey. You'll only make it worse."

He took her slight nod as agreement. She sipped a little of the whiskey from the glass he held to her lips, then closed her eyes. They flew open again at the touch of Jaret's lips on hers. He sipped the liquor from the corner of her mouth before kissing her eyes closed once more.

"Stay here and rest. Please. I'll be back to check on you."

Jaret pulled a second chair close so she could rest her feet on it, draped the blanket over her legs and left her alone.

Isabel closed her eyes and tried to get comfortable but the throbbing in her shoulder was getting worse. Just when she would doze off, a breath would cause her to put pressure on the wound and pain would yank her from sleep again. Perhaps she should give in and take some laudanum. She shifted again, searching for a comfortable position, but it was no use.

Easing her feet to the floor, she tried to stand but couldn't summon the strength. Just when she'd decided she'd have to do without the laudanum after all, a light knock sounded on the door and Lydia bustled into the room.

"Oh, little lamb, what are you doing? You should be in the bed, not sitting there."

The tears she'd fought since seeing her barn in shambles stung her eyes and spilled down her cheeks. "I thought it would feel better to sit up, but it doesn't and I was going to take some laudanum but I can't get out of the chair to get it." She knew she was whining like a child, but couldn't seem to stop. "It hurts so much."

"I know, *niña,* I know." Lydia slipped an arm under Isabel's uninjured shoulder and eased her from the chair. "Come now, I will put you to bed and make you comfortable."

Isabel let Lydia help her across the room. Lying on her good side, she fought the pain and tears while Lydia propped her up with pillows. This time when she let her body relax, there wasn't any pressure on her wound. She exhaled on a noisy sigh of relief.

"Now then, little one," she soothed. "Take this." Lydia held the bottle of laudanum. "I know you don't like to, but it will help you sleep. Your body must rest or it will not heal."

Isabel swallowed the generous dose of foul-tasting liquid without complaint. "Uck. It tastes even worse than usual." She handed the empty glass back to Lydia and tried to relax into the nest of pillows piled around her while Lydia bustled around, straightening the room and putting things away. The sounds she made as she worked were familiar and soothing.

The room began to spin around Isabel, and her vision faded around the edges. That had never happened before. Wondering if she was going to faint again, she took several deep breaths, but nothing worked. The room receded and the sunlight faded. Her skin grew clammy, but she felt as if she were burning up inside. Then her fingertips began to tingle.

She tried to tell Lydia that something was wrong, but her lips refused to form words. She fought the encroaching blackness, but wasn't strong enough to hold it off. With a soundless cry for help, she slid into the waiting oblivion.

Jaret sifted through the rubble of the barn looking for a clue as to how the fire started. So far everything he found pointed to someone setting it. The back wall of the barn seemed to have caught fire in several places at once. He tossed the charred piece of wood he held into the ashes and pushed to his feet just as a scream echoed through the structure. His first thought was of Isabel. He burst out of the barn at a run. Looking up, he saw Lydia leaning out of the bedroom window, screaming for help.

Jaret didn't wait to hear what she was saying. He raced

for the house with Manuel and two other ranch hands close behind. He took the stairs two at a time while the other men spread out to search the house. Lydia was waiting at Isabel's door.

Isabel lay on her side. She looked peaceful, as if the pain had finally let her rest. But her sleep wasn't natural. Fear squeezed his heart. He'd seen this before, he realized, when his mother decided she didn't want to bother with life anymore.

Jaret crossed to the bed and shook Isabel, calling her name. Lydia hovered near by, wringing her hands and repeating words in a panicked mix of Spanish and English he couldn't understand. Throwing pillows aside, he rolled Isabel onto her back. Her skin was clammy, her face slack. He called her name again, but there was no sign that she heard him.

"What the hell happened?"

"I put her to bed so she could rest. She was in such pain she wanted some of Don Enrique's laudanum."

Panic threatened to choke him. "How much did she take?"

Lydia was distraught. "Only a little, because she hurt so much. It wasn't too much."

He looked over to the chair where she'd been sitting. The whiskey was where he'd left it and by the amount of liquid remaining in her glass he didn't think she'd had any more after he'd gone. At least she hadn't created a deadly mix. But if she hadn't had too much alcohol, and she'd only taken a small amount of laudanum, why wouldn't she wake up?

Jaret reached for the laudanum bottle and tipped a little of the milky liquid onto the back of his hand. The skin instantly tightened where the drug touched. Dread filled him. He wiped most of it away and touched his tongue to the spot, but he already knew it wasn't only laudanum. He grabbed the bottle of water near the bed and rinsed his mouth.

"This stuff has been poisoned! I need warm water. Lots of it. We've got to get it out of her."

Lydia crossed herself, sobbing in fear. "Mother of God, what have I done to my baby? I was only trying to help her!" She grabbed at Isabel's hand, begging her to come back.

Jaret pushed her toward the door. "Now, Lydia! Hurry. And fetch Manuel. He's checking the rooms downstairs." The old woman hurried out, her ancient rosary clenched in her fist. Jaret turned back to the bed.

"Isabel." He shook her again. "Honey, open your eyes. I need to see your eyes, Isabel. Damn you, don't you quit on me, too!" He continued to call her name in a loud voice, alternately shaking her shoulders and gently slapping her cheeks.

The room seemed to shift and Isabel's face faded. Jaret fought the sensation, but couldn't stop the invasion of the past. He was a boy again and the worn out form of his mother lay on the bed.

He scuffed the toe of his worn-out boots in the dirt as he neared the front door. He was late and she was going to be mad, 'cause he'd been fighting again. It wasn't his fault, though. Darn that Billy Jenkins anyway, making fun of Mama that way.

Jaret shoved open the door, his excuse practiced and ready. But she wasn't in her usual chair by the window. "Mama?" The kitchen was empty; so was the backyard. Heading down the short, shabby hall, his steps slowed. Something was wrong. He eased open the door of her room. She lay all stretched out on the bed, wearing her Sunday dress and her best shoes. The blue bottle she always kept close was lying on the bed, the white liquid pouring into a puddle by her side.

"Mama!" He shook her, but she wouldn't wake up. He ran to the neighbors. Mrs. Harrison would know what to do. But she didn't. The old woman tried to send him for a doctor, but Jaret refused to leave. The doctor wasn't going to come to their house when they had no money to pay him. Instead, he'd stayed by her side and fought for the life his mother no longer wanted.

Jaret wrenched himself out of the past. He'd watched his mother slip away from him and had been helpless to stop it. He wasn't going to lose Isabel, too.

Lydia rushed in with a bundle of towels and two pitchers of warm water. Manuel followed on her heels with two more. Jaret's instructions were terse. Together the two men lifted Isabel enough for Lydia to slide in behind her back and support her head. Then Manuel filled a glass with water and Jaret began forcing it between her lips.

Most of the first glass ran out of her mouth and down her neck. It was the same with the second one. But Jaret refused to stop. Calling her name, holding her nose and rubbing her throat, he ordered her to swallow as he kept pouring the liquid into her. Finally her throat moved as she took some of the water, then again as she swallowed a little more.

Jaret's existence narrowed to Isabel and the glass. Vaguely he heard others in the doorway, asking what to do, how to help. He let Manuel talk to them. He concentrated solely on Isabel.

He coaxed and begged her to keep drinking as he poured the water into her, then held the glass out to be refilled. Over and over he emptied the glass and asked for more, but Isabel did no more than swallow when commanded.

Suddenly the remedy had the desired effect. Isabel's whole

body convulsed as she retched, expelling both water and poison from her body. When she stopped, Jaret eased her back against Lydia and began again, repeating the process, trying to get as much of the drug out of her as possible.

Time stood still as he watched Isabel for some sign that it was working. He kept forcing water into her, refusing to give up. Lydia had withdrawn into herself, stroking Isabel's hair and murmuring prayers while tears ran down her cheeks. Manuel didn't cry, but the pain was evident on his face. His skin was pale and he looked years older. And still Jaret poured the liquid into Isabel.

There! Did he imagine it or had she tried to refuse the water? Jaret leaned closer and Lydia fell silent. Then all three began calling Isabel at once. She'd moved. So slowly that it was hard to tell, she began to break free of the poison's grip. Her breathing grew deeper, her movements more obvious. Finally, after retching endlessly, she clamped her lips shut against more water and relaxed into a natural sleep.

Lydia kissed Isabel's hair, smoothing it away from her sweat-dampened face. Manuel put an arm around his wife and kissed her. Jaret stayed on his knees by the bed. He dropped his head onto his arms, hid his face and, for the first time since his mother died, allowed the tears to fall.

Manuel and Lydia didn't say anything while Jaret pulled himself together. When he lifted his head, a glass of whiskey appeared before his eyes. Thanking Manuel with a nod, he downed the contents. The liquor spread welcome warmth through him. He was so cold.

He'd come damned close to losing her. He'd come here to protect her and instead she'd nearly died. Tears were replaced with icy fury. Whoever did this to her would pay.

Jaret helped Lydia dress Isabel in a warm flannel nightgown before he carried her to his bed. While Lydia settled her, he took clean clothes and went out back to the water barrel. He needed to wash up. He hoped some of the images of the past hours would disappear with the mess.

The night was warm, with a dry breeze that rustled the leaves of the trees around the garden. Jaret stripped off his shirt, filled a bucket with water and doused his head and shoulders. Using his dirty shirt as a rag, he scrubbed himself clean and let the wind dry his skin.

From where he stood he could just see the rose garden. Their perfume filled his nostrils every time he took a breath. He knew the scent of roses would always remind him of Isabel.

Jaret glanced back at the house. Being away from her, even for a few minutes, tore at him. Someone had gotten to her, but who? How? What if they tried again and he wasn't there, watching over her, protecting her? Terror squeezed a fist around his heart. He yanked on the clean shirt and headed inside to check on her.

A single candle flickered on a table in the hallway outside the bedroom where Isabel rested. Jaret listened, but he couldn't hear anything but the wind. Going to the door, he eased it open, checking every shadow in the room as it was revealed. The opening was just big enough to ease his head in when the sound of a pistol being cocked cracked the silence.

"Show your face or I'll shoot you through the door." Coming from the darkness, Manuel's voice held the promise of death.

"It's Jaret Walker, Manuel."

Jaret waited until Manuel acknowledged him before pushing the door open farther. As he came into the bedroom, Manuel turned to go. A look of understanding passed between the two men. Manuel didn't want her unprotected, either.

When the door closed behind the older man, Jaret went to the foot of the bed. Isabel was asleep, her chest rising and falling with each breath. Lydia had brushed her long black hair and tied it back out of the way. Visions of what could have happened rolled over him, and a cold rage burned in his gut.

Jaret walked to the side of the bed and stared down at Isabel. How had she come to mean so much to him? He was a loner, never staying in one place too long, never getting attached to anyone who could leave him. But this woman had gotten under his skin. She mattered to him.

Isabel moaned in her sleep and Jaret reached out to stroke her hair so she knew someone was close by. He didn't want to admit that he needed it as much as she did, to reassure himself that she was alive. As he brushed her cheek, she quieted and turned her face into his palm.

Her trust was like a knife, slipping between his ribs to prick his heart. Jaret knew he would bleed when it came time to leave her. He pulled his hand away and a frown creased her brow. She shifted restlessly, her head rolling from side to side, as if looking for someone. When he put his hand on hers, she quieted again.

Giving in to his own need, he sat in a nearby chair to remove his boots, talking softly to her the whole time so she'd know he was close by. Then he eased onto the bed and gathered her close, careful not to touch her injured shoulder. She curled into him, seeking his warmth. Telling himself she didn't know it was him, that she just needed human touch, he tucked the blanket around her and held on.

What was he going to do? He was half afraid that, when the time came to leave, he wouldn't be able to ride away from her. But he was only here to pay a debt. Once Nick returned, he'd have to go. He didn't belong here.

Jaret knew he should just let her sleep, but, instead of

releasing her, he held Isabel a little tighter. This woman was making him think of family and future, things he'd given up on a long time ago. He couldn't have those things. He'd known that since he was eight years old.

It was time to get out of here. Once she found out the truth about him, why he was here, she'd throw him off the ranch anyway. As soon as he knew she was safe, he was riding out. He stared out the window at the darkened sky, praying the bastards who were trying to harm Isabel would show themselves soon, while he still had the strength to leave.

Chapter Eleven

Jaret settled his hat firmly on his head after climbing out of Lucifer's corral. He didn't need it, since the sun was still an hour from coming up, but he wanted to wear the hat Isabel had given him.

He glanced up toward the bedroom window where she slept. He hadn't been able to leave her alone in the darkness. So he lay awake all night, with her tucked against his side, missing the sound of her voice spitting fire at him when he made her mad, and wondering what a future with her would be like.

He turned away from the hopeless yearning. It was wasted time. A woman like Isabel would never have him. He was nothing more than a hired gun, good for some things, but not for keeping around.

A flicker of light caught his eye. It was coming from the little frame building Isabel called her schoolhouse. Another fire? He hesitated to shout the alarm. The flame, if that's what it was, looked small. He could probably handle it alone.

Jaret approached the building slowly. The door was ajar and he could hear voices coming from inside, a low, whispering rhythm. Slipping up to the window, he pulled off his hat so he'd be harder to spot and risked a look inside.

What he saw confused him. At the front of the room, on what he assumed was the teacher's desk, sat a statue surrounded by tiny candles. The long lace cloth beneath it glowed in the soft light. Kneeling in front of the makeshift altar were three women, heads bowed and hands folded, murmuring softly while pulling strings of beads through their fingers. Praying, he realized. They were praying. But why? It wasn't Sunday.

He hadn't been inside this building yet. He knew it was the schoolhouse most of the time, and doubled as the church on Sundays, but Jaret had sworn off both a long time ago. He didn't belong in there now, either. Whatever was going on inside didn't pose a threat to Isabel or the ranch, so he'd leave them to it.

Turning, he nearly ran over Miguel. In the waning light of the moon, Jaret could see signs of strain on his young face. More than any other, this child was special to Isabel. Miguel obviously felt the same way about her. "What are you doing up at this hour, son?"

"It's my turn."

"Your turn for what?" Jaret looked over his shoulder as the schoolhouse door eased open and one of the women slipped through the opening, patting the boy on the shoulder as she passed.

"At the vigil," Miguel explained. "We will all take our time here to pray until Miss Isabel is well again. All the men are here, too. Well," he hedged, "most of them. Some had to remain with the herds. You should come in, too."

The boy's innocence stabbed into Jaret. Miguel was too young to understand that a man like him would never be welcome in a church. "I don't think so, son."

"Why not? Don't you want her to get better?"

"Of course I do!" Jaret pulled his hat off and fingered the brim. "I don't belong in there."

"Everyone belongs in church. Father Perez said so."

"I don't know how to pray," Jaret blurted, then wished the words back.

The boy patted his arm. "That's doesn't matter. Mama says God knows what we mean, even if we don't know the words to say."

Miguel took his hand to lead him inside. Jaret could have pulled free, gone about his business, but instead he found himself standing in the candlelit room, staring at a tiny pottery bowl. "Holy water," Miguel whispered, then dipped his finger in the water and made the sign of the cross. When Jaret didn't do the same, the boy lifted Jaret's hand and helped him through the motions.

He motioned Miguel to go ahead and watched the boy move to the altar at the front. The murmured praying seemed to grow louder the longer he stood there. Marta knelt beside another woman on the hard wooden floor, and Jaret tried not to disturb them as he moved to the far end of the back row of chairs.

He didn't approach the altar. He didn't have the right. Still, he couldn't leave. Something held him here. So he chose a chair and settled down out of the way.

He turned his hat around and around in his fingers as he studied the room. The altar was just a table with a fancy cloth over it. The four windows were long panes of plain clear glass. The candles were the same as any others used on the ranch. But here, in this room, they became something else, special somehow.

He hadn't been in a church since the last time Mr. and Mrs. Harrison had insisted he go with them. They were the last folks who'd given him a home, a place to belong. He never understood why they'd bothered. He was an orphan, not their real son. What made them want to give him the family he was missing? Questions he'd avoided for years crowded in as he sat in the quiet room.

Why did he never feel a part of anything, that he didn't have the right to be happy? Why did the Harrisons, and the Wilkins before them, care what happened to him, the son of a gambler, a boy who told lies and stole, just like his father? Why did strangers care more about him than his own parents?

The whispered prayers faded into the background as Jaret considered his life, what brought him here to this place, to these people. He was living a lie and a few of them probably suspected it. Yet they welcomed him, included him as if he belonged.

Another woman entered and Marta rose to leave. As she passed, Marta patted his shoulder. "It is good you are here."

Was it? Unexpected tears burned behind his eyes. He wanted to follow Marta, ask her how she knew. Instead, he bowed his head and, for the first time since a rebellious boy had struck out on his own, he prayed. For Isabel, for the people he was learning to care about, and for himself.

By the time he slipped from the church, the eastern sky was showing some light. All around him, men slept anywhere there was a patch of grass. Miguel was right. The word of Isabel's injury had spread fast. There were men here that he hadn't seen before. As soon as the sun was up, he'd be sure to meet every one of them. Then he had to send them back out onto the range. Someone wanted this ranch to fail, and Jaret couldn't stop that from happening if all the ranch hands were here at the main house.

Jaret listened to the sounds of the ranch waking up. He'd almost forgotten how peaceful the morning could be. Since he was usually on the move, his minutes owned by somebody else, he rarely took the time to just stand still and watch the sky color up with the rising sun.

The scent of coffee and frying bacon, carried on the light breeze, made his stomach growl. As he headed for breakfast, two men he didn't know joined him.

"Morning, gentlemen."

A bear of a man with a graying mop of russet curls stuck out his hand. "Pleased to meet you, Mr. Walker. Folks around here call me Red. How's Miss Isabel?" The words were friendly, but the man's concern was obvious.

"She's going to be fine, I think." Jaret took a breath and looked at each man in turn. "It was a near thing."

The other man took half a step forward, forcing Jaret to stop. "Didn't think the fool horse kicked her that hard. She didn't look too bad when you carried her inside."

Red grinned in agreement. "She was hissing and spitting like a wet cat."

"True enough," Jaret replied. "She's got a gash on her left shoulder, and her hip and a couple of ribs will be pretty sore when she comes around. But it wasn't her run in with Lucifer that caused the problem." He eyed each man in turn. "The laudanum she took for the pain was poisoned."

Stunned silence reined for two heartbeats and then they started talking at once. Jaret answered every question as honestly as he could.

"How the hell did the stuff get into her room?"

Jaret faced Red. "I don't know, but when I find out, the man or woman who did it better be real good at hiding."

The men growled their agreement. The other cowboy offered a work-roughened hand.

"Name's Jim Easton. I've been here for going on twelve years, since Isabel's daddy found me wandering around in San Antonio causing trouble. Anything you need, you just ask."

It was the same with Red, except he'd come to the ranch when Isabel's mother was alive. Watching the two cowboys, he could see the same fierce protectiveness in their eyes that was evident in Manuel and Lydia.

Could he trust someone besides himself to take care of Isabel? He'd always worked alone. It was *his* promise, *his* word given to Nick Bennett. But to keep her safe, he needed help. Jaret made a decision.

"Someone around here doesn't want Miss Isabel to stay on the ranch. I intend to make sure they fail."

"Any idea who?"

Jaret had his suspicions, but they were only that. He couldn't prove anything yet. "I have one or two in mind. But I could use your help. Keep this to yourselves, unless you're certain the man you tell is loyal to Isabel and her brother. Someone slipped a rattlesnake into the barn where she'd be sure to come across it. Then they killed a horse to get Isabel and me away from the ranch long enough to set fire to the barn. Now the poison. It's someone nearby doing this, somebody we all know. From now on, trust no one you aren't sure of."

"How do you know you can trust us?" It was Jim Easton who spoke. Red waited for Jaret's answer with the calm of a man long used to being patient.

"I don't." He watched their spines stiffen and nodded. These men would do anything for Isabel. Even the suggestion that one of them would hurt her was an insult. "But then, I don't trust easily. I guess I'll have to learn."

The sound of the bell calling the hands to breakfast rang through the quiet morning. As one, the men turned toward the bunkhouse. Jaret was glad to see that both were armed. Each wore a pistol at his waist and a knife in his boot. Shotguns and rifles would be in a scabbard on every saddle. A man didn't last long in a place like this without knowing how to fight.

Since there were too many men to feed inside, breakfast

had been moved outdoors under the trees behind the bunkhouse. Marta and five other women tended pots and skillets arranged over an open fire pit. Jaret recognized the one who'd come out of the schoolhouse while he was speaking with Miguel.

As he neared the long line of tables set up under the trees, more men asked about Isabel. He kept his answers short, letting them know she was out of danger, but not mentioning just how close a call it had been.

As he looked at every face, he realized he was trying to figure out which one had done it. Was it one of the men who worked close to the house? The odds were with that choice. But none of the ranch hands would come into the main house unless they were sent for. That left the women and children, who had free run of the place, or Isabel's uncle.

Jaret looked back toward the house. He hadn't seen Don Enrique since yesterday afternoon, when he and Isabel had returned to find the barn nearly burned down. Her uncle had been in the house alone while everyone fought to save the structure. Abruptly Jaret stood. Several of the men nearby reached for their guns in an automatic response. Everyone was jumpy.

"Sorry. Didn't mean to move so fast," he reassured them. "Eat your breakfast. I'm going to check on Isabel."

"Mr. Walker, before you go."

Jaret looked back to see one of the two men who'd happened by the waterhole where he and Isabel had nearly . . . Jaret dug around in his memory until he came up with the man's name: Jedediah Wilson.

"There wasn't much of a chance to talk yesterday after we arrived." Wilson scuffed the toe of his boot in the dust. "I'd like to stay on, if you can use the help. I've got some experience swinging a hammer, could maybe help rebuild the barn. I sure could use the work."

"What about him?" Jaret glanced toward the man's silent companion, standing a few feet off, staring at the horizon.

"Harris wants to keep moving. Thinks he'll do better closer to the coast."

Jaret wanted both of them to move on, but wasn't sure why. Maybe it was because Isabel had said she didn't trust either of them. But they'd both pitched in to help as soon as they arrived at the ranch, according to Manuel. For that he owed them something. "All right. We can use you around here, at least for a few weeks. Then we'll see."

"Thank you, Mr. Walker." Wilson returned to his breakfast. Harris never even bothered to look at him. When Jaret glanced at Jim Easton, he found the cowboy watching the silent stranger carefully. Knowing Harris wouldn't go far without someone letting him know, Jaret gulped down the last of his cooling coffee and went to check on Isabel. He found Manuel sitting on the front porch.

"Morning. How is Isabel?" Manuel continued cleaning the shotgun he held open across his knees.

"She was fine when I left her an hour ago. I locked the hallway door and Lydia was in the next room, knitting."

Manuel nodded and reached for another cloth.

Jaret watched him work. The motions were practiced and soothing, peaceful, at odds with the necessity of carrying the gun in the first place. "Have you seen de la Rosa this morning?"

The older man looked toward the house, the wrinkles around his eyes becoming more pronounced as he thought back through the last few hours. "Not since yesterday," he decided. "Saw him around the horses just before my Lydia screamed. He's not in his room. I checked the whole house before I bedded down in the hallway last night. He didn't come in after that."

"Ask around, would you? I'd really like to know where he's hiding." Leaving Manuel to his task, Jaret headed inside.

The mid-morning sun shone through the open windows of Jaret's bedroom, glinting off the bottles on the dressing table and casting rainbows on the walls and floor. But Isabel was too upset to enjoy the display.

"What do you mean, I have to remain here? Lydia, I'm fine. I'll be even better when you let me get back to work." Isabel sat up in bed, with a light coverlet over her legs. "This isn't the first time I've been kicked by Lucifer. I'm only a little stiff and sore, nothing to be concerned about."

"Glad to hear it."

"Jaret." She smiled at the man she was sure would be on her side. "Please talk some sense into Lydia. I have too much to do to lie here all day."

Lydia huffed and crossed the bedroom. "You tell her to stay here, *Señor* Jaret. You're her husband. Perhaps she'll listen to you." The older woman closed the door behind her with a thump. Jaret's lips twitched under his mustache.

Isabel was captivated by the movement. His smile seemed to light his eyes from within. She had to force herself to concentrate on his words.

"I don't think I've ever seen her irritated before."

Isabel rolled her eyes. "You didn't grow up around her. I remember weeks when she wasn't anything but irritated." She waited until he crossed to her side. "Jaret, there is no reason for me to stay inside today. I'm fine, really. It's only a few bruises and one small cut. I've got to do something. I can't bear the thought of staying in this room all day."

When Jaret remained silent, Isabel decided she'd just make the decision herself. She tossed back the cover, swung her legs to the floor and pushed to her feet. With a deep breath, she took two steps away from the bed, then turned to Jaret and lifted her chin in defiance. She opened her mouth to tell him "I told you so," but the room took a slow turn around her and she swayed in place. She groped for the back of a chair to get her balance, but missed. Her knees buckled and Jaret barely caught her before she hit the floor.

She tried to protest when he lifted her, but she didn't have the strength. Jaret sat down on the edge of the bed with her on his lap and pushed her head down between her knees. When her vision cleared, she realized he had an arm wrapped around her waist, holding her in place. It had been a long time since she'd felt protected and safe, and she savored the feeling for a moment before trying to straighten.

"Feeling better?"

Jaret's voice was deep and rough, causing her to shiver. He tightened his grip around her waist. His arm pressed against her breasts, sending delicious warmth curling through her body.

Isabel nodded, the movement jerky. "Let me up."

When he complied, she sat up just enough to lay her head on his shoulder. This felt even better, she decided. She closed her eyes and took a deep breath. "You smell like leather and liniment."

She felt as much as heard his rumble of laughter. "That would be Lucifer's fault. We had a bit of a shoving match before he let me groom him this morning."

"How is he?"

"He's in better shape than you are."

Isabel straightened until she could see Jaret's eyes. "I don't understand why. He didn't kick me that hard. He's certainly done worse."

Jaret only stared at her.

"Well, it's true," she insisted.

"You don't remember."

Surprise was obvious in his voice. "Of course I remember. Lucifer was half crazy from the smoke and fire when I went to get him."

"Go on," Jaret urged.

"Once I had him safely in the corral, you yelled at me for doing what I consider my job. Then, when I needed to sit down, you completely overreacted, carried me to my room and bullied me until you had me bandaged and lying down."

Isabel looked around. "How did I get into your bedroom?"

Jaret dragged his fingers through his hair. Isabel was shocked to see his hand trembling. Needing to soothe him, she reached up and smoothed the sable strands back into place, then trailed her fingers down his jaw and brushed her thumb over his mustache. The beard stubble on his chin made her skin tingle.

Without any warning, Jaret pulled her close in a fierce hug. She cried out when he bumped her injured shoulder and he released her immediately.

"I'm sorry, honey. I didn't mean to hurt you."

"It's all right. I'd just forgotten it was there." Isabel pulled him close once more and snuggled into his arms. "I'm fine. Now answer my question."

Jaret made a sound that she thought meant he didn't remember the question, so she repeated it. "How did I end up in your bedroom instead of mine?"

"Because your room wasn't fit to inhabit after we got done saving your life."

Isabel sat up with a jerk. "What are you talking about? It was only a small cut." The bleakness in Jaret's eyes frightened her. "Jaret, tell me what I've forgotten."

He took a slow, shaky breath. "After we had you bandaged up, I went out to the barn to survey the damage. I wasn't there twenty minutes when Lydia screamed."

"Lydia?" It was Isabel's turn to stare. "Nothing frightens her, certainly not enough to make her scream."

"Believe me, she was scared enough." He threaded his fingers through hers, holding her close. "She'd given you some laudanum. Not too much, since you rarely take it. Just enough to dull the pain and help you sleep."

Isabel's brows furrowed as she tried to pull out the hazy memory. "I remember. I didn't even argue about taking it."

Jaret nodded. "Lydia said she turned away to straighten the room, and when she looked back you were reaching out for her. Then your eyes rolled back and you went under."

Vague panic clawed at Isabel's mind. "Go on."

Jaret's gaze was haunted. "The laudanum was poisoned."

She struggled to breathe. "That isn't possible. You must be mistaken. It's the same bottle I've had since my uncle came and I've taken some of it before."

"Maybe, honey, but this time it was poisoned. It took us a while, but we managed to get most of it out of you." Jaret didn't have to fill in the details. She could see most of them in his eyes. The blue was cold and bleak. He urged her head to his chest and laid his cheek on her hair. She felt his heart pound with remembered terror. "When we were done, I moved you in here so Lydia could clean up your bedroom. I thought I might do a better job protecting you if you were a little closer."

Of course Jaret would feel responsible. She tugged his

arm around her and snuggled closer. "That explains why my body feels like it's been stomped on by a whole herd of horses. But who would want to . . ." She wouldn't say it, refused to admit aloud that someone wanted her dead.

"I have a few ideas."

Isabel squared her shoulders, ready to listen and to defend her employees. "Tell me."

"Probably the same one who had your brother kidnapped and dumped into a Mexican prison."

"But that was Hardin, and he couldn't have put anything into that bottle. He was never in this part of the house. Someone would have seen him. Besides, he's gone."

Jaret nodded. "Maybe. But Hardin brought quite a few men with him and they aren't all gone. Then there's your uncle."

"No, Jaret, he's family. I refuse to believe he would try to harm me." Even as she said the words, she wondered if Jaret might be right again. Her uncle had become almost obsessive about seeing her married and off the ranch. "Let's find Uncle Enrique. Ask him what he knows."

"We haven't seen him since the fire."

Isabel stared at Jaret. "He was here when we got back."

"Yes, standing on the porch while everyone else was out of the house fighting to save the barn. He disappeared sometime after that and didn't return last night."

Isabel could feel the frustration and temper building inside Jaret. It matched her own. Who would want the land enough to kill for it? Or did someone just want her dead?

She decided to trust Jaret to find out who did this. She brushed a kiss along his jaw, hoping to distract him.

"Thank you for explaining how I ended up in your bedroom. Now tell me why you won't let me get back to work?"

Jaret's curses blistered the air. "Damn it, woman, you nearly died!" He buried his fingers in her hair, dislodging the scarf that held it back. His hands were warm against her neck, sending shivers down her spine. "If the poison had been a little stronger, or I hadn't been fast enough—" He bit off another curse and released her. "Don't you trust me to take care of your precious ranch for even one day?"

"Of course I do," Isabel insisted. She nearly smiled to see the glint of temper back in his eyes. "But I can't tolerate inactivity. If I have to sit inside all day, I'll go mad."

She softened the heat of her words by laying her head on his shoulder and planting kisses along the muscles of his neck.

"No."

His stern reply was softened somewhat by the sound of pleasure he made when she kissed him again. Jaret skimmed one hand from her shoulder to her hip and tightened his hold on her. Through the light fabric of her dressing gown she felt every one of his fingers. Wanting to feel more of him, she skimmed her fingers along his open collar, following the edge of his shirt until she touched the exposed skin of his chest above the first button. She pressed a kiss there, then pushed the button through the hole to give her more access.

He kissed her temple. "You're still not leaving this room."

"What?" Isabel lifted her head to look at him. For a moment she had no idea what he was talking about. She was completely caught up in him. When his words penetrated, she straightened, bumping into the hard bulge in his lap. For a second, she couldn't think. Then he grinned at her, obviously enjoying her predicament. She exacted revenge by wiggling back and forth a few times, settling closer to him with each motion. When he groaned and his fingers flexed, digging into her hip, she smiled. "Now, give me one good reason why I should stay here."

"Because whoever tried to poison you is still here and

they're liable to try again. I won't take that chance." Jaret nipped at her earlobe.

"You're not going to distract me, Jaret Walker." She moaned when he brushed his thumb just under the curve of her breast. "You don't play fair." Isabel pushed to her feet to pace and was dismayed to find her legs were too weak. She laid a hand on the back of a chair and forced herself to remain standing. "See, I'm fine. And there are plenty of men out there to guard me. If you don't trust any of them, *you* can guard me."

"Honey, most of those men were here yesterday, including me, but it didn't help. Someone still managed to sneak into the house and nearly kill you."

"Who do you think it was?" Isabel wasn't sure she wanted to hear him name a friend, but it was better to know your enemies than to be caught unaware.

Jaret didn't answer right away. Instead, he caught her hands and tugged her toward him until she stood between his knees. She put her hands on his shoulders to steady herself. "I don't know. I've got my suspicions, but for now that's all they are. I swear to you I'll find out, though."

"I know you will." She brushed at the hair that fell over his collar. "But what do I do in the meantime?"

"Rest." He nudged her back a little and stood, keeping her hand in one of his. He motioned her into bed with the other. "You're almost asleep on your feet."

Isabel protested, but did as he asked and sat on the mattress. Jaret lifted her legs from the floor, so she had no choice but to lie back. When she was settled, he pulled her slippers from her feet one at a time, caressing the arch of each foot as he went. Finally he laid the light coverlet over her, brushed his lips to her forehead and left.

Isabel lay still, staring at the ceiling. The sensations

that rocketed through her body at Jaret's touch made her tremble. What was she going to do about him?

Since thinking about him made it even harder to stay still, she concentrated on getting out of the bedroom. She had no intention of remaining locked inside while Jaret tried to find out who wanted her dead. She hadn't promised not to leave the house, but it wasn't fair to defy him in front of the hands, not when he was still getting his bearings.

Visions of the two of them on their pretend wedding night, and beside the creek, filled her mind. She knew what she'd like to do to pass the time, but how did she get him to cooperate?

Remembering the tremor that had coursed through him when she'd kissed his neck, and the reaction she'd felt in his body, she smiled. The sense of power she felt at being able to affect such a strong man was invigorating. But that would have to wait until he returned. So what could she do until he returned?

A laugh escaped as the answer occurred to her. Jaret wanted her to stay in the house, so she would. Reaching for the small bell that Lydia had left within reach when she'd taken away the breakfast dishes, she rang for whoever could hear her. Then she dampened the sound. What if Jaret was still in the house? What would she tell him? That she needed Lydia's assistance, she decided. Surely he wouldn't deny her that.

It wasn't Jaret that answered the bell. Isabel's smile broadened when Miguel stuck his dark head around the door.

"*Sí,* Miss Isabel?"

"Hello, Miguel. How is your puppy?"

"Oh, he is growing so fast." Forgetting his instructions to go no farther than the door, he scrambled across the room and plopped onto the mattress. Isabel barely managed to stifle a groan when his movement jarred her shoulder. "Every day he is a little bigger, I think."

The boy's legs were growing faster than the rest of him, making his movements a little awkward. The puppy wasn't the only one growing.

"Miguel, I need you to do something for me."

"Of course. That's why Mr. Jaret asked me to stay where I could hear the bell."

Isabel felt a twinge of guilt. If she asked the boy to help, he would very likely get into trouble with Jaret. Then she'd just have to explain to Jaret that it was her fault.

"I want you to run and tell all the children we'll have our lessons today, but since I can't get to the schoolroom, I want them to come to the house. We can all gather in the parlor. No," she corrected, "in the library." No one working in the yard or corral could see them in that room. "Have them come in through the kitchen. Go on, now. I don't want the children to be late."

Miguel hesitated, his brows coming together when he frowned. "Mr. Jaret said you are to rest."

"I promise to sit in a chair during the whole lesson. That's resting, isn't it?"

Clearly the boy was torn, but his loyalty to her won out. "I guess so." His face brightened. "I'll go get the others. We'll all be back before you ring the school bell."

With a grin, he bounced off the bed and raced from the room. Isabel bit back another groan of pain. She lay still until she heard the front door slam, then tossed aside the coverlet and dragged her legs over the edge of the bed. When she had difficulty getting to her feet, she began to doubt the wisdom of her plan. She gritted her teeth and forced herself upright. Once she was sure she could walk without falling, she crossed slowly into her own room.

It took her longer than expected to get dressed, but she managed to get into a loose cotton dress. The stiffness in her injured shoulder alarmed her. If she didn't start using it, she'd be useless for weeks. When her knees threatened to buckle beneath her, she held on to a chair until she could stand straight again.

She'd dragged a brush through her hair and found a bright blue scarf to tie it back with before she realized she couldn't do it herself. She simply couldn't raise her left arm up that far. In frustration, she threw the silk onto her dressing table. Now what? She couldn't sit down with the children with her hair free. Baffled she looked around for something she could use that didn't require two hands.

Sounds of a normal morning drifted in through the open window. She heard men shout and glanced out to see a colt make a dash for freedom. His bid was short-lived, however, as a cowboy tossed a rope over his head and pulled the noose tight.

Isabel smiled. She'd been tying that knot since she was five years old. Grabbing up the scarf, she smoothed it into a long column of silk. With practiced motions, she pulled the ends around and through and fashioned a bright blue lasso. Foolish pride filled her at the accomplishment. She threaded her long hair through the loop and tugged the scarf tight. When she was satisfied it would stay put, she headed for the door.

She half expected to find it locked, but it swung open easily. She looked around the hallway, but no one was nearby. Voices floated up from downstairs. Probably her personal guards. Well, they weren't going to stop her now.

Getting to the top of the stairs was easy, but her strength was already fading. Determined to get to the first floor, she held tightly to the banister, took a deep breath and descended one step. After the first one it got a little easier, but she was winded by the time she gained the hallway. From here she could hear the children already in the library.

"Miss Isabel." Harry Jenks stepped into her path. "What are you doing down here?"

She waved the man away. "I'm just going into the library. I won't try to leave the house."

Harry didn't look convinced, but he let her go. Isabel made it down the hall by holding on to the wall and whatever furniture there was in her path. Deciding not to stop in the doorway—she wasn't sure she would be able to get going again—she headed straight for the big leather chair one of the older boys had arranged for her to use. Dropping into it, she heaved a sigh of relief and exhaustion. Her face was damp with perspiration and she felt more than a little queasy.

"Miss Isabel, are you all right?"

She looked into the face of her youngest pupil. "Yes, Maria, I'm fine, but I would like some water. Would you get me a little, please?"

The shy little girl beamed with importance. She skipped through the gathered children to complete her errand, nearly spilling the water in her haste to return.

"Thank you." Isabel sipped the water, relishing the coolness on her dry throat. Leaning over to set the glass down on the floor beside her, she discovered she couldn't bend that far. One of the older girls nearby took the glass from her.

"I'll do it, Miss Isabel."

"Thank you, Rosalia. Now then, what did we study the last time we met?"

The morning of lessons passed swiftly. Isabel was unused to sitting still when she worked with the children, but they were all eager to help her, so she curbed her impatience at being so inactive. She got caught up in what they were doing and didn't realize it was lunchtime until the sound of the bell rang through the room. As one, twelve small heads popped up from their slates and looked at her expectantly.

"Tomorrow we will practice your numbers." She smiled at the groans and complaints that followed her statement. "Tomorrow. Come here to the library when you have finished your morning chores. Please put your slates over on that table as you leave." She paused, playing the game they all loved. The children strained forward, but not one moved. "You may go."

It was like releasing a herd of wild horses from a corral. They bolted for the door, piling their slates into a teetering stack on the table. She watched them through the window as they burst through the kitchen door and raced one another for the best spot at the table. With a sigh, she closed her eyes. She wasn't sure she had the strength to stand, let alone climb the stairs. But she didn't want Jaret to find her here when she was supposed to be upstairs resting.

Taking a deep breath for courage, Isabel heaved herself out of the chair. She swayed in place a little, but finally felt it was safe to take a step. She started toward the door, watching her feet to be sure they kept moving. She'd only taken three steps when a pair of boots appeared in front of her slippers.

Isabel looked up and braced herself. "Hello, Jaret."

Chapter Twelve

"I really ought to tie you to that bed upstairs."

Isabel smiled at him, but she looked exhausted. Dark smudges underscored her eyes and her cheeks were pale.

"Come on, you stubborn woman. Let's get you back to your room." He lifted her easily and carried her down the hall.

She heaved a sigh of relief, then wrinkled her nose. "You smell like smoke and soot."

"We started tearing down the back wall of the barn this morning." He climbed the stairs and passed her bedroom door without slowing down.

"Jaret, this isn't my room."

"I know." He sat her on the bed and dropped to one knee to remove her shoes, barely resisting the urge to stroke the strong curve of her arches.

"I can go back to my own bed."

"Not yet. I like knowing you're here." Jaret stopped. Where had that come from?

Isabel curled her toes in his hand, oblivious to the effect it had on him. "Where will you sleep?"

"Same place I did last night. Right here."

Her lips curved in a sleepy smile. "No wonder my dreams were so peaceful."

Jaret glanced at her, expecting to see that she was teasing, but she seemed sincere.

"I don't see how you fit here, though," she continued. She bit on her lower lip as a teasing grin lit her features. "I'm sure I take up most of the bed. Show me."

"Isabel, you don't want—"

"I don't believe you. Show me how you and I both fit on this bed last night."

Jaret looked away from the temptation. "I don't think that's a good idea."

"Then you didn't really sleep here. You're just saying that to scare me into staying put. If I think you'll be coming back any minute, I'll be less likely to get out of bed again."

"I might have tried that if I thought it would work." He tossed his hat into a nearby chair. "Nothing makes you do what you should."

She laughed at the frustration in his voice. "Lydia gave up on me years ago. She even tried telling me to do whatever I wanted, thinking I would feel guilty about disobeying her and do as she'd asked. That didn't stop me, either." She patted the bed beside her. "Now come here and show me."

Jaret rose off the floor slowly, his eyes never leaving hers. There wasn't a man alive who could have resisted her. When he put one knee on the mattress, she started to scoot away. "Stay still. You didn't move last night. You were unconscious."

Isabel subsided and just watched. He placed a hand on either side of her and leaned close. "First I checked to see if you were breathing." He lowered his head and brushed a kiss on her lips. "Then I checked again, just to be sure." He kissed her again, deepening it just a little.

"Then I stretched out beside you." He matched his

movements to his words. "I put an arm under your head and pulled you closer." When he tightened his hold, she came willingly, snuggling in just as she had done in her sleep. "And I just held you through the night."

"Shouldn't you check again to be sure I'm breathing?"

When he looked down, Isabel was watching him, her ebony eyes liquid with desire. Emotions poured through him, confusing him. Unsure how to respond, he reached out to touch her, almost afraid to believe she was real. When his fingers brushed over her lips, she kissed each one, then nipped at his thumb.

Heat ripped through him and pooled below his belt. Isabel took his hand and placed it on her waist, then took a fistful of his shirt and pulled him toward her. They met halfway. Jaret covered her lips with his and swept his tongue into her mouth to tangle with hers.

He tasted her sweet moan of pleasure. Reining himself in, he rolled her onto her back and buried his fingers in her hair. When he encountered her scarf he pulled it free and dropped it on the bed, fanning her silky hair across the pillow. He tore his mouth from hers and pressed kisses across her cheekbone, tasted the skin along her jaw, and traced her eyebrows with the tip of his tongue. When he nipped at her earlobe, her breath escaped in one long sigh, feathering the hair at his nape. A shiver of pleasure rippled through her and he felt it from shoulder to knee.

Jaret returned to her lips, filling himself with her taste. He was lost. He knew it and didn't even try to fight. With each kiss, she was pulling him deeper and he just didn't care. This was where he wanted to be. He'd think about leaving tomorrow.

The first giggle barely registered, but the second one dragged Jaret from the haze of desire. Frustration raged through him and he half turned to order whoever it was to get the hell out of the room.

The words died unspoken when he spotted three young girls, some of Isabel's pupils that had raced past him a few minutes ago. Or was it hours? The oldest of them carried a plate overflowing with food; another had a bowl full of amber-colored liquid. The youngest was trying to hold on to a pair of cups.

Jaret turned back to Isabel and buried his face in her hair with a groan.

"Jaret, do we have company?"

"Um-hmm."

Isabel muttered something decidedly unladylike in his ear and the warmth of her breath nearly made him ignore their audience and return to what they'd been doing. But when she nudged his shoulder, he rolled away and sat on the edge of the bed. He wasn't sure his legs would hold him yet if he tried to stand. Dragging in gulps of air, he worked at slowing his galloping heart.

"Come on in, ladies." That brought on more giggles, grating on his already raw nerves. "Why don't you put that stuff down right over there?" He indicated a small table near the window, flanked by two comfortable chairs.

When he glanced at Isabel, she was trying to tame her hair. Leaning across her for the discarded scarf, his arm brushed her breasts. Her swift intake of breath heated his blood all over again. Trying to pull himself together, he studied the knot she'd tied. "I wondered how you managed to tie your own hair back. You're pretty smart."

"How do you know *I* tied it?"

"Because that's a classic roping knot, one you could probably manage before you could walk. Besides, you couldn't ask Lydia. She'd never have let you out of this room." Loosening the knot, he tied the scarf around her hair for her, then brushed a kiss on her temple as he straightened.

The oldest of the three girls carefully arranged everything, just as she'd no doubt been instructed. While she was busy, the littlest looked up at Jaret from beneath the longest lashes he'd ever seen.

"What's her name?" he murmured to Isabel.

"This is Maria."

Maria's face split into a grin at the mention of her name, showing a gap where her two front teeth should have been. Jaret couldn't help but grin back. "Pleasure to meet you, ma'am."

Isabel motioned toward the others. "The young lady trying very hard not to look at you is Rosalia and the decorator is Christina. Both are Marta's daughters."

Christina smiled at him over her shoulder. Jaret nodded in greeting. "Ladies."

When everything looked just right to her, Christina turned to Jaret, fluttering her lashes in a practiced move. "Mama says to enjoy your lunch." With that she hustled the others out of the room and aimed another flirty look at Jaret before closing the door behind them. Jaret stared at it for a long moment before shaking his head and chuckling. "She's a pretty one."

"Maria is such an angel."

"I'm sure she is, but I was talking about Christina. Her folks have some worrisome days ahead."

Isabel shook her head. "I'm afraid you're right. She's one of the main reasons I started the school. Christina is very bright and quite lovely. All the boys notice her, which she enjoys. But she can be a troublemaker when she's idle. If I keep her occupied, she tends not to cause such a fuss around here."

The mattress shook as Isabel struggled to move to the far side of the bed so she could stand.

Jaret grabbed the fabric of her skirt to hold her in place. "Stay put. I'll get your lunch." He piled a couple of pillows against the headboard and helped her get settled. As he turned away, her hand brushed his thigh. Innocent touch or not, his body reacted instantly. Blood pooled between his legs, hardening him until there was no way he could hide his desire.

It took all his discipline to leave the bed and walk to the table. He messed with plates and napkins until he had regained a little control, then he picked up the bowl of soup and a spoon and carried them to Isabel. He put her cup of water within reach before he sat down to his own plate.

"Aren't you going to share?" Isabel eyed his heaping plate.

"I don't plan to."

She looked down at her bowl. "Why do you get to eat all that and I only have broth?"

"Marta must have figured your stomach was still a little touchy after yesterday." When she continued to watch him eat, he relented. "Would you like a bite?"

He held out a small chunk of roasted beef on his fork and watched as Isabel wrapped her lips around it. She chewed slowly, savoring the flavor. Her eyes drifted closed as she swallowed. When they flew opened, her expression was almost comical.

"What's the matter, honey?"

"It's very good, but . . ." She reached for her water and sipped twice before continuing. "Marta was right. I think I'll just have my soup."

They ate in companionable silence. When his plate was clean, he took Isabel's bowl and stacked it on the table. He had no doubt the girls would be back later for the dishes.

"Jaret, are you sure it was Uncle Enrique who poisoned the laudanum?"

"If I knew for certain, he'd already be dead." He swallowed the last of his water before turning his chair to face her.

He'd thought to shock her with his bald statement, but she didn't even flinch. After a moment, she nodded.

"I feel the same way about whoever hurt Nicolas."

Jaret's stomach churned. What would she do when she found out he was the one responsible? He shook the thought loose. Nothing could change the past and the future would take care of itself.

"I intend to ask your uncle if he was in your room while everyone else was fighting the fire, but first I have to find him."

Her brows furrowed. "Where is he?"

"No one knows. He was here when you and I rode in, but he hasn't been seen since. And your sorrel mare is missing."

She sat up in the bed. "He took Spring?"

"Looks that way."

"He'd better not hurt her. I've spent months training her to the saddle and my hand." Isabel flopped back against the pillows. "I love that little horse."

Jaret shook his head. She accepted his penchant for violence without blinking, but her uncle borrowing a favorite horse had her spitting nails.

Despite her best effort, Isabel couldn't hide her yawn. Jaret had to smile. She was certainly no pushover. "You need to get some rest now."

Isabel agreed with a nod. Jaret settled her in the bed, arranging the pillows to make her comfortable and pulling a light coverlet over her. Against his better judgment, he let her pull him down for a kiss. It took all his control to end it and step back. "Rest. I'll be back to check on you before dark."

He watched her for a few minutes, until he was certain she was comfortable. After her adventures this morning, she should be out for hours. Picking up his hat, he left as quietly as he could. He checked the other bedrooms on the second floor to be certain they were empty. Satisfied Isabel was alone in this part of the house, he went down the back stairs. Marta was busy in the kitchen, with one of the men who had been on the ranch for more than twenty years standing guard.

"Mr. Walker, I'm Henry Richards." The man greeted Jaret as he entered the room. "My little brother, Matt, is on the front porch. I'll be watching the back."

"Then get there." More words weren't necessary. The cowboy slapped his hat on his head and snagged a couple of biscuits from the pile cooling on the table as he headed out the door.

Satisfied Isabel was as safe as she could be without him, he grabbed a biscuit for himself. Still warm from the oven, Jaret ate it in two bites. Marta swatted his arm for getting in her way, then wrapped up two more biscuits.

"For Matthew," she explained when he just looked at her. Jaret took them and one more for himself, and headed for the front door. He was glad to see Richards reach for his gun before he recognized Jaret. He dropped it back into its holster with a smooth motion.

"The house is clear. Your brother is out back, chewing on the breakfast he charmed out of Marta. She sent some for you."

The man gestured with his chin. "Manuel said to tell you he'd be at the corral." He broke off a hunk of steaming biscuit. "Said something about another horse missing."

Adrenaline raced through Jaret. He jammed his hat on

his head and strode to the makeshift corral. Several of the horses had been taken out by the cowboys, and they'd added two more temporary enclosures to give the animals more room, but it was still too crowded and offered little shade. Jaret could see men working in the main corral. By nightfall, they should be able to move several of the horses there without risking injury from half-burned boards and charred nails.

Manuel was waiting near the rope corral. Jaret didn't waste time on pleasantries. "Which one?"

"The little gray mare, another one of Miss Isabel's. Hammond remembers leading her here and handing over the reins, but he doesn't know who took them. Too many people, too much chaos," he offered in way of explanation.

Jaret nodded. He couldn't fault a man for being more interested in saving the animals than in who was working where.

"There is also a saddle missing." Manuel kicked at a stone half buried in the dirt. "It was one of Mr. Nick's favorites. No other tack is gone, only one saddle, bit, and bridle."

Jaret absently rubbed the nose of a horse that wandered over hoping for a treat. The missing horse was the same gray mare Isabel had ridden the morning of the fire. She would be furious when she found out. "Post a guard on the remaining horses. We can't afford to lose anymore. Any of the hands missing?"

"I'm not sure. The men are scattered and I haven't been able to account for all of them yet."

Jaret didn't press. Manuel would figure out who the thief was. He had other things to worry about.

"How many are out riding the pastures today?"

Jaret quizzed the older man on numbers and locations until he had a little better understanding of the ranch's weaknesses. "We need to bring more of the men closer to the homestead. How many horses can we support?"

"We lost all the stored hay and some of our grain in the fire. The home pastures will support a hundred head, perhaps one hundred and fifty, for a few days, but no more."

"Damn." Jaret stared off into the distance. "They knew exactly what they were doing."

Manuel agreed. "The fire was deliberately set to wipe out our stores of feed."

"We'll have to make do." Jaret turned to the foreman. "Spread the word. I want as many horses as we can round up brought here by nightfall tomorrow, and all the men in closer."

"It will take ten riders to find all the teams. That won't leave many to do the work around here."

"Then those who are left will have to do the work of two."

Manuel shook his head at the idea that they could do more work than they were already handling. Jaret knew they couldn't keep it up for long. But he was betting they wouldn't have to. The showdown was coming. He could feel it.

He watched two young boys, about Miguel's age, step into the corral armed with brushes and picks. A young girl with her long black hair in pigtails struggled with the weight of a water bucket. Another was cleaning out the chicken coops. No one would be spared extra chores for as long as it lasted. Including him, he reminded himself. With a word of encouragement to the children, Jaret headed to the barn to get to work.

The afternoon raced by. The men ate dinner in shifts to keep the repairs moving ahead. Children ran back and forth, carrying water or ropes, depending on their age and strength. By nightfall, the little ones were bundled off to bed and lamps were lit to work by. Some of the men stopped to rest and others took their places.

Jaret didn't stop to eat. Three, maybe four hours and the barn would be secure enough to use. It was important he finish, since it also offered several good spots from which to defend the ranch when the attack came. Putting his aching back into the work, he pried off another charred board and began pulling out any nails that had been left behind.

He felt her before he saw her. When he turned, Isabel stood behind him, silent and pale. "What are you doing in here?"

"I needed to see for myself." She glanced around. "There's more left than I remember."

"Enough to be useful, though it'll probably have to be completely rebuilt when we can get enough wood." Jaret pulled off his filthy gloves and stuffed them into a back pocket as he worked his way across the rubble to her. He'd been at it longer than he thought. The older boys had gone to bed several hours before and without them hauling stuff out of the way, he was in danger of being buried. He had to stop and clear some away.

"You shouldn't be out here, honey. You need rest."

"I've rested all day. I wanted to get some air. Lydia and Marta are still in the kitchen, but they're both nearly asleep standing up."

"They've done more than I could have expected. All of them have, the women, the children. And the men are still working, taking turns catching a little sleep before coming back to spell someone else."

"When do you plan to rest?"

"I'm all right." Jaret looked back at the barn wall. "Another couple of hours and we'll have knocked down what can't be saved. Then we can rebuild a wall of sorts that will make this area usable again."

Isabel took his arm and Jaret felt her touch burn his skin through his shirt. The intense longing to feel her hands on more than his arm took him by surprise.

"It's late. Can't it wait until morning?"

"By morning, the horses should begin arriving." Placing a hand under her elbow to steady her, Jaret led Isabel from the barn. The moon was nearly full, rising over the horizon and spreading a ghostly light over the land.

"What horses?"

"We're moving the stock closer to the house where we can keep an eye on it. That will also bring all the men in and we need every gun we have."

When Jaret tried to turn Isabel toward the house, she resisted. Slipping an arm around her waist, they strolled around back to the rose garden instead. Her steps were steady but slower than normal. The heady fragrance of blooming flowers was heavy in the air. A soft breeze rustled the leaves in the trees, masking the sounds of their steps. Jaret glanced toward the house and saw the man still on guard there. With a wave, Jaret sent him inside to take a break.

He led Isabel to the same low bench they'd shared his first night on the ranch. It seemed impossible that it had been only a few days ago. She sat down, then tugged on his hand until he joined her. Once he was settled, she threaded her arm through his and laid her head on his shoulder.

"It seems ages ago, doesn't it?"

Jaret stared at her. Was she reading his mind?

"I feel like you've been here always instead of less than a week." Isabel inhaled deeply, and her breast brushed his arm with the motion. His body responded instantly.

"Don't." Jaret tried to remove her arm from his, but she just tightened her hold.

"Don't what?"

"Don't build dreams around me."

Her wide eyes reflected the moonlight. "Too late."

She was so beautiful. The soft light from the moon shimmered in her hair and made her eyes seem even darker. He could see himself reflected in them as she took his hat from his head. He was helpless to stop what was coming.

Isabel's hand sifted through his hair and along his jaw. He hadn't shaved since yesterday and he could hear the beard stubble scrape her palm. Her light touch warmed his skin and he could feel the embers of desire flare. He tasted her sigh as she slipped her hand behind his head and pulled him down for a kiss.

He knew he should stop her. Her lips were soft and so sweet, way too sweet for a man like him. When Isabel shifted, he told himself he only pulled her into his lap to keep her from falling, but lies never sat well with him. He wanted her right where she was. When he felt his control slipping, Jaret tried to end the kiss, but Isabel tightened her hold. When her lips parted and her tongue darted out to tease him, he was lost.

He eased her closer and mated his mouth to hers. He enticed her to explore, to taste him as he tasted her. The sounds of the night faded. Nothing existed in the world but the two of them. Isabel clung to him and matched him kiss for kiss, hunger to growing hunger. When he tore himself away, they were both breathing hard.

He stood with her in his arms, then released her legs and let her slide the length of him until her feet were on the ground. Her curves fit against him perfectly as she clung to him in the moonlight. He turned her toward the light until it illuminated her face. What he saw there had his burning need raging nearly out of control.

Her eyes were huge, their onyx depths luminous. Her lips were swollen and moist from their shared kisses. As he watched, they curved up at the corners. When she looked like she would speak, he pressed his thumb over their softness.

"How do you do this to me, woman? I swear to myself I'll keep my distance, but I can't stay away from you. I'm no good for you. You deserve a man who'll stay around and build a life with you, not a drifter who's only good for breaking horses and doing other men's business."

"Don't say that," she scolded. "You're a wonderful man." She stretched up to brush a kiss on his lips. "I'm not asking for promises, Jaret. I only want tonight."

He kissed her gently and smoothed her hair away from her flushed cheeks.

"Honey, are you sure?"

"Oh, yes," she breathed.

"This isn't a dream and I'm not your future. Your life is here."

"Yours could be, too. You've become a part of this place, Jaret Walker. You belong here."

"I don't belong anywhere."

She pressed her fingertips to his lips to stop his words. "Just for tonight then. No tomorrow, no promises."

Jaret stared into her eyes, searching for any hint that she was lying to herself, but all he saw was his own reflection, trapped in a need he couldn't outrun. Could he give her what she asked, just for tonight? Her fingers skimmed along his collar to the top button of his shirt. When he felt it give, he knew he was going to try. He couldn't deny her, or himself.

Capturing her hand, he turned her toward the house.

When she tilted her head to look at him, Jaret placed a kiss on her forehead, and another in her hair. Isabel sighed and snuggled against him, matching his steps. They climbed the back stairs and walked the hallway held tightly in each other's arms.

No one was around, but Jaret looked anyway. Satisfied that none of the shadows held more than darkness, he opened his bedroom door and led her inside. While he locked the door against interruptions, Isabel lit a lamp and trimmed the wick until a soft glow filled the room.

Jaret was surprised when she carried it to the bedside table. "Honey?"

"I want to see you." She faltered. "Is that all right?"

Desire slammed into him, weakening his knees. "That's just fine."

Her bravery slipped a little and she looked away. Tenderness flooded him. Her passion was so quickly aroused, whether in temper or desire, that it was easy to forget she was innocent. Her uncertainty helped him bridle his need. He would be gentle. She deserved that much. Later he would explore the passion she brought out in him so easily. Tonight was for her.

Jaret removed his gun belt and draped it over the bedpost. Then he tugged off his boots before crossing to shut the curtains facing the bunkhouse and barn. He quickly took off his filthy shirt and poured water into the washbasin to rinse off the day's work. As he reached for the buttons at his waistband, he caught Isabel staring at him. She looked away and busied herself straightening the items on the side table.

Wearing a clean pair of pants, but naked from the waist up, Jaret crossed to her and lifted her chin until her eyes met his. He kissed her, touching only her lips. There was sweetness here, honey and spice. He took the kiss deeper until they were lost in each other. When he tore his mouth away, she pulled him back for more. As her knees weakened, he tightened his hold. Finally, uncertain he could remain upright any longer, he lowered her to the bed.

Isabel's eyes were huge, their liquid darkness intoxicating. She held him spellbound with just a look. Jaret rained kisses across her cheek and forehead and began to explore. He shuddered when he felt her hands on his bare chest. As he nipped at her ear, she brushed questing fingers across one nipple. The shockwave rippled through them both.

"Jaret, let me up."

He didn't hear her words until she repeated them. Then he nearly howled in frustration. "What's wrong?"

"Nothing. Just let me up for a moment." She pushed at him and when he rolled aside she sat up and turned her back, dragging her fingertips down his chest as she went. "Help me with these." Isabel pulled her long hair over one shoulder and presented her back and a row of buttons from neck to hip.

Jaret knelt behind her. He cursed the first stubborn fastener, but recognized the gift he'd been given. As each button gave way, a new bit of skin was revealed. Jaret feasted on her with lips, tongue, and teeth. At the top of her chemise, he traced the softness of her back with his tongue. Isabel's breathing grew ragged. He explored the lush curves of her hips through the fabric covering them until she pulled away to stand beside the bed.

Facing him, her eyes on his, Isabel slipped her arms from the garment and let it slide to the floor. Her petticoat followed. His breath caught. In the flickering light of the lamp, her skin glowed like golden honey. The lace-edged chemise she wore skimmed her thighs above her knees, showing a length of leg that made his mouth go dry. His manhood hardened and throbbed with every beat of his heart.

Her full breasts rose from the filmy garment and Jaret's fingers itched to touch her. Still watching him, Isabel stepped from her slippers and her hands went to the tie of her chemise.

"No," Jaret stopped her. "I want to do that."

Her smile was beautiful. Jaret drew her onto the bed in front of him. He kissed each finger of the hand he held, then captured the other. Holding her in place, he worked his way up her arm, exploring the satin skin inside her elbow. He took a deep breath to drive back the urge to hurry, forcing himself to take it slow and easy.

Her shoulder was cool when he tasted her there, easing around the bandages. Isabel shivered when he kissed her neck, brushing the sensitive skin with his mustache. She tried to pull her hands free, but Jaret only laughed and held her wrists. He tugged at the ribbon tie of her chemise with his teeth until it loosened, then he used his tongue to unlace it top to bottom. When he nudged the fabric aside his breath caught in his throat and he sat back on his heels to look.

Her breasts were full and her skin was pale ivory where the sun had never touched. Moving slowly, he bent to her, filling himself with the feel and scent of her. Isabel whimpered when he brushed the curve of her breast. The sound slashed through him, hardening him even more. Reining his own need in with an effort, he kissed and tasted in ever-tightening circles until he reached the center. He suckled the tight bud of her nipple until she strained against him. Finally he released her hands so he could fill his palms with her.

Her fingers raced to explore everywhere at once. His hair, his shoulders, down his back to his hips and beyond.

The feathery touch nearly drove him over the edge and he gave that wildness back to Isabel.

His hands smoothed down her sides, past her waist, to her thighs. She stiffened a little when he brushed the mound of curls where her legs met, but relaxed again when he continued on, across the ridges of her hips and up the length of her back. So much soft, soft skin. Then it was his turn to experience sweet torture.

Isabel took the lead and explored his chest, tentatively at first, then with growing confidence. She moved lower and lower, until she encountered the waistband of his pants. Jaret's breath hitched when her fingers dipped inside, then retreated. As she loosened the buttons and pushed the fabric over his hips, he thought he would lose his mind. He let her work at removing the garment, until her pulling and tugging became too much for his control. Kicking the cloth from his ankles, he dragged Isabel against him and kissed her wildly.

When she collapsed onto the pillows, he followed her down, his weight pressing her into the mattress. The feel of her skin against his was incredible. His lips returned to hers, luring her tongue into a dance that hinted at the joining to come. Isabel's movements became increasingly restless, and she gasped as she crested the first peak. Jaret inhaled the scent of feminine arousal that perfumed the air. When she tugged at his hair, he reluctantly released her and looked into her eyes.

Isabel's breathing was ragged, her eyes huge in her face. Jaret kissed her cheek and nuzzled her neck, easing some of the anxiety he read in her eyes. When he filled his hand with her breast and bent down to lave the nipple, Isabel pressed him closer. His other hand moved slowly down her body, until he once more reached the apex of her thighs. This time she moaned when he touched her.

When he asked for access with gentle pressure on her legs, she gave it willingly. Her trust nearly undid him. He eased one finger between her soft folds and found her moist and ready for him. Slipping one knee between hers, he made room to explore, touching and kneading her soft center until her body jerked beneath his.

"Jaret!"

"I'm right here, honey." As he rose above her, he watched her face. The tightness he found as he eased into her made his control slip. That small amount of his seed eased his way a little more and he pressed into her until he met resistance.

He leaned close and nipped at her ear. "I'm sorry to hurt you, but it won't last long." Isabel's nod sent exquisite sensations through him. He took her mouth in a deep kiss and drove into her with one thrust, making her his own.

Isabel stiffened and cried out. Jaret held himself still, shaking with the effort. When she relaxed again, he moved a little. She was perfect. Never before had he felt so right with a woman. He rocked against her, lost in her heat. She was his. It was a gift he would never be worthy of.

He looked up at her gasp, but found wonder and desire in her eyes, not pain. Easing out a little, he pushed back into her and watched her eyes darken with growing passion. She grabbed at his arms as he increased the pace, lifting her hips to match his movements and driving them both toward the peak.

Jaret held off until he felt the first fluttering of her climax, then released the ruthless control he'd placed on himself and drove into her again and again, until his own release took him soaring over the edge.

Chapter Thirteen

Damn! Jaret slapped on his hat and strode across the yard. A couple of the ranch hands coming out of the barn called a greeting, but he ignored them. Two of the women looked up as he approached, then hurried to get out of his way.

He grabbed a currycomb and brush as he neared the temporary corral. He efficiently cut Sand Dune from the rest of the horses and started to groom her, but it wasn't until the animal shied from his touch that Jaret stopped.

"Double damn," he muttered. He was in a worse mood than he thought. Even his horse didn't want anything to do with him.

Jaret forced calm into the center of the storm raging in his gut. How did she do this to him? Since the day his mother swallowed enough laudanum to fall asleep and never wake up, he hadn't allowed anyone to get this close. More than once he'd been told he had ice for blood, but he didn't care. It was the best way to stay alive in his line of work. He'd never let a woman get under his skin.

Until now.

Isabel was fire to his ice. When she was near, he couldn't keep his distance. One touch, one word, and his rigid control melted. Her fragrant, velvety softness was irresistible.

Even when her temper sparked, he was drawn to her. How did she manage to tie him in knots with such ease?

With gentler motions, he groomed Sand Dune while she nipped at the brim of his hat. When he finished, he gave her legs a quick once over, looking for signs of strain or injury. Her hooves were trimmed and the shoes solid. Satisfied she was in good health, he led her to the small grazing pasture and removed her halter.

As he watched the mare trot away, he knew he had to do the same. He was getting too comfortable here. It wouldn't do for him to start feeling at home. A gun for hire didn't belong in a place like this, and that's what he'd been since he was old enough for people to take him seriously. He wasn't the type of man folks invited into polite company.

Maybe he'd head west when Nick was back and this was all over. He'd been offered work riding shotgun on a wagon train from St. Louis to California. The money was good, and it would keep him on the move for a while. It was the kind of job he usually couldn't wait to take on. So why did he feel lost at just the thought of it?

He looked up when a rider entered the yard. The man steered his horse in Jaret's direction, pulling to a stop beside him.

"Mr. Walker, we got trouble."

"That's nothing new." Jaret tipped his hat back so he could see the cowboy. The man's face was weathered from years in the sun, and his once blond hair was graying quickly. He searched his memory until he came up with his name: Mace Brinker. The man was a longtime hand on the ranch, one of the few that Manuel trusted completely.

The man swung out of the saddle and led his mount toward the water trough by the corral. "We've been cleaning out the stragglers in the west pasture and ran across a makeshift corral and a cold campfire."

"Rustlers."

"Looks that way."

Jaret cursed. Just one more way to take some of the men away from the house. "Go get some breakfast while I saddle up."

Ten minutes later the two were mounted and ready to go. Mace handed Jaret a small bundle wrapped in white cloth. The fragrance of fresh biscuits greeted him.

"Lydia said you hadn't been in to eat yet."

Jaret took a bite of the hot biscuit and spicy sausage combination the woman had sent. Now, if he had coffee, the morning would be complete.

As if he read his mind, Mace handed over one of the canteens hanging from his saddle. "She sent that, too."

Jaret looked toward the bunkhouse where several women were feeding a growing number of men. It seemed Isabel wasn't the only one on the ranch that could anticipate him. Wrapping up the rest, Jaret made short work of the biscuit in his hand.

"Manuel." He guided his mare to where the old man waited. "Assign a third man to watch the house while I'm gone." He hesitated. "Keep a close eye on her. I'll be back before nightfall." Jaret turned his horse west and lifted the reins, with Mace following close behind.

An hour out, they met up with the herd of horses being driven east toward the ranch house. Jaret estimated the number of animals to be no more than a hundred. That was at least fifty short, based on what Manuel said they should have found in that area. It was possible that there were more hidden in the cracks and crevices of the land, but the cowboys would never have missed that many.

As the roiling mass of men and horses neared, he caught sight of Miguel bouncing happily on the back of a yearling colt. The animal was obviously used to having a rider. As they got closer, Jaret saw signs of abuse. None of Isabel's hands would dare mistreat a horse. But someone had.

Jaret pulled a cloth over his nose and mouth as the herd passed. The dust was so thick behind them he couldn't see. Once it settled a little, he lifted the reins and followed Mace. It didn't take long to find the spot they were looking for.

The fire pit was no more than a couple of weeks old. A makeshift corral had been fashioned nearby to hold fifteen or twenty horses. The thieves were bold, branding the animals in plain sight. It didn't make sense. In this part of the world, rustlers were hunted down and strung up from the nearest tree or barn rafter. Who would risk death for so few horses?

"Choose two men you trust to stay behind with us, but be easy about it," Jaret ordered. "I don't want to alert the rest."

Mace reined his horse toward the retreating herd without a word and returned shortly with two caballeros.

They searched for three hours under a blazing sun before Jaret found tracks that hadn't been obliterated by the horses the Two Roses' hands had driven through. When he did, it only confirmed his suspicions.

"About ten men would be my guess." He studied patterns in the dust. "They took a couple dozen of our stock with them when they left, maybe more."

Mace dropped to his heels beside Jaret and held out a half-full canteen. "Any idea where they're headed?"

Jaret swallowed some of the water. He wiped the sweat from his face with the sleeve of his shirt and pushed to his feet. "Let's follow them and see."

The trail was almost too easy to follow. Jaret would have expected rustlers to stick to the rockier land so their tracks were harder to follow, but this bunch didn't seem to care. They rode at an easy pace, driving the small herd of stolen horses through the middle of the valley.

An hour later, Jaret found out why. The tracks joined up with another group that were headed west, through an arid section of land that ended at the border between Two Roses and the Williams spread. The dividing line was a ridge of rocks that stretched nearly the length of the Williams's property. They followed the trail of stolen horses until it disappeared into a tiny canyon.

The entrance was camouflaged with tumbleweeds and dry brush, but not very well. They all dismounted and Jaret signaled the other three men to fan out. Moving quietly, he climbed the rocks to one side of the narrow entrance, taking care not to be seen. Inside the enclosure he counted more than a hundred head of horses, all of them Two Roses stock. There were a couple of water troughs set up, but both were empty and he could tell from their restless movements the animals were getting thirsty.

Jaret examined the canyon thoroughly from his vantage point, but saw no evidence that anyone had been left behind to guard the herd. When he rejoined the others, they reported the same thing. Satisfied it wasn't an ambush, they approached the entrance, guns drawn just in case.

No one challenged their approach. Jaret examined the entrance for any sign of a trap. He found nothing but dust and rocks.

"Let's take down some of these weeds and get our stock back. You three take them back to the ranch house. I'm going to follow those tracks a while longer."

"You sure you want to do that alone?" Mace rolled a good-size rock out of the way.

"I'm sure. It'll take all three of you to keep that herd moving. I'll be careful."

One of the other cowboys pulled a pile of brush out of

the way. "You'd better be," he teased. "I don't want to be the one to tell Miss Isabel why you didn't come home."

Was it that obvious? Jaret glanced at the three men, but none seemed to mind the idea of Isabel being protective of him. The sense of belonging he felt was a little hard to accept.

They carefully dismantled a section of the brush fence large enough to drive the horses through. Leaving Mace and the two rancheros out front to control the herd as they came out, Jaret swung back into the saddle and worked his way through the milling animals. With whistles and shouts, he got the horses moving. In only a few minutes, the canyon was empty.

Jaret stayed where he was until some of the dust had settled. Then he repaired the makeshift fence and camouflage so it wouldn't be obvious from a distance that anything had changed, mounted and turned his horse in the direction the rustlers had taken.

The sun passed midday before he took a break. He found a small pool of water left from the rain a couple of nights ago where he could refill his canteen and let Sand Dune drink her fill. Dropping into the patch of shade beneath a couple of mesquite bushes, he pulled out the biscuits he'd been too busy to eat that morning.

Even though it was still early in the year, summer was well under way. Heat rose from the desert in waves, with a light so bright it hurt Jaret's eyes as he checked every patch of dust to be sure the wind had kicked it up rather than approaching riders. With his horse rested, he continued the search.

He'd only gone a short distance when he found what he'd been looking for. The tracks he'd been following converged with others and moved through a narrow opening in the rocky hillside. He expected to find another enclosure on the other end of it. He approached on foot, making sure he wasn't spotted. As he neared the top of the rocky rise, he dropped to his belly and crawled the last few feet.

Below him stretched an unexpected site, a valley with water. Someone had dug several small ponds to collect rain. Cold fire pits bore evidence the valley was used, but no one was around now.

Retreating the way he'd come, Jaret picked up the trail and backtracked for a mile before he found where they'd split up.

There were twenty distinct sets of tracks. He ignored the dozen he knew went into the valley and concentrated on the remaining eight. From the length of their stride, they'd ridden hard, going roughly east, toward the ranch—and Isabel.

Panic whipped through Jaret. He'd assigned plenty of men to watch Isabel, but he didn't truly trust anyone but himself with her life. What if she got it into her head to take that devil horse of hers for a ride? No one on the ranch would stop her. She might run right into the bunch of outlaws heading her way. He had to get to her first. Jaret spun his mount around, scanned his surroundings to get his bearings and chose the shortest route back to the house. He lifted the reins and kicked his horse into a wild gallop.

He hadn't gone far before common sense prevailed and he slowed to a safer pace. He couldn't run his horse flat out all the way back to the ranch. He was at least two hours out, maybe more. Manuel was with Isabel and the old man would die before he let anyone hurt her again. There was no reason to risk killing his horse or himself by racing hell-bent across the uneven ground. If the animal stepped into a hole and broke a leg, it would be some time tonight before Jaret could walk back to the house. That wouldn't help him protect Isabel. He picked a steady, ground-eating pace and settled in for the ride home.

Too bad common sense didn't apply to controlling the fear eating at his gut.

Isabel was in danger and he was supposed to be there, keeping her safe. Not that being close to her helped much. He'd failed her twice already. *Make that three times,* he reminded himself. It was bad enough that he'd let her deceive everyone she loved by pretending to have married him. By taking her to his bed, he'd probably ruined her chances of finding a real husband. He berated his lack of control with every hoofbeat on the dry ground.

The only way she'd be free of him now was when he was dead. He yanked his hat further down over his brow. Of course, with his choice of profession, that may not take long, but he was a careful man. It was how he'd survived this long.

Then again, he didn't really have to die, did he? Isabel just had to believe he was dead. A few weeks after he left Two Roses, he could have someone send a letter telling her he'd been killed. That would make certain he could never come back to this place or to her, and he figured that had to be for the best. As a "widow" she'd be free to marry a man who would give her what she wanted, what she deserved.

His gut twisted at the thought of Isabel in another man's arms. He didn't have the right to keep her for himself, but imagining another kissing her sweet lips, touching her satin skin, lowering her to the bed and . . .

Rage swamped him and overflowed in a string of curses that made his horse shy beneath him. There was no way he would allow another to have her. He loved her, damn it.

Jaret yanked back on the reins, pulling Sand Dune to a plunging stop. Love. "That's not possible." He was a drifter, never settling anywhere. But that didn't change how he felt.

"Damn it, Isabel, what have you done to me?" She'd changed him somehow. It wasn't such a stretch anymore to imagine himself with her years in the future, his hair white, surrounded by children and grandchildren who all looked like Isabel.

He tried to deny it, but he couldn't shake the certainty that he'd finally found what he'd been searching for without even realizing he was looking. Isabel belonged with him. He couldn't let another man have her.

Of course, when he told her the truth about why he'd come to Two Roses in the first place, she probably wouldn't want to see him again. He'd be lucky if she didn't shoot him where he stood. Hell, that might not be all bad. If she shot him, she'd have to nurse him back to health. That would keep her close by long enough to convince her she couldn't live without him.

"Come on, girl." Jaret bumped his horse in the ribs. "Let's head for home." He leaned forward in the saddle and increased the pace. Now that he'd realized he loved Isabel, he needed to tell her. He crested the hill overlooking the ranch and his heart missed a beat. A dust cloud boiled in the distance, riders heading for the ranch house in a hurry. Terrified he was too late, he kicked his horse into a gallop and raced toward Isabel.

Chapter Fourteen

Isabel felt surrounded by Jaret in the big bed. She had never expected to feel this way, glorious and free and desired. The night had passed in a delicious whirl of Jaret holding her, touching her, loving her. Isabel knew she could stay right here forever, as long as he was beside her.

The morning sun was a glow on the horizon. Isabel stretched, glorying in all the aches she discovered, blushing a little at how she'd come by them. When Jaret kissed her awake an hour ago to say good-bye, she hadn't let him go easily.

Isabel tossed back the covers and put her feet on the floor. Her injured shoulder protested a little, but she ignored it. She'd been banged up before. It was inevitable when you worked on a ranch. She searched beneath the mound of bedclothes for her nightgown until she remembered she hadn't been wearing one when she climbed into bed. Humming softly, she located the chemise she'd shed the night before, shook out the wrinkles and slipped it on.

It took a little longer to find the ribbon and thread it into place. Each time the ribbon brushed her skin, she could almost feel Jaret unlacing it with his clever tongue. With some of her modesty restored, she scooped up her dress and shoes and padded to her own bedroom to get dressed.

As she opened the connecting door she stopped and stared. There on her bedside table was an enormous bouquet of roses. A dozen different hues glowed in the morning light and their perfume sweetened the air. Delighted with Jaret's gift, she picked up the note leaning against the crystal vase and opened it.

Her smile faded as she read the words. *These should have been for your grave.* Isabel dropped the note like it had grown teeth. Who hated her so much? She forced herself to retrieve the note. It was nothing but paper and ink. But the roses meant someone had been in her room this morning while she and Jaret . . .

Isabel yanked on a blouse and split skirt, jammed her feet into her work boots, and tucked the note into her pocket. She would find Jaret. He'd know what to do.

The knock on her door made her jump. Pressing a hand over her racing heart, she scolded herself for being so nervous. Gathering her composure, she called out. "Come in."

Lydia bustled into the room, her arms filled with freshly laundered clothes.

"Good morning, child. Did you rest well last night?"

Isabel felt the warmth color her cheeks. How could she tell this woman just how little sleep she'd gotten?

"I'm fine," she answered. That, at least, was the truth. She felt marvelous.

Lydia stopped abruptly and stared at the bed, which so obviously hadn't been slept in. Then she glanced toward the connecting door. The look on her weathered face was a touching mixture of concern and triumph. The concern won out.

"Are you all right?" The words were spoken so softly that Isabel barely heard.

"I'm fine," she said again. "I'm wonderful. I feel . . . loved."

Lydia studied her face for a long moment, then nodded, silently accepting Isabel's decision. When she turned to rearrange the bouquet of roses, Isabel fingered the note hidden in the pocket of her skirt.

"Lydia, do you know who brought these flowers?"

The housekeeper looked puzzled. "Didn't Mr. Jaret bring them?" She adjusted one more blossom before stepping away.

"I don't think so." Isabel forced a smile. "But perhaps he did and didn't leave a note because he wanted to surprise me. I'll think I'll go find him and say thank you."

The beauty of the morning was lost on Isabel when she stepped outside. The wind had picked up and the scent of dust and dry grass permeated the air. The ranch hand assigned to watch the front of the house sat in the shade of a nearby tree, repairing a cinch strap.

"Good morning, Matt."

The man glanced up with a smile. "Morning, ma'am."

Isabel didn't approach him. Was he the one who'd brought the flowers inside? She hated that she suspected every man who worked for her of wanting her dead. "Have you seen Mr. Walker?"

"Saw him ride out about an hour ago, heading west. Manuel will know for sure."

Isabel reminded herself to breathe. This man meant her no harm. Surely she would know it if he did. Thanking him, she went in search of Manuel.

She found him arguing with her uncle in the barn. "Uncle Enrique, you're here."

"Of course I'm here, you daft girl. I live here, as I've been trying to explain to this old fool."

Isabel stepped between the men and faced her uncle.

"Be careful what you say, Uncle. Manuel has been here all my life, and a few years before that. He belongs on Two Roses."

She couldn't bring herself to add "too." Perhaps her uncle would get the hint that his welcome was wearing thin. She'd hate to have to throw a relative off the ranch.

"Where have you been? We've been looking for you."

"As I was just telling Manuel, I was unable to sleep, so I decided to go riding. I left just before dawn."

"I wasn't aware that you could ride, Uncle Enrique. You've never asked for a mount before, in all the months you've been here. Where did you go?"

He tugged his brocade vest down to cover his middle. "Of course I can ride, and where I went is no concern of yours."

Isabel felt her eyebrow arch. Not a good sign. "You disappeared on one of my horses and informed no one of your destination. I might have been worried."

Her uncle drew himself up to his full height and pasted a practiced look of disdain on his face, but the effect was ruined by his disheveled hair and the dust on his clothes. "I do not answer to you, or to any of these backwater ruffians. Now excuse me. I wish to bathe. Have hot water brought to my room at once."

Isabel's temper boiled over. "I'm sorry, Uncle, that won't be possible. Everyone is busy with more important things. You'll have to manage on your own." She ignored his gasp of outrage and turned her back on him, waiting until he'd stormed into the house before speaking to Manuel. "When did he ride in?"

"Just a few minutes ago. He was ordering one of the boys around when I got here."

Isabel stared after her uncle. He could have been the

one to put the flowers in her room. "Do you know where Jaret went?"

"Mace rode in early. There's a problem with the herd in the west pasture. Mr. Jaret went with him."

"When do you expect him back?"

"Not until this afternoon. Maybe close to nightfall."

Isabel nodded. She could wait until he returned, but decided against it. Any threat against her put everyone on the ranch in danger. She pulled the note from her pocket.

"Someone was in my bedroom last night or this morning. They left a bouquet of roses from the garden and a note." Keeping her voice low, she read him the hateful words. She felt him stiffen before his head snapped up and he stared toward the front porch.

"Someone got into the house."

Isabel nodded.

"And into your room."

Again she remained silent.

"Didn't you hear anything?"

Isabel flushed instantly. "I wasn't . . . that is, I was with . . ." She took a breath and blurted it out. "I wasn't in my room last night. I was with Jaret in his room."

Manuel continued watching the man guarding the house, letting no emotion show on his face. "When did you find it?"

She let out the breath she'd been holding, grateful that Manuel wasn't going to comment on where she'd spent the night. "An hour ago, when I went to my room to dress." She felt her cheeks blaze with embarrassment.

Turning away, Manuel called over one of the longtime employees of the ranch. "I want you to go relieve Richards. He has been guarding the house long enough. And send Mertz to take over the back. The only people allowed inside are Miss Isabel, Mr. Jaret, Mr. de la Rosa, Lydia, and me." The man nodded and strode off to do as he'd been asked.

"What was that all about?" Isabel watched the change of guard curiously.

"It fits."

"What does?"

"Your uncle rode in here a few minutes ago like the hounds of hell were after him. But the horse wasn't winded. Either he decided to kick it up to impress anybody watching, or that horse had a good long rest just before he got here."

"I don't believe Uncle Enrique is much of a horseman, in spite of what he said. I'm not sure he could stay in the saddle if he tried to show off. But what does that have to do with changing the men guarding the house?"

Manuel stared at the house. "Someone carrying a bunch of flowers walked right by one of them to get inside."

Isabel wrapped her arms around herself, shivering despite the heat of the sun. "But Henry Richards worked for Papa. He recommended we hire Matt. I've known them both for years." She wanted another explanation, but there wasn't one. "You're right. One of the guards had to let them inside."

Manuel agreed. "Stay close to me today. You don't go anywhere I can't see you."

Isabel didn't chafe at the restriction. If men who'd worked for her father could be in on the plot to steal the ranch, she didn't know who to trust anymore. "All right." She tucked the note away. "What are we going to do?"

"*I'm* going to start working with a new colt. *You* can stay out of trouble and watch."

Isabel groaned. "Not you, too." She turned pleading eyes on the man. "I have to do something."

He relented with a chuckle. "Never could say no to you. Go visit that horse of yours. He is feeling left out and making sure we all know it. Don't be gone long," he cautioned.

Lucifer pranced around his enclosure as Isabel approached, ignoring her in punishment for not coming to see him, but the lure of human fingers to scratch the itchy spots proved to be too great. She laughed at his show of masculine pride, then set to work making it up to him.

She was putting her tools away when she recognized the rattle of wagon wheels against the hard-packed dirt of the road. Men scattered around the yard, each carrying an armload of guns and ammunition, taking up positions they could defend. Isabel hurried toward the house and her shotgun.

Hearing hooves pounding the ground, she glanced back and saw Jaret ride hell-bent into the ranch yard just in front of a wagon carrying two men. She was halfway to the porch when he caught up with her. Leaping from his horse, he grabbed her arm and dragged her toward the house.

"Jaret, what is the matter with you?" Isabel struggled, trying to look over her shoulder at the buckboard rolling to a stop in the yard. There was something familiar about one of the men on the wagon seat. She stared at the newcomers, her eyes narrowed against the sun.

"Nicolas," she breathed. "It's Nicolas."

In spite of himself, Jaret turned back. It couldn't be, not yet. He still needed time to explain. All the things he wanted to say crowded his mind. Isabel wrenched free, screaming her brother's name. Jaret caught her before she could dash into the open. "What the hell are you doing?"

"Let go of me! Nicolas is back. Nicolas!"

"Who's the other man?"

Isabel fought him. "I don't care. Nicolas is home."

He pulled her up the front steps. Maybe he could get

her to listen long enough for him to come clean. But when a shout came from the direction of the wagon, Jaret knew he'd run out of time. He let go and watched Isabel run into her brother's arms.

Jaret closed his eyes against the pain. If he was smart, he'd mount up and ride out. Let Nicolas take care of things here. But he'd given his word. He couldn't leave, not when the war was just about to start.

Beating back the certainty he'd lost something precious, Jaret joined the crowd of men and women clustered around the siblings, welcoming home the prodigal son. The man who'd come with Nick stood back and watched. Jaret went to him first.

"You must be Jaret Walker," he greeted. "Nicolas told me all about you."

His voice was cultured, matching the cut of his clothes and the fashionable mustache. His hair was as black as Isabel's, with a streak of silver at the temples. And there was something about the eyes that seemed familiar.

"You have the advantage," Jaret replied.

The man stuck out a hand in greeting. "Enrique de la Rosa, sir." The name rolled off his tongue with the smooth silk of Spain. "My friends call me Rick. Their mother was my sister."

Surprise was too mild a word for the emotion that tore through Jaret. He shook the man's hand automatically. If this was Uncle Enrique, who the hell had been living in Isabel's house for the last six months? He motioned Manuel over.

"Where's her uncle?" Jaret kept his voice low.

"In the house. He came back a couple of hours ago. He should be well into his bottle by now."

"Find him and keep him there. We'll join you in a minute."

As Manuel headed for the house, Jaret turned back to the stranger. "I'd be obliged if you'd hold off the introductions until we get inside. It's important."

"May I ask why?"

"I'll explain inside."

Taking the man's silence as agreement, he approached the knot of people surrounding Isabel and Nicolas. They parted to allow him into the circle.

"Bennett." Jaret stopped in front of the man and waited.

"Walker."

The greeting was curt enough to have Isabel glancing between the two in surprise.

"Care to explain that tussle I witnessed on the porch?"

"Nicolas." Isabel was shocked at his behavior. "Jaret didn't recognize you. He was only trying to keep me safe. That's why you sent him, isn't it?"

"True enough." Nicolas didn't look at his sister. He kept his eyes on Jaret, waiting.

"Let's take this inside. Isabel needs to rest."

She protested. "Jaret, I'm fine."

"What's wrong with her?" Nicolas spoke over her words.

"That devil horse of hers nearly killed her three days ago and then someone tried to finish the job." The familiar feeling of failure swamped Jaret, even though the attempt hadn't succeeded.

Nicolas stared at Jaret before nodding once. "Inside." He turned toward the house, then stopped. A smile curved his lips. "'Bel, I almost forgot. You need to meet my guest."

Jaret interrupted. "Inside first."

Isabel's eyebrows lifted at his abruptness. "Jaret, there's no need to be rude."

"It's all right," the man soothed. "Introductions will hold until we are out of this sun."

Jaret turned toward the gathered men. "The rest of the reunion will have to wait. Those of you on guard, get to it. Divide yourselves up so half of you can get some rest. The rest saddle up and see to the horses. It's going to be a long night."

The men filtered away to do as he'd said. Jaret faced Nick and answered the question in his eyes with a shake of his head. He led the way into the house.

Manuel stood guard at the parlor door and lifted his chin toward the room when Jaret caught his eye. Nodding his understanding, he pointed the group in that direction.

A cry of surprise and delight came from above them. Lydia rushed down the stairs and into Nick's arms, chattering and sobbing in equal parts. Jaret let them be for a few moments, then signaled Manuel, who waded in and separated them.

"Mamita, let him go now. He is home to stay. You can smother him later."

As Manuel urged his wife toward the back of the house, Jaret took up the post at the parlor door. Glancing in, he was satisfied that dear Uncle Enrique, or whoever the hell he was, was too interested in his whiskey to pay any attention to the commotion in the hall. In fact, he looked like he was sleeping, a half-full tumbler balanced on his round belly. As Manuel rejoined them, Jaret motioned the group into the room.

Isabel was the first through the door. Her smile faded when she spotted her uncle. "Let's go into the library instead."

Jaret urged her through the door. "No. In here."

"But—"

"I've got my reasons, honey."

She relented and perched on the settee across the room from her uncle. Embarrassment colored her cheeks. When

Nick started to introduce himself to the stranger, Jaret stopped him. The man who'd ridden in with Nick crossed to stand at the hearth. Manuel stayed at the door. Satisfied no one would get in or out, Jaret woke up the sleeping drunk with a kick to his booted feet.

"What the—"

"Jaret!" Isabel surged to her feet.

"How dare you, sir? I am not a common cowboy to be knocked about at your leisure." He broke off when he realized there were others in the room. Huffing to himself, he set his drink aside and straightened in the chair. "My apologies. I was unaware we had company. Isabel, my dear child, would you introduce me?"

"Relax, honey," Jaret stopped her. "Let your brother do the honors."

Nick looked confused, but complied. "'Bel." He turned her toward the man at the hearth. "This is our uncle, Enrique."

Chapter Fifteen

Isabel stared in shock, then everyone began speaking at once. Jaret kept his eyes on the whiskey-soaked imposter, waiting for him to make a move. He didn't have to wait long.

The man moved damn fast for an overweight drunk. He was halfway out the window before Jaret got to him. Manuel came over to help and together they dragged the man back inside and shoved him into the chair. Isabel started across the room, wanting answers, but Jaret stepped in front of her to keep her out of reach. Wrapping an arm around her waist, he pulled her close, knowing it might be the last time she allowed it.

"Take your hands off my sister, Walker." Nick Bennett started around the settee as the room fell silent again.

"Stop it, Nicolas. I'm not a child. Jaret is only trying to protect me." She laid her hand over his where he gripped her waist and met his gaze. "It's all right, love." Her free hand brushed his jaw. "I won't get any closer."

The look in her eyes hit Jaret like a mule-kick in the gut. Love, concern, faith in him, it was all there. For him. He could see it—and knew those feelings would die when she learned the truth. He had to fight the urge to toss her over his shoulder and run away, where she'd never find out what he'd done.

Saying nothing, Jaret released her, but didn't move away. Isabel smiled up at him before turning to face the man who had been masquerading as her uncle. Her beautiful lips thinned in fury. "Who are you?"

The man sat motionless, perspiration pouring down his face. His bloodshot eyes darted from person to person. Isabel took a step forward, drawing his attention back to her. "I asked you a question. Answer me!"

He puffed out his chest. "Don't you dare speak to me in that tone of voice, young lady!" Evidently, he'd decided bravado was the way out of the mess he was in. "You know very well who I am. This man," he flung his empty hand toward the stranger, "is an imposter."

Nicolas started to speak but Isabel cut him off with a look. She moved away from the man in the chair before turning toward the stranger. "And you, sir. Who are you?"

The stranger smiled slightly and looked so much like Isabel that any lingering doubt Jaret had was removed. He moved closer to the imposter as the man replied.

"My name is Enrique de la Rosa, eldest brother of your dear mother, may she rest in peace. I am your uncle."

He said it with such quiet dignity that nearly every head in the room nodded in agreement.

Isabel looked at the family crest emblazoned on the ruby encrusted ring he wore. She studied his face, her gaze sweeping his features over and over. "You look like Mama." The hitch in her voice nearly broke Jaret's heart.

Nick took her hand. "I was trying to buy a horse and wagon from Colonel Kinney when he came into the livery. I'd never met him, but I would have sworn on the Bible that I knew him. Then I realized it's because he looks so much like Mama, and you." Nicolas hugged his sister. "He introduced himself and even his voice was familiar. Then he showed me the letters you'd written to him over the years."

"The last took several months to get to me," Don Enrique interjected. "I was at sea at the time."

"Are you a captain, then?"

His laugh was a warm, gentle rumble. "No, my dear, I discovered some years ago that I am a man who prefers the earth beneath my boots. But I have certain business interests that require my attention, and a ship is often the fastest way to see to them. When I returned to Galveston, I received word of the disappearance of your brother. My ship brought me as far as Colonel Kinney's trading post. I was trying to hire a guide to get me to the ranch when I found Nicolas."

He smiled at the two of them. "I recognized your mother in him the moment I saw him. Except for his hair, he is her image exactly." The man glanced away, clearing his throat. "I introduced myself and we got under way as fast as possible."

The stranger turned to Jaret. "Nicolas knows who I am. But I can give you more proof if it is required."

"No need. They believe you." Jaret dropped a hand on the shoulder of the man who'd been masquerading as Don Enrique, causing the man to jump and spill most of his whiskey. When he reached for the decanter, Jaret moved it out of reach.

"Now I think it's time we heard this man's story, don't you?"

When all eyes focused on the imposter, he began to bluster. "This man is a liar." He puffed out his whiskey-soaked chest. "I am Don Enrique de la Rosa, not this . . . this charlatan." He stuck out his chin, but shrunk back into his chair when Nick took a step toward him.

"Now, now, there's no need for violence." His throat worked as he tried to invent a story. When he realized he was trapped, he held up both hands in surrender. "Very well. My name is Roger Marks." His thick accent disappeared. "I'm an actor, a traveling showman from the east." He swallowed hard and gazed longingly at the whiskey Jaret held. When none was forthcoming, he dragged the back of his free hand across his mouth and continued. "I was in New Orleans when a man approached me about doing some work for him. Nothing strenuous, just pretense, he said. Only pretense," he repeated, almost to himself. "Of course, I accepted. There were bills to be seen to, and even a man in my profession has to eat."

He glanced around at each of them. "I'm not much of an actor, in truth. I could hardly refuse the opportunity to live in luxury, eat three meals a day, and earn a reasonable salary. The man paid me one half of the promised salary up front, with the remainder to be delivered once the charade was over."

Facing Isabel, he leaned forward in earnest. "I meant you no harm, my dear. I was only doing what I'd been hired to do."

Jaret stepped between them, blocking Marks's view of Isabel. "What *exactly* were your instructions?"

Marks looked at him. "I was to make myself a part of the family and ensure that Isabel chose a husband quickly, one that would take her away from the ranch for good. I was assured an appropriate candidate would present himself. I failed utterly, as you well know." He waved a vague hand in Jaret's direction.

Jaret interrupted before he could elaborate. "That's all, just encourage her? What about the poisoned laudanum?"

The man paled and shook his head frantically in denial.

"Poison?" Nick stalked toward Jaret. "What do you mean?"

Isabel stopped her brother with a hand on his arm. "He means that someone tried to kill me."

Nick looked like he wanted to tear something apart. Jaret knew the feeling well.

Isabel slipped her hand into her brother's and turned back to the actor. "Since marrying me off didn't work, you decided stronger measures were in order."

"No! I would never harm a woman. The laudanum was for your own good, to assist you with your headaches. It was my own supply, you see. I thought the whiskey would be a satisfactory substitute for my personal needs." He swallowed convulsively and the lump in his throat jumped. Coughing discreetly, he held out his empty glass. "Perhaps a bit now would assist this terribly dry throat I seem to have developed."

Jaret stared at him for a long moment, then relented and splashed a little into the tumbler. The man looked disappointed in the amount, but drank it anyway, swallowing it in one gulp.

"When the whiskey didn't help as much as I had hoped, I returned to taking the laudanum as well. That, of course, meant I would need more, with two of us requiring its medicinal effects, you understand." His gaze darted between Jaret and Isabel and back again. "I informed Hardin of my need, and he provided it. I merely replaced one bottle with the other. That way I was able to disguise any evidence of my having partaken of the medicine."

"When did you put the new bottle in my room?"

He stared at the floor, remembering. "Last week . . . no, the week prior, I believe. Yes, yes, that's right. The week prior. If the laudanum was poisoned, I had no knowledge of it."

Jaret watched the remaining blood drain from Marks's face as he realized the laudanum would have worked on him just as well. Whoever wanted the ranch didn't plan to leave witnesses.

"It's a good thing I never take laudanum, isn't it?" She glared at the imposter. "What about the flowers?"

Jaret looked up sharply. "Flowers?"

She glanced at him, her eyes fiery with temper. "Someone was in my bedroom last night or early this morning. They left a large bouquet of roses cut from my garden, and a note explaining how they'd planned on the flowers being for my grave."

The man tried to shrink into the chair. "I was only told to cut the roses and deliver them along with the note. I slipped in and out very early this morning, then staged that ridiculous attempt to arrive on horseback. The envelope was already sealed. I swear I didn't know what it said. I swear it."

Jaret's blood ran cold. Someone found it so easy to kill that they couldn't resist gloating. He had to find out who was doing this. "Who hired you? Hardin?"

"I believe Mr. Hardin is merely an employee, like myself. I have no idea who hired me. I don't," he insisted, when both Jaret and Nick crowded closer. "He paid in cash, which Hardin delivered to my hotel along with the message that my employer would be in touch when he wanted to see me."

"When are you to meet him next?" Isabel's eyes flashed as she took a step in Marks's direction.

Jaret thought she'd never appeared more beautiful. He took her elbow to keep her out of reach of Marks. "Where are you supposed to rendezvous?"

Marks's eyes widened as Nick flanked his sister. "Well now." He shifted in his chair. "I met with him just last night, actually, so I don't plan—" He broke off when all three closed in on him. "Now, now, violence is not the answer." He yelped when the cold steel of a knife pressed into his neck.

Manuel spoke very softly, very close to his ear. "You won't be seeing him again until Mr. Jaret says so. You won't leave this house without his permission. If you try, I will kill you. *Comprende?*"

"Yes, yes, I understand." Marks started to nod, then changed his mind as the blade bit a little deeper.

Manuel eased the knife from the man's throat, but held it where Marks could see it.

"Describe him." Jaret's voice sliced through the silence. "Tell me what he looks like."

"I've only seen him in the dark. It would be impossible to describe the man."

"There was a moon last night, Marks."

"But he concealed himself," the man whined. "I was only allowed close when I submitted to being blindfolded."

Jaret cursed. "What about when he hired you?"

Marks shook his head. "I'm afraid not. I was just returning to my lodgings after a performance. The moon was new and the sky overcast. He stopped me in a narrow street where there was very little light. It was enough to see the silver he offered, but nothing else. The second time I met him, he wore a hat low on his brow. I could see he had a mustache, but not much else."

Marks's brows furrowed as he searched through his whiskey-fogged mind for more. "He wasn't tall. Though he was stooped, I think he would stand a little over me. He was thin and rather unkempt. He smelled as if he hadn't bathed in some time and used a rather odious cologne to cover the oversight."

Isabel stiffened.

"Honey?" Jaret turned to her. "What is it?"

She stared at Marks. "I'm not certain, but I know someone . . ." She trailed off and shook her head. "No, it isn't possible. Never mind."

Jaret waited, but she shook her head. When he turned his attention back to Marks, the man heaved a sigh and closed his eyes. "I'm sorry, but I know nothing more."

The actor was probably telling the truth for the first time since he'd arrived here. He caught Nick watching him and nodded slightly. He could read the question in his eyes. The description closely matched that of the man who'd hired Jaret.

Jaret gave in to the need to move. He set the whiskey bottle on the mantelpiece with a crack and stalked to the window. The sounds of horses and men could be heard through the open glass. It all looked normal, if you didn't count the extra weapons and ammunition every man carried. Isabel was as safe as he could make her, but Jaret couldn't forget she was in danger because of him. Choices, he thought with a shake of his head. His choice, her life. It wasn't a fair trade.

"What's the matter, love?"

Jaret stiffened when Isabel touched his arm. Glancing at her, her saw worry and compassion combined in her eyes. It ate a hole in his gut knowing he'd put the first there and didn't deserve the second.

"Nothing you can change, honey." He brushed her cheek with his knuckles before looking away. "It's just something I have to live with."

She stood on her toes to kiss his jaw. "Maybe I can't change it, but I can listen while you tell me about it."

Jaret laughed without humor. "I don't think so."

"Now we know who this man is." Nick jerked his head

in Marks's direction as he crossed the room to resume his seat. "Do you want to explain the rest, Walker?"

Jaret led Isabel to a seat beside her brother, ignoring her protest. Once he had her settled, he lifted her hand and brushed a kiss across her fingers. He lingered over the scent of her skin for a moment, thinking of everything he was about to lose. "I'm sorry, honey," he whispered. Before she could question him, he straightened and faced Nick.

"The night after I arrived, I realized we'd underestimated the danger Isabel was in. I didn't know who to trust other than Manuel and Lydia, and the three of us weren't enough to keep her safe."

"Four," Isabel interjected. "In spite of what you think, I'm capable of taking care of myself."

Jaret didn't look at her. "Four," he amended, "although she didn't have a clue about what was going on around her. So I kidnapped her, intending to bring her to you."

"That would have left the ranch open to anyone who wanted to take it." Nick's voice raised a notch.

"I didn't give a damn about the ranch," Jaret bristled. "It was your sister that concerned me."

Nick nodded and settled back in silence.

"We didn't get far." He glanced at Isabel. "Manuel tried to buy us some time, but between dodging riders and chasing Isabel when she bolted, we were only a half day's ride from the house when Hardin and his men caught up with us."

"If you'd told me what you were doing, I wouldn't have tried to escape." Isabel raised an eyebrow, looking every inch the royal princess.

Jaret laughed. He didn't find much about the situation that was funny, but she still managed to lighten his mood. "Honey, by the time I realized that, it was too late to explain. I'm just grateful they didn't get a rope around my neck."

"They were going to hang you?" It was the first time Don Enrique had spoken since introducing himself.

"In these parts, justice is handed out by whoever feels the need. Hanging is the expected punishment for stealing, whether its horses or a woman."

Don Enrique nodded. "How did you escape their justice, as you call it?"

Isabel answered for him. "I told them we were married."

"What?" Nick jumped from his chair. "Married?" He started for Jaret. "What the hell have you done, Walker?"

Isabel grabbed at her brother's arm, holding him back. "Jaret had nothing to do with it. It was my idea." She urged him back to his seat. "He didn't know what I was going to say and there wasn't time to warn him. They had us surrounded. So I told Hardin and the others that we'd slipped away from the ranch to exchange promises. I surprised Jaret, but he recovered enough to play along or it wouldn't have worked."

"Why in the name of heaven would you do something like that, 'Bel?" Her brother stared at her. "Now everyone on the ranch thinks you're married to Walker. He's been living here in the house with you. What will you tell them when he leaves?"

"She'll tell them the truth, Bennett."

Isabel looked up at Jaret with dark, unreadable eyes. He wanted to get her alone long enough to explain, but he'd missed his chance. She frowned a little at the look on his face, then turned away when her brother spoke.

"Isabel, what made you want to save the likes of him?"

Isabel's eyebrows lifted in surprise at her brother's tone. "I thought he was your friend."

"Well, he is." Nick rubbed at his injured shoulder. "I'm just not sure I want him to marry my sister."

She laughed. "You sent him here."

"Not sent, really. Walker considered it his obligation after what happened. I didn't agree, but I took his help any way I could get it. He already had experience in kidnapping and I knew you'd forgive us both once I had a chance to explain."

Isabel looked confused. Jaret wanted to kiss her just once more, a taste to carry with him.

"Jaret told me where you'd been, and that you were too ill to travel."

Nick nodded. "I was recovering, but not from an illness, unless you consider fever from a bullet wound an illness."

"A bullet?" She grabbed at her brother's hand. "Were you shot trying to escape from the pri— that place?"

He shook his head. "We were an hour from the Rio Grande when we were ambushed."

"I don't understand." She looked from Nick to Jaret.

Nick stared at Jaret, his surprise and confusion obvious. He knew Nick thought he would have told Isabel everything, but the time had never seemed right. Jaret wanted to stop him, but the truth would come out eventually. He nodded for Nick to finish the story and went to lean against the mantel.

"'Bel, Jaret was hired to take me to that Mexican prison, probably by the same man who hired Marks. I'm sure the original plan was to leave me there to die while they stole the ranch from you."

Jaret watched the truth sink into Isabel as the color drained from her cheeks. Her feelings showed clearly on her pale face. When she looked at him, he knew he'd lost any hope of being able to explain.

"Jaret?"

He nodded, dread twisting his gut into a knot. "He's telling the truth, honey. I told you I was no good. You should have tossed me out when you had the chance."

"It would seem you were correct." She closed her eyes and rubbed her temple. "Nicolas, how did you escape?"

"Walker came back for me. He figured out he'd been lied to and forged a letter telling the general in charge there'd been a mistake. That and a sizable bribe convinced the general to agree. But Walker was followed. They tried to kill us both. Fortunately, they didn't succeed."

Isabel stared at Jaret, but he couldn't tell what she was thinking. "If he was responsible for putting you in prison, why did you trust Jaret enough to send him here?"

"Because he'd been set up right along with me. Walker recognized one of the men who ambushed us. He'd been there when Walker was hired to kidnap me."

Jaret interrupted. "Your brother took the bullet meant to silence me."

He hadn't realized how furious he was until she flinched at the tone of his voice. He wanted to go to her, to hold her close as he had through the night, but she wouldn't welcome his touch.

Isabel rose to pace the room, refusing to look at him. She stopped to stare out the window while the men waited in silence. When she finally spoke, her voice was flat. "Why would whoever is doing this want you dead?" She trembled as she said the word. It was all Jaret could do to keep his distance.

Nick leaned forward in his seat. "I think it's because of what I found when I visited the land office in Austin. I was looking into acquiring that piece of land to the north, the one I told you about? I'm sure there's water there, not too far underground. It would be the perfect place to expand one of the herds." Nick laughed in apology. "Sorry. You know I get sidetracked when I think about my horses. Anyway, I happened on some old government land grant information about Two Roses. About fifteen years ago, most of our land was signed over by the U.S. government to someone else, even though we've held title for generations."

"That's not possible." Isabel spun to face her brother. "This ranch is ours."

Nick held up a hand to stop her. "I know, and the government agreed, finally. The new grant was nullified a few weeks later, by a judge Papa knew. I think the other man didn't like the reversal, and now he's trying to get the ranch through us." Nick turned to Manuel. "Do you recall the time Papa went to the city to take care of some mysterious business? He wouldn't tell anyone why he had to go and insisted on going alone."

Manuel's brows lowered as he tried to remember. "I don't know that one trip stands out more than any other."

Nick grinned. "I only remember because I wanted to go with him. I'd packed a bag and was trying to saddle my horse when he rode out without me."

Isabel laughed, remembering. "You couldn't have been six years old. You were so angry at Papa for leaving you behind, you cried the entire morning."

Her brother ducked his head, embarrassed as his uncle and Manuel joined in the laughter. "I think he was heading for the land office. When I found the documents referring to the incident, they seemed more of a curiosity than anything important. Someone obviously disagrees. I planned to tell you when I got home, but I didn't get the chance."

Isabel shrank back on the sofa. Nick laid his arm across her shoulders, offering comfort. "Who was it, Nicolas? Who wants to steal our land?"

Nick shook his head. "I don't know. The name of the settler who'd been given our land had been crossed through so many times it was almost scratched off the paper, as if someone never wanted us to know who'd tried. Maybe Papa did it."

Jaret spoke up. "It's a damn shame, since it looks like they're trying it again."

Nick nodded. "That stands to reason. I've been racking my brain, trying to remember anything Papa might have said that would give us a hint as to who it is."

A sound at the door drew their attention. Lydia came into the room carrying a large tray. "I brought a cool drink for everyone."

She handed a glass of minted water to Isabel and Nicolas. Jaret accepted his and stayed close to Lydia as she held one out to Marks. The imposter took it, but cast a longing eye toward the whiskey bottle and set the water on the table with a thump. Lydia glared her disapproval before continuing around the room. She hesitated in front of the stranger, searching his eyes for a long moment before a small smile curved her lips. "I believe I know who you are."

Don Enrique inclined his head in a gesture of respect to the woman. "Nicolas has told me all about you, *Señora.* I thank you for your loyalty to our family."

The old woman nodded. "You are the *true* Don Enrique. Good. That one"—she pointed toward the imposter, her lips thinning—"he is too weak to be from the same parents as my Maria. You, I think, will do fine. Be welcome here."

Excusing herself, Lydia started for the door, pausing to take Nicolas's hand a moment. Releasing it with reluctance, she ran gnarled fingers down Isabel's hair and patted her shoulder, then hurried from the room dabbing at her eyes with one corner of her starched white apron.

Isabel broke the silence. "How do we know you aren't a part of this . . . this plot, Mr. Walker?"

"Isabel," her brother scolded. "I trusted Jaret with your life or he wouldn't be here."

She rounded on her brother. "But he never told me the truth. Why should I continue to trust him?"

Jaret straightened. "I never lied to you."

Isabel laughed, but it was a sound without humor. "No, you didn't lie, but you certainly left out a lot."

Jaret wanted to break something. He felt trapped. He had to get out of the room, out of the house, before he went crazy. He took a couple of deep breaths to try and calm himself. It didn't help much. He leaned back against the wall and crossed his arms over his chest and took up the story.

"After hearing Nick's side, I was pretty sure the man who'd hired me had others working at the ranch. I took a chance that none of them would know me or that I'd worked for whoever the hell is doing this. I kept quiet about my role in all of it because I didn't want anything to be overheard and reported back. Unfortunately"—he glared at Roger Marks—"I was a little too slow figuring out he'd put someone inside the house."

Isabel rose. "I want to hear the whole story, but right now we have other things to worry about. I want my ranch back."

Jaret didn't look at her. He couldn't. Instead he focused on the activity outside and began outlining his strategy.

"We brought in about two hundred horses this morning. Half of those had been corralled in a slot canyon close to the border of Williams's ranch."

Nick sat forward in his seat. "There should be another one hundred and fifty head at least."

Jaret nodded. "I also found a valley that's been used recently for rustling, but no men or horses were there. I don't want to risk sending men out to search for the rest of the stock. Besides, I don't think the ones doing this are really interested in the herd. It's the land and the water they want."

The men around the room nodded in agreement. Marks sat up a little straighter and risked opening his mouth.

"The man I've been working for has several loyal employees on the ranch. I know some of them, though not all. I will gladly identify those I can, if it would be helpful."

Jaret spun toward him. "You'd sell him out, just like that? What do you want in return?"

Marks shook his head before Jaret finished the question. "I require nothing from you. I owe it to Miss Bennett. I was duped into participating in this rather nefarious plot and I find myself wanting to get even."

"*That* I understand," Jaret muttered. "We need to know who they are, but we can't risk jumping them until we can get them all." Everyone agreed except Isabel.

"Why don't we make them disappear?"

"Isabel!" The shock on Nick's face would have been humorous at another time.

"Not like that." She turned to Jaret. "We could tie them up and keep them in the schoolhouse with someone to watch them. Then Nicolas and I wouldn't have to worry about tripping over one of them when we think we're safely among friends."

"Neither of you will have to worry about that," Jaret interrupted. "Nick needs to finish healing and you should be out of reach of anyone who wants to hurt you. You're both staying in the house."

She jumped to her feet, spoiling for a fight. "I refuse to sit inside and do nothing."

Jaret pushed away from the wall. "I can't spare the men to post a full-time guard on you. If you stay in the house, we know we only have to keep everyone else out of here."

Isabel wanted to argue. He could see it in her eyes.

But no matter how she pleaded, nothing was worth risking her life.

Jaret crossed the room to stand close to her. "Honey, please stay inside where I at least have a hope of protecting you." He kept his voice low so his words carried no farther than the two of them.

"All right," she capitulated. "I'll stay in the house, but only if you keep me informed of what's happening."

One corner of his mouth tilted up in a smile. "I think I can do that."

Jaret turned to the men in the room. "Bennett, go get some rest. Word of your return has probably reached whoever the hell is doing this and I have a hunch it's going to be a long night."

Isabel stepped around Jaret to her brother's side. "I'm sure Lydia has your room ready for you. Let me help you."

Nick yanked his arm from her grasp. "I know the way," he snapped, earning a smile from her and Jaret.

"You sound just like your sister, Bennett."

Laughter lightened the mood in the room and soon everyone was scattering in different directions. Roger Marks was trussed up like a turkey and taken to the kitchen where Lydia could keep an eye on him. He may have admitted his involvement, but that didn't mean they trusted him.

Isabel stopped Jaret before he could leave.

"Please be careful."

Jaret trailed the back of one finger down her cheek. "I plan to, honey."

Isabel watched Jaret walk away with a mixture of love and frustration. Shaking her head, she turned for the door and came face-to-face with her uncle.

"Are you all right, Isabel?"

She shook her head. "Even after what he's done . . ."

"Don't be too hard on your Mr. Walker. He was only given half a story, and not a very accurate one at that. If what Nicolas told me is true, he's been trying to fix this mess from the moment he realized he'd been lied to."

"Then why not tell me the truth, all of it?" That was an answer she wanted—needed to hear from Jaret. She crossed to look out the window, searching for a glimpse of him.

"You love him."

Isabel started to deny it.

Her uncle chuckled. "Don't bother. It shines from your eyes when you look at him. Has he realized it yet?"

"I don't think so." Isabel shrugged away the sadness weighing her down. "Thank you for bringing Nicolas home."

The man smiled gently at her. "You've had a difficult few months, haven't you?"

She shrugged. "There were days I considered tossing it all to the wind, selling out to Silas Williams and moving to Galveston. Thank heavens I had enough help and support to bring me to my senses in time."

Her uncle laughed as she'd intended. "You never considered accepting one of the many marriage proposals you must have received?"

"There weren't all that many, and none I took seriously."

"Why not?" He seemed interested, so she told him the truth.

"I want a marriage like Mama and Papa had. None of the proposals I received were from men I could fall in love with."

"Until now."

Isabel didn't realize she was staring through the window at Jaret until her uncle's soft question penetrated. She shrugged. "And he hasn't asked."

Enrique crossed to lay a gentle hand on her shoulder. "A love like my sister enjoyed is very rare. If you've found the one you want, don't give him the chance to escape."

Isabel frowned as she considered her uncle's words. A smile tilted her lips as an idea formed. "That's a marvelous idea."

He offered his arm to escort her from the room. "Walker doesn't stand a chance."

"No, he doesn't" Isabel slipped her arm through his. "Thank you, Uncle Enrique—"

"Call me Rick, child," he interrupted. "My American friends said Enrique took too long to say and the title sounded stuffy."

Isabel laughed in delight. "You're exactly as I'd always imagined." On impulse, she leaned over and kissed his cheek. "Welcome to the family, Uncle Rick."

Chapter Sixteen

The afternoon proved to be even busier than Jaret predicted. The hundreds of horses moved closer to the house provided a living barrier against those who might attack, but they had to be contained, which meant hours of work. The arrival of the herds also meant dozens more mouths to feed as exhausted cowboys joined those already in the bunkhouse.

Isabel hated that she couldn't be a part of the noisy, dusty, barely controlled chaos. She spent a few minutes staring out her upstairs window, but having to watch and not help frustrated her. She chafed at the inactivity, at being forced to stay inside when she knew how much work there was to be done, but she'd given her word.

At lunchtime, she prepared food for two. Before she got out of the kitchen, Lydia added extra meat, bread and potatoes for Nicolas. Balancing the heavy tray, she climbed the stairs.

"Come on in," Nick called.

"May I join you? I'm losing my mind being stuck inside."

"Try it for three solid months sometime," he groused.

Isabel crossed the room to set the food on the table near

the window. Settling into the chair opposite him, Isabel studied her brother. Pain had etched deep lines around his mouth and he'd lost weight. That, at least, could be remedied.

"I think Lydia and Marta are determined to fatten you up again." She set his plate in front of him.

He grinned and some of the lines eased. "It smells great."

"I told her you couldn't possibly eat all this, but her eyebrows lowered and she got that look that said I'd better watch my tongue, so I promised to try and convince you."

Under his shirt, Isabel could see the bulge of the bandages wrapping his left shoulder and back. "Are you still in pain?"

He looked up from his food. "Not much. The ride out here wasn't comfortable, but I'll survive. Lydia is satisfied that I'll mend."

"Then I'll stop worrying about that, too."

They ate in companionable silence, just glad to be in each other's company again. When Isabel finished her lunch, she leaned back in her chair and watched her brother down the mountain of food on his plate with relish.

"You eat like you're starving," she teased.

He chewed the bite, his enjoyment obvious. "I am. Mrs. Winston was a good woman, and she kept me alive, but I'm glad I don't have to eat her cooking any longer."

"Who's Mrs. Winston?"

"A friend of Jaret's. That's where he left me when he came to look after you."

Isabel turned to stare out the window. She wasn't surprised that Jaret knew other women, but she didn't expect the jealousy that snaked through her.

Nicolas put down his fork. "'Bel, she's a crusty old woman who could scare the skin off a snake from thirty paces. Jaret met her when he guarded a wagon train nearly ten years ago."

Isabel shrugged. "It doesn't matter to me."

Her brother laughed. "Of course it does. It's written all over your face." He leaned forward and reached for her hand. "Are you all right?"

She met and held his concerned gaze. "I'm fine." She gave his fingers a squeeze. "Will you tell me what happened?"

When Nick shoved his chair away from the table to pace, Isabel sat back with a smile. It was something Jaret would have done had she cornered him at the dinner table.

"Please, Nicolas." She wasn't too proud to beg. "I have to know."

He stopped at the window and stared at the activity below. He was silent for so long she thought he was going to ignore her. When he finally started talking, she had the feeling he didn't remember she was in the room.

"I was just playing cards, waiting for the storm to break. The saloon was crowded. Nobody wanted to be out in that gully-washer. There was an empty chair at my table. Walker came up and asked if he could use it. That alone should have put my guard up. Anyone else in town that day would have just sat down and to hell with what I wanted."

He raked his fingers through his hair, shoving it back like it was getting in the way of his memories.

"I liked him. There's a good man under that tough shell. Later I figured out he'd only joined me to find out where I'd be when he needed to find me.

"Once the rain let up, I headed to my hotel room. I got on the trail early the next morning. There were too many people jammed into that town and I wanted to get home to the new horses. When I rode out, Walker followed me.

"I recognized him as he got closer and holstered my

gun. Since I knew him, I didn't think I was in any danger." His bark of laughter held no humor. "I was pitifully easy to capture."

He paused and Isabel crossed to slip an arm around his waist. "You couldn't have expected it."

He raised a shoulder to block her words. "Doesn't matter. We kept riding south, into Mexico. Into hell.

"When Walker showed up at Perote Prison again, I wondered who else he'd duped, but this time he was alone. It took some fancy talking and a sizable amount of gold to convince the general in command to let me go. He brought Micah along for me."

Her brother's eyes lit with tenderness at the mention of his favorite horse. He felt about her the way Isabel felt about Lucifer. She laid her head on his shoulder and gave his arm a squeeze, but didn't interrupt.

"We were almost to the Rio Grande when we rode into a trap and the shooting started."

Nicolas flexed his left shoulder and pain crossed his face. With a gentle tug, she led him to the small settee nearby and urged him into it. She settled onto the floor at his feet.

"Walker figured out pretty fast that the ambush was a way to get rid of both of us. But for some ridiculous reason, he thought the bullet that struck me was meant to kill him. I told him there were several with my name on them as well, but he wouldn't listen. He still believes it's his fault I got shot. I think that's why he agreed to come here at all." Nick rubbed at his injury absently.

"He was able to kill most of the attackers. One got away, but I was in no shape to go after him and Jaret refused to leave me. He took me to Mrs. Winston, the one place he was certain they wouldn't find me, and couldn't get to me if they did."

Isabel interrupted. "Was Jaret hurt?"

Nicolas looked down at her and smiled. "You've got it bad for him, don't you?"

She opened her mouth to deny it but the words wouldn't come. She just nodded and let him finish his story.

"I'm not sure. It took almost three weeks before I even knew where I was. The minute my eyes focused, I tried to leave. I couldn't have stayed on a horse for more than ten feet, but I knew they would come after you next, and you had no idea you were in danger. I convinced Walker to come instead. The plan was for him to stick around and keep you safe until I could get here. I guess he decided it was too dangerous to remain, but he should have brought you to me."

"He tried." She had to smile at the memory. "I told him he had to leave—not in so many words, but he knew what I meant. The entire Williams family had come courting and after their tender care I swore off men completely, including Jaret."

"Both brothers? At once?"

"And Silas, too."

Nicolas gave a mock shudder, making Isabel grin. She nodded her agreement with the sentiment.

"Jaret left the next morning, but didn't go far. He surprised me in the barn that night and kidnapped me."

"He's too damn good at that."

"I didn't make it easy on him, I'm afraid." She rose to pour a cup of tea for each of them. It wasn't very hot anymore, but it tasted good.

"Unfortunately, Hardin had at least one very good tracker in the bunch. Even Manuel couldn't mislead him. They caught up with us and nearly hanged Jaret."

"So you married him to keep him alive."

"I *pretended* to marry him. He still hadn't told me where

you were and stringing him up from the barn rafters wasn't going to help me get the information."

She swallowed her tea and set the cup aside. "Jaret felt I was still in danger."

"He was right," her brother interjected.

"I know." Isabel was a little surprised at how easy it was to agree now. "It made sense to keep up the pretense when we returned to the ranch. And I was—am attracted to him. Since I'm never going to marry for real, I thought—"

"Of course you'll marry," he argued.

Isabel looked up at Nicolas, confused. "I refuse to marry a man who wants my land more than me. Since I'd never met a man like that, I decided to let you carry on the family legacy. You get married and have heirs, and I'll run the ranch."

He laughed. "That's ridiculous." A knock on the door forestalled an argument. "We'll talk about it later."

Lydia entered and broke up their reunion. Isabel left her to fuss over Nicolas and carried the lunch dishes to the kitchen. Once they were washed, dried, and put away, she wandered back to the library to find something to keep her occupied for the remainder of the afternoon.

She tried to work on the ranch's books, but couldn't concentrate on the numbers. When she added the same column for the third time and came up with a third different answer, she tossed down her pen in disgust and went to the kitchen to see if Marta would let her help. But the old cook was out helping feed the men. Even Roger Marks was gone, although she imagined he was still tied up and under guard.

Isabel wandered through the house looking for anything to pass the time. She dusted the parlor and the library, even though she hated the task. The kitchen floor didn't need sweeping, but she did it anyway. She rummaged through the pantry and found ingredients to make dinner, then remembered Lydia saying she would send food over for her and Nicolas.

Late in the afternoon she wandered into Jaret's bedroom and sat near the window to watch the sun set. The magnificent display of color was lost on her, but it signaled the end of the longest day of her life. Below her vantage point, the ranch settled for the night. She paid attention to which men were assigned posts to guard, and saw Manuel check on Lucifer as the last light of day faded from the sky.

She didn't see Jaret until well after dark. When she finally heard his boots on the stairs, she dashed across the room to open the door before he could reach it.

He looked surprised to see her, but entered when she stepped back and motioned him inside.

"Finally." She closed the door behind him with a thump. "I've been going crazy in this house."

Jaret just lifted an eyebrow and shot her a tired look.

Isabel felt like a petulant child. "I'm sorry. I didn't mean to sound so childish."

"What are you doing in here?"

She stared at him, confused. "Where else would I be?"

"After everything I've done to your family, I expected to find my gear dumped in the dust out back." He tossed his hat onto the washstand and poured some water into the basin. "You don't have to be here anymore. Your brother's home and the rest of it will be over soon. You should go back to your own room."

She stared at his back, stunned. It was all an act. He didn't care about her. Water splashed as Jaret washed the day off his hands and arms.

"Then none of what we shared meant anything to you."

He met her gaze in the mirror. "I didn't say that."

Relief swamped her.

"But I'm here to do a job and when it's finished—"

"Why is it so important that you complete it?" Isabel interrupted.

"Because I owe it to your brother, and you." He grabbed a towel and dried his hands. "The day my mother died, I was left to depend on the charity of others. The folks who took me in weren't able to afford another mouth to feed, but they'd made a promise to her and kept it. I decided I wanted to be like them instead of my own useless father. When I left, I swore to myself I'd keep any promise I made. I have." He shook out the towel and hung it back on the drying rack.

Even in the dim light, Isabel could see the exhaustion in his eyes. He looked stiff and sore as he headed for one of the chairs by the window. When he dropped into it, Isabel knelt in front of him and reached for a boot. Jaret hesitated, then leaned back and let her help. Dust and twigs slipped out with his feet to powder the floor.

"What on earth have you been doing, crawling through the countryside all afternoon?"

"Close enough. A couple of colts decided to explore a tiny slit in the rock in the east pastures, but they weren't bright enough to turn around while they still had room. I barely had space in there to think."

His socks followed the boots. Then she sat back on her heels and looked up to find him watching her.

"You shouldn't be here." His voice was soft and deep.

"I want to be with you."

"Isabel, you know I'm not right for you. Especially after what I did to Nick."

He leaned back in the chair and rubbed his hands over his face in a gesture so weary her heart ached.

"I meant to tell you everything, honey. The time just never seemed right."

"Nick told me the whole story this afternoon. I still

want to hear your side of it, but I think I understand." She leaned a little closer, making sure he was looking at her. "It doesn't change anything."

"It should. I'm a gun for hire. I'll do almost anything as long as it's legal and the money's right."

She laid a hand on his thigh. "I'm glad to hear it matters to you that it's legal. That tells me all I need to know."

"I'm no good for you. You shouldn't be here with me."

She rose on her knees and leaned forward to begin working loose the buttons on his shirt. "I'm sorry if you don't want me here. I'm not leaving."

"Why?"

"Hmm?" She was concentrating on getting the buttons open.

Jaret slipped a hand under her chin until her eyes met his. "Why are you doing this?"

"I think you know the answer to that question."

"Even after all I've done."

She smiled, hoping he could see the love in her eyes. She wasn't going to be the first to say the words, but surely he could tell how she felt. She nuzzled the hand that held her chin and nipped at his thumb before returning her attention to his shirt. Jaret didn't resist when she pulled the tail free of his pants and helped him remove it.

The shirt was nearly as filthy as his boots, sending a puff of dust into the air when she dropped it on the pile. He stood to remove his pants, but stopped with his hands on his gun belt and looked at her. With a blush, Isabel turned away to refill the washbowl with water and lay out a towel and a bar of the soap her father had always preferred. She sniffed the soap and closed her eyes as memories washed over her.

As a little girl, it had been her special job to get her father a towel and his soap when he came in from working with the horses. She would fuss until it was just right, then linger until he shooed her from the room so he could bathe.

Her smile faded and a strange feeling bumped in the pit of her stomach when she heard Jaret's pants join the pile on the floor. She took a breath to calm her jittery nerves as she realized he was just across the room, naked. She tried to turn around and face him. After all, it wasn't as if she'd never seen him naked before.

She took a deep breath, straightened her shoulders and lost her nerve. "I'll get some hot water so you can shave." Grabbing the water pitcher, she fled from the bedroom as fast as she could without breaking into a run. Jaret's laughter followed her out.

She had to solve a minor crisis in the kitchen before she could return. Juggling the full pitcher and a tray of food Miguel had brought for them, she hesitated at the bedroom door. She thought he should be finished bathing by now, but she had no idea how long he took. With a sound of impatience, she scolded herself for being timid for the first time in her memory. "If he doesn't want you to come in, he'll tell you," she muttered.

She knocked softly on the door, but Jaret didn't answer. She tried again, a little louder this time, but there still was no response.

Balancing the tray across her bent arm, Isabel set the water pitcher on the floor and opened the door to peek inside. Jaret was sprawled face-down across the bed, sound asleep. Tenderness filled Isabel. Closing the door softly behind her, she carried the pitcher to the washstand and set the food on the small table by the window. She turned down the wick in the lamp before going to the foot of the bed.

Jaret hadn't bothered to pull on anything other than clean pants. His bare feet hung off the edge of the bed even though he lay corner to corner on the mattress. She let her gaze roam freely across his broad shoulders and back, down the length of his well-muscled legs.

Had it only been last night that he'd shown her the marvels of man and woman? It seemed like days had passed since he'd touched her. Isabel knew she wanted to feel that way again, but didn't know how to tell him. Being direct was her usual way, but somehow that didn't seem quite right.

An idea formed when he shifted in his sleep and groaned at some hidden ache or other. Isabel smiled. That should get her point across.

Trying not to make a sound, she searched through her father's things. Even though he'd been gone for years, there were some things she hadn't been able to bring herself to remove from the room. She went through the drawers of the bureau until she found the liniment he'd always kept there.

Her mother had used it when Papa complained about the aches and pains left by the day's work. She could still remember the soft laughter that usually followed when Mama applied the liniment. It was years later before she understood what their laughter signified. Now she wondered if it might have the same effect on Jaret. She certainly hoped so.

When Isabel turned, she found Jaret watching her.

"What are you doing?"

"Looking for this." She held up the small ceramic pot.

"What is it?"

Returning to the bed, she settled onto the mattress beside him. "Just something to take away a few of those aches for you."

"What are you planning to do with it?"

"Lie back down and I'll show you."

He eyed her for a long minute before complying. Shifting a little closer to his side, she opened the container and sniffed. "This was my father's. A miracle, he always called it. He said it took away all of his pains in no time."

Scooping up a small amount, Isabel warmed it in her hands, then spread it across Jaret's nearest shoulder and began working it into his skin.

This time when Jaret made a sound, it was one of pleasure. Isabel smiled to herself. It was working already.

"What did you do this afternoon," she asked. "Lie in the dust and let those horses walk all over you?"

"Nearly." He groaned as she worked at a knotted muscle. "Lucifer got a little testy with another stallion when one of the men put them too close together. They both took some convincing that it wasn't necessary to kill each other before the sun went down."

"It must have been one of the new hands. Those who've been here for a round-up know better than to have Lucifer in the same county with another stallion." She pressed her fingers hard onto tight, tired muscles. "You could have sent for me."

She expected a quick retort about how she needed to stay locked up in the house, but he surprised her. "I considered it. By the time you could have gotten there, I'd managed to coax Lucifer out of most of his temper."

"How did you do that?"

"I think I promised him warm baths and sugar candy for a month. Do you think he'll hold me to it?"

Isabel laughed. Jaret opened one eye and grinned at her, then closed it again and seemed to drift to sleep.

She worked her way across both shoulders, investigating all the marks that life had left on him. At least one she was certain had been caused by a bullet. She swallowed hard. She might have lost this man before they'd ever met.

Her fingers discovered faint marks on his back that looked like they'd been made by a strap. She frowned. From what he'd said, his childhood hadn't been a happy one, but he hadn't mentioned beatings. His father truly was a beast if he'd beaten his four-year-old son.

When she tried to reach his other arm she found it wasn't possible from where she was. She considered moving to the other side of the bed, then changed her mind. Hiking up her skirt and petticoat, she climbed farther onto the mattress and, after a brief hesitation, straddled his hips.

Jaret mumbled something into the pillow, but she shushed him and went back to work. When she had spread all the liniment in her hands over his back, she leaned forward to get more from the pot set on the tiny table near his head. Her breasts brushed across his skin. This time the sound he made was not one of pain. Isabel took a little more ointment onto her fingers and set the pot back on the table. She felt Jaret shift and when she turned her head she found herself looking into his eyes.

"Turn over."

"I don't think that's a good idea, honey."

"I disagree."

"Your brother is home, Isabel. We don't have to pretend anymore."

The flash of pain that stabbed through her was a surprise. She'd told Nicolas only hours before that the marriage wasn't real, but it still hurt to hear the words coming from Jaret.

"I'm not leaving."

Jaret reached for her arm, threatening to dislodge her. Isabel stopped him with a hand on his shoulder.

"Jaret, I know exactly what I'm doing."

The flash of heat in his eyes had her insides melting. Still Jaret hesitated, searching her eyes. Isabel lifted her weight off his hips and waited for him to decide. Finally he rolled over beneath her in one fluid motion. Without taking her eyes off his, Isabel settled high on his thighs, nearly moaning aloud as the rigid proof of his desire pressed into her most sensitive flesh.

His eyes blazed with such heat she wondered that she didn't go up in flames. She shifted to get better balance and Jaret's hands shot to her hips to hold her steady. For an instant Isabel wondered if she really did know what she was doing, but she'd come this far and she wasn't going to stop now.

Leaning forward she began rubbing the liniment into his skin. His chest was lightly furred with hair the color of night. Here, too, there was evidence his life hadn't been an easy one. Old scars marked his skin along with some blossoming bruises.

"Lucifer tried to head butt you out of the way, I see."

The sound of agreement Jaret made vibrated under her hands. Her palms tingled and heated. The hair on his chest tickled the sensitive skin on the inside of her wrists. Isabel explored slowly, enjoying the sensations. His skin was tanned all the way to his waist, evidence he sometimes worked in the sun without his shirt. She decided that was something she wanted to see. With lighter and lighter touches she learned his contours.

When her fingertips brushed one of his nipples, Isabel felt Jaret jerk beneath her. A smile crept across her lips and she returned to the sensitive place, circling it as he had done to her in the dark of the previous night. Watching him for his reaction, she plucked at the rough nub. When she heard his breath catch, Isabel gave in to temptation and leaned forward.

Jaret's fingers dug into her hips when her tongue slipped out to taste him. Isabel braced herself on his shoulders with both hands, brushing kisses across his chest. She felt Jaret's hand move to her hair and pull the scarf loose, freeing her hair to fall and cover him. When she turned to his other nipple, Jaret's hips moved, caressing them both. Isabel couldn't prevent a moan of pleasure.

Slipping a hand between their bodies, Isabel quickly unbuttoned the front of the dress she wore and unlaced her chemise, eager to feel Jaret's skin touching her own.

Jaret helped tug the garments from her shoulders, baring her to the waist. When his fingers closed on her breast, her gasp changed to a low sound of need. Lost in her own desire, Isabel pulled her dress over her head and threw it aside. Nothing separated them but the fabric of Jaret's pants and her own thin undergarment. Her fingers struggled to free him, clumsy in her haste to feel him beneath her, inside of her.

Jaret's fingers closed on hers, stilling her frantic movements. She looked at him, ready to beg him not to stop. The look on his face made it clear that was not his intention. He dealt with the fasteners that had given her such trouble with one hand while the other slipped between the folds of her drawers to drive her wild with need. When he was free of his cloths, Isabel lowered herself as Jaret guided himself into her. She bit her lip against a cry of pleasure and settled more fully onto him.

Jaret's fingers dug into her hips and showed her the motions she was desperate to discover. She tried to tell him how it felt, how she loved him, but the fire stole her breath and drove her toward the peak. Jaret thrust into her again and again until, with cries of triumph, they flew over the edge together.

Isabel drifted back to reality slowly, savoring the feel of Jaret beneath her. She was sprawled across his chest and his heartbeat pounded in her ear. Smiling with satisfaction to know she'd had an effect on him, she opened her eyes to meet his. They were the blue of a dusky evening sky, with flecks of stars shining through.

"Are you all right?"

The low hum of his voice filled her with contentment. When she didn't answer, he tucked a finger under her chin and urged her head up.

"No, I'm not all right. I'm wonderful."

Concern clouded his eyes then cleared just as quickly. "We should both get some rest."

"All right." Isabel snuggled closer with her ear pressed over his heart and let her eyes drift closed. When Jaret moved, she protested. "Lie still. I'm trying to sleep."

"Don't you want a pillow?"

She kissed his skin and teased him through the mat of dark hair. "I have one. Besides, this way you can't get away and leave me to sleep alone."

His rumble of laughter warmed her to her toes. Lifting her face, she found his lips and melted into the kiss. When he released her, she kissed his fingertips and nuzzled the hand he curled around her jaw. With a smile on her face, she drifted to sleep, knowing this was how they would spend every night for the rest of their lives.

Chapter Seventeen

With her arms wrapped around him, Jaret didn't think he could get out of bed without waking her, but he had to leave and fast. Even though she'd just soothed away his aches and taken him to heaven, he wanted her more than he had before. If he was honest with himself, he knew he'd never stop wanting her—and that terrified him. He was a drifter, a loner who didn't belong anywhere, certainly not with someone like her. But that didn't stop him from getting hard whenever he thought of her, which was often.

Moving slowly, Jaret tried to separate himself from Isabel. As he shifted to the side and began to ease away, the silky hands holding him tightened. He looked over and found himself staring into the most beautiful eyes God ever put on the earth.

"Going somewhere?"

The huskiness of her voice scraped along raw nerve endings, hardening him even more. "I've got work to do."

"Don't go yet. It's still night." Before he could stop her, she skimmed one hand down his naked body and wrapped her fingers around his stiff shaft. Jaret jerked at her touch then forced himself not to move. She couldn't know what her touch did to him. He got lost in the pleasure, forgetting he needed to leave.

Cursing in silence, he reached for her wrist, intending to pull her hand away, but her tongue flicked across a nipple and he was lost. With a curse he yanked her closer and rolled until he was looking down at her. Fusing their mouths together, he stabbed his tongue between her lips and plundered.

Desire exploded between them and Isabel matched him touch for frantic touch. She moaned and he drank the sound from her lips. Not giving her time to catch up, Jaret pushed her thighs apart and thrust inside her. He tried to slow down, but he was beyond reason. With a harsh sound he pounded into her, racing toward the heights and dragging her with him. He shattered into a million pieces, with her close behind.

Reality drifted back much more slowly this time. When he could think, he lifted his head to look at her. He expected to see shock and pain. The shock was his when he was greeted by her contented smile.

"Oh, my," she whispered. "Where has that been hiding all this time?"

"Are you all right?" Jaret knew he'd been too rough, but he seemed to lose control whenever she touched him. If he thought about it, he hadn't really been in control since he'd seen her standing in the shadows of the porch when he first rode onto the ranch. It wasn't something he liked to admit. "Did I hurt you?"

She laughed, a soft feminine sound that raced through him and heated his blood again.

"No, I'm not hurt. Just the opposite, in fact. I had no idea it could be like that." Her fingers explored his chest and arms. "No idea I could feel so wonderful."

"I'm sorry."

Her hands stilled. "For what?"

"I shouldn't have been so rough with you."

She smiled. "I'm not complaining, Jaret."

"Maybe you should. I don't know how to treat a lady. I shouldn't be here."

The smile faded and her look turned serious, almost angry. "Stop saying that. You belong here as much as any man does, more than most. I want you here, Jaret. I need you."

It was what he'd longed to hear and feared she would say. His body hardened in a rush inside her and Isabel gasped as he filled her again. She shifted to make room for him, but he stilled her movements. Gritting his teeth, he forced himself to separate from her heat. Not giving himself time to change his mind, he rolled off the bed and to his feet.

"You only need me around until this mess I created is over. But you don't want a good-for-nothing drifter hanging around your ranch or you."

"Stop it," she snapped. "Don't tell me what I want!" She scrambled off the bed and faced him. "You didn't create this mess, whoever hired you did. You only did what you were paid to do. You were used, Jaret. When you realized it was wrong, you tried to fix it."

"Don't make me into a hero, Princess. I just said yes to the wrong job. I don't leave my mistakes for others to clean up, but when this is over, I'll still be a cowboy taking work from the one with the fattest wallet."

"It doesn't have to be like that. You can stay here and—"

He cut across her words. "And be a hired hand? As well as you treat your employees, I don't see myself working for you."

"In the eyes of everyone here, you're my husband."

"That was a mistake, too, honey. All of it was."

"It was not!" She stomped across the room, naked and glorious. Jaret ached to wrap himself around her again.

Tightening his hands into fists, he forced himself not to move.

"What we shared was wonderful, beautiful." Isabel spit out each word between clenched teeth. "It wasn't wrong."

"It was great, Princess, but dangerous. Families begin from a lot less than that and I can't risk that."

"What is so bad about being married to me?"

The hurt in her voice shocked him. He tried to correct her, tell her it was him that made it wrong, but she didn't give him the chance.

"I'm sorry I don't measure up to your expectations, Mr. Walker." She reached for her discarded dress and tried to cover herself. "Consider your debt paid in full. You're free to go wherever you choose. I won't try to stop you. I never want to see you again."

Isabel spun on her heel and ran to the bathing room. The door slammed behind her, followed by the one to her bedroom. Jaret winced. That hadn't come out right. He started after her. No, better to give her time to cool off, then he could try to explain that it wasn't her. He just didn't dare let himself believe that he'd found his future here.

He dressed quickly, fastening his gun belt with practiced motions, and straightened the bed. He didn't want anyone to know Isabel had been here. She didn't deserve the speculation or the pity. The food she'd brought filled the hollow spot in his belly. He ate everything and covered the empty plate with the cloth that had been on it. He blew out the lamp and went to the window. Sliding back one edge of the curtain, he let his eyes adjust and then checked all the places there should be men on guard. The shadows by the schoolhouse seemed empty. He waited and finally saw movement. Dropping the curtain into place, he decided he'd given Isabel enough time. He wanted her to understand before he got back to work.

Jaret knocked softly on the door to Isabel's bedroom. When he didn't get a response he knocked again, a little harder. The silence grew deeper. Turning the knob he was a little surprised to find the door unlocked. "Isabel?" He entered the dark room, searching the chairs and bed for her.

"Damn." His whispered curse echoed in the empty room. Where had she gone? As the question formed, he heard a horse whinny. Lucifer. Where else would she go when she was upset?

No one was moving in the house as he went down the stairs and through the front door. The man on the porch had him in the sight of his long gun when Jaret stepped outside, but quickly relaxed his stance.

"Did she head for the horses?"

"About fifteen minutes ago."

Jaret nodded his thanks and strode toward the corral. The weather was perfect for an ambush. A sliver of a moon provided very little light and the breeze stirring leaves and grass would hide the sound of approaching men until they were nearly on top of the ranch yard. The hair stood up on the back of Jaret's neck. He could sense the time of waiting was almost over. If only he knew what they were planning, he could finish it and keep Isabel out of harm's way.

Veering to the main barn, Jaret woke one of the men catching a nap before he had to go back on guard duty. "Go to all the stations, but be quiet about it. Tell them to look sharp. It's coming tonight. I can feel it."

The man didn't argue with the look in Jaret's eyes. With a nod, he checked his weapons and ammunition and slipped out of the barn. Jaret woke two more men and sent them to double the guard behind the house. Satisfied there would be ample warning when the attack came, he went to find Isabel.

As Jaret passed the schoolhouse he looked again for the guard that should be there. The shadows were empty. He stood very still at the corner of the building and listened. He nearly missed the muffled moan at first in the sighing wind. When it came again his first thought was of Isabel. Slipping his revolver from its holster, he dropped his hat in the dust and inched up to the open window.

His heart pounded so hard he couldn't hear much else and he wasted precious seconds bringing it under control. Icy, gut-wrenching fear dulled his senses even more. He had to protect Isabel. He loved her, damn it. And he couldn't let her go. But first he had to find her. He forced his worry into the recesses of his mind. Exhaling slowly he came to his feet and looked through the window.

The man lying on the floor was gagged, bound hand and foot, and bleeding badly. Jaret made certain there was no one else there, waiting to pick off the next man who came through the door, before he moved. He was easing his way toward the door when he felt someone watching him. Spinning around, he dropped to the ground and cocked his gun at the same time.

Manuel stood only a few feet away, but Jaret hadn't heard him approach. Shaking his head at his own carelessness, Jaret jerked his head toward the schoolhouse. Manuel moved to the door without a making a sound, waiting for Jaret's signal.

Unable to see anyone inside except the injured man, Jaret nodded to Manuel to cover the shadows while he slipped in the door. No explosions of gunpowder and metal came from the dark corners. Jaret checked the room until he was satisfied no one else was there. A match flared and a lamp wick caught the flame. Jaret went to the man on the floor.

Blood oozed from a cut at the base of his skull, probably caused by a rifle butt. The worst bleeding was from a knife wound in the man's side. Manuel went for help, while Jaret tried to staunch the flow and find out about Isabel. Every touch brought a moan of pain from the semiconscious man, but he wasn't able to answer Jaret's questions.

Fear knotted in Jaret's gut. Something was wrong and Isabel was caught in the middle of it. He was almost wild with worry by the time four others crowded into the schoolroom.

"Get him to the bunkhouse and wake Marta. I've got to find Isabel." Five men turned to him as his words registered.

"Miss Isabel is gone?" "When?" "What happened?"

Jaret ignored their questions. He turned to go when the injured man finally got his attention. He had to crouch down close to the man to hear.

"She was . . . far enclosure . . . I heard . . ." He had to stop every couple of words to drag in air. "I tried . . . hit from behind . . . at least two . . . couldn't . . ."

Jaret stopped his frantic words with a hand on his shoulder. "I'll get her back." He turned to the others. "Get everyone to their posts but do it quietly. No lights, no noise. Let's not tip them off that we know they've been here. I'll find Isabel. When we come back, we'll circle around and follow the creek in. If anyone comes in from another side, shoot first and then ask questions."

Jaret sent Manuel to the house to wake Nick and his uncle, then began searching for Isabel's tracks. The wind that had blown all day had smoothed out most of tracks made by the dozens of boots that passed this way through the day. It had backed off at sunset, so only the newer prints showed. She'd been heading for Lucifer, so he started looking in that direction. He found her tracks and followed the trail around the schoolhouse to the makeshift corral set up between two storage buildings.

Lucifer paced up and down the rope fence. Jaret whistled softly and the big horse paused, but almost immediately resumed his frantic movements.

Jaret could see where Isabel's tracks stopped at the fence close to where he stood. She'd probably done as he had, called Lucifer over to let him know who was here. Then her tracks moved to the building on the right where the ropes were tied off to secure the enclosure. More tracks, larger ones, joined hers there. But these were scuffed as if a struggle had taken place. Then hers disappeared completely.

Jaret followed the bigger boot tracks around the storage building and into the desert. A short distance away, horses had been hobbled out of sight. That's where boot tracks ended. Jaret went back to the barn. Manuel was already saddling Sand Dune.

"There were only two. She put up quite a fight. It looks like they carried her to their horses. They headed west. Let her brother know what happened."

Jaret slipped the reins over the horse's head and paused before swinging into the saddle. "I was hoping there wouldn't be a need for any of this."

"*Sí,* Mr. Jaret," Manuel agreed as a cheerful grin creased his weathered cheeks. "But then we would've missed all the fun."

Jaret was surprised he could laugh. Fear for Isabel was choking him, making it heard to breathe.

He checked that both his belt guns were fully loaded and swung into the saddle. "You know what to do." Without waiting for a reply, he set off in pursuit of Isabel.

Chapter Eighteen

The desert air was cold. Isabel tried to spit out the cloth tied around her mouth and twisted against the ropes binding her wrists. She was furious with herself for walking right into the hands of the two hired guns waiting for her near Lucifer's corral. But anger wouldn't help her get free of the man whose horse she was forced to share. She glanced down at the hairy arm circling her waist.

As if he could read her thoughts, her captor tightened his hold, fondling her hip as he pulled her closer between his thighs. Isabel's stomach turned. She longed to put more space between them, but the man's obvious physical pleasure the last time she'd struggled against him kept her from moving. She ignored the hard ridge pressing against her backside and concentrated on getting away.

The man's free hand loosely held the reins of a very well-fed mount. The horse was walking along a trail that had been beaten into the dry ground. Obviously, they'd been this way many times in recent weeks.

Isabel knew where they were, at least in relation to the house. After riding due west for an hour, they'd turned southwest. She was certain they were on the Williams spread, but she didn't think they were heading for the ranch house.

She now knew Silas was the one trying to steal Two Roses. Because her captors had been discussing the reward he'd promised to pay for her. Then they'd laughed about how easy it had been to earn the money.

Now that she thought about it, she was disgusted that she hadn't realized sooner that Silas was involved. This morning, when Roger Marks mentioned the man who hired him wore horrible cologne–and lots of it–she'd been reminded of Silas Williams's first visit to see her. Why hadn't she told Jaret?

Silas made his first move a week after her father died. He'd shown up at the ranch and offered to marry her so she wouldn't lose the ranch. She'd refused him on grounds that it was too soon to think of marriage. She thought he'd taken her words to heart when she didn't hear from him again. But he'd returned on her birthday the next year with a handful of flowers and a ring. It had been the same every year since.

After her last, more forceful refusal, Nicolas disappeared and the imposter pretending to be her uncle arrived. Then Williams's sons had jumped into the fray, pressing her to choose one of them to marry. At the time she thought it was because they considered her the only marriageable female in the county. It galled her to realize she'd been blind to their real intent.

She was jolted back to the present when the horse stumbled. Grabbing at the saddle horn for balance, she looked up and realized they'd left the trail and moved into the rocky ground nearby. The rough whispers of her captors told her why.

"Are you sure you heard somebody back there?"

"No, I ain't sure, but I don't want to take the chance and turn out to be wrong."

"Maybe it's the boss."

"Could be, and maybe not. We're pretty close to where we're supposed to meet up, but they shouldn't be behind us."

They were being followed and she'd bet anything it was Jaret. This was her chance to get away. Pretending to faint, she slumped forward in the saddle and pinched the neck of the horse hard at the same time. Her sudden move and the horse's reaction were enough to unbalance the man who held her. As he struggled to control a suddenly unruly mount, she dove from the saddle. She bit back a cry of pain when she hit the ground. Giving her captors no time to react, she rolled to her feet and ran.

The ground was uneven and rocky. Isabel skidded on the pebbles underfoot. She darted to the right. If she could work her way back to Jaret, she'd be safe.

As she jumped onto a small outcropping, her skirts tangled around her ankles, nearly pitching her headfirst into the rocks. She gathered the fabric in her hands, but that made keeping her balance difficult. Glancing over her shoulder, she could see one of the men chasing her. The horse he rode wasn't having trouble with the terrain and its four legs were gaining on her rapidly.

Changing direction, Isabel stuffed the hem of her skirt into the waistband as best she could and headed deeper into the rocks. Throwing herself around boulders as big as she was, she clawed her way up the hill. The curses from the cowboy chasing her grew fainter until she couldn't hear him over the sawing of her own breath.

Risking a look back, she was relieved that neither man was in sight. Maybe they'd given up the chase. She took a moment to work free of the gag and the ropes binding her hands.

The moon was mostly obscured by clouds. Her father and Manuel had taught her to find her way using the stars, but there wasn't enough sky visible for her to pick out the ones she needed. Hoping she was right about where she was, Isabel began moving through the rocks and boulders in the general direction of the ranch.

Going slowly, trying not to make any noise, she worked her way along the ridge, taking care to stay hidden from the men chasing her. Every few minutes, she looked up, both to be certain she was still going in the direction she wanted, and to search for Jaret. The third time she began to get irritated. If he was close enough to make those men nervous, she should have found him by now.

Isabel crouched down among the large rocks as another thought occurred. What if it wasn't Jaret? It didn't make sense that the two kidnappers would have been nervous about their fellow outlaws following them. But then, they hadn't known who was back there. Maybe they'd found out it was their friends after she escaped and now they were all tracking her, three or four, or a dozen men, slowly herding her into a trap. Isabel panicked.

Jumping to her feet, she ran through the rocks. They were smaller than before, but the footing was still treacherous. When she knocked loose a small slide of stone, the adrenaline in her system made her change direction, running away from the sound. It wasn't long before she was hopelessly lost.

Exhaustion finally forced her to stop. She threw herself down into a small indentation in the hill, between two large boulders that she hoped would keep her hidden from view. After wedging herself in, she remembered how the snakes loved just this type of place to hide out of the cold air at night. Her heart kicked up another notch as she searched every shadow.

She lectured herself silently on the stupidity of anyone who forgot the desert rattler. She was breathing too hard to hear if anything shared her hiding spot, but she doubted it.

She'd have been bitten long before now, since the big snakes weren't known for their even temperament. Saying a silent thank you for saving a frightened female from her own foolishness, Isabel looked around for familiar landmarks.

The wind harried bits of dust and rock across the hard-packed ground and down the rocky slope. The skittering of a rodent came from her left as the tiny animal searched for food and tried to avoid the desert hunters. Once she thought she heard the sound of a horse, but she couldn't be sure of the direction it came from or if she'd heard it at all.

Isabel shifted positions on the hard rock, trying to get comfortable. She looked up at the sky for the tenth time in as many minutes, wishing the sky was cloudless. She shoved back the panic that clawed at her and tried to remember everything she knew about surviving in the desert. The night was passing slowly, but it would end. She'd make it through. Then she would figure out where she was and find her way back to the ranch.

The deep darkness of the night began to lessen as dawn approached. In the increasing light, Isabel saw the faint signs of water on the land. It had to be the creek that ran through her ranch. All she had to do was follow it home.

Anxious to be on her way, she searched the rocks for the best way down. She didn't know she wasn't alone until something brushed her arm.

Screaming, Isabel fought off the hand that tried to hold her and darted away. She heard a shout that might have been her name, but she couldn't be sure. Running blindly, she threw herself downhill, toward open ground and the tiny watercourse that would lead her home.

When the ground leveled out, Isabel ran as fast as she could. When her skirt began to slow her down she gathered it into her fist and kept going. As she rounded a rocky outcropping that she hoped hid the tiny ribbon of water, she tripped over a man stretched out in a bedroll on the ground. His shout of surprise made her dart away. She veered right but found another man lying nearby.

Turning quickly, she tried to avoid yet another man bunked down on the land, but he was quicker. A hand closed on her ankle and she fell headlong onto a fourth man. Fortunately, his round belly cushioned her fall.

Isabel tried to scramble to her feet as beefy hands closed around her waist, holding her in place. She flailed at her captor with fists and feet, but he was much too strong. With a quick motion, he rolled over and pinned her beneath his considerable bulk.

"Take it easy, girl. I ain't gonna hurt ya. Just settle down now."

Isabel struggled to catch her breath. "Let me go."

"Yes, ma'am." He rose, lifting her with him, and set her on her feet in the dust. She had to look way up to see his face. She studied him for a moment, but couldn't place him. Turning away, she looked out over the camp she'd stumbled into.

In the increasing light, Isabel could see the valley that had been hidden from view over the ridge. This must be the rustlers camp Jaret found. Horses surrounded the dozen men that were now on their feet and trying to find out what had awakened them. Nearly half the horses sported Two Roses' stylized double rose brand.

"What are you doing with our stock?"

A snicker came from behind her and several other faces split with ugly grins. Before she could question them further, a wiry figure strode toward her from the far side of the camp.

The overpowering scent of his cologne reached her before he did. Silas Williams. "Well, well. Miss Bennett. Where did you come from?"

She hesitated before accepting the arm he offered to escort her toward a campfire being stirred to life a short distance away. Dawn turned the eastern horizon a rich pink and shed enough light to make walking easy as they picked their way around bedrolls and saddles. When Silas stopped, she looked around at the faces of the men staring at her.

"Look what stumbled into camp."

The hair on her neck stood up. "Hardin!" She nearly spat out the name. She whirled to Silas. "What is he doing here?"

"Nothing worthwhile! He should still be working for you, but he ain't anymore 'cause the damn fool lacks patience. But I didn't raise him, so I can't take the blame, although he's a lot like my other boys, I suppose."

Isabel stared at him, confused.

"You know, Miss Isabel, if you'd just married me when I asked, all this could have been avoided." He spit in the general direction of the fire. "Any one of the four of us would have been a fine choice."

"Four?"

"Yep. You already know two of 'em. Let me introduce my other boy." He pointed a dirty finger at Hardin. "This here's Henry Hardin Williams, Hank to you. Until he showed up at my door, I didn't know I'd left little Ellie with a souvenir. We'd been in the habit of getting together whenever I went to Galveston, you see."

When he paused to spit again, Isabel tried to take a step away, but he held her arm tightly against his side. Patting her hand, he continued his story.

"My dear wife, God rest her, never knew about Ellie. When Margaret died after birthing Eli, I went to Galveston one more time, for the comfort, you understand."

Silas stared down at her with half-crazed eyes. "I never went back after that. There was too much to do here, running the ranch and raising two boys. And Ellie never told me the scrawny runt hanging around her was mine."

Isabel looked from him to Hardin. The resemblance was so obvious she wondered how she'd missed it.

"Yeah," he cackled. "If I'd looked closer I'd-a figured it out. But I wasn't there to look at boys."

A few rough laughs greeted his words. Isabel flinched. She'd almost forgotten the other men surrounding them.

"About a year ago he showed up at the ranch with a letter his ma wrote to me. Since I couldn't deny being his daddy, lookin' like he does and all, I took him in. He learns faster than these other two. The problem is I don't have enough land to split up between three boys. But Hardin here already had it all figured out. He found a way to get close to you, so he could help you run the ranch when your brother *disappeared*."

The four Williams men laughed. The identical sounds grated on her already strained nerves.

Isabel faced Hardin. "You hired Roger Marks."

Hardin sketched a cocky bow. "That's right. I dressed up in some old clothes of Pa's, so he wouldn't recognize me when I showed up as his foreman. I hired Walker, too, but I had someone handle that transaction for me." He spit into the fire as his father had done, but his aim was better.

"Good thing Walker never saw my face. When he turned up at the ranch, I figured he'd turned on us. Then I realized he didn't know who I was at all. I tried to convince him to leave, but you fixed him up and he stuck around."

"You see, Isabel," Silas interrupted. "I tried to get the land legally a few years ago. That judge had no right to give it back to you and yours. After my claim was rescinded, I made sure your daddy had an accident of the permanent kind."

A shiver went through Isabel. He spoke so calmly of murder.

"I couldn't stake my claim right away or somebody might-a got suspicious that I had something to do with your daddy's rather untimely demise. I decided to offer for your hand instead, but you were too high and mighty for that. Then Hardin here gave me the idea of how to get your brother out of the way.

"You should have married me when I asked. We could have added your land to mine and everything would have been fine. There'd be plenty to split between all my boys and start them all out proper in life." One corner of his mouth lifted beneath a filthy mustache. "Course, if we'd had more kids, we'd have needed even more land, but I would've figured that out later."

Silas held out his free hand for a cup of coffee and paused long enough to swallow it in a few noisy gulps. A river of brown ran down his chin, leaving a pale line in the dirt on his neck as it disappeared beneath his collar. "I planned to do the vowing tonight, but since you're here, we can just take care of it right now."

Isabel yanked out of his grasp. "I'll never marry you or any of your sons. And I certainly wouldn't tie myself to an animal like Hardin."

Silas's laughter was an ugly sound. "I don't think you understand. You ain't got a say-so. We were going to take the ranch this morning while everyone was either sleeping or feeding their faces. I still got enough men on your spread we could have done it without killing too many. But now I don't have to go to all the trouble. The priest is ready and waiting. All you got to do is pick one of my boys. If you won't, you'll marry me."

Isabel looked in the direction he indicated and saw a rather stunned Father Perez standing at the edge of the camp.

"What did you promise Father Perez to get him to agree to this scheme of yours?"

He grinned, showing rotting yellow teeth. "I just didn't tell him you weren't a willing bride."

Isabel was a little relieved. The priest was a good man and an old friend. She hated the thought that he could sell her out for a bag of silver.

"It is an interesting plan, Silas, but you've forgotten one thing. I'm already married."

"No you aren't." Hardin stepped toward Isabel. "That pretty speech about exchanging promises in the desert was nothing but a pack of lies."

Hardin grabbed for her arm and the sound of several dozen weapons being cocked shattered the morning air. As one, Silas, Jacob, Eli, and Hardin lifted their hands well away from their gun belts and looked around. Their moves were mirrored by the other cowboys in the camp.

"Touch her, Hardin, and I'll kill you where you stand."

Isabel spun toward the voice and saw Jaret standing just beyond the ring of men, silhouetted by the rising sun.

"You aren't going to shoot, Walker, not with her standing in the middle of us." Hardin lunged for Isabel, but she had no intention of becoming a captive again. Lashing out with a booted foot, she connected with his knee and he fell to the ground with a howl of pain. Isabel didn't hesitate. She turned and ran, snatching a revolver from Silas's belt holster as she passed.

There were too many men between her and Jaret to make it safely, so Isabel spun back and faced the Williams family. She knew the weapon was loaded. On one of his courting visits, Silas had lectured her for more than an hour about an unloaded gun being the most useless thing on earth. Calmly she pulled the hammer back and pointed it at Silas.

"You won't shoot," Hardin taunted, favoring his injured knee as he lurched to his feet. "You're too much of a *lady* to kill a man."

The sarcasm in his voice set her off. Taking casual aim, Isabel shot the hat off his head. Hardin dove to the ground again, screaming in pain as his injured knee connected with the rock-hard dirt.

"You bitch!"

"You may be right, Hardin. I probably wouldn't shoot a man, but you're such a sorry excuse for a human being, I'm not sure you'd count. And mind your language," she added as she turned to point the weapon at Silas again.

"Tell your men to drop their weapons."

Silas was furious. "You can't mean to leave a dozen men unarmed out here."

"Yes, I can. Now empty those gun belts, damn it!"

The older man stared at her for several long seconds before rasping out a command, leading the way by pulling out his own remaining belt gun and dropping it into the dust.

"The knives, too, and move real slow while you do it." Isabel puffed at a lock of hair that blew across her face. She didn't dare take her eyes or her aim off Silas.

Isabel waited for the silence to return before raising her voice enough to be heard by everyone in the valley. "All of you take a couple of steps away from those guns."

The shuffling of feet and grumbling of men followed her order. Out of the corner of her eye, she saw Jaret making his way to her. When he slipped a hand around her waist, she sagged in relief. It was almost over.

Lifting her chin, Isabel glared at the rancher. "Silas, I'm only going to say this one more time, so listen very carefully. Two Roses is not for sale and neither am I. I'll never marry you or any of your offspring for any reason. I'll notify the authorities of what went on today, so they'll be keeping an eye on you. If you try to steal my land or my stock again, I'll put buckshot in your backside and they can arrest what's left. Now mount up and get the hell out of my sight!"

She'd had enough. This man and his sons had pushed her too far. When Silas didn't move, her finger tightened on the trigger and she considered shooting him for the horse thief he was.

"It's all right, honey, he'll leave." Jaret skimmed his hand up and down her back. "You don't need to shoot him."

"But I *want* to," she spit back.

Her desire to do just that must have been obvious, even to Silas Williams. Turning, he gave the order to break camp. All the men he'd brought with him headed for their horses.

"Make sure they leave all of the Two Roses stock." Jaret put Mace Brinker in charge. "And find out which men on the ranch are working for Williams."

"Yes sir, Mr. Walker," the cowboy acknowledged.

Most of the Two Roses hands mounted horses that were brought out of hiding from the rocky hillside and escorted Williams and his bunch out of sight. Only a few remained behind. When the last one turned to the west, Jaret gave Isabel's shoulder a gentle squeeze.

"It's over now, honey. Give me the gun."

Several seconds passed before Isabel lowered the weapon. She was dismayed when she started to shake, but she couldn't seem to stop. Jaret took the revolver from her and dropped it into the dust at his feet.

Murmuring words she didn't understand, he gathered her into his arms and held her while she cried out her anger and exhaustion and fear. Isabel stifled her sobs so the men wouldn't hear, but tears ran down her cheeks and dampened Jaret's shirtfront.

When the storm was finally over, Isabel took a couple of deep breaths, memorizing the feel, the scent of him. She loved being in Jaret's arms, but now that the trouble was over she no longer had the right. He would be leaving and her life would return to normal, or as close to it as possible. Nothing would ever be the same.

"Are you all right?"

Jaret's voice made her feel safe and warm.

"Yes, I'm fine." To prove it she straightened her spine and tried to step away. Jaret's arms tightened and held her in place. She knew she should insist, but she wanted to stay right there forever. With a sigh, she snuggled closer.

"You gave me one hell of a night, woman." He tightened his arms around her.

"Me!" Isabel lifted her head to glare at him. "All I did was get kidnapped again and spend the night hiding in the dark in the rocks. How did I give you a bad night?"

Jaret settled his hat lower on his forehead. "I was the one trying to catch up to you."

Isabel tilted her head back until she could see his face. What she saw in his eyes made her want to smile. "I knew that was you I heard."

His brows lowered into a frown. "You didn't hear anything."

"I heard someone behind me in the rocks," she insisted. "That's why I kept running. I thought it was one of the two who dragged me out here." She fought not to smile.

"Those two idiots were already hogtied and stashed in the rocks. Manuel came on them just before you woke up. That's how he knew he'd found us."

"If you had them before dawn, why didn't you stop me from running into the middle of that bunch?" She jerked her chin in the direction the Williams clan had taken.

Jaret looked away and his brows dropped even lower. “I couldn’t find you.”

Isabel stared. Had she heard correctly? “But the men all say you’re the best tracker these parts have ever seen.”

“I may have met my match.”

Isabel grinned in triumph. She couldn’t help it. “I can’t believe I managed to hide all night from you.”

“Not all night.” Jaret’s blue eyes glinted in the morning sun. “I knew the general area where you’d gone to ground, just not the specific hole. When I figured you were there to stay for a while, I went back for Manuel and the others.”

He looked over her head and across the valley. “I got back just as you were waking up. Your white petticoats were easy to see once there was a little light. I touched your arm to let you know I was there, but you screamed and took off like the hounds of hell were snapping at your heels. Before I could call you back, you were climbing over the rocks and into Williams’s camp.”

Isabel couldn’t stop the satisfied smile that curved her lips. She was better than she thought if she’d been able to hide from an accomplished tracker like Jaret Walker. She was still enjoying her success when his lips covered hers.

The biting kiss was hard and brief, but it told Isabel just how worried he’d been. When Jaret tried to end the kiss, Isabel threw her arms around his neck and pulled him back for more. He didn’t resist.

She threaded her fingers into his hair and held on as Jaret bent her back across his arm and plundered her mouth. The sounds of men and horses faded away.

She jumped when someone nearby cleared their throat. The other men gathered around laughed and Isabel felt her cheeks heat. She turned her head and tried to put a little space between them. Jaret held on until she looked back, and he captured her lips again. With a sigh she melted into him. His lips burned a trail along her cheek to her ear. He whispered something that she didn't understand, then buried his face in her hair and held her close for a long moment. Finally he loosened his hold and stepped back, nodding toward someone behind her. "I think he wants to be sure you're not hurt."

Smoothing her rumpled skirt, Isabel turned around and was enveloped in long male arms. She realized with a start that her baby brother was grown up.

"Don't scare me like that again, 'Bel. Damn it."

She held Nicolas tight. "I'm fine, truly. I think it's finally over."

Nicolas nodded as he released her. "Those Williams boys are worse than their daddy and he's no better than a rattlesnake. They won't take no for an answer, neither from Papa or you."

Their uncle joined the group. "Before we left the trading post, I sent word to an old friend, a former Texas Ranger, to join us here. I can see now he isn't needed. We have Walker." He extended his hand to Jaret in thanks.

Nick mirrored the action. "When he arrives here, he can make sure the entire Williams family understands they no longer have a choice. They have no claim on our ranch. And if that doesn't work, I'll shoot the first one I see on Bennett land."

"Nicolas." Isabel was shocked. The gentle boy who'd left to buy horses only a few months before had changed. He was learning to be tough enough to stand up to the land. Even his laughter was different, she noticed, as he joined the men in planning ways to keep the neighboring rancher in line.

"Excuse me."

The quiet voice interrupted the reunion. Isabel turned

to greet Father Perez. "Good morning, Father. Welcome back to Two Roses."

Nick greeted the man like an old friend before introducing their uncle and Jaret.

"My dear child," the priest addressed Isabel. "I must apologize for my unwitting participation in this unfortunate affair. Had I considered it more carefully, I would have realized you are much too wise to accept an offer of marriage from anyone in that family. I was just so pleased that you had finally given up that notion of being a maiden aunt to your brother's children and decided to marry. Now I'm told that you may already have wed."

The priest turned to Jaret. "I understand from some of the men with Mr. Williams that you and Isabel exchanged promises of marriage. Others thought it was only a ruse to divert unwanted attention."

Isabel spoke up before Jaret could. "It was necessary to let everyone believe we had wed, Father. Otherwise Jaret would have been hanged."

"Hanged? Whatever for?" The priest looked genuinely shocked.

"Kidnapping and horse stealing." She shook her head at the priest's expression. "It's a long story."

She felt Jaret's low laugh as much as heard it and she had to fight the urge to move closer to his side.

"When Hardin and his men caught up to us, I had to stop them somehow. Since I had been thinking earlier in the day that I would enjoy having Jaret as my husband, it was the first thing that came to mind."

"You would?" Jaret took Isabel's arm and turned her to face him. She looked into his eyes and couldn't remember what she'd just said. A smile curved his lips and the sounds of all the men gathered around faded away again. She swayed toward him, eager for another kiss.

"Isabel?" Jaret traced her jaw with a thumb.

"What? Oh." His touch broke the spell and she glanced around, her embarrassment growing when she realized everyone had heard what she said. "I mean, a man *like* you would . . . You would make . . ." She took a deep breath and tried to stop stammering. She looked into his deep blue eyes. "You're a good man, Jaret Walker, and you'd make a good husband. I keep telling you that you belong here, but you don't want to be tied to one place."

"I don't know anything about being a family. Mine was a real poor example to go by. I wouldn't know how to start."

"Fine." She stepped away and stiffened her spine. She wouldn't beg. "Your debt to Nicolas has been more than paid. I appreciate all you've done for us—for me."

"Now hold on a minute."

"You've told me time and again you don't plan to marry. Neither do I. That works out well for both of us."

Jaret grabbed her arm. "What the hell kind of man do you think I am? We're married in every way that counts and I don't walk away from my responsibilities."

"I am not your *responsibility*!" She yanked free. "If I ever want to get married, I will, but it will be to someone who loves me the way I love you."

He looked like he'd been kicked in the head by a mule. "You can't love me."

"Don't tell me what I can't do. We didn't exchange vows or promises or anything else. You're free to go back to the life you've chosen, as am I. You don't need to worry about me any longer."

Nick protested. "'Bel, you can't just—"

She rounded on her brother. "You stay out of this! If you'd been more careful, he would never have come here in the first place."

Isabel stormed off toward one of the horses grazing nearby. "I'm going home."

"Hold on, Princess."

"Don't call me that!" She scrambled into the saddle and pointed the mount toward the ranch house. The landscape blurred. She was grateful the horse knew the way, since she couldn't see past her tears.

Chapter Nineteen

Why couldn't Jaret love her?

Furious with Silas Williams, with Jaret, with herself most of all, Isabel rode hard for the ranch. She wanted to lock the bedroom door and never come out. When she reached the long, flat wagon road leading to the house, she leaned closer to the horse's mane, whispering to the animal, urging it to run faster. The scarf holding her hair came loose and her long hair streamed behind her as they raced into the yard.

Hauling back on the reins, she slid from the saddle before the exhausted horse even stopped. Matt Richards met her and she tossed him the reins.

"Glad to see you back, Miss Isabel."

Isabel was so intent on getting into the house she didn't see anyone until her arms were grabbed from behind.

"What are you doing? Let me go!" She twisted in the grip, trying to see who held her.

"Not this time." Matt leered at her. "Mr. Williams will want to see you as soon as he arrives. And when he's done, I wouldn't mind a little time with you myself."

Her temper exploded. Yanking free, she spun to face the

man. "Silas Williams won't be coming to my ranch. We know what he tried to do, but he failed."

"I don't think so, missy."

"Silas?" Her anger died and a creeping fear took its place. She glanced around for help, but none of her ranch hands were in sight. Where was everyone? She began to take in details: a dozen horses in the corral, all saddled and sweating from a hard ride; the cook fire blazed near the bunkhouse, but there was no one tending it. She'd ridden into a trap.

"You didn't think I'd give up that easy, did you? I got me too many years invested to quit now. I want this land, and I'm going to have it."

Isabel faced Silas, willing herself to remain calm. "What have you done with my employees?"

"The few dumb enough to fight me after we left the valley might be a bit slow getting back here." He cackled. "God damn, you were pitiful easy to fool." He spit a stream of brown at her boots. "Most of the ones around here ain't been hurt. How long that's true is up to you."

How could she have been so foolish? With all the warnings Jaret had . . . Jaret!

"Don't count on being rescued this time," Silas sneered, as if he could read her mind. "I've got men posted all around the house. Your brother and Walker won't get within a hundred yards of you." He leaned closer, staring at her with wild eyes. "Say a prayer for them, 'cause they won't see another sunset."

"No!" She backed away, bumping into Matt Richards. "Don't hurt them. Please. I'll do whatever you ask, just let them go."

Silas cackled. "You shoulda said that before, girl. It's too late now. They gotta die."

The words were matter-of-fact, cold, as if life meant

little to him. Isabel wanted to scream. Her knees went weak and it took all her concentration to stay on her feet. She considered begging, but she refused to give him the satisfaction. "What do I have to do?"

He spat into the dust at her feet. "Agree to marry me."

"I'm already married."

Silas backhanded her. "You may have convinced some folks with that little farce you two played out, but not me. You probably bedded him, but that don't matter. Just means you won't bleed so much our first time together."

Nausea hit her like a fist. "I would rather die than let you touch me."

"That can be arranged," he hissed, the promise of violence glittering in his gaze.

"Riders coming." Henry Richards sprinted toward Silas. "About a dozen, from the west."

"Get to your places." Matt Richards followed his brother to the barn. "You all know what to do," Silas hollered, looking around the perimeter of the yard. "Kill them all except Walker. He's mine."

Silas dragged Isabel toward the house. She struggled to get free, dragging her boots in the dust. He turned and struck her again, so hard she saw stars.

Gunshots erupted all around them, from beyond the barn and behind the house. "Jaret!" Isabel screamed his name, struggling against Silas's hold on her wrist.

A shout came from beyond the schoolhouse. More shots cracked through the air. The shooting abruptly stopped.

"Jaret," she sobbed. He couldn't be dead.

"Let her go, Williams!"

Jaret's voice came from behind her. He was alive! Isabel turned, desperate to see him, but Silas twisted her arm behind her back until her fingers nearly touched her shoulder blades.

"She's mine now, and so is the land."

Silas wrenched her arm even higher, lifting Isabel to her toes. She couldn't breathe for the pain. He hauled her back a step. A shot rang out, spitting up the dust just behind him. Silas cocked his revolver and laid it against her neck. "She'll be dead before I am, Walker!"

Silence spread across the yard. Out of the corner of his eye, Jaret saw Manuel and Jim Easton take up positions in the shadows.

Silas used Isabel as a shield when Jaret stepped out of the barn. Cold sweat trickled down his spine. He held his hands out to the sides, fingers loose, poised over his belt guns. "It's over, Williams. You're surrounded. Your boys are dead."

Silas jammed the barrel into her jaw. "You lie!"

Jaret kept coming, step by step, closing the gap between them, making himself an easy target.

"No, Jaret. Get back," Isabel begged. "He'll kill you."

Isabel whimpered when Silas lifted her higher, pulling her off balance. Jaret halted. He wanted to reassure her, but he didn't dare look away from Williams.

"Jacob? Eli, answer me!" Silas waited for his sons to respond, to let him know his plan had worked. Silence was his answer. "Hardin?" He looked around, panic beginning to show in his eyes. "Where the hell are you, boys?"

"It's finished." Jaret stayed perfectly still, waiting for an opening.

"No! If you murdered my boys, it'll never be finished." He swung the barrel of his gun toward Jaret.

"Get down!" Jaret drew and fired, the sound of both shots deafening as they fired simultaneously. Silas's arm jerked as a bullet slammed into his shoulder and Isabel fell to the ground. Jaret felt a bullet burn through his arm, but he rolled to his knees and fired again, this time striking

Silas Williams in the chest. The man collapsed into the dust, sightless eyes staring into the cloud-strewn sky.

Jaret's heart stopped. There was blood on Isabel's face and clothes. Stumbling to her side, he scooped her into his arms. "Honey?" *God, please,* he prayed in the silence of his heart. *She has to be all right.* "Talk to me, Princess."

"Don't call me that," she mumbled into his shirt.

Relief made him weak and he sat down hard. Wrapping her tighter, he rocked back and forth, trying to get his breath. He didn't realize he was crying until he felt her fingers brush at his cheeks.

"Shh, love. I'm fine." She pressed her lips to his chin and then relaxed in his arms. Her fingers curled around his neck, connecting them. "Tell me it's over."

Jaret nodded, unable to speak around the lump in his throat. He'd nearly lost her, before he had a chance to tell her how much he loved her.

"What did you say?" Isabel stared at him, shock reflected in her beautiful eyes.

"I didn't say anything." He smiled at her frown, love warming his insides. Touching her with more tenderness than he knew he possessed, he brushed her tangled hair away from her face, letting his fingers linger on her skin. She turned her head and nuzzled his palm. He didn't know what he'd done to deserve her, but he wasn't letting this chance at happiness get away. He hugged her close and kissed her, then helped her to her feet as Nicolas and Manuel joined them.

"'Bel, are you all right?" Nicolas turned her to face him. "You're bleeding!"

"It's not mine."

Manuel reached for Jaret. "Must be his, then."

Isabel cried out when she spotted the blood soaking Jaret's shirt.

"Take it easy, honey. It's only a scratch. I've had worse. I'm glad to say Silas's aim was terrible."

She helped wrap the wound to stop the bleeding. When she was satisfied, she leaned into Jaret, burrowing into his side.

He wrapped an arm around her waist. "Are any of the men hurt?"

"We lost three men, another has a gunshot to the shoulder," Manuel reported.

Isabel gasped. Jaret hugged her closer. "I'm sorry, honey."

"It is always terrible to lose friends, *pequeña.*" Manuel patted her arm and turned back to Jaret. "The women and children were locked in the bunkhouse, out of the way. Her uncle went to free them."

Isabel straightened. "Silas said the ones you sent with him would take a while to get here. He must have them tied up somewhere between here and that valley."

"Henry Richards already told me where to find them."

"Henry is on our side? But Matt . . ."

He smoothed a strand of hair out of her eyes. "When Henry realized what his brother was up to, he asked to get in on the act, all the while planning to let us know before the attack came. He managed to slip away from Silas long enough to double back and warn us."

"Come on, 'Bel." Nick reached for her hand. "Lydia will want to see you."

Jaret stopped him. "Not yet, Bennett. I need to talk with your sister first." He turned Isabel to face him. "I'm not getting down on one knee."

Isabel glanced at the dirt. "Why would you do that?"

"Isn't that how a man usually asks a woman to marry him?"

Isabel's mouth opened, but she didn't say anything.

"Then again, nothing about us has been usual." He brushed her cheek with his fingers, because he had to touch her.

"You want to marry me?"

One corner of his mouth kicked up. "You'll make me crazy, since you never do what you're told, but I think I can get used to that."

She laid her hands on either side of his head, holding him still. "But why?"

"I guess you've kind of grown on me." He grinned as fire flashed in her eyes.

"So does a puppy."

Jaret tightened his hold when she tried to get away. "Take it easy." He took a deep breath. Pulling her a little closer, he stared into her eyes. "I want to marry you because . . ." He hesitated. He hadn't expected it to be so hard to say the words.

Isabel didn't make it any easier, just smiled and waited for him to continue.

Jaret huffed out a breath and dragged in another. "Because I love you," he blurted.

She knocked the hat from his head when she threw her arms around his neck.

"Is that a yes?"

"Yes," she whispered in his ear. He jerked a little at the tiny word and she tossed her head back and laughed. She covered his face with kisses until Jaret captured her lips in a soul-deep kiss. The sun broke through the clouds and flooded the land with golden light as the men around them cheered. Isabel leaned away enough to look into his eyes. He could see his future shining there.

"Welcome home, Jaret Walker. You've finally found where you belong."